THE JOSHUA

25 March 1946

Edward Fairfax stood in front of his platoon waiting for Major Rattigan to give the order for his company inspection to begin. He felt grand. The sight of the Paras lined up *en masse* on his left and right was splendid. This had been his first real posting. More than that, Palestine had been a first for everyone but the tiny handful of veterans of the North African campaign who had passed through the country during the war. Their job, now a seemingly endless round of riot control, road blocks and searches, was hardly what Edward had bargained for, but it was a new experience for everyone, even the old hands, and gave the satisfaction that they were all on the same footing, especially in face of an elusive enemy.

About the Author

Mark Bles is well qualified to write about war and insurgency.

Educated at Sandhurst and Oxford, he has served in the Royal Green Jackets and 22 Special Air Service Regiment. After leaving the regular army, he worked for several years as a kidnap negotiator. He drew upon this experience to write his acclaimed first book THE KIDNAP BUSINESS. His second book is CHILD AT WAR: The True Story of Hortense Daman from her young career in the Belgian Resistance, to her survival from Ravensbrück concentration camp.

THE JOSHUA INHERITANCE

MARK BLES

CORONET BOOKS
Hodder and Stoughton

Copyright © Mark Bles
1992

First published in Great Britain in
1992

A Coronet Paperback
original

The Joshua Inheritance is a novel. All of
the characters are invented and none is
intended to portray a real person, living
or dead. Certain names of well-known
places or individuals or institutions and
historical facts are merely used to give
a realistic background to the story.

The right of Mark Bles to be identified
as the author of this work has been
asserted by him in accordance with
the Copyright, Designs and Patents
Act 1988.

This book is sold subject to the
condition that it shall not, by way
of trade or otherwise, be lent, re-
sold, hired out or otherwise circulated
without the publisher's prior consent
in any form of binding or cover other
than that in which it is published and
without a similar condition including
this condition being imposed on the
subsequent purchaser.

No part of this publication may be
reproduced or transmitted in any
form or by any means, electronic
or mechanical, including photocopying,
recording or any information storage or
retrieval system, without either the prior
permission in writing from the publisher
or a licence, permitting restricted
copying. In the United Kingdom such
licences are issued by the Copyright
Licensing Agency, 90 Tottenham Court
Road, London W1P 9HE.

British Library C.I.P.
A CIP catalogue record
for this title is available
from the British Library

ISBN 0-340-56534-9

Printed and bound in Great Britain for
Hodder and Stoughton Paperbacks, a
division of Hodder and Stoughton Ltd,
Mill Road, Dunton Green, Sevenoaks,
Kent TN13 2YA (Editorial Office: 47
Bedford Square, London WC1B 3DP)
by Clays Ltd, St. Ives plc

TO REBECCA

CONTENTS

Book 1 – *JOSHUA*
1 Betrayal *4 October 1944–12 January 1945* — 3
2 VE-Day *8 May 1945* — 21
3 The Victims *May–June 1945* — 28
4 Summer Dance *28 July 1945* — 47
5 Deployment *August–September 1945* — 53

Book 2 – *STORM*
6 First Moves *October–November 1945* — 83
7 Strategic Reserve *7 November 1945* — 101
8 The Storm Brews *November 1945–February 1946* — 107

Book 3 – *JERUSALEM*
9 Course Logic *25 March 1946* — 153
10 Jedburgh *April–July 1946* — 157
11 Jews and British *May 1946* — 179
12 Kidnap at the Astoria *June 1946* — 199
13 Cordon and Search *29 June 1946* — 225
14 The King David *22 July 1946* — 253
15 No Flowers *27 July 1946* — 277

Book 4 – *FUEL TO THE FIRE*
16 Special Squads *February–March 1947* — 285
17 A Little Holiday in their Hearts *4 May 1947* — 330
18 Exodus *July–August 1947* — 334
19 Full Circle *September 1947* — 363
20 Funkspiel *September 1947* — 384
21 The Cemetery at Marmoutier *September 1947* — 406

Epilogue — 421

BOOK 1

JOSHUA

Now therefore arise, go over this Jordan, thou and all this people, unto the land which I do give them, even to the children of Israel.

> The Book of Joshua, 1:2

1

BETRAYAL

4 October 1944–12 January 1945

George Fairfax waved cheerfully at the German soldier as he rode past Maursmünster police station on his motorbicycle, and immediately regretted it. He was in an excellent mood after his reconnaissance in the mountains but, after four miserable years of Occupation, people did not wave at the Germans any longer, even in Alsace-Lorraine.

His embarrassment soon faded in the satisfying burble of the bike's exhaust echoing off the stone walls of the houses as he twisted and turned through the town's narrow cobbled streets. The place was deserted. It was a cold, damp October afternoon and those with work to do stayed inside. He turned finally into a long road lined with cheaply built red-brick workers' cottages in little fenced gardens, where they had been hiding for the last three weeks in the last house which offered a fine view of the approach from its gable-end bedroom window. He left his bike at the side, hidden from view in a delapidated shed, let himself in through the kitchen door at the back with a key and went upstairs two at a time. The top floor squatted tight under the sloping roof and he bent his head on the turn of the stair before barging through a coarse matchboard door on the tiny landing.

Inside, a thin man in a baggy brown suit wearing a

jersey under the jacket was crouched behind the bed pointing a big .45 automatic at the door, his fist clenched white round the pistol grip. The mass of grey hair on his head and the intense expression on his narrow face made him look older than his forty-five years.

'Goddam it! Why don't you use the agreed signal before coming in? Shit, I had the goddam set out!' He waved the pistol furiously at a leather suitcase on the table.

'Relax, Romm, old thing,' Fairfax replied seriously, refusing to match the other's temper. 'You heard the bike, didn't you? Who else could it have been?'

Romm snapped back, 'And quit the goddam "old thing" routine.' He dropped the automatic on the bed and stood up. He looked tired. Living in Occupied France, always with the threat of being caught by the Sicherheitsdienst, or SD, was taking its toll, Fairfax thought. He said, 'You shouldn't get so worked up! You'll wear yourself out.'

Romm did not reply. With what he knew of the area, he thought he ought to be running the operation, not this solidly built Englishman whose every action seemed guaranteed to attract the attention of the Germans.

'Bloody cold out,' said Fairfax and slumped down on the end of the bed. He began to unbutton his outer coat. He said, 'Saw a lot of vans and other motors round the police station as I came through town. Wonder what the sods are up to now?'

Romm paid no attention. He went back to the suitcase on the table, opened it and looked at the B2 clandestine radio neatly fitted into four compartments inside. He checked that a Bakelite switch on the right was turned to 'battery', lifted a loose floorboard under the table, pulled out two wires from the hole and connected them into the set. The workman's cottage had no mains electricity and Romm was using a truck battery hidden under the floor. Without stopping he asked, 'Just tell me about the

The Joshua Inheritance

landing strip. Is it okay? We've got to get this message off right now.'

Fairfax watched him and nodded, 'Yes, the place is perfect. No doubt about it. Even for a big twin-engined plane like the Hudson. We can bring the team in there, no difficulty. D'you want the grid?'

'No. I've got it,' Romm replied. He fished in his trouser pocket and pulled out a small rectangular object, the emergency radio crystal with a daytime frequency of 6,123 kilocycles. He plugged it into the radio at the back, in the centre compartment. 'I knew the place up there would be okay so I've coded the whole message already. I wanted to be ready to send at once.'

Fairfax raised an eyebrow. 'I know there's nothing like local knowledge, old chap, but that's a bit forward, eh? After all, it's my operation.'

'Bullshit,' said Romm bluntly, his back to Fairfax. 'We don't have time to waste.' With feverish haste, he continued to set up the radio. He reached over to the window in the gable-end wall for the aerial wires which were concealed along the roof outside, just above the gutter, and connected them inside the suitcase. Without pausing, he began to stuff the jackplugs of the headphone and Morse key into their sockets.

Fairfax watched, wondering if there was another reason why the American had been so keen to come on this operation apart from his excellent local knowledge. He shrugged. Sitting in a safe house about to send a clandestine message back to England was no place for a clash of personalities. The Germans had excellent direction-finding equipment to locate their position. He simply confirmed his earlier orders, 'Okay. But have you told them to cancel the team till we're ready? I want to be sure that they won't send the boys in that bloody Hudson till I am good and ready. Are you sure you've got that?'

Romm nodded, one hand holding the headphone to

his ear. 'And I've added that we'll confirm the grid at that time too.' He concentrated on the tuning signal in his ear, his other hand on the knob in the suitcase.

Fairfax hesitated. The message was now rather long. One-time-pad coding was totally secure but they ran the risk of being pin-pointed. The system's main fault was that it produced too many groups once encoded, which took a long time to tap out on the Morse key.

Romm sat down. He was ready to send, the single headphone held over one ear and his right hand on the Morse key on the right side of the radio. He began to concentrate on the scruffy piece of paper in front of him, with its lines of grouped numbers written on it in pencil. Fairfax shrugged and said, 'Okay, Axel, send away.'

Romm nodded vaguely. He was totally absorbed in his work. Fairfax admired him for that. On the radio at any rate he was a perfectionist. Romm's fingers began to twitch over the Morse key and the bare room filled with the precise musical cadence of the snapping key and silent puffs of breath condensed on the cold air. It was strange, Fairfax reflected, to find comfort in the mathematical beat of the Morse, an exact score of pulses, longs and shorts, but this was their only precious and vital contact with home. He turned to the grimy window under the eaves to keep watch on the empty street outside.

In a large high-ceilinged room in Paris in a secret Gestapo headquarters, three hundred cathode ray tubes glowed green in the subdued lighting and the room was filled with the hum of radio receivers. These panoramic receivers contained the very latest Telefunken electronics and constantly monitored the wavebands for every single frequency which could be used by illegal transmitters. Anywhere in Europe. Special duties signallers in the black uniforms of Department IV of the Schutzstaffel, or SS, watched the screens, calmly waiting for someone, somewhere, to give themselves away. The system was well tried and efficient. Two signallers talked in low voices but did not let their eyes stray from the screens.

A bright spot appeared on one screen. One of the signallers immediately picked up a telephone and in clipped tones he read off the frequency which had appeared on the apparatus under the screen, '*Achtung! Sechs, eins, zwei, drei Kilohertz.*' He waited for acknowledgement the other end and put the telephone back on its cradle. At the same time, with his other hand, he set the receiver to the same frequency and a wire recorder added its noise to the humming machines around, registering every flick of Axel Romm's fingers on his Morse key.

Two minutes later, four different direction-finding stations, at Brest in Brittany, and in Germany at Augsburg, Nuremberg and Berlin, were tuned to the same frequency and the SS signals staff were reporting exact compass azimuths back to the headquarters in Paris.

Alerted by the pickup, the Gestapo duty officer joined the two signallers in the Paris operations room. Impatiently glancing at his wristwatch, he waited as the minutes ticked past. Still the transmission continued and the wire recorder hummed. One by one the four bearings came in and four bright lines lit up across a vast map of France which covered one whole wall. They were criss-crossing a small area at the top end of the Vosges mountains, west of Strasbourg.

'*Interressant!*' the officer remarked quietly, pleased to see that earlier preparations seemed to be paying off. He snapped an order, but the signallers were already in action. The four azimuth bearings clearly marked a small area around Maursmünster about eight kilometres square, the same place they had identified in the past two weeks. They scented success. The day before, after yet another transmission from the same area, the SD had moved special direction-finding teams into three police stations in the area, disguised as telephone repair teams.

They were parked up, ready to go on constant twenty-four-hour watch. The signallers grabbed a telephone each and were instantly put through to Maursmünster and Wasselnheim, five miles south. The Gestapo officer picked up another telephone to Zabern in the north.

In Maursmünster, the SD officer slammed down the telephone in the bare squad room and shouted, *'Achtung! Raus, raus!'*

'Jawohl, Herr Standartenführer Denkmann!'

Within a minute four men in blue overalls tumbled out of the side door of the building into a square Citroën 11 van and passed the frequency to the signaller on duty inside. His fingers twiddled the dials on the radio equipment racked up in the back of the van while the driver gently eased the van on to the road.

'Er überträgt jetzt!' the operator exclaimed exultantly. Romm was still sending. The Citroën moved unsteadily on the cobbles and the operator struggled to get a fix, his face a mask of concentration. Behind the SD officer followed them in a Mercedes with three others wearing overcoats.

Seconds later in Paris, the light in the green tube suddenly went out and the wire recorder stopped.

'Scheisse!' the younger of the signallers blurted out and immediately apologised.

'Kein Problem,' said the duty officer indulgently. He knew that the clandestine station had only closed down while its base station in England decoded the message, worked out a reply, coded it and then sent it back. His eyes gleamed. When that message was sent, the clandestine station would have to come up again to acknowledge receipt. If the local direction-finding teams had managed to get a fix in the previous two minutes they could narrow the search to a few hundred yards or even less.

'I hate the waiting,' George Fairfax remarked as he stared through the little gable-end window at the damp reflections on the cobbled road. Nothing moved in the grey afternoon light but he was thankful Romm had finished sending. He had taken too long. He cursed himself. Five minutes was a maximum and they had taken seven. Two minutes too long.

Romm sat back on the wood chair, lit a cigarette and inhaled deeply. 'Don't worry, Fairfax. The tootsies in Buckingham will have no problems decoding my message.'

'How d'you know?'

Romm grinned. 'Because I know one of the girls there, and I'm a good operator. They get every group first time from me, no corruptions.'

'You could be faster.'

'Horseshit!' Romm snapped back angrily and Fairfax regretted making the remark. They had a long way to go together before the operation was done.

Romm had no such reservations and went on, 'At least I follow the goddam procedures. I bet you never checked if you were being followed before you came blundering back in here?'

George Fairfax ignored him. He knew he should not have waved at the German soldier by the police station, but he was sure he would have seen anyone following him on the narrow mountain roads he had used to recce the landing strip. He checked his watch. Over twenty minutes since England received the message. They should have decoded it and sent it by landline to Baker Street. No doubt Colonel Haike was reading it at that moment. He pulled a face.

Romm started to pace up and down the little room, his steps beating out a hollow rhythm on the boards. 'Good thing I use a battery on the radio. The Krauts sometimes switch off the mains to see if the signal stops when they get close.'

Fairfax grunted. 'If you're worried they're getting that close to us, we shouldn't be sending at all.'

'They'll only be close to us if they followed you!' Romm replied and resumed pacing back and forth across the room. He was conscious this was his first operation. He was a novice compared to Fairfax, but he hated the Englishman's casual attitude.

The Germans in the Citroën 11 which left Zabern were not quick enough to record a bearing before the transmission stopped, but the operators in Maursmünster and Wasselnheim triumphantly reported theirs on the radio. The SD officer in the Mercedes listened to the bearings on his radio, plotted them on a large-scale map of the area and nodded. There were only two plots but they tallied with previous results and indicated a poorer quarter on the west side of Maursmünster, near the railway line. He grabbed the radio to redeploy the three Citroëns to obtain the best triangulation when the transmitter came back on the air. In minutes the Citroëns and Mercedes were racing along the straight flat road towards Maursmünster.

'*Die Engländer warten auf die Antwort,*' said Standartenführer Denkmann on the radio as the big Mercedes swung round the town into position, explaining that the British agents were waiting for a reply. Following his instinct and knowledge of Maursmünster where he had been born, Denkmann instructed the other arrest teams in the Mercedes cars to road junctions where he could cut off the agents' escape. Then they all settled down to wait.

Romm looked out of the window again. The street was quiet. His attention was distracted by the sound of a train on the railway track. He did not see a fat man in an overcoat cross the top of the road and slip out of sight into an alley between two houses.

Fairfax was looking at his watch again. An hour. One of the girls would be encoding the reply. Without looking round at Romm he said sharply, 'You should sit down and get ready to receive. We're off the second this is over. Time we left this nasty little house.'

Romm sat down at the radio. 'You're only saying that because it's somewhere I suggested.'

Fairfax sighed and said nothing. Romm was probably right. But they had spent too long in the same place. That was dangerous and he felt guilty about it.

Romm put on the headphone and listened to the burbling noises on the ether. Somewhere out there was a message from him. It seemed odd that it was coming from England, from safety straight into the heart of Occupied Europe where they were surrounded by enemies.

In Paris, the bright spot lit up again on the green screen and at once the wire recorder began to hum. Simultaneously the equipment in the three Citroëns in the streets of Maursmünster registered the signal and the radio net buzzed with activity as the SD radio operators alerted the arrest teams and the three apparently overweight men deployed on foot with field meters hidden under their overcoats. Everyone waited expectantly for the clandestine station to acknowledge England's reply. At that moment, speed and pin-point accuracy would be vital or the agents would get away.

Romm was totally absorbed, listening and writing down the letter and numbers of the reply message. Fairfax paid no attention. The message was meaningless till it was decoded. He stared through the dirty windowpanes.

Behind him Romm's fingers started working the Morse key, tapping out his acknowledgement.

At once, the SD radio net rippled with messages of alert, like a spider's web around the fly. This time all three Citroën operators fixed the location and the three men on foot began to walk with poorly disguised urgency along the pavements round the houses by the railway. Every few seconds they checked the meters on their wrists, made to look like watches, to see if they were getting closer or further away from the signal.

George Fairfax began to relax. Soon they would be away from the claustrophobic little house. He enjoyed being in France when he was active, like that afternoon checking out the landing strip in the hills for the Commando team to join them later, but he hated being cooped up while the Germans used invisible scientific trickery to locate him. He frowned. Romm seemed to be taking a long time to acknowledge base station's reply. As he turned to cut him off, he caught sight of a man in a large grey overcoat sixty yards distant at the top of the street.

'Gestapo! Stop sending!' he shouted as he glimpsed another man behind the first.

'I don't goddam believe it,' Romm said in astonishment. He stepped across the short distance to the window and leaned over Fairfax to see for himself.

'Shove off!' Fairfax shouted, shaking him away. 'Get that bloody set packed up and leave me to deal with this.' He pulled a Sterling sub-machine-gun from under the pillow on the bed, flicked off the safety catch and gripped the long black silencer on the end of the SMG as he aimed at the nearest man. He knew Romm would need all the time he could give him to get away.

Romm had the set dismantled in seconds and crushed the lid shut on the wires. 'What about the aerials?'

The two men in overcoats were walking briskly up the road towards the house. Beyond them Fairfax saw a large black Mercedes saloon turn slowly round the corner.

'Do you want to clamber on to the roof and fetch them? For God's sake, get away and we'll meet at the emergency rendezvous as planned.'

Romm glared at him for a moment and was gone, crashing down the wooden stairs three at a time. George Fairfax heard the kitchen door slam and then his attention was diverted by the Germans in the street.

The Joshua Inheritance

One nearest the house pointed into the gardens. George Fairfax picked him up in his sights, squeezed the trigger and shot him dead.

The other Germans never heard the dull noise of the silenced SMG or the thin glass in the window which crumpled round the bullet hole, like shattered ice, and fell in slivers from the sill. They stared at the dead man, unable to tell where the attack was coming from while George Fairfax smoothly switched his aim to the Mercedes and fired again. The crump of metal inside his SMG was drowned by the Mercedes' windscreen exploding and the shouts of the men inside. The driver collapsed over his wheel and Fairfax shot two others before the car careered out of his sight through a fence into one of the gardens. With no more targets in view, George Fairfax decided it was time to move.

Outside, there was chaos. One German on the road had spotted the broken gable window and was screaming at the others to fire at it. As George Fairfax tumbled out of the kitchen door and sprinted up the garden, a volley of bullets found their mark on the little room upstairs ripping the woodwork to shreds and tearing plaster from the ceiling.

George stopped breathless at the top of the garden. He looked back, gasping fresh air into his lungs and wishing he was younger. At least he had got the action he wanted, he told himself ironically, though he was far from out of danger yet. Two Gestapo men in suits ran round the back of the house next door and he opened fire at them at once. That was the way Romm had gone and at all costs he had to dissuade them from following him. Romm had the radio and, so long as he escaped, the operation could go on. The two men disappeared from view. He thought he had hit them but the light was fading and he could not be sure. He swung over the fence and ran through rough grass and brambles towards the railway regretting he had ever agreed to stay in the little house. It would be too easy for the Germans to cut him off on the embankment.

He stopped again. The shouting was coming closer and several bullets smacked overhead. At least he had drawn them his way. Romm should get away and the worsening light would suit them both. Even the best soldiers shot too high in the dark. He ran on underneath the embankment and an increasing weight of fire began to whine in his direction. As long as they did not have dogs. If he could cross the line, he had a chance, through the woods on the other side and then into the hills.

But before he ran for it, he knew he must make certain of drawing all the Germans in his direction. It would be fatal if the radio and codes fell into German hands. He looked for a target. Three men in suits were climbing over the broken wooden fence about fifty yards away. He shot one in the stomach and fired a burst at the others when they dived for cover. He was rewarded with a mass of gunfire over his head at the embankment. The Germans could not hear his SMG firing but they were taking casualties.

Doubled up, he ran on a short way while the Germans plucked up courage to follow. Between breaths he sympathised. It was no fun chasing a gunman who could not be seen or even located by the sound of his firing. He glanced round. The Germans were firing as they came, to give themselves courage. George Fairfax forced himself not to think of bullets and scrambled up the stones to the embankment. He reached the top and slipped on the wet granite ballast, recovered his balance and was hit. The bullet struck him only a glancing blow on the side of his knee but it felt like being smacked with a sledgehammer. He went down at once, cursing at the pain, but rolled and pulled himself over the railway lines and down the other side of the embankment.

'*Halt!*'

The Joshua Inheritance

He looked up. Through the gloom, a patrol of grey-uniformed Wehrmacht soldiers approached, drawn by the shooting and knowing they were in dead ground from the fire the other side of the railway embankment. They were well spaced out among the trees covering each other as they moved. Experienced troops.

George Fairfax dropped his Sterling and hoped that Romm had had more luck.

12 January 1945

Colonel Haike marched briskly up the pavement from his office in Whitehall through Trafalgar Square to Pall Mall, wrapped inside a heavy black coat with the velvet collar turned up to his bowler hat. He had been brought up to believe that hands in pockets was sloppy, so he swung his arms vigorously and occasionally beat his gloved hands together to keep the circulation going. He hoped the Allied bombers attacking German troops in the Ardennes were enjoying the same brilliant blue skies as London that day and he longed for spring. Spring, summer and the end of the war. He stamped his feet as he walked and wiggled his frozen toes inside nothing more robust than a slim pair of hand-made black brogues, wishing he had worn something thicker than silk socks. He was relieved when he reached his club, the Travellers, at No. 106 Pall Mall.

The porter greeted him, 'Morning, sir!' and they exchanged views on the weather. Colonel Haike nipped up the steps into the hall where he reluctantly stripped off his coat. The club was never kept particularly warm and after nearly six years of war there was a shortage of fuel. He strode through the pillared hall straightening his dark pin-stripe suit and adjusting his Guards tie. With automatic gestures he smoothed his neat black moustache and hair which he kept brushed straight back from a sharp widow's peak, then pushed back his cuff and checked his watch. He was precisely on time and decided to go straight up to lunch.

John Peregrine Fullerton, also in a dark suit, was already waiting for him at a members' table in one corner of the long dining-room and reading the club wine list. As soon as he saw Colonel Haike he stood up and they shook hands like old friends.

'Septimus, my dear chap,' said Fullerton effusively. 'Good to see you.'

Colonel Haike disliked displays of *bonhomie* almost as much as he disliked Fullerton's smooth Foreign Office manner but they had known each other a long time and had worked together during the previous year. He extracted his hand from the other's grasp and replied, 'Yes, indeed, John. I hope I haven't kept you waiting?'

'Not at all, dear chap,' said Fullerton easily as they both sat down. 'I did get here a little early and spent an agreeable half-hour chatting to a newish member of the club called Philby. Very nice young chap, I'd say.'

'Recruited into your lot from MO-1(SP),' said Colonel Haike as he began to study the scanty menu.

'Yes,' agreed Fullerton, irritated that Haike knew. 'I think he's got a future in the Firm.'

Colonel Haike grunted dismissively, so Fullerton decided to plunge straight into the reason for meeting quietly in the club outside their respective offices. Leaning slightly forward across the polished mahogany table he said in a low voice, 'There's going to be an internal inquiry on "Joshua". They're looking for a scapegoat.'

He had the satisfaction of seeing Colonel Haike look up sharply.

'What?'

Fullerton deliberately put a finger to his lips and disguised the gesture by scratching his nose. 'Yes. They're not happy that the Hudson was lost to enemy flak. There have been serious irregularities.'

'What're you talking about?' asked Colonel Haike, his

The Joshua Inheritance

dark eyes watching Fullerton's expression very closely indeed.

'Let's order,' said Fullerton waving for the head waiter. He wanted to let Haike stew for a moment. They ordered steak and kidney pie, a speciality of the Travellers even under tight food rationing, and Fullerton chose a fine d'Angludet 1928 claret. Throughout the war he had refused to let the Germans upset his passion for good wine and was delighted that their imminent defeat meant the French vineyards could get back to full production again. Thinking of Operation Joshua, he remarked to the wine waiter, 'Perhaps now the Germans have been flung out of Alsace we'll see some more of those very elegant white wines which I enjoy so much.'

The wine waiter smiled dutifully and slid away, and Colonel Haike spoke at once, 'What the devil is going on?'

Fullerton was delighted with the reaction to his news but the situation was serious for both of them. He frowned.

'No-one knows exactly, and the problem is that we should. The whole area has been liberated by the Americans, Patton's Third Army, and yet the chaps on Joshua have not surfaced as we expected them to. The Hudson flew in at the start of November with the entire Commando team, as you know, but it never returned. We all assumed it was hit by enemy ack-ack, or fighters, or crashed in the mountains. However, there's been no sign of anyone on the operation at all. Except, that is, the American member.'

'Axel Romm,' said Colonel Haike. 'I never thought he should have been allowed to go. Your department was quite insistent, though.' He enjoyed scoring a point of his own.

Fullerton said defensively, 'Romm's knowledge of the

area was impeccable. And he was fluent. He lived there before the war.'

'That's probably what let them down,' Colonel Haike put in. In his view, emotional attachments to people or places were far too dangerous on operations. 'I did warn you, old chap.'

Fullerton switched tack and retorted, 'The problem seems to have been less in the choice of personnel than with signals procedures from the field.' He had the satisfaction of seeing Haike go immediately on the defensive.

Haike said carefully, 'I admit we've heard nothing from them since the end of November. We assumed that Romm and Fairfax are either both still alive, but prisoners somewhere in Germany, or both dead. What's new to change that?'

Fullerton delayed his reply while the wine waiter opened the claret for him. He tasted it, enjoying the rich flavour as much as the look of frustration on Haike's face. The wine was poured and Haike was about to speak when Fullerton explained, 'Romm's report has shed new light. He blames George Fairfax for betraying the whole set-up to the Germans. Way back in October.'

Colonel Haike was appalled. He gasped, 'You mean we sent the Hudson to a German reception party?'

Fullerton nodded grimly. 'Looks like it.'

They both sat silent for several moments. Haike fiddled with his tie and Fullerton twisted the stem of his wine glass. He continued, 'The dates in Romm's report make it clear that the Germans must have been running the radio themselves. They signalled us to send the Hudson in November and we obligingly sent fourteen men to their deaths or a Gestapo prison.' The waiter interrupted with the steak and kidney and Fullerton began to eat at once, exclaiming, 'This is excellent!'

Colonel Haike was still grappling with the revelation that the whole operation had been compromised.

The Joshua Inheritance

He demanded incredulously, 'What about the security checks on the signals?'

'They were all there. I've looked,' said Fullerton. 'They stand out like a pikestaff, in retrospect of course, and you overlooked the whole lot, Septimus.' He forked in a mouthful of pie and sipped more wine, watching Haike start his food with automatic gestures and a distant look in his eyes.

'You chose the bloody radio operator,' said Haike sharply but his accusation was without malice. He was on delicate ground and needed support.

'I agree.'

Colonel Haike covered his surprise at Fullerton's consent. He detected a measure of compromise, even complicity, and gently moved on with, 'What else does this American chap of yours, Romm, say?'

'He lays the blame square on George Fairfax. Says George was captured and bubbled the whole Op to the Jerries.' Fullerton sipped his claret.

Colonel Haike grunted, 'Was Romm captured?'

'His report is rather vague on that, actually. I assume so, or the Germans wouldn't have had the radio but it's impossible to say. Romm appeared in American lines on 12 December and categorically refuses to have anything to do with us any more. He says after working with George Fairfax he's had enough of the British.'

'Bounder,' said Colonel Haike with feeling. 'But I don't visualise George as a traitor.' He knew the family well. The son, Edward, had just gone to an Officer Cadet Training Unit and had volunteered at once for the Airborne.

'Nor do I,' said Fullerton, letting his words come out slowly. 'Except that he's disappeared entirely from view, which lends support to Romm's theory that he's too embarrassed to show his face again.'

'Probably still a prisoner.'

Fullerton shook his head and looked cunning. 'No.

He gave himself up to the Americans too, the day before Romm, but instead of staying he borrowed a Jeep and hasn't been seen since.'

'Ah,' said Colonel Haike. Being absent without leave was a serious matter. Especially after a disaster like this.

Fullerton continued lightly, 'If Romm is wrong, George Fairfax should come storming back to put the record straight, don't you think?'

'Damn right,' Haike said. He nodded gratefully as Fullerton poured him some more claret.

'George Fairfax was always a cavalier sort of a devil,' Fullerton went on smoothly. 'So Romm may be right. He says Fairfax gave them away through sheer carelessness. If so, he'll have the book thrown at him. And if Romm is even halfway right, Fairfax is digging a very deep trench for himself by not coming home.'

Haike declared, 'He'll take the blame in any event, eh?'

Fullerton sat back and nodded gently. 'For everything, I'd say. Operating procedures, signals procedures.' He let the words trail.

After a pause, Colonel Haike looked Fullerton straight in the eye and added, 'Choice of personnel too. Yes. No doubt about it.'

Fullerton nodded. He noticed the wine was nearly finished. It had been an excellent bottle.

'Almost best if George doesn't come back at all, wouldn't you say?' Colonel Haike leaned back and wiped his moustache with his napkin.

'Best all round,' agreed Fullerton. 'We shall see when this bloody war is over. Won't be long now.' He relaxed and looked up at the three huge sixteen-branch chandeliers hanging from the high ceiling above them. 'Good show, wasn't it, that the club never succumbed to taking down the chandeliers.'

2

VE-DAY

Tuesday, 8 May 1945

Edward Fairfax did not share everyone else's wild enthusiasm for celebrating the last day of the war in Europe. For five years, the war had uprooted the lives of millions of people all over the world while he had passed exams at a school in the country, safely away from the Blitz and the buzz-bombing in London. Impatiently he had waited to join up like his father, and tried to curb his frustration by studying the details of every campaign in the newspapers. Finally, he had enlisted, passed his War Office Selection Board and basic training, where his determination to join the Paras was rewarded with a transfer to the parachute training depot at Hardwicke Hall, near Sheffield. Now, at the very moment he had finished his training and had proudly pocketed his first posting order to a Para battalion, the German Army had surrendered. Worse, in the early afternoon, Colonel Haike had invited him to his office in Whitehall and what he said was brief but devastating.

He looked Edward straight in the eye and stated, 'Your father is missing.'

'In action?'

'No.'

Colonel Haike was sitting bolt upright behind his large oak desk with his hands resting gently on the leather top. He grimly shook his head; 'I wish I could say so, but it appears he is absent in circumstances of great disgrace. There is talk in the War Office of a court martial.' He paused and added more kindly, 'I'm sorry, Edward, but I'm sure you understand that I'm bound by security. Need to know and all that. I shouldn't really have told you anything, but I've known your father a long time, and your mother too of course. And I know you see quite a bit of my daughter Diana. I thought it best to tell you myself, rather than allow you to be hit by a bombshell of an official letter.'

'I don't believe it!' Edward said instinctively, forgetting this was no way for a junior officer to address a full colonel and an officer of the Imperial Staff. 'He was on the "Q" side, resupplying a tank brigade, wasn't he?'

'Yes, well,' said Colonel Haike vaguely, ignoring the tone. He had known Edward since he was a boy, and liked him. Instead, he shoved his heavy oak armchair back across the carpet, stood up, and walked with neat steps across to the tall windows. His whole appearance was polished. His beautifully tailored service dress was of the finest barathea, and the toe-caps of his hand-made shoes gleamed.

He opened the windows with precise movements and listened to the sound of the crowds gathering in the street outside. 'We shan't be needing these any more,' he said, pointing with genuine pleasure at the wall of sandbags which had been piled on the balcony since the beginning of the war.

His attempt to lighten the atmosphere failed. Edward was oblivious to the noises of celebration, the shouts and laughter floating up from Whitehall below. Tense and confused, he stared at Colonel Haike and insisted, 'What are these circumstances you mention?' It seemed impossible that his father could have disgraced himself.

Colonel Haike paused before replying. Perhaps he had been unwise to pre-empt the official notice that George Fairfax was posted missing. Young officers could be dangerously impetuous and, though Edward was talented and ambitious, he was often forcefully independent.

Colonel Haike unconsciously made a minute adjustment to the knot of his tie. 'I'm very sorry, Edward, but there is nothing further I can say.'

He watched the mixture of confused emotions on Edward's earnest young face and by force of habit began to inspect Edward's uniform – his neatly pressed battledress top and trousers; one bright white pip on each shoulder proclaimed him a very newly commissioned second lieutenant. His shirt and beige cloth tie were carefully ironed, though Colonel Haike had always disliked the standard issue khaki shirt for himself. His belt-buckle brasses glittered satisfactorily on a correctly blacked belt but his boots were not as shiny as Colonel Haike would have liked. He approved the Parachute wings on Edward's arm, which Edward had personally sewn on with enormous care and pride, putting on the battledress top several times to check their exact position in the mirror. Fit and enthusiastic, Edward was rearing to fight the enemy on the field of battle, but he was untried and this made him vulnerable. Not for the first time, Colonel Haike thought it would be best all round if George Fairfax were dead, perhaps killed in a motor accident in that damned Jeep he had taken from the Americans.

'Surely you can tell me at least where he is and when he was last seen?' Edward burst out finally, his mind a turmoil of questions, unconsciously screwing up his red beret in his hands.

Colonel Haike pursed his lips and said, 'Sorry, old chap. All I know is that he's absent without leave. That's bad enough in all conscience, especially for officers, but apparently what he left behind was a simply frightful stink.' Colonel Haike emphasised the words and flicked his hand over his moustache. 'The pity of it is, I don't know a damn thing more. I had it strictly on the q.t., from one of the boys in the personnel machine, as a favour you understand, but he was tight as a drum about passing on any more detail.' He gave an awkward smile of encouragement, walked over and took Edward's arm in an almost paternal way and turned him towards the door of his office. 'I promise that if I hear any more, I'll let you know. And, remember, if you need advice, do not hesitate to ask. I'm always here and ready to do what I can to help.'

Edward nodded. He allowed Colonel Haike to see him out on to the spacious landing where they said goodbye and he tramped down the wide stairway, filling the empty hall with the booming echo of his studded boots clattering on the stone treads. Colonel Haike leaned on the banister and looked down on him as he walked across the marble floor beneath. He observed Edward's back straighten as he pulled his red beret firmly down on his blond head and turned back into his office thinking that there was much in the son that was like the father, only it was as well that the son had not realised that yet. With luck he never would.

The corporal on sentry duty saluted the young Para officer and flung open the heavy wooden doors to the street. He said, 'Innit grand, sir! A piece of 'istory. You'll never forget VE-Day as long as you live.'

Edward saluted automatically. He did not need reminding, but the corporal was undaunted and added cheerfully, 'Five years I've waited for this!' With peace, he would soon be demobbed, a civvy again and then sod the Army and all its officers for good.

Edward stood on the steps looking at the crowd which filled Whitehall from pavement to pavement, shouting and talking excitedly. Cars were marooned in the middle of the road, unable to move, the occupants clustered on the black roofs. People kept looking at their watches and staring expectantly at tannoy loudspeakers which had been tied with wire to the Victorian lamp posts. He felt lost. He had nothing in common with these cheerful masses. The very act of German surrender and the declaration of the long-awaited peace immediately and irrevocably placed him apart. Instead of being just another soldier among the millions who had joined the war, he was now the first of the peacetime British army and already, he reflected bitterly, he was blighted by trouble. He wished Colonel Haike had been able to be more explicit about his father.

The sonorous tones of Big Ben chimed three o'clock, hushing the hubbub of voices. The deep notes from the tower itself in Parliament Square, just a few hundred yards down Whitehall, echoed tinnily in the loudspeakers with sharper urgency. The last excited chatter stilled. Everyone stood in utter silence, fearful they might lose even one syllable of the message they had waited so long to hear.

After a slight pause the familiar gravel voice of Winston Churchill boomed from the tannoys. 'The war in Europe is over! The German generals have surrendered unconditionally. Today, Tuesday, 8 May 1945, the conflict in Europe will end at midnight.'

There was a roar of cheering and people hugged each other ecstatically. Distantly Edward wondered how long the celebrations would last and muttered under his breath, 'What a bloody time to get my first posting!'

He stumped down the steps into the crowd, uncaring of the jubilation around him. He was filled with the injustice of Colonel Haike's vague but serious accusations against his father so much so that he was hardly conscious of barging through the people milling around him in the road.

'Careful!' called a voice beside him.

Edward turned, automatically apologising and saw a girl in uniform, her dark hair tucked under a soft khaki cap. She was rubbing her arm but to his relief she was smiling.

She took in his grumpy expression, waved her hand at the cheering crowds and said, 'You not celebrating?'

He shook his head, not bothering to match her light-hearted tone and excused himself by saying, 'I've just had some rather grim news.'

In spite of Churchill's speech, the girl nodded. So many people had had bad news during the war that the excuse needed no enlarging.

Edward noticed how attractive she was. Suddenly he felt churlish and introduced himself.

'I'm Carole,' she replied shaking his hand and, just to balance matters, added seriously, 'I've had some bad news too.'

'I'm sorry.'

'It doesn't matter,' she shrugged. 'I'm a nurse and used to this kind of thing. I guess in war the best one can say is that it was expected.'

He hesitated. 'Are you American?'

She nodded, smiling at him again, and Edward asked dryly, 'Do Americans always look so cheerful about bad news?'

Her smile widened and he found himself cheering up. He said, 'Since we've both just had bad news, why don't we have a drink together?'

'Drown our sorrows?' she asked looking at him sideways, her eyes large and dark.

'Everyone else will,' said Edward shrugging slightly, beginning to laugh. She let him take her by the arm and they weaved through the noisy masses filling the road. A group near them sang a popular hit at the top of their voices: 'Mairzy doats and dozy doats and little lambsie divies,' and the deep notes of a brass band reached them from the top of Whitehall. The government had removed all restrictions on licensing hours and the VE-Day celebrations had all the makings of a long night. After five years of war, the serious business of thinking about the future could wait till the following day.

3

THE VICTIMS

May–June 1945

Edward rolled out of his camp bed early in the half light of dawn, determined not to be late on his first morning. He washed in cold water, breakfasted on army sausage and beans and walked over to the Company Office under a flat grey sky which threatened rain. As he crossed the parade ground, he returned the salutes of several Paras, feeling very new.

The battalion was occupying a brick barracks in Wismar on the Baltic coast which, until the week before, had belonged to Hitler's Wehrmacht. The buildings were largely undamaged but showed the bullet strikes of strafing attacks from the air and its occupants had fled with the remains of the German army, abandoning Wismar to its fate. Edward's battalion had reached it just before the Russians who were now camped on the outskirts, to the east.

Edward waited in a bare room in one barrack block and looked round at the British Army field tables and chairs which were the only furniture. He pictured the Paras using them over the last years, the maps of famous actions spread over the tables – North Africa, Sicily, Normandy – the men dressed in fighting order, camouflaged, faces blacked, their weapons at their feet, arguing and fixing the attack plans for battles they had fought and died in, the battles which he had missed.

The Joshua Inheritance

He heard boots stamping on the concrete floor. His company commander, Major Rattigan, came in. He was tall and thin, only twenty-six years old, but he had a hard lean face which had seen a great deal of fighting in the previous five years. Edward noticed the purple and white ribbon of the Military Cross above his battledress pocket. Rattigan flung his beret on a table, brushed a hand through his dark hair and said, 'Admiring our tables and chairs? We've only had them a week! Whole bloody war with nothing, but as soon as peace breaks out they give us the chairs to sit on! Marvellous, isn't it?' He laughed and waved his arm at the emptiness. There were shadows on the walls where cupboards had stood. 'Bloody Krauts looted everything. For firewood, I dare say. They're strapped for the lot round here. Food, fuel, clothing. All gone.'

He shook Edward warmly by the hand, welcomed him and briefed him on the situation. 'Last week, we were fighting the Boche, now we're nannying them,' Major Rattigan said without a trace of complaint and ignoring the chagrined expression on Edward's face. As far as Rattigan was concerned this was part of British Army life, fighting one moment, helping the next. 'I'll introduce you to your platoon and then I want you to take a convoy of rations to a refugee camp near Lübeck. A place called Poppendorf. You'll find all sorts there, Germans of course, Czechs, Latvians, Russians, Poles and Jews, what's left of them. They all seem to have come from the east, scared to death of the Reds.' He grabbed his beret. 'Food's the priority. Poor buggers are desperately short. Doc Kelly will go with you.'

They left the office and walked across to the vehicle park. A thin drizzle had started. Groups of soldiers were cleaning and maintaining Bren gun carriers and Jeeps. A troop of Sherman tanks was parked on one side, engines running, mechanics peering inside the engine compartments.

'We just finished muster parade before you arrived. Sergeant Hodgson is over there with your platoon. He joined us when we were in North Africa, where he won a very good DCM.'

Sergeant Hodgson, like the others, wore rough khaki serge battledress, red beret, blancoed belt and anklets over his black boots. Edward guessed he was much the same age as Major Rattigan. Sergeant Hodgson turned to meet the two officers, slamming his boot down on the gravel, and saluted smartly, his face expressionless.

Major Rattigan, as the senior officer of the two, returned the salute less energetically and introduced Edward. 'Mr Fairfax is your new platoon commander, Sergeant Hodgson. Get him settled in as soon as you can. I'm damned sure we're going to be on the move in the near future and I want to be absolutely ready.'

'Sir!' Sergeant Hodgson replied. The single word conveyed at once complete understanding, agreement and the intention to comply. He scrutinised Edward. He had seen a series of young platoon commanders during the war, and not all of them good.

Major Rattigan hoped that Edward would have the good sense to learn from Sergeant Hodgson. He looked at the two of them, platoon officer and platoon sergeant, separated by only a few short years but a wealth of experience. He said, 'The platoon's all yours, Edward, I'll leave you to it.' It was always the same. There was nothing more to be said. It was up to Edward and Sergeant Hodgson.

There was more saluting and Edward was on his own, facing the platoon. They stood to attention, their eyes seemingly straight to their front, but he knew they were watching him closely, waiting for him to act, to order their lives. Three lines of men, thirty-one soldiers. His platoon.

For a moment Edward was at a loss for what to say. Somewhat to his embarrassment, he found his eyes had

The Joshua Inheritance

involuntarily slipped to the DCM ribbon on Sergeant Hodgson's chest.

'Would you like to meet the men, sir?' Sergeant Hodgson enquired tactfully.

Edward agreed. This was right. Keep it formal to start with and then maybe, as time progresses, hope to get to know his platoon sergeant better.

Edward walked slowly down each rank, Sergeant Hodgson following and introducing every men by his rank and name – the three section commanders, all corporals, the section second-in-commands, all lance-corporals, and the men. Britain's Army, the Army of the British Empire, numbered three million men at the end of the war, deployed all round the world, and in Edward's platoon all but a few were conscripted men. He had a few words with each, asking where they came from. He would have more time later when he interviewed each man individually in private, a useful idea his instructor at OCTU had suggested.

What struck him at once was how young they all were, though half had fought through Europe since D-Day. Only a year or two separated the youngest from those who had been on operational parachute drops in Sicily and Arnhem while three, having fought in North Africa, were eligible for the Africa Star. The section NCOs were the 'old men' of the platoon, in their mid-twenties. Two had oak leaves on their ribbons signifying they had received a Mention in Despatches for gallantry. One stocky, muscled private with a square jaw had the Military Medal.

After the parade, the senior section commander, Corporal Jacobs, marched the platoon away to load the trucks and prepare the convoy to go to Lübeck.

'How did Private Brogan get his MM?' Edward asked Sergeant Hodgson.

'I'm not exactly sure, sir. He wasn't with us at the time, he was fighting in France behind enemy lines with a special airborne unit. I believe he fought off the Krauts with his anti-tank gun even though he was wounded.' As his own personal contribution to Brogan's citation, Sergeant Hodgson added simply, 'A good man.'

'Why hasn't he been promoted?'

'He was, sir, to lance-jack,' Sergeant Hodgson replied with a brief smile. 'But 'e was busted down again to private after a couple of months.'

'Drunk?'

'Fighting, sir. 'E was on leave from this 'ere unit of 'is, in England, and got into a brawl in a bar. The Military Police turned up and made a fuss, so 'e got busted and sent back to us. There're always a good few who go up and down the junior ranks before they settle. If they do. Brogan's like that. He 'as to keep busy. In action, I mean.'

Edward felt Sergeant Hodgson did not disapprove of Brogan's behaviour, in fact even looked upon it as showing good form. Clearly, there were unexpected standards of behaviour behind the disciplinary steel of the British Army. Thinking of regulations reminded him uncomfortably about his father. He hoped Colonel Haike had been wrong. He did not want to start his career under the shadow of his father's court martial. He wondered where he was, and why the hell he had disappeared. Perhaps he was somewhere in Germany, near here?

An hour later, when the trucks had been loaded with rations and medical supplies for the refugee camp, Edward had the pleasurable experience of telling his platoon what to do for the first time. He had to decide who should travel in which trucks. These were hardly earth-shaking decisions but vitally important for a new officer. Sergeant Hodgson hovered discreetly at his shoulder and nodded approvingly when Edward put three men in each truck, section NCOs in the front with the drivers and two in the back as guards. Sergeant

The Joshua Inheritance

Hodgson offered to go in the rear vehicle. Edward climbed in the front truck, so he could map-read and chat to Doc Kelly.

The convoy turned out of the barracks gates and headed west along the coast road from Wismar to Lübeck, crossing the flat country which stopped a few miles north at the Baltic Sea. Edward could smell the salt on the damp air. They made poor time. The road was cluttered with refugees in drab little groups, brown and black shadows of people standing on the edge of the road and in the ditches as the trucks passed, the women in long skirts and headscarves protecting silent children with pinched faces and big eyes, their husbands in caps looking after horse carts, hand carts or bicycles piled with the few meagre belongings they had salvaged: mattresses, pots and furniture and endless tattered suitcases.

'Poor buggers,' said Paddy Kelly. He was a powerfully built, bluff, red-faced GP from County Cork who played Rugby for the battalion. He had served with the Paras and sewn them up in numerous battles through Africa, Sicily, Normandy and Holland.

'It's the same picture all the way from the coast,' said Edward, wanting to show he at least knew something about the war in Europe. In the spring of 1945, the roads of Europe were clogged with millions of refugees.

'You arrived yesterday?'

Edward nodded. He kept his story short, acutely conscious that crossing the Channel from Harwich to the Hook of Holland on a passenger steamer and trundling through the Low Countries on a train would hardly grip the imagination of a man who had followed the fighting over the same route since the breakout from France.

'It'll take the world a while to settle down after this terrible war, you know,' remarked Kelly thoughtfully in his gentle Irish brogue.

They stared out through the flat windscreen at the

straggle of refugees along the tree-lined road and bounced on their canvas seats as the Service Corps driver struggled with the steering wheel on the pitted road. After several miles Kelly asked, 'Now tell me, is your father a cavalry officer, Major George Fairfax?'

'Yes, that's right,' Edward replied, looking sharply at the doctor. He felt a sudden twinge of excitement.

'I met him not so long ago.'

'Where?' Maybe Colonel Haike had been wrong.

'In Belsen concentration camp.'

Edward just stared.

'He wasn't an inmate,' Paddy Kelly said reassuringly, seeing the expression of shock on Edward's face; 'he was helping. He helped us set up tents where we could give the poor devils some medicines. We put up food tents and other places where some of the worst could die in peace.'

'Why were you there?'

'Sixth Airborne all passed terribly close to the place, liberated it so to speak, and the commanding officers of every battalion in the division were ordered to send their doctors to do what they could. We found over forty thousand people. Well, they were hardly people by the time we got there. In the last stages of starvation, most of them. I remember talking to one fellow, and the next moment, right in the middle of a sentence, he just fell to the ground and died, right there at my feet.'

Edward struggled to think of something to say. The usual adjectives of horror sounded trite.

Paddy Kelly went on, 'I'm told the Paras said they could smell the place from two miles away, and I can believe it. I showed our Intelligence boys round so they could take photographs. The local Germans thought they were propaganda. Well, they did till we marched them in to have a look for themselves.' For a moment the doctor's eyes glazed, staring into the distance of his mind's eye, seeing the long wooden camp huts slimed inside with human excrement where the wretched inmates had been too weak to move elsewhere.

'I can't think why your father should have been there at all.'

'Did he say why he was?'

'There wasn't much time for talk, not the usual sort, you understand. But he did say he was looking for someone. Possibly more than one person. We were all very busy but your father never seemed to stop. As if he wanted to check all the poor devils in the place. In the end, he drove off as he'd come, in his Jeep.'

'Jeep?'

'Aye. He had an American Jeep.'

'Did he say where he was going?'

'Not a word.'

'Or where he'd come from?'

'He did not,' said Paddy Kelly bluntly. He glanced again at Edward and added more gently, 'Don't misunderstand me, Edward. Your father was charming, but something seemed to be driving him, some sort of terrible, fierce rage. I'd say he was a hard man to see inside.'

In the pale overcast sun of mid-morning that same day, Paul Levi trudged exhausted on to the Baltic coast road and turned his face towards the jagged, bomb-shattered roofline of the German town he could see in the distance. He guessed this was Lübeck and wondered if he had walked far enough. He was young and had been fit once, but there was little to distinguish him now from the other refugees who straggled along the road. He wore a ragged grey overcoat which hung from his narrow shoulders almost to his wooden clogs and provided some protection from the cold wind off the sea to his right. He had taken the coat, and the filthy shirt and trousers underneath, from a dead German civilian he had seen killed in a Russian air attack two days before. Before that, he had escaped from the Germans when the Russians swept across the rolling German plain north of Berlin and he had been walking ever since. In the confusion of sudden peace nothing was settled between the Red Army and the West and he was determined not to be a prisoner again, least of all of the Red Army.

He concentrated on putting one foot in front of another and eventually reached the outskirts of Lübeck. The old Hanseatic town was wrecked. The conical roofs over the massive brick gates pierced the sky like broken black egg-shells; the tall, narrow houses with stepped brick façades were shattered by endless Allied bombing; and the streets were a mess of water-filled craters and mounds of red-brick rubble. Little groups of people clambered about on the debris of their homes trying to salvage their belongings, wraiths among the smoke from fires which still smouldered in the ruins. He plodded on, picking his way through the chaos, heading for the centre of the town, without any idea of what to do after that.

Near the Marienkirche, a man sitting on a pile of broken stones watched him approach. He was middle aged, stocky and wore a filthy old suit over his vest. He drew heavily on a hand-rolled cigarette, to combat the acrid smell of dust and rot around him. As Paul drew level he said, 'Where are you from?'

'From?' Paul stopped his rocking shuffle forward and stared, trying to relate the stunning normality of the question to what he had been through.

The man guessed. He could see Paul's dark hair had been cut to his scalp and was beginning to tuft again like a black brush above the expanse of pale skin of his forehead. As he sucked on the last scrap of tobacco, scorching his throat, and flicked the saliva-stained stub to the ground he asked, 'Which camp were you in, my friend?'

Paul registered the friendly tone of the older man.

The Joshua Inheritance

'We were on a march,' he replied. 'I escaped. Near a place called Goldberg, I think. So many died.' His eyes glazed over.

'Then you have come from Orianenburg,' the man stated. He knew about the death march from Orianenburg, a concentration camp just north of Berlin. Frightened by the Russian advance, the SS had fled the camp, driving the inmates along with them, afraid to leave the evidence of their atrocities. Some five thousand, he guessed, had died on that pointless march west.

He asked, 'What is your name?'

'Paul Ephraim Levi.'

'And where are you going?' So many refugees had no idea.

'I want to go to Eretz Israel!' Since his capture he had thought of nothing else but reaching the Land of Israel.

Paul's reaction took the man by surprise but he said simply, 'Then you have arrived.' He spread his hands like a magician able to conjure up the wildest ambitions.

Paul looked round at the desolated main square as if he could be fooled into thinking he had somehow been transported to the sun-baked citrus groves of his dreams. He stared down at the stranger. He was too tired for useless conversation and said coldly, 'How?'

The man offered him a cigarette and told him, 'Sit down, Paul Levi. I will tell you how. First, you need to eat and sleep. Later you will travel to Israel.'

Paul had no reason to trust anyone. Bluntly, he asked, 'Who are you?'

'My name is Zvi Shkolnik. I am in the Haganah, the army of Eretz Israel.' A slight smile creased his lined face. 'The underground army, that is. My job is to find men like you among our people who have survived the Nazis, the hundred thousand that's left out of more than six million. We need you. The British promised us a national home but they've refused to let us in. The Haganah is committed to ending the diaspora, the dispersal of our people, and to bringing Jews to Israel. That's why we need you.'

'Then I have arrived,' said Paul Levi simply. Shkolnik offered a roll-up. Paul took it and sat down. 'Food,' he said practically. 'I need food.'

Shkolnik knew that Paul had subsisted in the camp on a diet of only one piece of black bread a day. He nodded. 'And sleep. Were you in Orianenburg for long?'

'Long enough.'

Shkolnik grunted. He would learn more about Paul Levi in due course. 'There's a refugee camp not far from here. Run by the British. They're supplying food and clothing.'

Their conversation was interrupted by a convoy of British Army trucks rumbling through the broken town, gleaming headlights reflected off the puddles in the road. They slowly followed the narrow twisting lane which had been opened between the piles of bricks fallen out from the houses, lurching and splashing in and out of potholes and forcing Paul and Zvi to clamber across the rubble to avoid being soaked.

Shkolnik swore. As they stood in the roofless shell of someone's home Paul watched the Paras in the back of each truck, neat figures in serge battledress and red berets. He noted the professional way they held their sub-machine-guns, loose but alert, their hands on the pistol grip, thumbs by the safety catch. The war was over, but only just and there were still German soldiers about, armed and ready to kill for the rations they carried.

Paul pulled on his cigarette and felt his head spin. 'I know all about the British,' he said, 'They're always doing what they call the "right thing". By the goddam book.'

'What book?' Shkolnik asked, scratching his grizzled

neck. He was Polish, recruited into the Haganah by a Jew who had come from Palestine. He had never had any contact with the British.

'The book of the law. Their law. They write it themselves,' replied Paul. 'And they change it to suit themselves whenever necessary.' He wondered what lies had been told about him in London or if there would be a time in his life when he would shake free of the British. Perhaps one day in Israel. There was so much to do first. He said, 'I'm grateful to you, Zvi Shkolnik. You are the first man I've met in years who is a real friend. We come from the same background, you and I.' He gestured at the ruined house and the rubble-filled street and seized Shkolnik by the shoulders. 'We have nothing now. We are uprooted, but we'll beat the British and their bloody Empire. They've won the war, but they're tired. I've seen it.' He took a last deep pull on the butt end of his cigarette and added bitterly, 'God knows, I've experienced it. They're morally drained. But we have the spirit, and we shall win!'

He flung the smoke away, feeling giddy. The nicotine was too strong for him after so long on his feet, marching so many miles without food. He had to recover. Zvi watched the bright tip curve into the ruins of the house.

Paul said quietly, 'Take me to this refugee camp. I may hate the British, but there's nothing wrong with their food.'

Shkolnik said, 'The bridge is down over the River Trave, so we'll have to follow those trucks through the town.'

Poppendorf refugee camp was on flat sandy land near the big Luftwaffe airfield of Travemünde, where the murky river Trave mixed with the cold Baltic sea. The icy winds from the north-east raked across the sand bars and whined through the wire fences round the wooden huts. A line of refugees approached the camp from the direction of the railway line which ran past to the airfield, while hundreds more struggled for space between the huts, gaunt-faced men settling their families as best they could, helped everywhere by British military policemen, medical orderlies and harassed officers who tried to make lists of everyone who came in through the gates.

One officer, a burly British major in his forties, had had enough. His Jeep was parked by the wire-and-wood-frame main gate and he stood with his hands on his hips, fists bunched on his webbing belt. He looked round the camp for the last time, searching the faces of the refugees, knowing it was hopeless. None of the names of the inmates was one of the ones he wanted to see. He shook himself, admitting it was unlikely he would find the people he wanted in a refugee camp but he had had to try. Now he climbed into his Jeep, started the engine and drove through the gates. He paused at the main road which ran parallel to the railway, leaning on the steering wheel, undecided.

Far down the road to Lübeck, he saw a line of British Army trucks approaching. He wondered for a moment what brought them to this desolate limb of land and then decided to avoid them. He let out the clutch and turned north, away from them, towards Travemünde. There might be officers among the troops on the convoy who would want to see his movement authority. Officialdom was already creeping in only days after the end of the war, and besides, he was not ready to answer questions. There were other camps he had to check first.

Edward's convoy reached Poppendorf about midday and for several hours he was busy supervising the unloading and fair distribution of food. Sergeant Hodgson quickly developed a good working relationship with the Military Police who ran the camp. He directed the platoon to set up tables between the huts, to prevent

The Joshua Inheritance

their being surrounded by a mêlée of people, and soon had orderly queues of refugees waiting patiently for the rations. Sergeant Hodgson stood with his SMG slung, hands behind his back, easing up and down on the balls of his feet, as if on parade, watching the queues with a fatherly eye. Quite soon, he spotted a young boy trying to take a second issue. He waited till the boy had moved up the queue near to the table, then he stepped swiftly forward, grabbed him by the ear and pulled him out in front so all the refugees could see. Raising his voice, he bellowed, 'Come along now, my lad. There's others waiting for theirs.' He pulled the boy's face close to his, glaring at him as if he were a new recruit on the square at the Para depot, and bellowed. 'Stealing another man's rations is a court martial offence! We won't do that again, will we?' He let go and the boy scuttled off rubbing his ear. Few of the refugees spoke English, but the message was clear.

Paul Levi and Zvi Shkolnik reached the camp late in the afternoon, on a wagon pulled by two black mares belonging to a family who had walked from Trakehnen in East Prussia. Shkolnik was chatting to some other Poles he recognised standing near the wire gates and immediately told Paul, 'I'll get your ration. But you must see the doctor.'

Paul pulled his ragged coat round his shoulders and joined another queue. Queues were part of life in concentration camps, in refugee camps, in army camps and he blamed the British. Everyone in England queued for everything and he decided that the British Empire, like Hitler's Third Reich, was nothing more than a vast camp, staffed by the Colonial Office and guarded by the British Army. He hoped that no-one queued in Israel.

'Next!' A shout from inside disturbed his thoughts and he stepped up into the wooden hut. An army medic took down his name and nationality. Most refugees had no other personal details to give. There was no way of checking and Paul automatically gave a false name.

He waited on the bare boards in the middle of the room. The doctor was standing with his back to him, dressed in rolled-up shirt sleeves and braces and scrubbing his hands in a white enamel bowl with a blue rim. Paul observed the doctor's broad back and felt detached.

'I'm Dr Kelly,' said the doctor turning round and wiping his hands on a small khaki towel. 'D'you speak English, Irish or one of these funny lingos like Polish, German or Russian? In other words, my friend, do I have to find the bloody interpreter again?' It had been a long day.

Paul hesitated, surprised not to feel more animosity toward the doctor. He was the first British officer who had spoken to him since he had been arrested. He said, 'I speak English.'

'And damned good by the sound of it,' said Paddy Kelly appreciatively. 'Tell me, now, you being a Pole. Where did you learn that?'

'I learned it. That's all.' His past was none of the doctor's business.

'Alright then. Alright,' Dr Kelly replied soothingly. He ushered Paul to sit down and stuck a thermometer in his mouth, talking as he worked. 'You've no idea how it warms my heart to talk to a patient in my own language after a day diagnosing more exotic diseases than a Cork general practitioner would see in a year, in people from more countries than the Dublin passport office sees in a decade.' He told Paul to strip and checked his lungs, blood pressure and muscles, dictating notes to the medic sitting at a portable desk in the corner.

'You know I found a case of the common cold in a Latvian lady but, through the medium of a Pole who spoke no English and a Russian who spoke no Latvian, I think she got the idea she had terminal tuberculosis.' He stood back, hands on hips, and demanded, 'Anything particular wrong with you?'

Paul stared.

'Don't look so insulted, man! Spit it out! You don't have TB, typhoid, typhus, cholera, jaundice, pneumonia, tetanus, or even the common cold, so you've nothing seriously wrong with you. You're run down, you've got terrible blisters on your feet and you're thin. Awful thin. But you're in good shape compared to some of the poor devils I've seen. Nothing that food and rest can't cure. I'd say you're a lucky man.'

'Lucky! What d'you know about luck?' Levi burst out.

Dr Kelly ignored the outburst, looked him straight in the eye and said, 'I think you'll get by. You've survived the camp, haven't you?'

'What d'you know about camps?' Paul asked surprised but bitter.

'Never mind. I've seen a few like you before,' Paddy Kelly replied in his soft lilting brogue. He had no time for one man's bitterness. His concern was with the sick and the ones who waited outside. He turned away to wash his hands in the enamel bowl. 'Now, I've got other patients to see, if you don't mind, worse than you. Just remember, if you want to go on living, it's a terrible help to be alive in the first place.'

As Paul stamped out across the boards to the door, his fury lost in the doctor's strange logic, he bumped into a young British officer coming in and snapped rudely in Polish, '*Pacz gze idczes!*'

Edward apologised and quickly backed away to let Paul out of the hut. In his hurry Paul stumbled on the step, his feet painfully blistered and he took it out on Edward, '*Ti kurwa!*'

'I say, hold on!' Edward said, quickly putting out his hand to steady him.

Paul shook free, embarrassed and angry. He hurried

away, feeling sick in his stomach. Edward watched him disappear around the corner of the hut, his clogs spitting up tails of sand on the bare ground. He supposed there must be a volume of resentment when so much had been lost. Thoughtful, he went back in to see if Doc Kelly was ready for the drive back to barracks.

A week later in Kensington, Edward's mother, Anne Fairfax, was sitting bolt upright in a wing-backed chair in the drawing-room of her flat. She was wearing a severely plain dark grey dress and her fair hair was pulled into a loose bun at the back of her neck to conceal the streaks of grey and show off the excellent skin of her face. She concentrated as she poured tea into bone china cups.

'I wish there were lemons in the shops again,' she said to Diana Haike. 'We haven't had them for five years and I have always preferred lemon to sugar in my tea.'

Diana nodded and crossed her long legs. Even sitting down she was obviously an attractive young woman with an excellent figure and waves of blonde hair. It crossed Anne's mind that her son always picked the best, in appearance at least, even though Diana's determination to make her relationship with Edward permanent was sometimes unnecessarily blatant. Of course, the families had known each other for years, but she hardly thought Edward was ready to settle down.

'D'you think rationing will go on long?'

'Now the war's over, it ought to end soon,' said Diana with a slight frown. She had come to find out about Edward and wished his mother would be less formal. Diana guessed that Anne Fairfax was in her mid-forties but she looked younger, with smile lines around the corners of her mouth which suggested she could be fun. Diana needed female support. Her own mother lived in Scotland, separated from her father, and neither Colonel Haike nor her brother Roger took the slightest notice of women.

'Surely the ships can get here now?' said Anne, passing a cup to Diana. It rattled in the saucer. 'After all, the German submarines aren't sinking our vessels any longer and I gather there are extensive citrus fruit plantations in Palestine.'

There was a moment's silence while the two women sipped tea. The large clock on the mantelpiece was ticking slowly and soporifically. Diana looked over at Edward's photograph on the piano, among all the other family photographs. He was wearing his new uniform, one pip up and his wings showing.

'Any news of Edward?' she asked casually, brushing her hair back from her face.

'Yes, I've had one letter,' Anne replied, ready to talk now that the ritual of afternoon tea had begun. She smiled at Diana, folded her hands softly in the lap of her dark dress and said, 'He's arrived safely after a long slow train ride through the Low Countries. He says there are signs of the fighting all the way. Burned tanks and, of course, refugees everywhere. Those poor people.' She sighed. 'He's somewhere on the Baltic Coast now. Rather cold, I should imagine.'

Diana nodded, willing Edward's mother to go on, to say if Edward had talked about her.

Anne Fairfax continued. 'Apparently they are inside the eastern part of Germany which is to be controlled by the Russians. He says the Paras are going to pull back.'

'When? Did he say when?'

'In a matter of weeks, I think. They have to come back to England. He says Germany is devastated. I suppose one should feel sorry for the Germans, but I must confess I don't have much sympathy. It's all too grim. Let's hope this will be an end of conflict for a long time.' She did not mention her husband's trouble. The whole business was mortifying and Diana did not need to know. At least not yet, and she fervently hoped George Fairfax would turn up soon to clear himself of the allegations, whatever they were. Her spirits had been hugely lifted by Edward's mentioning that the Regimental doctor had seen his father. Perhaps she should tell Colonel Haike? He was being tremendously helpful but Edward had not elaborated and she decided to leave it till he returned to England.

Diana did not notice the little frown cross Anne Fairfax's face. She wanted to know whether Edward had written about her. She picked up her handbag and made a show of looking for something inside it. Trying to sound as offhand as she could, she asked, 'Did he mention me at all? I mean, whether he'd got my letter?'

Anne Fairfax knew perfectly well what was going through Diana Haike's mind. 'He hasn't had your letter yet, or mine.' She paused a moment, watching Diana fiddling with the handbag. 'But he did say he was looking forward to seeing you when they come back to England.'

Diana looked up quickly with a radiant smile. When she saw Anne Fairfax's amused expression, she burst out laughing.

4

SUMMER DANCE

28 July 1945

Two days after the announcement of the result of the General Election, when the British electorate rejected Sir Winston Churchill and the Tories in favour of the Labour Party under Clement Attlee, and a week after the wartime 'blackout' was finally lifted in London and the south-coast resorts, the colonel of the battalion had decided there would be a summer dance in the Officers' Mess. On their return from Germany they had moved into Bulford, on the edge of Salisbury Plain, and everyone had been reunited with wives and girlfriends for the first time since the end of the war. Mindful that the Japanese were still fighting on, and that there was every expectation that the Paras would be sent to the Far East, the Colonel wanted a splendid occasion to celebrate the battalion's success in Northern Europe.

As the guests arrived, the Regimental Band played a selection of marches. Everyone wore battledress, except a few older officers with their own Mess dress from pre-war service, and Edward had taken care to look immaculate, his trousers ironed to a knife edge and his brown leather shoes gleaming. He could not help noticing that most other officers, and some soldiers in the band, had medals, ribbons on their chests, campaign medals and awards from Africa or Italy, mute statements that they had served in the war he had missed.

'Who d'you ask tonight?'

Edward looked round. Aubrey Hall-Drake had slouched over, his hands typically in his pockets, wearing his usual benign grin. He brushed a strand of straight dark hair away from his eyes. He was the other subaltern in the Company with Edward and they had immediately made friends, even though Aubrey had joined in time to see the last action in the war, earning a very brave Military Cross. He was quite unaffected by the honour. Tall, charming and lazy, he had considerable private means and took life as it came.

'Diana Haike,' Edward replied. 'Major Rattigan's found her a place to stay with some friends of his who are coming.'

Aubrey's grin widened. 'Well, I've asked one of those nurses we saw the other night. What if she tells her friend about this Diana of yours? Might spoil a good thing there, eh?'

Edward shrugged. 'There will be others.'

Aubrey wagged his finger. 'You'll be caught out one of these days, Edward Fairfax, mark my words.' He frowned and added, 'Haike, you say? No relation of that toad Roger? Chap in the Gunner support lot.'

'Yes. Roger's her brother.'

'Hope she's better looking.' Aubrey slipped a Turkish cigarette from a silver case in his jacket. He offered one to Edward who declined. A large Austin shooting brake had pulled up on the gravel below the Mess steps and Edward spotted Diana inside. He went down the steps to meet her.

She was stunning. Her fair hair fell in soft curls over her bare shoulders and a rich cream dress clung to her figure, cascading in gentle folds to the tips of her shoes and shimmering when she moved. She knew she looked good and enjoyed the looks of admiration when she walked up the steps into the Mess.

'I say,' breathed Aubrey to himself. He put his

The Joshua Inheritance

cigarette back in the silver case and ambled forward rather more sharply than usual to meet her, putting out his hand. 'What a simply delightful way to start the evening.'

Edward introduced Diana, smiling broadly. He knew they were the focus of attention and though he was acutely conscious of being the most junior officer in the Mess, he felt intensely pleased with himself. Diana was perfect.

As they went to find a drink, Aubrey whispered to Edward, 'I can see why you weren't bothered about the nurses, old boy, with a model like this one in the garage.'

Edward hissed, 'For god's sake, Aubrey! Can it!'

Aubrey Hall-Drake put his hands up in an expression of mock horror: 'My dear chap, you don't think I'd give away boys' secrets! The nurses, God bless 'em, are purely for fun. Medical study and all that. I assure you.' He gestured surreptitiously in the direction of Diana's bottom shimmering voluptuously in front of them as they walked into the bar, 'This one, though, is serious stuff. No wonder you keep her hidden away.'

Edward laughed. 'Go away, Aubrey.'

'I must, old chap. Got to pick up my poor little nurse. See you later.'

Diana was in a sparkling mood, wildly excited by the splendour of the occasion, the uniforms, the flowers, the glittering chandeliers reflected in the polished regimental silver on the tables and the music. After dinner, they danced, swinging through several fast numbers and when the band played a soft waltz, she moved closer, into his arms. She was breathing hard and her pale skin was flushed pink. Edward felt a sudden rush of blood in his veins and wondered if she realised how much he wanted her. He slipped his hand as far round as he dared without attracting attention and, after two slow dances, he pulled her away and outside through the french windows into the garden.

She followed happily, saying, 'I'm going to miss you awfully if you have to go away.'

'And I will miss you,' said Edward.

'Really?' she asked, searching his face. Even though their families had been friends for years, and the two of them had played together as girl and boy on shared holidays at Frinton-on-Sea before the war, she was not sure how well she knew him now that he had become a man.

'Yes, of course,' he smiled and leaned forward to kiss her on the lips. He had said the same to lots of girls, but this time he was sure he meant it because she looked so beautiful and because the occasion made them important together.

The night was warm and they sat on a low stone wall in the garden looking at the still waters of a pond, silver in the moonlight. Edward slipped his arm round her waist and she wriggled closer, tucking herself into his side, happy that her plans for the evening had worked out so well.

A loud voice behind them shouted, 'There you are! Looking everywhere for you!'

Edward's heart sank. He whispered, 'Your brother has a knack of turning up when he's least wanted.'

Diana put her finger gently on Edward's lips and said in a husky voice, 'Maybe he'll go away if we don't say anything.' She had never got on with her brother. He was older than both of them, and still bullied her, but the days at the seaside when he had sat on Edward and hit him were long gone.

'He's being damn nosey.' Edward refused to look round but he could hear Roger Haike coming down the steps.

'Thought I'd find you two lurking in the garden,' Roger shouted as he stopped to slurp from a glass

The Joshua Inheritance

of champagne. He joined them, blocking their view of the pond, and announced cheerily, 'I wanted to know if you'd make up an eight for the reels? They're starting soon.'

Edward looked at Roger standing stiff as a mannequin in his pressed battledress. Roger was small, wiry like a terrier, and his dark hair was smoothed back from his forehead, copying his father, but he had none of his father's sophisticated poise. He sported a small black moustache which he thought suited someone who had seen a bit of action at the end of the war. He had been lucky enough to join Operation Varsity in an artillery battery supporting British troops crossing the Rhine, and never stopped talking about it.

'We'll come in shortly, Roger, and sort something out then,' said Edward, hoping he would go away.

Roger did not go away. He continued with false enthusiasm. 'Jolly well better come now, or the eightsomes will all get booked up.' His eyes became accustomed to the pale moonlight of the garden. 'I say, you're not up to hanky-panky with my sister, are you?'

Edward guessed this was the only reason Roger had come out to find them and said, 'Go and do a reel if you want to, Roger, but we're staying out here for a while.' Diana giggled.

Roger snapped, 'I know what you're like, Edward Fairfax. Up to no good.'

Edward took a deep breath to control his temper. He eased off the wall, with his arm round Diana, to lead her away, leaving Roger standing by the pond.

'You're making a terrible mistake, Diana,' said Roger pompously. 'I've been watching Fairfax and that lay about Hall-Drake since we got back from Germany and they're like a pair of dogs on heat.'

Edward stopped as they passed Roger, and said, 'Bitches, Roger. Bitches get on heat. Not dogs.'

'It's not funny, Diana,' said Roger crossly, trying to

look round Edward at Diana who was grinning with amusement. 'There's an awful lot of venereal disease about after the war.'

'Damnit, that's beyond the pale!' Suddenly furious, Edward reacted at once. He pushed the flat of his hand on Roger's chest and shoved hard. Roger staggered back, his heel tripped on the uneven flags and he fell full length backwards into the pond.

Water washed out of the pond, cascading everywhere. Diana put her hands to her mouth in surprise and a roar of laughter from the terrace made Edward spin round. Aubrey Hall-Drake was watching, one arm round his nurse. With him was the Adjutant, Captain Ian Fogg, known to all as 'Phileas' and his wife. To Edward's relief, 'Phileas' was hugely amused and Aubrey called out, 'Wonderful! Hope you don't mind, but I knew there'd be fun as soon as I spotted Roger on his way out to find you.' Roger sat up in the fish pond, his hair plastered flat with water, soaked to the skin.

Diana was crying with laughter too and said, 'Come on, Edward, come on! Let's go before he gets out!' Roger was speechless with amazement as she pulled Edward away. They ran off into the darkness before Roger could recover his breath, deeper into the garden, where she could have Edward to herself uninterrupted.

'Bastard!' Roger exclaimed at last. 'I'll get the bastard for this. My god! I promise it.'

5

DEPLOYMENT

August–September 1945

Paul Levi sat outside the gates of Poppendorf camp, his head in his hands. He was muttering, 'I have to get away.'

Zvi Shkolnik and the others sitting round with him nodded. Nationalities in Poppendorf naturally grouped – Russians, Latvians, Poles, Prussians and others with a common language – but the Jews grouped because of their faith; their faith in the past, the diaspora, and, unlike the others, the faith they had in the future: Zionism. Europe held nothing for them any longer but they looked to a new life, in Palestine, in Eretz Israel, the country which the League of Nations had entrusted to the British under the Mandate of 1922.

'We all want to go,' said Zvi. 'But you're not really strong enough yet.'

The food in Poppendorf was good, regular and balanced, they slept and they slowly recovered their energies which had been drained by their experiences. The British medics did their best. They had been given 'new' old clothes, suits, shirts and vests, which they wore without complaint, though some repeated a black joke that these were the clothes taken from the victims of the death camps.

'For god's sake, I can't stay here,' said Paul. He looked round the windswept landscape and the bearded faces of the men sitting with him. 'I know the gates of this camp are always open, but it still reminds me of Orianenburg.' He mentioned the concentration camp without qualms, because he was among men who understood. 'We are fed and watered, like cattle, but the Russians are moving closer from the east, to take over all this part of eastern Germany, and I don't trust the British. I've had enough.'

'They promise us we'll get papers soon,' said one, a married man in his late forties with a beard and black skull-cap who, to his own surprise, had survived the Warsaw ghetto with his wife. His children had not.

Paul replied harshly, 'That's a euphemism for saying they'll release us when they want to.'

Zvi added, 'The last thing the British want is a flood of Jews arriving in Palestine. They've cut the immigration to fifteen hundred a month.'

A young man asked worriedly, 'When will we be allowed to go?' He had survived Buchenwald with the thought that his parents had already succeeded in reaching Eretz Israel and he was desperate to join them.

'I'll get you there, Selig, don't worry,' Zvi said.

'I want to go now,' Selig insisted. 'I'll go with Paul.'

Paul had watched Selig carefully during the last weeks. He was dark, slightly built and young, so he had recovered his strength quickly. He would be a useful companion, if a little over-enthusiastic. It would not pay to draw attention to themselves during the journey through Europe.

'You're not worried about going?' Shkolnik said. 'There will be checks and always the chance of arrest.'

Paul shrugged. Shkolnik had seen others who were as determined as Levi, but Levi's attitude suggested he knew more than most about avoiding the police.

'I'll tell you what I can,' Zvi Shkolnik said.

Paul nodded, smiling. Selig ought to hear, if he was to leave Europe for Eretz Israel too. He leaned forward and listened closely while Shkolnik explained about the controls which had been imposed throughout Europe by the British, American and French armies, and how to pass through them with the papers he would supply. When he finished, Shkolnik had the impression he had been wasting his breath. He asked Paul, 'Were you on the run long? Before they caught you?'

'Actually no.' Paul's face clouded with remembered pain, but he did not want to reveal his personal humiliation. 'Let's just say I've learned a lot since.'

Imperial Japan had still to be defeated and 6 Airborne Division was going to be thrown into the battle. The prospect was bloody. In June, 7,000 American soldiers had died taking the island of Okinawa for General MacArthur. The Japanese, fighting for every foxhole, lost 110,000. The Paras knew they must train as never before.

Edward was delighted at the prospect of action, but worried how he would react under fire. No-one really talked about how they coped with being shot at, and Aubrey Hall-Drake was typically vague about his own brief and intense experience. Plainly, everyone had to deal with the event in their own way, so Edward adopted an attitude of quiet confidence which he did not always feel, and ignored the twinges of apprehension as deployment to the Far East loomed closer.

The Headquarters of 5 Parachute Brigade was flown to Bombay, as an advance party, and there was endless talk of operations in the jungle. No-one had been to the Far East and Edward realised that even those who had seen plenty of fighting against the Germans were worried about taking on the Japanese in the jungle. There was a good deal of talk about the sweltering heat, the dark vegetal gloom of the forest, insects, snakes, disease and getting lost. There was no chance of getting lost on the open grassland slopes of Salisbury Plain where they had to prepare for their move east, but Major Rattigan took the training seriously.

'The company will carry out a Jewt on Salisbury Plain,' he said during a company 'Orders Group' in the Victorian brick-built barracks on the edge of the Plain. Edward was now used to these 'O' Groups, which were the essential medium of communication in the Army. With the other company officers and senior NCOs all in battle kit, he sat taking notes on how the forthcoming training would affect his platoon. Carefully, he extracted the details of Major Rattigan's orders which he would later use in his own platoon 'O' Group to Sergeant Hodgson and his Section corporals.

Aubrey Hall-Drake interrupted, waving his pencil, and drawled, 'I say, sir. What's a Jewt?'

'Quiet, Drake! Questions at the end!' Captain Scarland snapped. He was the company second-in-command, built like a bull, with a broad face and a prominent square chin he liked to stick out. Edward thought he looked very like Mussolini.

'The name's Hall-Drake,' Aubrey replied very quietly, perfectly well aware that Captain Scarland was jealous of his MC.

Captain Scarland glared back and retorted, 'Don't interrupt the OC during Orders!'

'I shall continue,' said Major Rattigan pointedly. He followed the approved Army procedure for giving orders, with an explanation first of the area. 'The Ground,' he stated solemnly. 'All of you are well aware that Salisbury Plain is a vast, treeless feature of rolling grass hills, where visibility can be several miles, assuming, that is, the driving rain holds off for a moment. Whereas the jungle is, so I'm told, very steep and thickly covered in trees which severely restrict visibility.'

Edward looked up at his company commander, detecting irony in his voice.

The Joshua Inheritance

'The Army obliges us to train on Salisbury Plain for operations in the tropics, so the exercise we're going to do is called a JEWT, a Jungle Exercise Without Trees.' He paused for the laughter, and added, 'Gentlemen, you will use your imagination to bolster the scenario.'

Edward and his platoon trained hard, advancing and withdrawing across the Plain in hot sun and sudden drenching summer showers, digging trenches in the warm chalky turf and then filling them in again.

During one terrible night exercise the rain sleeted horizontally across the Plain. Major Rattigan was away and Captain Scarland had ordered the company to 'defend' a hill. He put Edward's platoon next to Hall-Drake's on one side and the third platoon over the hill behind them. Company Headquarters was in the middle. Edward laid out the positions of the trenches with Sergeant Hodgson at last light, and the Paras began to dig on a gentle turf slope which might have been an agreeable place for a picnic on a sunny day, but that night was black, wet and miserable. As usual, just beneath the grass was solid chalk. By midnight, everyone was soaked to the skin, slimed with mud and chalk, but no-one was near the regulation depth of four feet. Edward doubted whether anyone would finish the job before dawn. He staggered over to see Aubrey Hall-Drake.

'What a bastard,' Aubrey declared feelingly, raising his voice against the wind.

'D'you mean Captain Scarland or the weather?' Edward asked. 'Your lot going to finish these bloody trenches before first light?'

'Doubt it,' said Aubrey. 'We'll have to fill the buggers in anyway. Scarface is bound to move us all somewhere else then. Have a brew.' He reached under a glistening wet tarpaulin where he and his signaller had lit a small fire in a tin, and produced a mug of steaming hot tea. Edward held the mug in frozen fingers and was enjoying the scalding warmth of the tea sliding down his neck and spreading across his chest when Captain Scarland appeared out of the night.

'What the devil you doing here, Fairfax? Can't you cope with your own platoon?' Captain Scarland peered closely at Edward, trying to read his expression in the darkness and spotted the mug of tea. He shouted, 'Tea? You're supposed to be tactical. No cooking or lights allowed!'

Hall-Drake felt responsible and diplomatically pointed out, 'I don't really think the light can be easily seen on a night like this, sir.' Especially not under a tarpaulin, Edward muttered to himself. Water was pouring off his helmet and down his neck.

Captain Scarland deliberately turned his back on Hall-Drake and shouted at Edward, 'Idiot! You wouldn't have got away with a trick like that fighting the Germans.' The remark was unanswerable and Captain Scarland knew it.

Scarland's hand whipped up, knocking the mug out of Edward's hands and he watched Edward closely, his chin jutting out, daring him to react. Edward held his temper in check.

After a long moment while the rain poured off their helmets, Captain Scarland snapped, 'Show me your platoon, Fairfax,' and he squelched off through the mud. Edward glanced at Aubrey, who pulled a face and shrugged, and hurried to catch up. He did not want Captain Scarland causing trouble with his Paras unless he was there to take the heat and arrived as Captain Scarland began to storm round the platoon position criticising everything, swearing at the men who were still digging in, soaking figures bent over in their shallow trenches hacking at the stubborn chalk in the bottom. Sergeant Hodgson appeared out of the dark and Edward sensed his fury. He had approved Edward's layout of the platoon and Captain Scarland knew it. Edward realised this was Captain Scarland's way of

The Joshua Inheritance

showing that Sergeant Hodgson's greater experience of the war did not count where rank was concerned.

The weather worsened in buffeting gusts of rain, making everything invisible except close to. The three approached the last group of trenches. Through the blackness, Edward caught sight of Private Brogan in his trench. Amazingly, Brogan had finished. He was leaning casually forward on the parapet of his trench with his sub-machine-gun sticking out from under his cape, on sentry duty. Edward dropped to his haunches and said, 'Looks good, Brogan. All done, then?'

'Ah well, sir,' Brogan replied evasively, glancing past Edward at Captain Scarland looming over his trench.

'This soldier proves my point,' Captain Scarland shouted into the wind. 'Why can't the rest of your useless lot do the same?'

Ignoring the water running in icy rivulets down his back, Edward peered into the trench. Through the dark, he could just see Brogan's feet under the cape. His heels, not his toecaps. Brogan hadn't dug any more than anyone else.

Edward looked up. Standing, Captain Scarland could see nothing in the darkness of the trench. He shouted, 'Get a bloody grip, Fairfax. I want the rest like this before dawn.'

In spite of the weather, Edward smiled. He was fed up with Captain Scarland. Only Brogan saw him smile. In a deliberately puzzled voice, Edward said, 'Like this? Are you sure?'

'Of course I'm bloody sure!'

'Right ho! Then perhaps you'd make doubly certain, Captain Scarland. You know, jump in and see for yourself.' Edward almost laughed out loud at the expression of shocked appeal on Brogan's face.

'First sensible thing you've said all night,' growled Captain Scarland and leaped in. He expected to land four foot down. Instead he thudded in at two foot, jarring his spine and driving the air from his lungs. He collapsed on the parapet, gasping for breath. Edward stood up and watched, saying nothing. Sergeant Hodgson beside him said nothing. Brogan, still on his knees beside Captain Scarland, wished he was somewhere else. The rain poured down on Captain Scarland who was wriggling about in the muddy spoil of Brogan's trench struggling to his feet and swearing terribly. He clambered out, glared at Edward and, without a word, stamped off through the puddles into the darkness back to Company Headquarters.

Edward said lightly, 'Keep up the good work, Brogan,' and turned away. Sergeant Hodgson followed him, saying quietly, 'Come over to my trench, sir. I've got a brew on. I 'spect you'd fancy a nice cup of hot tea now. Eh?'

Suddenly the rain did not matter any more.

As his train crossed from Germany into Austria. Paul Levi's depression lifted. The Alps rose to rocky snow-capped peaks and blue sky on both sides, the carriage rocked hypnotically in the warm sun and Paul felt the malaise of France and Germany gradually lifting as he travelled south. Selig sensed the change too so that, after a week travelling together, he finally plucked up courage to ask, 'Paul, have you got any family?'

Paul stared out of the window at the lush Alpine pastures and little wooden houses for a long time before answering. He told himself Selig was not prying, just trying to relate to his own experience, so he said, 'Not any more.'

Selig looked embarrassed and said in a rush, 'I'm sorry. Leave it.' He had heard too many painful stories and did not want to hurt his new friend whom he instinctively trusted and liked.

Paul waved away his objections. Crossing the Alps was symbolic. He was leaving the memories behind and

The Joshua Inheritance

maybe sometimes it was good to talk. He started slowly: 'My father took the family away from Warsaw, to our house in the country. He foolishly thought we would be ignored there, but of course someone denounced us and a SS Einsatzgruppe patrol found us. I was collecting wood in the forest, as we dared not go into town to buy coal, and I heard the shooting. I ran back, but I was too late.' And helpless. 'They were all butchered. Against the farmhouse wall.' Where he remembered happy summer parties, eating outside, laughing and gaiety. He stopped. The pain was too acute, fuelled by the guilt of survival. He still wished he had run over to his mother and father, and been killed with them.

The compartment door rattled open and a British lance-corporal barged in from the corridor, his .303 rifle slung over his shoulder.

'Papers, please!'

Paul and Selig looked up in surprise. They thought they had left the British behind in North Germany, where they had been on the left flank of the Allied invasion armies. They had passed through the American sector in the south and did not expected to see British soldiers again in Austria.

Paul dug inside his second-hand suit for the little oilskin package which contained all that was important to him in his new life: the money Zvi Shkolnik had given him, his identity papers, and his authority to travel. He handed the papers to the lance-corporal.

'Mr Levi, Paul Ephraim,' the lance-corporal read out. His dark blue beret sat large on the side of his head as he bent to inspect Zvi Shkolnik's forged documents. 'So you're a Frenchman, are yer? Very good. What yer doing in Austria?'

'I am on my way to Italy. To find business,' Paul replied. He noticed the insignia of the Desert Rat on the man's shoulder. He remembered one of the team in England saying that the British 8th Army had finally stopped its advance up the eastern flank of Italy in Austria's southern provinces.

The lance-corporal eyed Paul's brown suit and the battered suitcase on the luggage rack above and declared, 'Well, if yer speak as good Eytie as yer do English, yer'll do alright.' He saw no point cross-examining all the passengers. Thousands of ragged-looking people were on the move in Europe. They all had papers which were all different and all the writing was foreign. As far as he was concerned, they could do what they liked provided they caused no trouble. He was a soldier, not a bloody ticket inspector and certainly not a bloody policeman. He handed Paul his papers and ticket, checked Selig's cursorily and left, slamming the compartment door.

Paul and Selig had a three-hour wait in the Hauptbahnhof in Innsbruck where another patrol of British soldiers checked them in the station canteen as they were tucking ravenously into a bowl of vegetable soup and chunks of brown bread. They found a train south and more British soldiers checked them again at the top of the Brenner Pass, at the border with Italy.

Paul wondered if the whole world was occupied by the British.

'Levi's a Jewish name, ain't it?' the soldier asked. Paul nodded. The soldier grinned, 'Thought so. Well, you'll 'ave no trouble doing business then, will yer?'

Paul stared out of the window, furious, and for hours refused to talk even to Selig.

The train moved at a snail's pace through the Dolomites because Italian partisans had blown the track in so many places that the Germans had been able to do no more than rudimentary repairs at the end of the war. Gradually the hills sloped away into the purple distance and tall junipers filled the landscape, like steel-green soldiers marching along the roads and standing guard over the grey-walled villages. They changed trains in Verona, which showed little sign of fighting apart from

The Joshua Inheritance

some bomb damage, and bought cheese and bread and a bottle of beer each, to celebrate leaving the German Reich, in a little mobile canteen on the platform. They ate in the shade, keeping out of the hot sun which seemed to bake the life out of everything in the flat Po valley. After another three hours' wait, their next train made better time across the northern Italian plain and by nightfall they reached Trieste, where they tramped the dark streets until nearly midnight to find a cheap place to stay.

Paul could see that Trieste deserved its reputation. For centuries, the port had been tucked into the corner of Christian Europe and its merchant seamen had traded the roughest routes, risking their lives to do business with the Ottoman Turks. At the end of the war, Tito had tried to grab Trieste for Yugoslavia. The British and New Zealanders had intervened with a show of bombers and the Yugoslavs withdrew, but Zvi Shkolnik had thought the continued political uncertainty made it a perfect place to hire a boat. He assured Paul there would be no difficulty finding a sea captain willing to take them to Palestine.

'Jews, are you?' the skinny landlady demanded in a high voice when she counted the money Paul gave her, an exorbitant price for the grubby little room. He pushed her out on to her landing and shut the door. He and Selig looked round at the bare room, the single bed, the thin mattress and the plaster peeling off the walls. He wondered whether Zvi Shkolnik had been right.

Edward was travelling from Salisbury up to London to see Diana's father in Whitehall. Colonel Haike had proved difficult to pin down. On the rare occasions Edward had been able to contact him, he had kept saying how much work he had to do with the post-war programme settling the division of Europe. Edward felt very junior and uninvolved, but he persisted. He left the train at Waterloo Station and walked to Whitehall wondering if he would find their meeting had been cancelled. In the event Colonel Haike greeted him warmly and then sat down behind his massive oak desk like the captain at the helm of his ship. He said, 'So, you've found evidence your father was at Belsen, you say? Most interesting.'

'That's what Paddy Kelly said,' Edward replied, standing in front of the desk and holding his beret in both hands, like a supplicant.

Colonel Haike frowned.

Edward explained, 'He's the battalion doctor. He saw him there.' He clung to the faint chance that this news would overturn the official tag 'Absent without leave'.

'The camp was liberated on 15 April,' Colonel Haike mused, shifting some buff-coloured documents on his blotter. 'I managed to get these files sent up when you rang about this. Let's see, your father would have been there with the doctor for what? A week, say?'

'The doc said he last saw him six days later, on 21 April.'

Colonel Haike said nothing for a moment, carefully reading the files, sitting with his back straight, neck bent, peering at the documents. A frown darkened his narrow features now and again as he made minute adjustments to his tie and cuffs.

Edward wondered what else was in the files. It was hoping for too much that information so easily come by should change everything. He had not dared tell his mother that George Fairfax had been in Belsen camp, even when he saw her on his return from Germany, for fear of frightening her. Everyone had seen the ghastly photographs in the newspapers.

Colonel Haike finally looked up and said, 'I'm sorry, Edward. This report says he was last heard of after the

21st. In fact, he reported to a British Army signals unit three days later somewhere south-east of Hamburg.'

Edward was badly disappointed, but not really surprised. 'Isn't there anything else in those files?'

''Fraid not, old chap,' said Colonel Haike. He closed the folder, pushed it dismissively to one side and changed the subject.

'Seeing my daughter again this evening?'

His father's case hung over Edward like a black cloud. He forced a smile and said, 'Yes, I've got tickets for *Henry V*.' In spite of being with Diana, the film would match his mood. 'Best to see it while we can. Most people down in Bulford seem to think we'll be sent to fight the Japs quite soon.'

Colonel Haike screwed up his eyes knowledgeably. 'Very probably. As you know, I'm in Intelligence so mum's the word and all that, but it's no secret the Nips are fighting on and they've got to be stopped. V J Day, when it comes, really will be the end of the war.'

Colonel Haike came to the top of the stairs to show Edward out and brightened at a sudden thought. 'By Jove, there won't be much left for us to do after that, will there, eh?'

At the beginning of August, on Monday the 6th at 8.20 a.m., Hiroshima was devastated by an A-bomb. Three days later Nagasaki suffered the same fate. A week after, on Tuesday 14 August, the young Emperor Hirohito surrendered unconditionally. Japan was finished. The Prime Minister, Clement Attlee, declared VJ Day and two days of national celebration to mark the final end of the war.

The same day, Major George Fairfax arrived back in London, tired out and frustrated by failure. He went straight to Whitehall, forcing his way through the celebrating crowds just as his son had done on VE Day in May. He passed the sentry on duty at the door, who saluted, took the marble stairs two at a time and barged straight into Colonel Haike's office without appointment.

'Septimus, what the devil is all this talk about court martial?'

Colonel Haike looked up, thoroughly startled, and it was a moment before he recovered his wits to reply. Automatically, he fell back on a social catch-all and declared loudly, 'George! Glad to see you!'

'Rubbish!' George Fairfax knew Septimus Haike only too well.

Haike sounded shocked. 'Really! We thought you must be dead!'

'Maybe it would have been easier all round if I were.' George Fairfax stated bluntly. He walked over to the desk, put his hands on the edge, fingers straight, loomed over Colonel Haike and demanded, 'Just what's been going on while I've been away?'

Colonel Haike, immaculate in his uniform as usual, felt at a distinct disadvantage looking up at George Fairfax whose borrowed battledress and boots were worn and dusty and quite out of place in the calm atmosphere of Whitehall. He pushed his chair back and retreated to the open window where the noise of the crowds was filling the air. He fixed a concerned expression on his face and began, 'I must be frank, George.'

'That would be nice, Septimus, for a change.' George Fairfax folded his arms and waited.

'The fact is, George, things went wrong.'

To Colonel Haike's surprise, George Fairfax laughed out loud. 'That's a bland way of describing the death of a dozen good men. And the poor bloody crew.'

'Eleven, actually,' said Colonel Haike ignoring the Hudson's crew. 'Axel Romm has been accounted for by the Americans. He has made a statement to them but he refuses to see us.'

The Joshua Inheritance

George Fairfax snapped at once, 'Where's this statement? I must read it. Was he captured, or did he escape? I must know.'

Colonel Haike made a slight deprecating movement with his hand and replied, 'I am sorry, George, the file is *sub judice*, depending on whether the Chiefs of Staff decide you must face court martial.'

George Fairfax exploded. 'What? How the hell can I find out what happened to my team if you won't let me see what that pedantic bastard says?'

Colonel Haike shrugged, feeling bolder the longer the conversation went on. 'You should have been in touch before. Not gone off on your own.'

'Who else was going to find what happened? Romm ran off and the rest were picked up, according to a local man I spoke to. That only left me. I was team leader and it was my responsibility. I've looked in every damned prison, camp and barracks in Germany for those men.' He stabbed a finger at Colonel Haike. 'I checked Natzweiler, and dozens of other concentration camps in the British and American sectors, including Belsen. There's a bloody statement for you.'

Colonel Haike looked apologetic. 'But how will the chaps in the department know they can believe you?'

George stared at him, amazed. 'I filled up the Jeep in virtually every damn military POL point in Germany. Dozens of people have seen me.'

'But is there any proof of that?'

George Fairfax mellowed his tone. They both knew that in the chaos of the war's end, with military units scattered all over Europe, transport NCOs kept no records of single vehicles needing fuel. He changed tack and insisted, 'I'm telling you, Septimus, there is no sign of them. Nothing. The lads were betrayed and murdered somewhere. Must've been. It's the only thing left. The bloody Krauts didn't just stumble on them. There would have been more evidence. They were betrayed, Septimus. And I want to know who's responsible.'

Colonel Haike agreed. 'A mistake was certainly made, but your absence is seen as a measure of your sense of guilt. In other words, they think you ran away.'

'Then why the hell d'you think I came back?'

'You have a family.' Colonel Haike shrugged and brushed his little black moustache with one finger and thumb.

George Fairfax continued to stare while the full realisation sank in of what had been happening while he had been scrabbling round the camps. Quietly he asked, 'Septimus. You were with us on the planning for this operation. You know the whole story, from this end at least, from the control-room side. D'you believe me, or do you take the official view?'

Colonel Haike gave a brief smile. 'Of course I believe you. That's why I told Edward.' He explained quickly what he had said to Edward weeks before. 'Does the boy know you're back?'

George Fairfax shook his head. He had heard enough. He pulled himself together and started for the door. 'I'll see myself out.' He could see the odds stacked against him. People in England had been busy saving their skins while he had been away. He had a lot of work to do.

He paused at the door and looked back. Colonel Haike had not moved from the window. George Fairfax said, 'I shall fight this, Septimus. All the way.'

'What about Edward? And Anne?'

'What about the lads who died?' George retorted and slammed the door behind him.

It was raining hard, a torrential summer downpour, and after several weeks in Trieste, Paul Levi was beginning to regret his offer to Zvi Shkolnik to collect a group together, lodge them and find them a ship to sail to Israel.

He hopped along the narrow back streets avoiding the puddles. At the entrance of a small café, he ducked through the multi-coloured beads hanging in the doorway and stood inside shaking water off himself. He had tramped round every dive in the port and the shabby little bar was familiar, frequented as it was by men off the merchant steamers. He had found that lodging only a dozen Jews in dirty rooms was hard enough, but locating a captain to take them to Israel was nearly impossible. The Italians had quickly learned the Jews would be illegal immigrants and brazenly racked up the prices to match.

Conversation had stopped when he walked in but, once everyone saw the newcomer was as badly dressed as they were, the hum of talk picked up again. Paul turned his collar back, loosened his tieless shirt where the rain had stuck it to his chest, went up to the bar and ordered a small glass of white wine. He looked round for his contact. Several men, obviously sailors, sat drinking at wooden tables. Paul saw the man at a table in one corner.

'*Buon giorno, Capitano Angelo*,' said Paul sitting down. The Italian grunted. He was unshaven and a dirty white vest was tightly stretched over the bulk of his stomach, which spread comfortably over his wide-spread legs, almost concealing his blue cotton trousers.

'When do we leave?' Paul asked after he had bought the captain a beer.

'The repairs, they are not finished,' the Italian grumbled. 'I need more time.'

Privately Paul thought that no amount of time or repairs would make the slightest difference. The Captain's tramp steamer was at least sixty years old, blackened with coal dust and she hung low in the water. Paul was no sailor, but he was certain the ship had a permanent list to one side. He was not looking forward to the trip, but he had been quite unable to find anyone else to take them.

'When?' Paul persisted quietly, sunk on his elbows on the table, sipping his wine.

'Soon,' the fat Italian said and wiped beer froth from his lips.

Outside, the rain stopped and the hot July sun glared on the coloured bead screen. Steam rose from the cobblestones in the street. They heard boots marching up the alley and an unmistakeably British voice calling out, 'In 'ere, Sarge?'

Paul and the Italian watched the café doorway. The shadow of a British soldier wearing a steel helmet fell across the strings of beads hanging in the entrance. They heard another voice, 'Nah, we done that one yesterday,' and the patrol moved on down the street.

The captain of the tramp steamer caught a faint expression on Paul Levi's face and grinned. 'You may not like my price, but we both agree about the Inglesi.' He flicked one fat hand under his chin and spat on the stone floor. 'Stronzo! What are the British doing here in Italy?'

'Keeping Tito's Communists from marching back into Trieste,' said Paul dryly. In the weeks he had spent in Trieste he had been amused by the easy-going attitude of the Italians but despised their lack of drive.

The Italian shrugged. 'The Yugoslavs? Trieste is Italian. We don't need the British any more.'

'I'll drink to that anyway,' said Paul. The Italian laughed, his belly shaking, and they clinked their glasses together.

Like everyone else, Edward had been astonished by the complete destruction of Hiroshima and Nagasaki, but now a sense of anti-climax had set in. He taxed Sergeant Hodgson while the platoon was firing on the ranges. 'I expect there's some disappointment in the battalion that Japan has given up after the A-bombs?'

'No, sir. I doubt that,' Sergeant Hodgson replied in a quiet and serious tone of voice. 'I know those bombs must've been terrible. But it's saved us a lot of hard work.' Sergeant Hodgson looked sideways at Edward and seeing the young officer was puzzled, he went on, 'The Yanks 'ave taken some terrible casualties fighting for Okinawa and Iwo Jima. Don't get me wrong, sir, we've got first-class soldiers.' He glanced along the firing point at the Paras who were lying down behind their Bren Guns, the Light Machine-Gun workhorse of the British infantry platoon. The butts were tucked firmly in their shoulders, the distinctive thirty-round box magazines on the top curved forward towards the conical flash hider on the muzzle, and the staccato bursts rattled down the six-hundred-yard range with deadly accuracy. 'The best, but I fancy them who've seen action before will not be heartbroken that the Nips 'ave thrown in the towel.'

When Edward got back to the Mess, he found a telegram from his mother in his pigeonhole. His father was back. He went straight to the company office to see Major Rattigan and ask for time off, thankful he did not have to speak to Captain Scarland. Major Rattigan willingly gave him the following afternoon off and, when Aubrey Hall-Drake heard why he was going up to London, he insisted Edward take his Morgan sports car.

'Save all the hanging round on drafty platforms, old chum. Besides, nothing worse than having to leave a jolly dinner reunion when you're checking the watch all the time to dash away and catch the last train down.'

The reunion started well enough. Edward had a fast and glorious drive up to town in the red Morgan, the top down pressing along at speed through the narrow main roads and overtaking slow lorries with ease. Petrol rationing was still in force and there was very little traffic on the roads. He reached London in good time in the early evening in excellent spirits and cruised through the streets feeling marvellously grown-up, out on his own in a smart car, free and independent, going to meet his father for dinner. For the first time in his life he felt they would be on equal terms. Edward had come to help him.

He parked off Kensington High Street and rattled up in the old lift to the fifth-floor apartment. Fighting a sudden flood of apprehension, he rang the bell. This was his home but for the first time he felt like a stranger. His mother opened the door and hugged him at once. 'Darling Edward, you're looking so well,' she said, stepping back to see him properly. 'And I love your uniform. You look very handsome.'

'Yes, Mother.' His mother always made him feel somewhat like a mannequin in a shop window. 'Is Father here?'

She smiled and nodded towards the drawing-room. Edward tossed his red beret on a little occasional table in the hall and walked through. His father was standing at the fireplace, dressed in a dark suit, white shirt and his club tie, and toying with a glass of sherry. Somehow Edward was disappointed not to see him in uniform.

'My dear boy! How are you?' George Fairfax took a couple of steps towards his son as Edward came into the room and they shook hands, George clasping his son's hand with both of his. Edward could not remember when his father had last shown such affection.

'It's been a long time, Father, nearly two years. We haven't seen each other since you were posted and I joined up.'

'I know. Too long, but let me look at you,' said George Fairfax, standing back to admire his son's uniform. 'The Parachute Regiment chaps are fine soldiers. You look well. And the wings are splendid.' He lightly touched the blue wings on Edward's arm with his fingers and

The Joshua Inheritance

Edward grinned, feeling proud in spite of himself. His father had always had a way of making him feel good.

'Were you frightened?' George asked, screwing up his eyes a little, smiling inquisitively.

'No,' Edward answered, but too quickly.

His father noticed the fleeting expression on his son's face and knew the reason. 'Even a bit? From the balloon?'

Edward grinned, 'Well, maybe a little.'

'I can imagine,' said George Fairfax, wishing he could tell Edward more of his own experiences. He walked over to the drinks cabinet with his glass, set out another glass and poured sherry from a decanter, the driest Amontillado, which he loved. 'I've saved a few bottles, to celebrate,' he said over his shoulder.

There was so much to talk about. Edward wanted to ask where his father had been, why he had been out of touch and what had made Colonel Haike talk about disgrace, but where to start? He plunged in: 'Father, there's so much news to catch up on,' but before he could say any more, George Fairfax handed him the glass of sherry and said, 'There certainly is, my dear boy. And a new life to talk about for the future. Have you made any good friends yet?'

The question threw Edward off balance but for a time he was happy to talk about the battalion, about his platoon and Hall-Drake, and his father plied him with questions. His mother called them to the dining-room for dinner, three round the table using the family silver, and they ate, not well, because rationing was getting worse, but sufficiently well. George Fairfax continued to ask Edward about the Paras and his mother joined in, happy to hear Edward's stories, although she never quite knew herself what to ask Edward about Army life.

Normally, Edward would have loved telling his father about his first weeks in the Army, but he began to realise his father was deliberately avoiding all talk of himself. From the sitting-room, Edward could hear the drawing-room clock ticking on and the pressure built up, as it had when he was a boy, when he wanted desperately to talk about something but his parents refused to discuss it.

'You know which train you've got to catch?' His father asked.

'I drove up,' Edward said and explained. Silently he thanked Aubrey for lending him the Morgan.

After dinner, they went back to the sitting-room, Edward and his father alone. George Fairfax produced a packet of cigarettes. He offered one to his son, 'You smoke yet?'

Edward shook his head. He wanted to concentrate. As his father lit his cigarette, he asked abruptly, 'Diana's father told me you were in trouble. Can you tell me about it?' He immediately regretted the bluntness of his outburst.

George Fairfax exhaled slowly, his face disappearing behind wreaths of smoke and replied, 'It's nothing serious, dear boy.'

'But Colonel Haike said you might have to stand a court martial. I'd call that pretty serious.'

'Hardly worth bothering about, really. Just a misunderstanding. It'll all clear up now I'm back.'

'But why have you been away so long without keeping in touch?'

'I've been damned busy,' George answered, his face hardening behind the cigarette smoke. He had seen too many dead and dying in the endless prisoner lagers and displaced persons' refugee camps. But never the people he wanted to find.

'But it was May when Colonel Haike told me to come and see him. On VE Day actually.'

'That long ago?'

Edward nodded. He knew so little what to ask and his father's reluctance grew like a wall between them. The

The Joshua Inheritance

frustration was too much and Edward snapped crossly, 'He said you were missing. What were you doing?' In spite of trying to keep calm, to discuss the thing man to man, he felt like a boy again, daring to confront his father. His voice rose, 'Why won't you tell me? After all, it could affect me too.'

George Fairfax looked at his son for a long moment without speaking and Edward tried, without success, to read his expression. Then he turned to the fireplace, drew heavily on his cigarette and exhaled, a long soft breath against the relentless ticking of the mantelpiece clock.

At last, George Fairfax said, 'I can't.' He did not look round.

'Can't?' Edward asked rudely at his father's back, speaking as plainly as he would to Hall-Drake, aware he had at least scratched through his father's usual reserve, though the formal barrier which stood between father and son were not down. 'What about Belsen? What were you doing there?'

George Fairfax did not look round but his head dropped slightly. He said stubbornly, 'Edward, I can't tell you anything about what I've been doing.'

'Why not? Maybe I can help in some way.' There was something in the slope of his father's shoulders which told Edward his father needed to talk.

George Fairfax laughed shortly at the impossibility of the offer and turned back to face his son. He said lightly, 'I can't because I'm bound by rules of security to say nothing. I am not allowed to tell you.' He smiled the condescending smile of a father fond of a wayward son who has not quite understood something adult. Edward knew at once that he had lost his advantage as fast as it had been won. 'But it's a nice thought, my dear boy. Sweet of you.'

Edward left soon after. Like his mood, the weather had changed and the drive back to Bulford was miserable.

Rain poured off the canvas hood and fogged the windscreen all the way as he churned over the whole problem, hardly knowing the questions, let alone the answers. By the time he reached camp, he was tired out.

At muster parade the following day, Sergeant Hodgson announced to the platoon with impressive clairvoyance, 'Listen in, lads. Don't kid yerselves that just 'cos the Nips 'ave packed in, there'll be no more fighting. Just 'cos someone's invented a bigger and better weapon, like that 'ere bomb, never made no difference in the past, did it now? You mark my words, lads, there's been too much killing in the last five years all 'rand the world for it to stop overnight. So I don't want you 'orrible lot thinking you'll 'ave plenty of free time to misbehave wiv all the lasses 'ereabahts and start punchups in the pubs! Sure as eggs is eggs, we'll be off somewhere policing the Empire, and I don't doubt we'll find fings 'ave changed a bit in the meantime.'

The Imperial General Staff at the War Office in London seemed to agree with Sergeant Hodgson's assessment. However, they did not anticipate any sort of fighting and phrased themselves differently. Less than two weeks later, however, they ordered 6 Airborne Division, including Edward's battalion, to move by sea, not to the Tropics, but to the Middle East, to Palestine.

The posting took everyone by surprise. Expectations of the exotic east were over and Edward listened with trepidation to old Africa sweats talking of sand and desert flies so numerous a man could hardly feed himself without eating them clustered on his spoon. The generals and politicians wanted the Division to be the strategic reserve in the Middle East. Talk of war was replaced by talk of peace. The Paras were in for a quiet period of training in Palestine which offered air training facilities and airfields considered better than those in Egypt. Besides, the Chiefs of Staff were conscious that the Egyptian government was anxious to get rid of the British Imperial presence.

Arab interests were vital. The Foreign Secretary, Ernest Bevin, was keenly aware of the importance of Arab oil in the Middle East and the millions of Muslims in the Indian Empire. He viewed Palestine as critical to British interests in both areas and therefore to the survival of the United Kingdom itself. The Foreign Office focused on the Arabs and no-one took much note of the bubbling cauldron of Jewish nationalism. Nor did anyone seem to connect Palestine with the bitter experience of the Jews in Germany.

Frantic preparations began for the move by sea. The battalion moved to Southampton and boarded the M.V. *King Edward* in the docks. Edward's farewell with his parents in London had been painful, his mother upset and in tears, his father distant, like a schoolmaster seeing off a boy leaving the school for the last time, but Diana came to see him off at the quayside. She had suddenly realised how far he was going and was desperate to keep in touch. They parted on the dockside, promising to write, and she held back her tears till he walked up the gangway and turned to wave as he ducked inside the ship. She waited for ages with the other women and children left behind on the quay, waving at Edward who hung on the rail looking down. At last, the ship's horn blasted, the hawsers dropped free and the ship began to slide away from the dock. They waved furiously at each other till he could no longer distinguish her in the rest of the crowd and the boat rounded a bend in Southampton Water, but her golden hair and slim figure stayed etched in his memory as he watched the grey coastline of England fall away over the horizon. Diana was a focus of everything which remained unsettled in England; yet he could not help being lifted by the sheer excitement of a sea voyage.

All enthusiasms died in the sickening swells of the Bay of Biscay. Edward and Aubrey retired to groan and heave in private misery in their shared cabin but recovery was swift when they refuelled in two days of welcome calm under the Rock of Gibraltar, symbol of Britain's imperial power. They sailed the last leg of their journey across the blue Mediterranean sea under balmy late summer skies, past the British island of Cyprus, to the port of Haifa on the Palestine coast.

Paul Levi had finally agreed a deal with the Italian captain, and after a long and uncomfortably oily crossing of the eastern Mediterranean hiding below decks in the baking-hot steel hull of the old steamer, they stood off the coast of Palestine under cover of darkness in the middle of the night. Further north, British troops disembarked in good order in the heat of the day on the quayside of Haifa port, welcomed by a brass band, but Paul prepared for a landing unannounced, on a sandy beach south of the town, in secrecy.

The moon was low in the sky casting an orange glow across the still water, providing just enough light for the Italian sailors to follow his directions and row the tramp's longboat towards the dark line of the shore. He told them how to slip the oars silently on the approach to the beach and glide in with the waves. He felt sick with excitement as the dark shape of the land ahead loomed larger and he began to make out the grey shapes of trees and rock outcrops further up the beach. This was his new home, Eretz Israel, the land of Israel, spoiled by one important factor. British occupation. He smiled at the irony, for it was the British who had taught him all he knew about clandestine operations, in a special school in England two years before.

When the longboat broke through the surf and struck the beach, he and Selig leaped out. Selig grabbed the boat's painter but Paul struggled past him through the

The Joshua Inheritance

foam to the hard, fell to his knees and kissed the sand as the waves ran away past his face. He pushed his fingers deep into the sand, grasping handfuls. Wet grains stuck to his lips but to him the salt was the freshest taste in the world. He had arrived at last. Eretz Israel.

BOOK 2

STORM

'The tragic task of saving the Jewish people was not one to be borne by Palestine alone.'

Ernest Bevin, November 1945

6

FIRST MOVES

October–November 1945

In the pale light of the stars, Paul Levi could only just make out the rising shape of the railway embankment above him, stretching away left and right across the flat gravel plain north of Gaza. It was midnight and the end of October, but the dry heat from the rocks and sand gave him no chance to cool down after the long march from the village. His shirt was soaked with sweat. Moisture was running down his chest and his back was drenched where he carried the rucksack. He wiped his face with the shemag hanging loosely round his neck, like a rag.

He checked his watch, finding it hard to see the faint phosphorescence in the darkness. The march had also taken longer than he wanted, partly because the four men with him had been nervous on their first job and partly because he had not realised he would take so long himself to recover full fitness. So there was no time to delay.

Earlier, during the day, he had done everything by the book. He had carefully planned every move, described it all in detail to his team using a little model drawn in the dust behind the house in the village, and then rehearsed the whole operation out of sight of the village on a goat track which he pretended was the railway line. Now the preparation would tell.

In the darkness, he whispered urgently, 'Phase two. Move!'

They moved at once, scrambling up the embankment. At the top, on the edge of the track, a man slipped off silently on each side, keeping the bulk of his body below the top, just in case anyone saw the skylined shape moving through the night. They disappeared quickly into the blackness but Paul knew they would stop about thirty yards away and lie down, invisible among the ground-shadows, watching out for danger along the line. One man stayed under the bank as rear protection in case they had been followed. The stars gave no light but Paul could see his target: the two wheel-polished railway lines which glinted at his feet and faded quickly into the dark in both directions.

The fourth man came up close, and rasped in a low voice, 'Can you see enough?'

Paul grinned in the dark, already swinging his rucksack to the ground. 'Selig, my friend, I could do this blindfold.' He had practised enough in the past and was enjoying himself, knowing the operation was going well. He pushed Selig's arm, meaning him to take his position as lookout on the other side of the line and Selig obeyed at once.

His cover men were out, protecting all four sides in case they were disturbed, and Paul knelt down beside the line, put his rifle on the ground, and set to work. He could not see much but he knew what he had to do. He removed the charge from the rucksack, tied it with cord inside the web of one steel line and twisted a piece of wood round to tighten the knots. The best effect could only be obtained if the plastic explosive was tight against the steel. Then he fitted the initiation device, the detonator and safety fuse, and held the fuse match ready. Complete control. He was in command, the only one with the matches, the only one who could set off the explosion, when he was ready. He looked up. He could just see Selig's shadow lying on the other side of the line. Paul breathed out a low whistle. Selig looked round, scrambled to his feet and came over.

Paul repeated his whistle between cupped hands, facing up and down the line. After a worrying delay he heard answering whistles. In moments, the two lookouts appeared at a crouching run from either side and Paul waved them back down the embankment with the third man. Paul had deliberately planned that they deployed from his position at the centre of the ambush and withdrew the same way, so he knew they were all four back safely below him before he blew the charge. There must be no confusion in the darkness. Alone on the line, in a moment of peace before he lit the fuse, Paul felt an intoxicating thrill of apprehension and danger mixed with the wonderful scent of success.

He held the match firmly in one hand, the striking board in the other, closed one eye so he would not altogether lose his night vision, and struck the match. In the darkness, the glare seemed massive, enough to alert the whole Yishuv. Without hurry, he held the glowing red tip against the end of the safety fuse and waited till he was sure it was alight. Then he picked up his rifle and rucksack and walked away, remembering the lesson never to run. To trip in a rush and fall near the charge would be fatal. He slithered down the embankment and found his men waiting, not in a cluster like the inexperienced men they really were, but lying down as he had trained them with their rifles at the ready, all looking outwards in case they were surprised at the last minute.

Dropping to his knees, Paul warned in a hoarse voice, 'Wait for it!' just as his instructor had always done, and recalled his amusement at the words which suggested there was some way of stopping the chemistry he had started with the fuse. He hoped the detonator was good and wished he had been able to use two in his initiation set as he had been taught, so there was a back-up if one failed.

A roar of light and sound above them on the track showed his fears were groundless. Instinctively, they all flinched and moments later were showered with pieces of stone and wood. The thrill of success was instantly laced with fear. Such an explosion must have alerted the entire district, troops would soon be converging on them from all sides and the men were appalled when, instead of ordering their instant withdrawal, Paul said he wanted to check the charge had done its job. He grabbed Selig, who was nearest him, and the two ran up the embankment, their nostrils filled with the stench of cordite. The place where Paul had laid his charge was obscured by pale smoke which hung about in the windless hot night but he could clearly see the shattered line and broken sleeper underneath. Selig shouted fiercely and slapped Paul on the back. Paul felt the same surge of savage pleasure. Neat and tidy. No-one hurt. This was the way to force the British to take them seriously.

'Come on, Selig,' he said. 'We have a long walk back.'

They ran back down the embankment and quickly moved off in line, their rifles at the ready, moving fast across the barren countryside towards the mud village they had left hours before. Paul noticed he was sweating heavily once more but he pressed on. They had to reach the village before first light or risk being spotted by the British planes which would be out looking for them. Paul laughed to himself. Everything had gone according to the book. Sergeant Royle would have been proud of him.

'It's outrageous!' Aubrey Hall-Drake exclaimed, flopping down on his camp bed on his side of the square khaki frame tent they shared.

The Joshua Inheritance

'It was the Jews apparently, not the Arabs,' said Edward sitting on his bed. He pulled his .38 revolver from his canvas holster, emptied the chamber of bullets and began to clean it. He reached for a piece of four-by-two, the traditional rifle-cleaning rag which was four inches broad with red threads every two inches so that even the simplest mind knew where to tear off a piece the right size. He dipped it in rifle oil and began to wipe dust off the blue metal. Their tent was uncomfortably warm, baking under the midday sun, and smelled of rifle oil and hot coir matting. He added, 'You know they blew up more than 240 bridges all over Palestine, and attacked the oil refinery at Haifa last night?'

'How d'you know that?' Aubrey asked, appalled.

'I overheard Captain Scarland talking to the Intelligence Officer in the Mess when we got back. The whole rail network is at a standstill.'

'What the devil d'these people think they're doing?'

'I've no idea.' Edward was genuinely nonplussed. No-one had yet told them of any reason which accounted for such widespread and obviously co-ordinated destruction. The British administration had been taken by surprise.

'It's a bloody outrage,' Aubrey burst out. 'Who do these sods think they are? This is the bloody British Empire!'

Edward continued to work on the pistol, rodding out the barrel. He lifted it up to a sliver of sunlight shining through a chink in the tent flap, squinted down the barrel at the gleaming steel and grunted with satisfaction.

Suddenly he felt terribly tired. They had been dragged out of bed at midnight to pursue the gangs who had blown the railways. They mustered on the square to hear Major Rattigan's orders under a vast canopy of ice-white stars in a black sky. So many were visible in the clean desert air that Edward wondered how the Three Wise Men could ever have picked out the Star of Bethlehem.

His platoon had driven at top speed to the railway line north of Gaza in trucks which had given their best during the battles against Rommel only three years before. They met a patrol of the Palestine Police, a strange mix of Arabs and Jews working together, left their vehicles under an armed guard, and hastened on foot up the line to find the break. They found the place, on an embankment, just after dawn. A large black hole in the stone base, shards of timber sleeper scattered everywhere and a yard of steel line missing. Edward had looked round the gravel plain but there were no signs of the sabotage team's footprints on the sun-baked stony ground. Edward made sure that the policemen with them marked the right place on their map and gave the order to return to base. There was nothing else they could do.

'I'm shattered.' Aubrey Hall-Drake kicked off his boots, dragged off his tie and battledress top and flung them in the corner of the tent. 'This was not what I expected to find in Palestine at all. Bathing parties on the beach, yes. Just the job to get fit after sitting about on that ship on the way out, and probably the only entertainment in this God-forsaken desert. Shooting parties, yes. I've seen plenty of snipe and quail. Jolly biblical to nab quail, too. I was even looking forward to a spot of training. A few para drops and platoon work. Especially since old Rattigan has decided we can take our chaps into the desert and work independently, away from that idiot Scarland. But chasing after bally amateur explosives experts is not what we're here for.'

'They weren't amateurs, Aubrey. Sergeant Hodgson said they'd done a very professional job.'

Aubrey grunted. He undid the buttons of his shirt and inspected his broad but hairless white chest. He announced, 'I stink. 'Spose I better have a shower in that dreadful wriggly tin box they call the ablutions.' He grabbed his towel and wash bag and stamped out of the tent. Edward listened to him grumbling into the distance along the dry path between the khaki bell tents of the officers' Mess lines. It was typical that the Paras had been dumped in the driest, flattest and apparently dullest part of Palestine. He wondered which fortunate units were based in the lush citrus groves of the Plain of Sharon which they had passed during the train journey down from Haifa.

He put his revolver back in its holster, tucked it under his pillow and slumped on to his camp bed. He rubbed the dust from his eyes. He was exhausted and dirty, badly in need of a shower, but he wanted to read the letter from Diana first. He pulled it out of his shirt pocket and enjoyed again the jolt of real pleasure that she had written to him.

My darling Edward, I miss you terribly. It seems ages since we had that simply wonderful evening together at the Trocadero. I shall never forget it, the glittering candles, the romantic music and the way we danced. I want to do it again, soon, but we can't, can we? It's not fair!

Life is very dull in England now, especially without you. I'm trying to keep busy (though I promise I shan't forget you!). You remember my telling you I was toying with the idea of helping a friend decorate her flat? No, probably you've forgotten, but I have, and I've decided to help her make the curtains. So, I needed to buy a sewing machine! Well! I ordered it from Selfridges and do you know what they said? There's a three-year waiting list. Well. I'm used to rationing (at least I tighten my belt, as rationing is getting worse, believe it or not) but this is ridiculous.

Edward stopped reading to look at the photograph she had sent of herself and reflected that her figure needed no tightening at all. But this photograph, he realised suddenly was the closest he would come to her for a long time to come.

He read on: There's a dock strike on. Again. It's a pity they didn't strike before you left, and you might still be here with me. Isn't that typical rotten luck?

Her letter was eleven pages long, written as he could hear her speaking, with endless detail about what she was doing, including that she had been to see Edward's mother again, and she intimated that his father was thoroughly morose and uncommunicative about his impending court martial.

Aubrey barged back into the tent, smelling of soap and dripping water all over the sandy floor. He said, 'We should call this poxy little tent of ours the "Sandpit". There's more than enough of the stuff about to justify that and the place is certainly a pit.'

Edward grinned without taking his eyes from his letter. 'At least half of the mess is yours.'

Aubrey noticed Edward's letter and remarked, 'Judging by the number of pages she's written, she obviously misses you. Looking at the state of you, I can't think why, but do you miss her?'

Edward smiled. 'Of course! And mind your own business.' He continued to read but Aubrey was not going to be put off. He said with a knowledgeable air, 'Of course you do, old chap, but these are early days. Will you still miss her when we've been here a couple of years? Eh?' He rubbed his hair with his towel, his head on one side, smiling quizzically at Edward.

Edward looked up. Two years, or even three, the usual length of a posting, was a long time. How would her photograph look then? Would he still want to read her letters about England?

Aubrey said, 'Bit of social life is all we need. Nothing serious, of course.' He grinned, lighting one of his Turkish cigarettes. 'We'll have to have a look round, eh? With all these troops about, there must be a hospital.'

The Joshua Inheritance

'There's one at Nuseirat,' said Edward. 'Dodgy though. Lots of senior officers about. All the HQ elements are based there.'

Aubrey was not bothered by senior officers. 'Good show. Where there's a hospital there's a nurse. Or two.'

Edward laughed. 'You're just obsessed with the uniform.'

Aubrey looked shocked, 'Not at all. I like their dedication!' He threw his towel at Edward and said, 'Go and clean up. I've managed to get hold of a Land-Rover.'

In London, Anne Fairfax set out from the flat in Kensington by bus to meet an old friend, John Peregrine Fullerton. She needed his special talent for knowing a wide circle of people in useful places, but had no idea that he knew her husband and Colonel Haike, except socially. On the telephone, he sounded delighted to meet her and suggested lunch at the Connaught Hotel.

Fullerton ordered champagne as they took their seats at a quiet table in one corner of the richly decorated dining-room.

'Please, John, not for me,' Anne said, delighted but rather embarrassed as the lunch had been her idea.

He smiled at her. 'Then for me, Anne. You see, I always forget what a beautiful woman you are. How can we drink anything else?'

'I'm supposed to do all the flattery today,' she replied, hoping her pleasure was not too obvious. She had known Fullerton since they had met at dances during the Season when she came out, and he had proposed to her as soon as he came down from Cambridge.

'I was a fool to let you go,' he smiled, enjoying himself. Many of the people he met socially were ghastly, but Anne Fairfax was most certainly not one. She still had an excellent figure and looked most attractive in a loose-fitting pale grey jacket and mid-length pleated dress. The colour suited her blue eyes and fair hair which was as usual gathered at her neck.

'Dear John, you always say that,' she smiled and he remembered with pleasure her fantastic complexion. 'We were close, but a long time ago. A great deal has happened since.'

He nodded. He had guessed what Anne wanted to ask him, so he could relax in her company, a wonderful change from so much of his socialising which was pure work, as tedious as any Foreign Office meeting. He sighed, 'True. A long and unpleasant war, and you have a son. How is he?'

She told him Edward was in Palestine.

Fullerton grew excited. 'He's there, is he? That business the other day was appalling. Blowing up railways all over the country! No-one was hurt, of course,' he said hastily, seeing the expression of alarm on Anne's face. He leaned forward confidentially. 'Ernie Bevin was very shocked. He summoned Chaim Weizmann, the Jewish leader, and told him that if this meant the Jews had declared war on Britain, then we would stop our efforts to find a solution in Palestine. As you know, the Balfour Declaration and the League of Nations Mandate oblige us to settle the situation between the Arabs and the Jews.' He paused and added thoughtfully, 'How we can do that and retain our interests in the area is, frankly, beyond me.'

'You're supposed to be a Foreign Office star,' Anne laughed.

'I know,' he smiled, rather pleased. 'Silly, isn't it, but we've got to think of the Arabs. Too many Muslims in India, m'dear. Weizmann tried to have us believe that the Jewish Agency condemned violence and then had the neck to blame us for causing a lot more Jews to support violence than before.'

'Why?'

'He says we're not letting enough of them emigrate there.'

The Joshua Inheritance

Anne was worried about Edward. She asked, 'What will happen?'

'Oh, I don't think the Jews will get much change out of Bevin,' said Fullerton casually. 'He's expected to make a statement on Palestine soon, and I suppose they thought they could sway him with all this unpleasantness. Well, it was damned shocking actually, but it won't do, y'know. I'm not a great fan of the Labour Party, as you know, but Bevin will certainly use the troops if necessary. I always feel that using soldiers to solve political problems is a frightful admission of failure, but it worked for the Arab Revolt before the war.'

Fullerton thought that the world would work much better left to diplomats and had always blamed the generals for starting wars. He had already taken to citing the last war as a supreme example. The Arab Revolt in 1938 was another, when the Arab soldiers, as they called themselves, had tried to usurp British control and about five thousand had been killed. He thought it best not to mention these figures to Anne and went on, 'The Jews want us to let in more than a hundred thousand to Palestine. I know they've had a rotten time in Germany, but I ask you, Anne, where would that leave the indigenous Arabs? Why can't they go to America? Why do they all have to go to Palestine? No, it's really out of the question.'

The champagne arrived and the wine waiter made a special show of presenting and pouring it. Fullerton was a rich and regular guest.

'It's delicious,' Anne exclaimed, delighted, sipping from her glass. They ordered and Fullerton leaned forward again, speaking with intimate sincerity.

'Well now, m'dear, enough of Palestine. I'm sure your Edward will do jolly well. What interests me is how I can help you?'

This was her chance. The outcome affected the whole family. The accusation struck specifically at her husband

George but the blast would reach and damage her son too.

She said, 'George is in trouble.'

'Really?' Fullerton was past-master at concealing his thoughts. He made sure he listened attentively as Anne explained what little she knew about her husband's work in the last stages of the war. George Fairfax had steadfastly refused to tell her any details, but she just could not sit idly by doing nothing. Her voice broke at the thought of what was happening to her family and she finished lamely, 'It seems he's got to face a court martial.'

'What a rotten show!' Fullerton declared, nodding, delighted she knew so little. Apart from any earlier feelings of jealousy which had long faded, he had always found George Fairfax too direct a person for his personal taste. However, Anne was badly upset and without hesitation he stated expansively, 'I'll do anything I can to help. Just let me know.'

Anne did. She wanted him to put her in touch with any friends or contacts who might be able to stop George being put on trial.

He was taken by surprise. 'Just like that?'

Anne snapped at him, 'What d'you expect?'

To his chagrin he realised she was serious. He disliked being in a cleft stick, but Anne needed someone to talk to and it would be a splendid excuse to see her more often. In the end he surprised her by saying, 'Don't worry any more about this, m'dear. I've a list of disreputable characters who might help, but I couldn't possibly have you wandering about the streets and bars of London by yourself.'

Anne was ecstatic. She clasped his hand on the table with both hers. 'John Peregrine, you're the sweetest man in London,' she exclaimed, and then added with a quizzical smile, 'You don't hang about in streets and bars?'

The Joshua Inheritance

'Well, not exactly,' he said, laughing at the thought that the other members of the Travellers would not be pleased to hear their club described as a bar. 'Leave it to me. I know one or two people who might be useful.'

After a hot day's work ploughing the stoney white soil in the fields round the kibbutz, Paul travelled to Tel Aviv by bus, with the smell of the orange harvest in his nostrils from the groves along the road. He had an important meeting in the old quarter of Neve Tedek. The police were still trying to find the gangs which had attacked the railways on 31 October, stopping people on the street for questioning, comparing faces with photographs of suspects, but Paul was not worried. He had good papers, he was not armed, and the police did not have a photograph of him.

He walked briskly from the Central bus station towards the Great Synagogue of Tel Aviv, cutting across the Jaffa Road and Rothschild Avenue through the narrow streets and alleys. After several minutes he checked his watch and stopped at a corner on Nachlat Binyamin Street. He was precisely on time. At two minutes to three he moved forward and stood on the corner, leaning against the wall. He had already circled the area and was satisfied there were no police about in civilian clothes. Having suffered in France for trusting someone else, he had no intention of being caught out a second time. Anyone in Palestine who was convicted of carrying a weapon or being involved in attacks on the British administration could be hanged.

An elderly rabbi shuffled down the pavement, pausing from time to time as if drained by the warmth of the day. He stopped near Paul, gazed at him from behind his thick white beard and said, 'Shalom, my son. There is so much to do, don't you think?'

Paul nodded, feeling the excitement grow in his

stomach, and replied, 'Yes. The oranges will rot on the branch if they are not picked.'

The rabbi nodded sagely, his kindly brown eyes studying the young man carefully, taking in his tatty suit and open-necked shirt, his lean figure and the shock of dark hair above his pale earnest expression. Very softly, as if saying a prayer, he said in a deep voice, 'Follow me at a distance and find shelter at the third door along this street. A brass jug stands outside.'

Paul, waiting impatiently for the old rabbi to totter far enough ahead, tried to control the tension stirred up by the pre-planned meeting going exactly according to plan, then he pushed himself off the wall and walked casually along the pavement in the direction of the Great Synagogue. The third door was ajar, the brass jug on the step. Paul went straight in, as though he had always lived there, without a glance around. He knew the organisation would be watching him from the windows of one of the other small two-storey houses in the street, in case anyone were following him.

Inside he was in complete darkness, blinding after the bright sun outside. He sensed he was standing in a stone-flagged hall and struggled to adjust his eyes.

'Welcome, Paul Levi,' said a full rich voice. A broad shadow approached and shook him by the hand. The man's hand was thickly muscled. 'Come upstairs and we can talk.'

Paul followed the man up old wooden stairs which creaked at every tread and into a plain whitewashed room furnished with only a table, two chairs, and a chest of drawers against one wall. A brown striped blanket made of goats' hair hung across the far wall. Light filtered through the shuttered window which Paul guessed looked out on the back of the house.

His companion was perhaps in his late thirties and a figure of great physical power, with a strong round face, thick neck and barrel-shaped torso which Paul guessed

The Joshua Inheritance

might eventually run to fat when he no longer had to lead the life of a clandestine fighter constantly on the run. He smiled, creases lifting at the corner of his mouth. 'My name is Yudelmann. Why d'you want to join us? The Irgun?'

Paul put both his hands on the table. He looked Yudelmann directly in the eyes and told him, 'I've come a long way to be here. I have the experience you want. I am one of a new generation of Jews. I am a fighting Jew and I want this country to be our Nation, our State.'

Yudelmann did not reply at once. He nodded, his eyes screwed up, shrewdly examining his young guest. All those were good, pat answers, but he wanted more and waited. He knew from his own painful experience of arrest by police, the Cheka in Russia, that quite as much can be obtained during an interview by not speaking as by a barrage of questions.

Paul recognised the silence between them and they both sat relaxed, waiting, listening to the stairs creaking back into place. Paul was sure he could hear something else, breathing, and strained his ears. The blanket drew his attention.

Yudelmann grew tired of waiting and watching and finally, 'Why don't you want to stay with the Jewish Agency, with the Palmach in the Haganah? I understand you did well for them. On the railway, two weeks ago.'

'You're well informed,' Paul said quietly. He was pleased. He did not want to commit himself to another organisation shot through with inefficiency and security leaks. 'The Haganah is fine but I can't stay with them. They are obsessed with the immigration problem. The British can't stop the wind and the rain from landing on this country and they can't stop the Jews. I came from the camps in Germany. I can tell you our people there will immigrate, whatever the British do. They can't be stopped. What's more important to me now is what happens when they arrive. The Haganah wants to carry out attacks and then they sit back to see if the British will give up. But the British are not going to give up. They are stolid, unbending, conservative. We must batter them continually. It's the only way. The Irgun does this, so I must be in the Irgun.'

Yudelmann was impressed, but he said quietly, 'I thought you had good friends in the British Army?'

'How d'you hear that?' Paul asked sharply.

'There are Jews everywhere in the world sympathetic to our cause,' said Yudelmann shrugging aside the question. He persisted. 'Well? Are they your friends?'

Paul laughed. A hollow noise. He brushed the mop of dark hair back from his forehead and told Yudelmann shortly, 'We worked together, some British officers and I, and they abandoned me. D'you think they can be my friends?'

Yudelmann followed up with another question, kindly put but crucial: 'Would you mind killing them?'

Paul hoped these questions did not last. He had long before considered the problem of killing his fellow man, when his family was massacred. He considered the question out of place between men who had come further down the road of commitment than that, and simply said, 'Listen, Yudelmann, I suffered in Germany and I killed Germans. They were my enemy then. And I risked my life at it. I'll do the same here, where the British are my enemy. More so, because now I am fighting for my country, not for someone else's country. My experience with the British in Europe only hardens my resolve here. We must do whatever is necessary to make the British give us our country. It's our Land, Eretz Israel. It's not our fault if the British can't, or won't, recognise the march of history, and it's not our fault if some British soldiers are killed.' He paused.

'Yes?' Yudelmann asked, softly because the young man was filled with the energy of fresh hatreds and

The Joshua Inheritance

burned on the short fuse of past personal humiliations.

Paul realised the older man was on his side. He was with friends who sympathised with his feelings and who would understand. He said, 'There is certainly one who must answer for his actions before God. If I don't stumble over him first.'

Yudelmann laughed, a deep belly laugh. 'Someone who betrayed you?'

Paul nodded vaguely and said no more. It was all far away and no business of Yudelmann's, nor of the struggle in Eretz Israel. He became brusque and said, 'Will you have me in the Irgun Zvai Leumi or not?'

Yudelmann's smile spread across his face. 'I'm supposed to be interviewing you!' He could see his young visitor's face had closed on personal revelations for the time being.

Paul looked past Yudelmann at the coloured blanket which hung down the far wall. 'What does he say, the man behind the blanket?'

Before Yudelmann could reply, a voice spoke up from behind the blanket. 'You are welcome, Paul Ephraim Levi. Experience like yours is invaluable. Give him the cover-name of Joshua, Yudelmann, to use when he's working for us.'

'Not Joshua,' said Paul. 'I don't care what you use, but not Joshua.'

The man behind the curtain paused, evidently not used to being contradicted, but he conceded, 'Alright. Yudelmann will choose a name for you, then brief you. He and I have discussed the plans for which your skills are singularly appropriate.'

'Plans?' Paul queried.

'I'll explain later,' said Yudelmann.

On an impulse Paul said, 'Thank you for the opportunity, Menachim Begin.'

The man behind the blanket chuckled. 'You made the opportunity yourself, Paul Levi. Now we are equal.'

'I'm impressed,' Yudelmann said, grinning. 'How did you guess?'

The unseen leader of the Irgun said, 'Remember, Yudelmann, he's played this game before, against the Nazis. You and I played the Soviets. Now we pool our resources against the British.'

7

STRATEGIC RESERVE

7 November 1945

'Stand up!' the airloadmaster bellowed, cupping his hands to his mouth against the roar of the Dakota's engines and of the wind outside. He glanced through the open door. The aircraft was levelling out at six hundred feet and he could make out the rocks and occasional scrubby tree on the dry sand of the Negev desert. He looked up the body of the aircraft. Cramped together, the helmeted Paras were struggling to their feet, weighted down by their heavy equipment and weapons slung across the front of their legs from 'D' rings on their parachute harnesses.

Edward was first in line. He looked up for the hawser which ran the length of the plane above their heads. This thin steel wire was their lifeline. The drills were precise. He clipped his static line hook on to the hawser. In theory, when he jumped, the weight of his body in the slipstream pulled the parachute from the pack on his back, provided the static line hook stayed clipped to the hawser, and provided the hawser did not break. Apprehension flooded his stomach at the thought of what would happen to him if either broke.

'Tell off for equipment check!'

Way behind him near the front of the aircraft, Edward heard Sergeant Hodgson start the answering chorus of shouts: 'Number one okay!' And slap the shoulder of the man in front of him to indicate he was hooked up on the hawser running above his head and ready to jump.

'Number two, okay!'

'Number three, okay!'

The rhythmic sequence was repeated all the way down the line, rolling from one man to the next, louder and louder, the slapping hands rising and falling from one shoulder to the next, till Brogan shouted in Edward's ear and his hand fell like a blow on his shoulder. Secure in the drill, Edward put his thumb up and shouted to the despatcher, 'Number twelve, okay! Stick okay!' He felt better for the shouting.

The despatcher nodded and returned the thumbs up.

The Dakota rocked and shook as it turned for its final run over the drop zone. Edward looked at the despatcher, who was listening intently to the metallic voice of the pilot through the plane's intercom in his leather headphones, and braced himself.

The despatcher looked up with surprised amusement. He lifted his hand and blew across the palm. The wind. Then he held up his hand, fingers spread wide, three times. Fifteen, thought Edward. Fifteen knots, ground wind speed. Marginal wind speeds for safety landing. The despatcher held up his hand again, this time with only three fingers. My god, Edward thought, eighteen knots! That was more than marginal. His surprise must have showed because the despatcher grinned. He was thinking of the rocky ground below and thankful he did not have to jump himself wearing only shorts and a shirt.

'Stand by!'

At this the entire line of Paras began shuffling towards the door, Edward in the lead, until he stood in the open doorway with Brogan and the rest pressed up behind him. He put his right hand on the edge of the door to stop himself falling out as the plane steadied for the run in.

The Joshua Inheritance

The despatcher was staring down, listening to the little voice in his headphones.

Edward's heart began to pump hard, the adrenalin surged into his veins. He looked down at the dusty ground flashing beneath, rocks, low hills and the blue sky on the horizon in the distance.

'Red on!' The despatcher jerked his hand at the red light which burst alight on the left of Edward's vision, just on the left edge of the door.

'Green on!' the despatcher yelled, thumping Edward on the arm. The single word 'GO!' blazed into his consciousness. In the fury of the moment, Edward hardly heard the start of that short command as he drove his body out through the door into the empty air, and he certainly never heard the frantic trailing syllable as his body was whiplashed sideways by the slipstream, feet upturned in violent switchback to the sky, and was tossed downwind like a morsel of chaff till the wrenching jolt of his opening parachute hung him like a shaken doll in the calm upwinds over the Negev drop zone.

Edward forced his head back against the straining risers to check his canopy. The parachute arched in a silent dome above him, flapping gently in the wind, perfectly inflated, its myriad cords falling to the points on his shoulders where he was held safely in his harness. He looked round. First out of the Dakota, he could not see anyone else for a second. Then another 'chute, which he took to be Brogan's, floated quite close, happily drifting sideways, safely away from him.

Next, his mind snapped to his equipment. To land with the fifty-pound weight attached to his legs would break them. Especially if the winds were high. He grappled for the release catches in the angle of his groin, found them and shoved them open. The heavy sack fell away and yanked his harness on the end of the thirty-foot rope.

Hundreds of yards away, he could see the tiny black figures and vehicles of the drop zone safety party but the ground below was coming up fast. He spotted whirling dust clouds racing across the sand. The despatcher had not been joking. The wind was high. Too high, driving him across the desert. He braced himself for the landing, jamming his feet, knees and elbows tight together.

Then he spotted the tree.

It was the only tree in the landscape – a thorny acacia tree, capable of growing tall and rounded in the barest desert soil. The proud spiky branches of this specimen spread high and wide, as if celebrating the singular achievement of growing in such an inhospitable and remote place as the Negev. Covered in dusty grey leaves, the tree provided the only shadow for miles around. Silently, Edward plunged towards it.

There was no time even to swear. He desperately pulled on the risers lifting from his shoulders, hoping to guide his parachute away, but the wind was too strong. He accelerated towards the tree, closed his eyes and braced himself again.

He crashed through the top branches. Thorny twigs and leaves lashed at his legs, arms and face. He smashed into solid branches which drove the breath from his lungs, bouncing him back and forth, like a pinball in a seaside machine on Brighton Pier, till he stopped.

He opened his eyes. He was hanging helplessly suspended from his parachute, which, above, had entirely enveloped the top of the tree, leaving his feet swinging only a few tantalising feet from the ground, where an Arab was lying on his back staring up in terror, rudely awakened from his siesta in the shade.

For several minutes, it seemed, Edward stared at the barefoot, curly-haired Arab in his brown and white striped jellaba, and the Arab stared back, trying to understand how the white man had suddenly materialised in his tree. The only sound came from the parachute

The Joshua Inheritance

lines creaking against the dry branches as Edward swung gently back and forth.

'Awfully sorry,' Edward began uncertainly as he tried to open his harness release catch, embarrassingly aware for the first time since arriving in Palestine that he spoke nothing of the local language. The catch was jammed. He battered it with his fist but it stayed locked.

This seemed to galvanize the Arab. He leaped to his feet, glanced rapidly down the drop zone where they could see the others landing in swift succession and produced a small knife from the folds of his cloak. Edward thought he was about to be rescued; cut down by a poor Arab peasant desperately grateful to be of the smallest service to a commissioned officer of Britain's Imperial power. Instead, the Arab grabbed both Edward's feet, tucked one boot under one arm while he slashed the laces of the other boot, yanked it off and repeated the process for the second boot. Edward, hanging like meat in a butcher's shop, was helpless and in seconds watched the Arab step back with a pair of new boots, one in each hand.

'They won't fit you!' Edward yelled.

'British army! Very good,' grinned the Arab. He lifted the boots, waggled them delightedly, and set off at a fast run across the desert.

'Bloody Arabs!' Edward yelled as the thief disappeared over a ridge. Suspended in his stockinged feet, he stared into the empty desert, bursting with frustration. The full realisation of his humiliation sank in. He even forgot the stinging pain of his cuts and bruises, and the blood running down his arms and legs where the thorns had lacerated the skin. All he could do was wait till the drop zone safety party rescued him in its Land-Rover. In the silence as he swung gently to and fro, a ragged figure in socks hanging in a tree, he could already hear the story being told at his expense, the laughter of Roger Haike and Captain Scarland. This first piece of training did not augur well for his tour of duty in Palestine.

8

THE STORM BREWS

November 1945–February 1946

After a week in which Edward threw himself into platoon training with such vigour that even Captain Scarland stopped joking about parachuting into trees, the Foreign Secretary in London made his long-awaited announcement about Palestine. Against a background of flippant remarks, that the Jews should not ride roughshod over Arab opinion and that they should read the Koran as well as the Bible, Ernest Bevin set his mind against Zionism and refused to condone any increase of Jewish immigrants from the camps in Europe. On 14 November the Jews in Palestine learned that the figure was to remain at only fifteen hundred a month and that Britain had no intention of bringing about a Jewish State. That afternoon, thirty thousand angry and frustrated people gathered in Tel Aviv.

By evening, the agitators in the mob had set fire to the post office, the income-tax office and other government buildings. The Palestine police were stretched beyond their limits. For the first time in years, the police called on the army to 'aid the civil power' to control a large demonstration. The army commander called on the Paras.

Edward's battalion was scrambled into action and, by dusk, he was sitting in the lead truck of his platoon in the column of sand-coloured trucks winding through the outskirts of Tel Aviv. The growling engines echoed off the walls of the houses and shops. Windows were shuttered and doors bolted against the riot. The streets were eerily deserted. They jolted to a halt near the city centre, in Colony Square, where Edward jumped down from his cab and at once heard not far off the deep roar of people on the rampage. The sound was disturbing, a chorus of anarchy which at the same time triggered the fear that he had to confront them, and echoed the gut excitement that drove the rioters themselves.

'Get moving!' Sergeant Hodgson shouted at the Paras tumbling out of the back of the trucks. He chivvied them into lines by sections, forming a square, like the Redcoats of old. This time, however, the square was khaki and formed to face civilians, not trained soldiers.

Edward kept glancing over his shoulder. Above the flat roofs of Colony Square, he could see the menacing glow of flames reddening the evening light.

A police lieutenant joined them with a small squad of policemen carrying batons and wearing steel helmets, like the Paras.

'How many d'you think there are?' Edward asked.

'Thousands,' the young man grinned, amused at the expression of surprise on Edward's face.

Edward reflected that forty men was hardly the number he would have put against thousands. He shrugged. The rest of the company would not be far away, and he guessed that Major Rattigan could always radio for reinforcements. All the same, the police had clearly received a battering. Their uniforms were dishevelled, and several were cut or bruised about the face. He told the police lieutenant, 'We'd better get on with it! Get your lot into the middle, with me.'

The police officer nodded. He was exhausted and grateful for the support. He waved at his men to go into the centre of the Paras' square where Corporal Jacobs was waiting in command of the platoon snatch squad.

The Joshua Inheritance

Edward took up his position near them with his runner and Private Brogan whom Edward had detailed to carry the banner.

Brogan nodded his head in the direction of the noise beyond the square. 'They're mad, sir! Think we'll have to use this?' He tucked the banner under his arm.

'No doubt about it,' the English police lieutenant butted in. 'They've gone too far this time.'

'I don't understand what all the fuss is about,' Edward shrugged. It was hard to reconcile the brown-faced old men he had seen in little whitewashed villages and soporific-looking donkeys trotting along with with sacks of oranges on their way to market with the frantic violence of the mob he could hear only a few streets away.

The lieutenant laughed dryly, 'They don't tell you anything in the Army, do they? All the Jews who survived Hitler want to come here. They see it as their national home.' He jerked his thumb at the pall of smoke which was rising into the indigo-blue evening sky over the modern three-storey buildings of Colony Square. The rich smell of burning drifted over on a warm breeze. 'The way they see it, Bevin won't let the Jews go home.'

Brogan chipped in, 'He won't let me go 'ome either, to me old mother in Sligo.'

'Shut it, Brogan,' Sergeant Hodgson hissed sharply, passing by. 'Get yerself in position and keep quiet.' Sergeant Hodgson moved on round the platoon, constantly checking the men, giving the odd quiet order to make one or two concentrate. A sudden roar made them all look up. The riot was coming closer.

Captain Scarland marched briskly across the square under the sycamore trees, his jaw jutting out beneath his steel helmet. He had orders from Rattigan.

'Get on with it, Fairfax,' he shouted while still some way off. 'The old man wants to form a base line of defence around Colony Square. Your platoon has got to stop these lunatics from coming down that street at the top end of the square. If you cock it up, the whole company will fold up.'

Edward seethed. Icily he demanded, 'Where are the other platoons?' He needed to know so he could gauge the extent of any new threats if the rioters suddenly changed direction.

'Don't see what it's got to do with you,' said Captain Scarland, but he knew the question was a good one. Reluctantly, he added, 'Hall-Drake is in the middle of the square with Major Rattigan and Three Platoon is on the other side. Now get going.'

Edward took a deep breath to control his anger and turned to Hodgson. 'Ready to move, Sergeant Hodgson?'

'Ready, sir.'

'Lieutenant?'

The young police officer nodded, his face grim.

'Platoon!' Edward shouted. 'Platoon, quick march!' Whatever might happen in the next hour or two, he felt intense pride at that moment, marching his platoon up the street. Even if they were not going to face a real enemy, like the Germans, there was certainly trouble ahead. He wheeled them into the street which Major Rattigan wanted him to hold, and gave them the order to halt. As if on cue, the front of the mob appeared a hundred yards away at the other end of the street.

A froth of young men headed the marchers, some only boys of ten or less running back and forth shouting, waving their arms and dancing with manic energy. The crowd slid menacingly up the street, like the waves of a rising tide beating along a rocky cliff. The noise echoing off the walls of the houses was deafening.

Edward stared at the riot advancing on them, like a bird stares at a snake. He guessed it was the sheer chaos which was so fascinating, and the contrast between the

The Joshua Inheritance

soldiers and the mob. Silent, the Paras stood in a thin khaki line across the width of the street, 'at ease', holding their rifles in their right hands. A picture of solid order. Their faces were expressionless under their steel helmets. Edward wondered if some of them were thinking of the last time they had been in action, street-fighting in Germany against the Wehrmacht when they had fought house to house, blasting each room with a high-explosive '36' grenade or even a Gammon bomb, and dashed in firing a burst of automatic fire through the door or window at anything left alive. Their stolid composure facing a mass of crazed civilians gave him confidence.

A volley of missiles sailed over. Bottles, stones, nuts and bolts hailed down on the Paras who hunched their backs and lowered their heads, like men walking into a storm, using their helmets as best they could to cover their unprotected shoulders. The range had closed to some forty yards and stones were coming over thick and fast.

Now the Paras could make out what the mob was chanting.

'Nazis! Nazis! British Gestapo!'

There was a noticeable murmur of shocked anger among the soldiers standing in the square.

'Steady!' Sergeant Hodgson called out warningly to the men near him, more to cover his own surprise than because he thought the Paras might have broken ranks without orders.

The crowd sang in English, 'Red poppies with black hearts!'

Edward turned in amazement to the police lieutenant and shouted in his ear, 'What the hell do they mean?'

'It's a Hebrew song called "Kalanyot",' he shouted back over the din. 'The poppies are supposed to be your red berets.'

The stones showered over, clattering down on their

helmets and the road. A Para in the front line staggered back. Sergeant Hodgson stepped forward at once, grabbed his rifle and pulled him back out of the way with a handful of his battledress, shouting for another man at the back of the square to take his place. A Jewish boy at the front of the crowd threw his hands up, jubilant with his accuracy.

The crowd shouted louder than ever, 'Nazis! Nazis! Nazis!'

Edward swiftly crossed the inside of his square to see the injured man, taking care not to run or give an impression of panic. The police lieutenant had formed his police into a wall behind the front line of Paras to conceal the injured man from the mob. Brogan was kneeling beside him wiping blood from a deep cut on his jaw.

'I can't understand it, sir,' said the private, sitting on the road. He was not so much upset by his wound, which was bleeding all over his shirt, but mystified. 'We was on their side, wasn't we? In Germany. We beat the Krauts, and let the Jews out of all them camps. Belsen and the like.' He paused. 'Why 'asn't no-one told these bastards?' He looked up at Brogan.

'Sean, you know what I'm talking about. I lost a good mate fighting the Krauts. Didn't I?'

Brogan just nodded, his face bleak and hard, a window on the determination which had won him his Military Medal in France.

Edward winced as a large rock landed on his back. This was not France, nor Arnhem, nor the Rhine. The enemy this time was not German, but he had had enough. He said, 'Time to charge them.'

'Waste of time,' snorted the young police lieutenant. 'We've spent all day doing that. It'll take more than a quick smack over the head to disperse this lot. Bastards should be shot, in my view. Someone will get badly hurt in a minute.'

The Joshua Inheritance

Edward was shocked. The idea of opening fire at a mass of civilians was repugnant, even though several of his platoon were bleeding under the rain of missiles. A charge had to work. The alternative was too awful to contemplate. He ignored the police lieutenant, checked that Sergeant Hodgson was ready and bellowed an order. The Paras in the front line suddenly parted and Edward's snatch group charged out of the square with the police.

They crossed the short distance to the crowd in seconds. Caught off balance, the younger ones at the front spun round and began running back into the mass behind, where people could not see the danger. Most were too slow. Edward's snatch squad reached them and they began laying about with their batons. Without thinking, Edward joined in, carried away by the exhilaration of the charge, the release of tension in action and venting his anger at being stoned. He slammed his baton over the shoulders of a young man he saw carrying a handful of nuts and bolts to throw at the Paras. The young Jew screamed, dropped his missiles all over the street and was promptly seized by two policemen who dragged him off by his feet for questioning.

The crowd fell over itself getting away. The momentum of the charge faded. Edward stopped running forward, ready to give the order to retire back to the square. A tunnel momentarily opened through the maelstrom of fleeing people, like the parting of waves in the Red Sea, and he saw a young man man staring at him. The intensity of his eyes in the pale face under a shock of black hair was riveting and disturbing, somehow personalising the violence on the street between them. The tunnel closed again and he disappeared from view. Edward frowned, something familiar nagging at the back of his mind. Then he ordered his men back to the square.

The police had several prisoners. They frog-marched

them through the Paras' square and round the corner out of sight of the crowd to a holding 'cage', which was really no more than thick rolls of barbed wire pulled round on the road. While the riot continued, other police interviewed them at tables in the street, one by one, checking their identities against lists and photographs of men suspected of being involved in the railway attacks: the Stern gang, the Irgun, the Palmach or the Haganah underground groups.

Edward felt rather pleased with himself. The crowd had retired a safe distance down the street and the baton charge seemed to have blunted their enthusiasm. Irritatingly, the police lieutenant was dismissive. Moments later he was justified. The mob began to move back up the street, chanting again, 'Nazis, Nazis! Gestapo! Red Poppies and Black Hearts.' The air darkened with missiles and soon the cobbles were littered with debris.

The see-saw sequence of missile throwing, abuse and answering charges continued up and down the street for another exhausting hour during which last light faded into night. The glow from burning buildings elsewhere in Tel Aviv could be seen over the rooftops lighting the faces of rioters and soldiers a hellish red. Edward was drenched in sweat, his face covered in grime and his initial excitement had long gone. The situation was desperate. After yet another charge, he stood near Sergeant Hodgson catching his breath and looking round. Far from being frightened off by the charges, the mob had gained confidence and retreated less far each time, taking advantage of the dark. Instead of running, the young Jews were fighting back fiercely with improvised weapons, metal railings, pipes and broken furniture, and all the time more people were pushing into the street from behind. On their side, the Paras were tired. No-one had escaped injury and several were being patched up behind in Colony Square by the police medics. It finally dawned on Edward that all their

The Joshua Inheritance

wartime experience would count for nothing if the mob, hundreds strong, launched an attack of its own. Edward tested his thoughts on Sergeant Hodgson.

'Couldn't 'ave put it better meself, sir! Bunch of 'ooligans.'

There was no time to enjoy the flavour of Sergeant Hodgson's understatement. A sudden raging cheer from the mob signalled another policeman down, stuck by a brick. Edward despatched his runner on the double to Major Rattigan to ask for support. He wanted a flanking movement through side streets to dislodge the crowd in front of him. Reluctantly, with the police lieutenant's eyes on him, he also asked for permission to open fire if necessary.

The runner never reached Rattigan's position in Colony Square. Major Rattigan had already appreciated that Edward's platoon was out of its depth and joined Edward behind the thin front line of his square.

'Under pressure, Fairfax?' Rattigan grinned encouragement at his young platoon commander, sticking his head close so he could be heard over the noise from the crowd. 'Things are rough with the others as well. Hall-Drake and Three Platoon are fully engaged, like you. Even Company Headquarters is committed. I've sent a sitrep to the Colonel asking for support. He says the rest of the battalion is on its way and I shan't be surprised if the entire Brigade isn't deployed before tomorrow.' He ducked as a chunk of wood came sailing over, pulling Edward out of the way. Then he said grimly, 'Looks like we'll have to open fire.'

He saw the expression of distaste on Edward's face and nodded, 'I know, but there's no option at this stage. It's us or them. Good luck!' There was no time for discussion. He slapped Edward on the back and disappeared through the rear of the platoon heading back to Colony Square. He was an officer with considerable combat experience who expected his orders carried out without supervision. He had full confidence in Edward. He had once said, 'Don't have a dog and bark yourself!' He made it perfectly clear that junior officers were ranked with the dogs and should look out for a severe hiding if their bark were not fierce enough.

Edward turned to face a sea of faces not thirty yards from his men. The young Jews were frantic with hate, mouths open, screaming and beating their sticks on the ground. Major Rattigan was right. Edward took a deep breath. The questions could come later. Now he had to deal with the problem. He just wished his first action had been against a real enemy, not civilians.

Sergeant Hodgson was about to speak when Edward shouted at Brogan to unfold the banner. Brogan and a policeman lifted the banner in record time.

'TITPAZER OO NIRAY!' was written in Hebrew in huge capitals across the banner, 'Disperse or we fire!'

The crowd booed and catcalled, 'British Nazis! Gestapo!' and they never changed the beating tempo of their inching advance on the soldiers. A volley of stones, bottles and pieces of metal flew over the square at the banner, folding it up. A great cheer of derision went up before Brogan could yank it out straight. The rioters moved forward another couple of yards. Some of the bolder young men were less than twenty yards away.

'Front rank!' Edward shouted at the top of his voice, to make himself heard over the roaring crowd. 'Ready!'

Instantly, the Paras shifted their stance, holding their rifles across their chests, poised to ram them into their shoulders and fire, or use them as clubs, whatever was ordered. Like Major Rattigan they had confidence in their Company. Edward noticed a different set to their backs. Alert like boxers, they stood ready to strike back after long hours standing like Aunt Sallies in a coconut shy.

Feeling caught in the inevitability of a nightmare, Edward shouted at the policeman with the loudhailer,

The Joshua Inheritance

'Give them the warning!' The man lifted a loudhailer to his mouth and bellowed, first in English, 'Disperse or we will open fire!' and then in Hebrew, *'Titpazer oo niray!'* Edward doubted very much whether the crowd could even hear the words but the drills demanded that the warnings be given.

The crowd crept forward, snarling and almost within striking distance of the thin khaki line across the street. Edward turned to Corporal Jacobs who was standing near him in the centre and told him to take aim.

'What at, sir!'

The reality of shooting someone hit home. Edward swung round and stared into the crowd, seeing nothing more than a milling sea of brown faces, shadows in the darkness. Then he saw the man who had stared at him before, standing on one side in the cover of a doorway, his pale face and shock of hair clear above the rest. Edward guessed at once he was a ringleader. He pointed.

There was no time for heart-searching. The crowd roared suddenly and rushed forward. For a moment Edward was transfixed, fascinated by the mob which surged up the darkened street, threatening to swamp them. Sergeant Hodgson whipped round at him, the police lieutenant stared at him, his mouth opening to shout.

Edward bellowed, 'Fire!'

The explosion of the Lee Enfield rifle shocked the rioters to a standstill. The echoes boomed back and forth across the narrow street, bouncing off the white stucco walls, and died away. For a fraction of time no-one moved and the silence was broken only by the thin metallic sound of Corporal Jacobs smoothly working the bolt on his rifle to chamber another round.

Edward was all action now. The first man had disappeared from sight and he pointed again, at another of the men he had seen organising the riot at the back. 'Thirty yards, man in white jellaba in doorway! Fire!'

Everyone heard the order and Corporal Jacobs's trained response to a target indication and fire order. 'Seen,' he said coolly, lifted his rifle, aimed and pulled the trigger.

The echoes of the second rifle shot had hardly died away when a woman screamed deep within the crowd. Instantly, the mob came to life again, galvanised by the reality of death. They turned and fought to get away, running and stumbling over each other, all their jubilant aggression turned to panic.

Edward wanted to see who had been shot. He caught sight of a group of young men struggling along in the escaping crowd. They were dragging something. He shouted for another baton charge. They must be quick. He sprinted out ahead of the snatch squad but the mob was evaporating with astonishing speed and he nearly fell over a man and a woman kneeling in the dust, like rocks left on the beach as waves sweep back to the sea. Beside them was the body of a small boy. Edward stopped in his tracks. He could clearly see the blood thick on the boy's soft brown skin where he had been shot clean through the neck. About the height Corporal Jacobs would have aimed to hit his target in the chest. The woman was weeping hysterically. She clutched her hands to her breast, pulling mindlessly at her crumpled bloodied dress. The man kneeling with her was the one Corporal Jacobs had tried to shoot.

Paul Levi dragged his eyes off the dead boy and looked up at the young Para officer. His voice deadly quiet, he asked, 'Why?'

Edward could not meet the other's terrible gaze. Accusation screamed from his black eyes, in the bleak expression on his thin white face and in the sheer vulnerability of his position kneeling in front of the soldiers.

The Joshua Inheritance

'He was nine years old. The only son she had left. Why?'

Edward felt sick. A terrible mistake had been made. He knelt to look at the boy more closely.

'Forget it,' Paul said harshly. 'He's dead. Why?'

'You know bloody well why,' Corporal Jacobs butted in, angry that he had hit the child instead of the man. The fellow's calm accusation after all the violence of the past hour and a half was infuriating. 'More to the point, mate, why's this youngster 'ere in the first place?'

'This is his nation's fight for survival,' the man replied softly.

'Wouldn't let my missus bring the kids to a shindig like this, whatever it was,' Corporal Jacobs retorted. 'They'd stay at 'ome.'

'This is our home,' said Paul with fierce intensity. 'Eretz Israel is our home. You have no right to be here. You're killing us, men, women and children, in our home, like the Nazis killed six million of us in Europe.'

Brogan stepped forward enraged, his arm raised, but Edward stood in the way, shouting, 'Enough! There's been enough violence already.'

Paul laughed unpleasantly, 'Enough? What is enough? D'you seriously think that you can kill the sons and call halt to their families? This isn't a game of cricket that you can leave the pitch for tea in the pavilion when it rains.'

Edward's feelings of shock and guilt at the boy's death faded quickly at the bitter reference to Nazis again and the surprising unreality of a young man in a riot in Tel Aviv knowing anything about cricket. Suddenly he felt terribly tired and confused. The rest of the mob had vanished down the street, leaving them alone in relative quiet. One boy was dead, a sacrificial lamb, and it was over. Edward waved his hand and said distantly, 'Take the boy away.'

Paul's anger bubbled over at the imperious dismissal and he opened his mouth to shout his rage.

Edward bellowed, 'Go! Take the woman and her son away, before I change my mind and have you arrested!'

For a long moment Paul stared at the Para officer, pulling his anger back under control. Then he bent down and gently scooped up the dead boy. He stood up and walked away through the litter of stones and broken bottles towards the remnants of the mob who waited in small groups at the bottom of the street. The boy's mother pulled herself to her feet and followed, staggering alongside the man, blinded by tears and unbelieving. She gently touched her son's dusty, bloodied forehead with her fingertips as it lolled and swung disjointedly over Paul's arm.

'Nazis!' a voice screamed from the back of the crowd.

Edward turned away too, followed by Corporal Jacobs and Brogan. They walked back to the platoon leaving the field of battle empty. His first engagement. He had won. He supposed it was inevitable, but at what cost? There was no sense of victory or achievement. Just disgust. He felt too tired to ask himself who was really responsible for the death of that boy. The politicians in London, or ringleaders like the young man who carried the boy away, or was he, Edward Fairfax, responsible for giving the order to Corporal Jacobs? He felt hollow and badly let down.

The chaos subsided after the first shots that night but the crowds did not go home for three days and Edward had no time to think. Major Rattigan was proved right when the whole of 3 Parachute Brigade deployed into the city to help the police restore order.

Finally they returned to El Bureij camp. Edward and Aubrey sat on their beds in the 'Sandpit' and discussed the situation endlessly. Neither came up with an answer.

* * *

The Joshua Inheritance

The demonstrations in Tel Aviv lit the fire of public dissatisfaction throughout the Jewish community in the Yishuv, and the Arabs, still two-thirds of the population, stood back on the sidelines and watched. There was no further need to open fire but the Jewish crowds turned sullen and unco-operative and there was no let-up for the army on internal security duties. The original plans to train for the job of strategic reserve were shelved and riot duties, patrolling and curfews kept Edward's battalion busy into December.

Finally, they were given a forty-eight-hour leave pass. Edward and Aubrey managed to persuade the battalion MT officer to let them take a Land-Rover and they set out in the middle of the morning on a jaunt to Jerusalem, which neither of them had had the chance to visit.

Aubrey drove while Edward relaxed, pleased to be away from the confines of El Bureij and the 'Sandpit' and looking forward to a couple of nights in the officers' hostel in Jerusalem in real beds. Their spirits rose as the bleak scrubby desert south of Gaza town gave way to pleasanter and greener countryside in the foothills rising towards Jerusalem.

'How long d'you think these riots and disturbances will go on?' Aubrey asked. He had come to respect Edward's opinion.

'I don't know,' Edward answered. 'The IO thinks the Jewish underground won't be able to stand the pace. Especially once more troops come out here.'

'But I thought we were trying to demob the conscripts and send them home?'

'So did I. There always seems to be an inevitable "but". I think the Intelligence fellahs are wrong. There's something extraordinarily committed about the Jewish demonstrators and their attitude to us. The British, I mean, not just the Army. I don't think it will be easy to crush feelings that strong.'

A slow-moving horse and cart loaded with fat green melons swerved erratically into the road and Aubrey pulled the wheel to avoid them, swearing under his breath.

'Have you gone soft because of that boy?' Aubrey looked sideways at Edward's angular profile, his face browned in the sun, lean and fit. Feelings among the soldiers about the Jews had changed. The sympathy they had felt for the wretched survivors of the Nazi concentration camps in Germany was fading fast.

'No,' replied Edward thoughtfully. He looked out of the window. The road had started to rise in sweeping curves into hills topped by rocky outcrops. Even for December the sun was hot and he imagined the lizards basking on the rocks. Palestine seemed to him a harsh place, with no room for mistakes. Had he made a mistake killing the boy? Or was it the boy's mistake? 'I admit the boy's death was a shock. I felt completely responsible at the time.'

'You were furious.'

'That's true,' Edward replied frankly. He would not normally have been so open, but he and Aubrey had become good friends. 'That fellow who carried him off unnerved me. I can't shake off the peculiar sensation that I've seen him before.'

'Guilt,' Aubrey said, casually, the single syllable piercing Edward like a knife.

'He was obviously a ringleader. I wish I'd arrested him now. He's as responsible as me for killing that boy.'

'Not at all. Silly little bugger shouldn't have been out on the streets on a night like that.'

Edward reflected it was easy for Aubrey to cuff a remark like that. He had not been the one who ordered the boy killed. He said, 'That's what Corporal Jacobs said. It seemed right at the time, but on reflection how can you stop a youngster, maybe ten-years old, doing something he really wants to?'

'Lock the little bastard in his room.'

'Never stopped me doing what I wanted at that age. If the young ones feel strongly enough, they'll join in.' Edward looked directly at Aubrey and added, 'What's more, we can't blame them.'

'Why the devil not?' Aubrey demanded, thinking that Edward was absurdly keen to offer the other side of the argument. 'I'm fed up with being screamed at by women in black headscarves and stoned by trainee bandits in their teens.'

Edward laughed. 'How I agree! But it's the older ones who are to blame, like that dark-haired chap. He knows what he's stirring up. He knows the law. The young ones don't, so we can't blame them.'

Aubrey grunted. 'What about our lads being hurt?'

Edward shrugged. This was something he had never expected when he joined the Army and certainly never wanted. 'Piggy in the middle, Aubrey. The army we've joined has stopped being the vengeful striking force against Nazi world domination. You were lucky enough to catch the end of it. But now we're piggy in the middle, just like Sergeant Hodgson says, policing the bloody Empire.' Edward had thought a good deal about Sergeant Hodgson's remarks and wondered sadly if his entire career was going to be spent doing the sort of thing they were doing now in Palestine.

They crossed the Tel Aviv-to-Jerusalem single track railway line. Stone terraces banked away up the hills on both sides, harbouring grey-leaved olive trees. The road was busier. They passed a few ramshackle trucks straining up the hills, but most travelled on foot, or on tired horses and mules dragging carts, while colourful Arab tribesmen wobbled along on small donkeys, looking like their ancestors might have when Herod was Governor of Jerusalem.

They drove through a dusty village. 'They're all up to no good,' said Aubrey with feeling, waving his hand at two very old men with creased brown faces sitting in the sunshine on chairs outside a mud-brick house. 'Those two might not blow up the bridges themselves but I bet they know who's doing it. Buggers won't tell us. Typical Old Testament stuff. Don't look and pass by on the other side.'

'New Testament actually,' grinned Edward. 'The Good Samaritan.'

'Really? Amazes me how you remember all that sort of thing.'

The road left the village, winding alongside the River Soreq, drawing them closer to Jerusalem. Edward was not particularly religious but he could not help a growing feeling of excitement at visiting the Holy City. Perhaps it had to do with the thought that soldiers from every European nation had fought in the Holy Land during the Crusades to free Jerusalem from the Arabs and centuries later from the Turks.

They rounded a sharp bend and almost ran into a stationary truck. Aubrey stamped on the brakes, swearing, and Edward nearly hit his head on the windscreen. Ahead, cleverly concealed from approaching cars in a fold in the hills, was an Army road block. Two Land-Rovers were parked across the road to form a chicane and several Paras wearing their distinctive red berets stood in the road with their .303 rifles at the ready while a motley collection of trucks, cars and livestock milled about waiting to pass through the check.

'I'm not queueing with the bloody natives,' said Aubrey crossly. He reversed away from the truck, pulled out and slowly pushed through the people milling about in the queue. Seeing red berets in the Jeep, the Paras waved him on with thumbs up. This gave Edward a pleasing sense of belonging and he reflected that 6 Airborne was beginning to get rather good at internal security work, even if no-one liked it.

In the centre of the road block, on the apex of the bend

The Joshua Inheritance

in the road, Paras were searching a large black sedan belonging to four Orthodox Jews wearing black felt hats and long curling sidelocks hanging down by their ears. They kept glancing uncomfortably behind them at the inevitable roll of Danette barbed wire which had been pulled round in a circle on the ground to form a 'cage'. Two Palestine policemen sat stolidly at a collapsible camp table, their black peaked hats placed neatly at either end, questioning another man wearing a simple white shirt and slacks. A tall dark-haired girl, about twenty years old, stood by him with a string bag full of vegetables at her feet. Her large companion was waving his arms, clearly frustrated.

'I'd lock the devil up, if he got stroppy with me,' said Aubrey, pointing. 'Fling him in the cage, eh?'

'You can't arrest everyone, Aubrey, for God's sake.' Edward wondered what it must be like being interrogated and searched by foreign soldiers on your way back from the shops.

'Stop being so bloody reasonable, Fairfax.'

Their attention was diverted by the corporal in charge of the guard party. He wanted to see their identity cards. He checked them and waved them on. Aubrey Hall-Drake began to accelerate.

'Wait!'

Edward turned round. The dark-haired girl was waving furiously, trying to dodge the corporal who had stopped her running after the Land-Rover.

'Let me go!' she called out frantically. 'Hey! Eddy!'

Edward recognised her. He grabbed Hall-Drake by the arm. 'Hang on, Aubrey! I know that girl.'

She shouted again.

Aubrey grinned at Edward. 'Eddy?'

Edward looked embarrassed. 'Yes, well. She's American. They talk like that.' As Aubrey reversed the Land-Rover, Edward explained, 'We met on VE-Day, in the crowds in Whitehall outside Colonel Haike's office.

Just after he told me the news about my father.' For some reason she had decided to cheer him up and he recalled they had drunk rather a lot together.

Aubrey braked and looked at the girl. She was in casual clothes, a simple blue and white cotton dress and flat shoes and he admired her excellent figure, giving a low whistle. 'I say, old chap! She's got the most wonderful brown eyes! What's her name?'

'Carole,' Edward told him as he got out of the Land-Rover. 'And as far as you're concerned, it's hands off!'

He walked over to talk to the Para corporal who was scrupulously polite but it was obvious he found it very hard to believe that an officer in the Parachute Regiment could, or should, know civilians in Palestine.

'They won't let me through because I forgot my ID,' Carole said, putting her hand on Edward's arm in a friendly way. 'It's really ridiculous but I was only shopping, with Yaacov. He's Daddy's driver.'

The driver was an American Jew, an enormous man with a crewcut and no sense of humour. He had a diplomatic pass but the platoon commander, a lieutenant, refused to be bullied with talk of the American Consulate. The Irgun had dressed up as British soldiers several times and used false identities to bluff their way into camps to steal arms. Edward explained how he knew Carole and the platoon commander seemed content.

'I never would have recognised you,' Edward said, introducing her to Aubrey. 'I seem to remember you were in the uniform of some women's volunteer unit when we met in London?'

'And very attractive I should think too,' Aubrey drawled before she could reply. They shook hands and he added, 'But I think I prefer you as you are.'

She laughed. 'I must admit I'm delighted to be out of uniform. I hated the restrictions.' She looked at Edward happily and put her hand on his arm. 'The end of the

The Joshua Inheritance

war seems so long ago but it's only like yesterday that we met.' She had never expected to find him again.

'Isn't it extraordinary luck meeting like this?' said Edward. He felt he was meeting an old friend and was flattered that she appeared so pleased to see him. They looked at each other for a moment, then both spoke at once and they burst out laughing.

'What are you doing here?' Carole asked.

Edward said, 'What d'you think?' He gestured at their uniforms.

'And you?' asked Aubrey, lighting a Turkish cigarette. He was completely taken by Carole's eyes.

'I've been to Haifa today, with Yaacov. We were shopping and I found some nylons in the stocking salon but they were very expensive.' She pulled a face. 'They cost sixteen hundred mils.'

'No, I mean where do you live?'

'In Jerusalem,' Carole replied. 'My father was posted out here in August. He's on the American Consulate staff.'

For Edward, this was excellent news. Palestine might be bearable if he could get away from the Army from time to time and see Carole. He said, 'Maybe we'll be able to meet?'

Carole nodded happily. She said, 'Where are you two based?'

Grinning broadly, Edward suggested, 'We'll give you a lift to Jerusalem and tell you on the way.'

She agreed and ran over to speak to Yaacov who was waiting beside a large blue Ford saloon.

'What a simply delightful girl,' Aubrey breathed, watching her talk to the enormous driver. He exhaled a cloud of cigarette smoke.

She was back in a moment. 'He's a bit grumpy, but there's nothing unusual in that. He said he'll follow us back to Jerusalem.'

'To see we don't molest you?' Aubrey teased.

'Of course.' Carole gave them a rapturous smile. Edward noticed she wore no make-up. Her skin was lightly tanned and flawless.

Aubrey took the wheel again and they all squashed together on the front seat. Carole's warm side pressed against Edward and he slipped his arm round her shoulders to give her more room.

She looked about inside the Land-Rover, 'Can't the British Army find you anything better than this Jeep thing?' She wriggled about next to him trying to find a comfortable position and he found her closeness unnervingly pleasant.

He advised her, 'You have to sit on one buttock at a time.' She smiled at him and sat so she was tucked under his arm. He watched her cross her long legs to keep out of the way of Aubrey grappling with the gear stick. They were smooth and brown and he wondered how he had managed to completely forget all about her after VE night.

'What news of your father?'

'My father?' The question took him by surprise. Although Captain Scarland never let slip an occasion to pass an unpleasant remark, in Palestine his father's problem seemed remote.

'Don't you remember? In London. You said you didn't know where he was.' She noticed his puzzled expression and said, 'I'm sorry. So many good men never came home.'

Edward shook his head, 'No, no, Carole. He's alright. He's back home now.' He glanced at Aubrey and said, 'He's fine. Really.'

Carole knew immediately he was lying, but she did not pursue the subject, not wanting to spoil the good fortune and sheer pleasure of seeing him again. Aubrey asked her what there was to do in Jerusalem and she was happy to see Edward quickly recover his good humour as she talked about the various diplomatic

The Joshua Inheritance

clubs and officers' Messes where there were frequent parties. Edward surprised himself by feeling a pang of jealousy. There could be no shortage of men willing to take her out.

After climbing the narrow Soreq valley, the road levelled out on the high ground and they approached the outskirts of Jerusalem along the Jaffa Road past old houses with balconies in a mixture of colonial styles betraying the centuries of Turkish rule. Carole directed Aubrey towards the centre. At the bottom of the Jaffa Road, Aubrey drove into Allenby Square, named after the general who had taken Palestine from the Turks in the First World War. There Edward caught his first glimpse of the Holy City. The old walls of Jerusalem rose massively beyond the bare ground beside the road, topped by solid rectangular battlements and dominated by the towers of the Citadel. The place looked impregnable, yet Edward remembered that soldiers of nearly every European nation and all the great faiths of the region had ruled there.

The white and yellow stone curtain walls reared above them, pitted with age and the noise of countless seiges over the millenia, from the times of the ancient Assyrians, through Persians, Romans and Arabs to the British. Jerusalem was still the centre of three great religions and Edward felt the atmosphere was almost tangible as they passed into the Old City, into the cool shadows under the Jaffa Gate and bounced over the cobbles of the street which bordered the Christian and Armenian quarters. It was crowded over by tall buildings and filled with polyglot peoples of all kinds and religions. Arabs in their long white jellabas passed Orthodox Jews in black with hats perched on the back of their heads, businessmen hurried along in drab suits of grey and brown, groups of British soldiers in twos and threes were easily visible in their ubiquitous khaki, their peaked hats bobbing among Arab shemags, trilbies and Jewish skull-caps and everywhere Edward noticed priests and nuns and monks. Religion and war, he reflected, was a terrible mixture. He had already experienced the intense passions which could be generated in the Holy Land in the riot in Tel Aviv, and he had the feeling that worse was to come.

'What an awful smell,' said Aubrey distastefully. 'Hot bodies and rotten veg. Not a lot of washing goes on here, I'd say.' He took a deep pull on his cigarette and hooted the horn for people to clear the road.

'Spices of the Orient, Aubrey, not rotten veg,' said Carole.

'Is that what you call it?'

She smiled and gave him direction to her house in Hezron Street.

Edward looked up through the flat windscreen past the pale stone houses with their arched windows and snatched glimpses of a fantastic skyline of chaotic rooftops pierced by the individual shapes of monasteries, churches, synagogues and mosques reaching above the city; the onion domes of the Russian Orthodox church, Romanesque bell towers, the round pinnacles of Muslim minarets topped with the crescent moon of Islam, and finally, as they turned a corner into the Jewish quarter, a splendid view of the huge golden sphere of the Dome of the Rock, the Mosque of Omar, high above the Holy City, and glittering in the midday sun.

Carole had seen it all before, but she watched Edward's face and asked, 'A penny for your thoughts?'

He said, 'I was thinking how sad it is that Muslims, Jews and Christians are so bitterly divided when they all revere the same piece of ground.'

Carole nodded. She wanted to find out more how he felt, but there was no time. They had arrived.

'This it?' Hall Drake asked frowning. They had stopped in a dusty side street in the Jewish quarter. Houses of white stone rose on either side, clustered like

The Joshua Inheritance

tenement blocks, with heavy wrought-iron bars over the dirt-encrusted windows. Carole pointed one brown arm at double doors under an arch. 'Yup. This is home. I assure you it's not so bad inside.'

Yaacov passed them in the blue Ford and pulled up at the double doors. He got out, opened the doors and then drove the Ford inside. Edward was about to see her out when she suddenly turned and said, 'You must both come to supper tonight, please?' She put her hands on his leg, grasping his knee, and he noticed how strong her grip was. She looked pleadingly at him and then at Aubrey. 'You will, won't you?'

They needed no second asking.

'Wonderful!' she said and jumped down. She stopped at the paint-faded wicket door in the archway to wave once and disappeared inside.

Aubrey and Edward left the walled city and headed towards the YMCA in Julian's Way. The YMCA was a huge white stone building looking like a Byzantine university with a tall central tower and rows of arched windows which reached out to two solid wing blocks at each end. It dominated the horizon. The British used it as an officers' Mess since it had the advantage of being conveniently opposite the King David Hotel which housed the British Army Headquarters and the Governor's civil administration.

'By Jove, Carole's a strong character,' said Aubrey. 'Did you notice she has the most wonderful mouth? A little wide perhaps, but delicious to taste, I bet.'

'Yes,' said Edward.

'I suppose you did,' said Aubrey dryly. 'Just what did you two get up to on VE night?' He turned right-handed up Mount Zion and into King George Avenue. The tower of the YMCA rose above the rooftops.

'We swopped state secrets,' said Edward.

That evening, wearing smartly pressed service uniforms

and polished Sam Browne belts they returned to the winding side street in the old city. Yaacov opened the door, now neatly dressed in a white shirt and black trousers. Carole was behind him, smiling and radiant. The classical strength of her face was softened by just a hint of make-up around her big brown eyes and a delicate shade of pink on her lips. Her dark hair hung in shining waves down her back over a simple evening dress, locally made with beautiful hand-stitched smocking at the waist to emphasise her slim figure.

Edward was amazed. 'You look wonderful,' he told her with complete honesty.

She smiled happily at him and said, 'Come on in and have a drink.' Aubrey was amused that, although she included him with her smile, her interest was entirely in Edward. He did not mind. The evening had all the signs of being a considerable and welcome change from the Mess in El Bureij camp.

Inside, they took off their Sam Brownes and were immediately struck by the contrast with the dirty street outside. The ceilings were high, the white rooms spacious and on the walls hung a rich selection of Oriental art forms: Turkish and Mughal miniatures, wonderfully coloured silk carpets from Egypt and Persia, and icons from Russia.

'It's like a museum,' said Aubrey, much impressed.

'Most houses are like that here,' Carole explained. 'Ghastly on the outside and paradise inside. You find the same all round the Mediterranean. They're built as havens from the harsh conditions outside, the desert and the heat.'

'I'm sure they're not all like this,' said Edward emphatically, waving his hand round at the collection of paintings and ornaments. He had no experience of anywhere else in the Middle East, but he was sure he was seeing something unique.

'My father has collected all his life.' She led them

The Joshua Inheritance

through a pillared arch from the drawing-room into a courtyard in the middle of the house, open to the pale night sky. Water trickled from a small fountain on one side.

'Where is he?' Edward asked.

'He'll probably be late,' Carole answered, pulling a face. 'He's always working, or meeting people.' She poured them wine from a decanter and handed out the glasses. 'This is excellent red wine. From the Lebanon. Let's drink, to the good fortune of meeting.' She clipped her glass against Edward's and Aubrey's and sipped, watching Edward as he replied to her toast.

Edward asked, 'Your father doesn't mind you entertaining men in the house on your own?' In England, he doubted Colonel Haike would take such a liberal view with Diana.

Carole laughed, 'Women have the vote now, or haven't you heard in England? God, you British can be stuffy at times. I noticed that when we were in London. No, my father wasn't at all bothered when I said I had two officers coming to dinner. Besides, I'm a qualified nurse and working girl.'

'You're a nurse?' Aubrey asked.

She nodded and Edward grinned 'He's obsessed with nurses' uniforms.'

Carole smiled 'Typical male. I trained in New York straight out of school, but I hardly did much nursing there because we came over to England during the war. That's why we met in London,' she told Edward. 'When my father was posted here I thought I should stay with him and, to make myself useful, I work at a hospital off the Jaffa Road. We passed it on the way in this afternoon.'

They heard a noise inside the house and Yaacov came out to the patio with another man. He was of medium, spare build with a narrow face and a thick head of prematurely grey hair which made him look much older. Edward put his age in the late forties. He wore a lightweight grey suit and heavy black shoes with thick welts.

Carole walked briskly over to greet him with a kiss on the cheek and then turned to Edward and Aubrey. 'May I please introduce my father Axel Romm?'

'Daddy,' Carole went on cheerfully, 'these are the two officers I called you about. Edward Fairfax and Aubrey Hall-Drake.' She frowned. Her father had made no move to shake hands. He seemed to have frozen and his dark eyes were fixed on Edward.

'Who?' Axel Romm asked. His expression was a mixture of shock and distaste, like a scientist who has discovered an unwelcome antibody in the culture he is examining.

Aubrey stepped forward and put out his hand, smiling genially, 'Lieutenants Hall-Drake and Fairfax, sir. Delighted to meet you.'

Axel Romm ignored him. He repeated flatly, 'Fairfax. Are you any relation of Major George Fairfax?'

'Why, yes,' said Edward. 'What a coincidence! He's my father.'

Axel Romm exhaled a long breath and Carole put her hand on his arm, thinking that he must be overworked. She was about to ask when he took them all by surprise and said, 'Then I must ask you to leave. At once.'

Edward was stunned. The evening, which had promised so well, had collapsed. Without being told, he guessed this extraordinary situation had to do with his father's disgrace, though he had no idea how.

Carole was saying, 'Father! You can't ask them to leave. They're our guests!'

'Not mine, Carole. I can't explain but Mr Fairfax must go. This other officer will presumably leave with him.' He turned away and walked across the patio to help himself to wine. As far as he was concerned the incident was closed. It had to be, or the anger swelling inside him threatened to upset the control he exercised over the humiliation of the operation in France.

'How extraordinary,' drawled Aubrey. He had long thought the Americans had no idea how to behave.

At Aubrey's remark, Edward snapped out of his surprise and asked as politely as he could, 'Has this got something to do with my father and the war?'

Axel Romm nodded. He watched the water fall from the fountain. 'It has. We worked together. If I just say we did not get on, then I would be guilty of goddam understatement on a magnificent and typically British scale.'

'You're an American,' said Aubrey, disbelieving. 'What were you doing in the British Army?'

'More a Jew fighting the Germans.'

'I see,' replied Aubrey, embarrassed but refusing to show it.

Axel Romm rubbed it in with heavy sarcasm. 'Some Jews did fight you know.'

'Of course,' said Edward. Corporal Jacobs in his own platoon was just one of thousands. He added in a rush, 'Hasn't there been a terrible misunderstanding? I'm sure my father never did anything wrong.' If Romm knew something about his father's operation in the war, he desperately wanted to know.

Romm laughed bitterly. 'What the hell do you know about it?'

'Nothing, really. That's the trouble. Can't you explain?'

'You're not permitted to know.' There was no regret in Romm's voice.

Edward stared at him. 'What d'you mean?'

'Security. Your rules, not mine.' His tone was final, his face taut and unhelpful and Edward noticed his jaw working. It was plain they were wasting their time.

Aubrey was the first to move. 'Come on, Edward. Let's go.' His sense of form was outraged by Axel Romm's behaviour and his patience gone. He pulled Edward away by the arm.

Carole was caught between the two, not knowing whom to support. She cried out, 'Please, wait! Father, they're my guests.' She took a step towards him. He turned round, ignoring her and shouted, 'Yaacov! These two British officers are leaving. See them out!' As Edward and Aubrey left the patio, he added directly to Edward, 'And of course, I don't expect you to see Carole again.'

Edward burst out, 'Listen, please! Tell me about my father!'

Aubrey pulled him again. 'Forget it, Edward, old chap. We're not wanted here. Time to go.'

Edward's fight collapsed. He allowed Aubrey to lead him into the house. 'What about Carole? We must say goodbye.' He was sure she was as shocked by her father's attitude as them.

'Not the right time, old chap,' Aubrey said as he propelled Edward through the hall. Out of the corner of his eye he saw the tall figure of Yaacov standing silently along a passage. 'Not after a barney like that with her old man.' They grabbed their belts off a table and he pushed Edward through the wicket door under the arch while Edward's resolve was still weak. 'Not the right time at all. See her some other time.'

In the street, they stood on the dusty cobbles buckling on their Sam Brownes and Edward said incomprehendingly, 'You heard her father. How?'

Aubrey said coolly, 'Of course. Very rude fellow indeed. Typical American, if you ask me. They all seem very anti-British from President Truman down. Something to do with the Jewish vote in New York, I believe. I suppose this cove Romm had some beef about your father, but I'm not used to being flung out of chaps' houses. Not at all.' He patted his pocket and grinned. 'Still, not to worry. You know me. I was so taken with Carole, I couldn't help slipping one of their

The Joshua Inheritance

cards in my pocket as we passed the telephone. So, you can phone your pretty Jewish girl and make a plan to see her somewhere else.'

'At the hospital perhaps,' said Edward recovering. He was determined to see Carole again and find out what he could from her about his father and Axel Romm.

Edward did succeed in seeing Carole at the hospital but they had time only for a short chat. He was delighted to find she did not share her father's attitude to him and she promised to find out what she could about the wartime operation which Axel Romm and George Fairfax had been on together. However, events combined to keep them apart. She worked long hours at the hospital and at home her father had instructed Yaacov and his wife to prevent all contact with Edward.

At El Bureij the Paras were busier than ever on internal security duties. December passed through Edward's first Christmas away into the New Year with attacks by the Irgun on more railway installations, on a British Army camp where they stole all the rifles from an armoury, and on the Palestine police headquarters in Jerusalem and in Jaffa. There was no let-up. The police could not cope with the level of violence and constantly called on the Army to help them out. At the same time Captain Scarland worked the company hard on training and getting away from El Bureij seemed impossible.

By accident, Roger Haike, whom Edward had been avoiding, gave him the opportunity. One morning at the end of January, they passed each other at the camp gates. Edward had driven in with his platoon after another stint on road-block duty near Tel Aviv, and Roger was on his way out. The gunners had become full-time escorts for road convoys after the Jewish underground started to mine the roads.

'I say, Fairfax,' Roger shouted, waving a route map

from the cab of the lead truck. 'Keeping your nose clean?'

Edward ignored him. He was tired and dirty after forty-eight hours out of camp and in no mood to put up with Roger Haike.

Roger was not easily put off. 'What's the matter, old cock? You haven't shot another of those Jew-boys, eh?' He laughed. The gunner with him in the cab smirked. The story was well known.

Edward forced himself to control his fury.

Roger saw the shadow cross Edward's face, leaned out of the cab door and shouted, 'A chip off the old block, you are, Fairfax. Find the easy way out and shoot the boys. Just like your old man.'

Roger's laughter capped the insult. One or two soldiers unloading stores at the guardroom stopped work to watch. Arguments between officers were always entertaining. Furious, Edward crossed to Roger's cab, unsure what he was going to do when Roger added, 'I shall tell my father when I see him next.'

'Tell who?' Edward demanded looking up at Roger Haike's narrow grinning face. 'Is Colonel Haike in Palestine?'

'Oh yes,' Roger said with a note of pride in his voice. 'He's in Jerusalem, Head of Intelligence.'

'Where?' Edward's anger faded with the germ of a plan.

'In the King David Hotel, of course. You don't know a bloody thing, do you, Fairfax? "Headquarters British Troops in Palestine and Transjordan" is in the King David, with the Civil Administration.'

Edward had all he needed. He snapped, 'Pity your father never passed on his brains to you,' and slammed the cab door shut in Roger's face. Roger fell back into the truck clutching his nose. The gunner at the wheel looked away to hide his broad grin.

Edward started working on his plan at once. He spent

The Joshua Inheritance

weeks cultivating the Battalion Intelligence Officer who became impressed with the young platoon commander's interest in what he liked to call the 'big picture'. Towards the end of February, the IO said, 'Things are getting worse, Fairfax. You know we've got camps for Jewish dissidents in Eritrea?'

Edward nodded, although he had never had the slightest idea that the British were even in Ethiopia, let alone sending Jewish immigrants to camps there.

The IO continued, 'There was a riot there in January. Several Jews were killed in the fighting and the news has finally got out. Frightful how-de-do in the papers.' The IO rolled his eyes at the ceiling. 'We're accused of murdering them all out of hand. Anybody would think it was us who killed the whole six million, not the bally Jerries.'

'So what's new?' Edward shrugged. The Paras had become thick-skinned about comparisons with the Nazis, but he asked, 'Is that why they attacked all those police stations again two days ago?'

'Of course!' The IO said. 'Look, Fairfax. Tomorrow, I'm going to Jerusalem to watch the funerals of the four Haganah men who were killed in one of those raids, on the Sarona police station. Would you like to come along?'

This was what Edward had been waiting for. He casually mentioned he would like to drop in on the Head of Army Intelligence in the King David Hotel. The IO was impressed. He said, 'I'm sure I can swing it with Major Rattigan. He's mustard keen on Intelligence.'

On 24 February Edward and the IO drove to Jerusalem in a Land Rover. As soon as they entered the city they noticed an atmosphere of menace. Thousands had flocked to attend the four funerals and the streets were seething with angry people. All British soldiers had been ordered to keep a low profile to avoid inflaming the situation, so the IO and Edward climbed the stairs to the roof of a tall building outside the walls to observe what they could of the funeral procession without being seen. In the street below, the coffins were carried on a river of bare heads flowing between the houses, like tree trunks on the floodwaters of a storm. Watching the mourners, Edward reflected that the real storm was yet to come.

Later – in his office in the King David Hotel – Colonel Haike was outraged. 'Fifty thousand joined the procession! And the damned Chief Rabbi at the front. A funeral for four criminals killed during an attack on a police station under the jurisdiction of His Britannic Majesty, King George!'

His office was on the second floor of the seven-floor hotel. He strode with neat angry steps to the tall windows and glared at the walls less than half a mile away over open ground in front of Herod's Palace. The King David stood on a slight rise and there was a splendid view across the old city.

'Monstrous!' he fumed. 'It's rather like the Archbishop of Canterbury taking the funeral of four members of the IRA shot while trying to blow up Scotland Yard.'

Edward agreed but said nothing. He had not come to see Diana's father to discuss the Jews. Colonel Haike glared. He found it impossible to understand why the British Empire was not taking a stronger line to suppress the Jewish dissidents. He fiddled crossly with the knot of his tie and muttered, 'Damn Jews!' Then he turned around and changed his tone completely. 'Edward, my dear boy, it's nice to see you again, I must say. Diana sends her love, though I know you two write to each other a good deal so I expect she's told you that, eh?' He gave a brief embarrassed laugh, like a cough, unsure how to handle the sexual innuendo of correspondence between young people.

He switched to safer ground, flattering his young

The Joshua Inheritance

visitor with, 'I know you chaps in 6 Airborne have been busy. Good of you to take the trouble to drop in to see me.'

'Any news from England?' Edward asked.

'Not much. It's damn cold, rationing gets worse and the bloody Labour government keeps telling us all to tighten our belts.'

Privately, Edward knew that the National Service soldiers in his platoon would have given anything at that moment to be back in England, whatever the conditions. Demobbing the service conscripts after the war was going far slower than anyone expected. Some had been kept on because of the worsening situation in Palestine, while the dust, heat and antagonism only strengthened their desire to go home.

Edward wanted to talk about the family. Specifically, he wanted to ask about his father, but he started obliquely with, 'Have you seen my mother?'

Colonel Haike paused before saying, 'Yes. Yes. I have. Several times.'

'Is she well?'

Colonel Haike nodded. Anne Fairfax always looked wonderful and he had always been puzzled why such a beautiful and charming woman had agreed to marry someone like George Fairfax. He said awkwardly, 'She's splendid.'

To Edward this seemed an odd remark to make about his mother, as though she were a statue in a public place, or a seaworthy boat. But he pressed on, wishing that Colonel Haike could be more forthcoming. 'And my father? I hoped you might be able to tell me why his case is so secret?' He did not understand what could possibly be secret about the work of a cavalry major in charge of stores, ammunition and equipment for the tanks.

Colonel Haike sat ramrod straight in his armchair, his lightweight uniform without a crease and smoothed his dark hair. There was a slight odour of pomade in the air. 'I'm not sure, my dear chap. I did my best to find out. You know, on the old boy net, but I was sent out here before I got a sniff.' He picked up his pen as if he wanted to get on with some work.

Edward noticed but he looked out of the window. He was determined to do something to help his father. On the right, the walls turned away on Mount Zion which was dominated by the solid structure of the Church of the Dormition by the site of the Room of the Last Supper. Just inside the walls at that point was Axel Romm's house.

Edward plunged in. 'Does the name Axel Romm mean anything to you?' After all, Colonel Haike said he had read all the reports about his father's disappearance.

'Axel Romm?' Colonel Septimus Haike slowly put his pen down again. 'Doesn't sound English.'

'He's American. A Jew. He's on the American Consulate staff here.' Quickly Edward explained the little that Romm had mentioned about working with his father during the war, at the start of 1945. 'Could he have been involved with my father?'

'A number of foreign Jews did join the Army,' said Colonel Haike, speaking slowly as if he were trying to remember little-known facts. 'That is apart from the good chaps back home, the British Jews who were enlisted like everyone else.'

Edward persisted. 'His daughter mentioned her father had parachuted into France.' It was all Carole had had time to tell him about her father's work in the war.

'Really?' Colonel Haike looked carefully at Edward. 'What else d'you know about this chap?'

'Nothing more.' There was something about Colonel Haike's questions which made Edward feel he had stumbled on something important, but he had no idea how to proceed. 'Could Romm have been in my father's unit?'

'What on earth for?' Colonel Haike stood up and

The Joshua Inheritance

walked back to the window, his hands clasped behind his back as though he was on the parade ground. 'I suppose your father might have arranged the supplies for this fellow Romm's operation in France, but it seems unlikely Romm could have been in the cavalry. Not an American. Not if he parachuted anywhere.'

'He certainly parachuted,' said Edward. Carole had been definite about that, proud of her father, as Edward was of his.

'All kinds of chaps dropped from planes all over the place,' said Colonel Haike vaguely, talking more to himself than for Edward's benefit. 'Rather embarrassing now. Bloody nuisance the whole damned thing and a bloody rum lot, in my view, but we trained 'em all. We took ordinary chaps, civilians a lot of them, and turned them into snipers, saboteurs and experts in street tactics. We showed them how to use the clandestine wireless, to gather intelligence, and we taught 'em how to do it all undercover.'

'You mean the Resistance?' Edward asked.

'Yes. The underground. I said it was a damn fool idea at the time. Never liked it. Bunch of ill-disciplined scruffs.'

Edward was astonished to hear such a straightforward attack on the public's romantic vision of the Resistance. 'I thought they were a good lot, you know, really contributed to beating the Germans?'

'I don't think the results were all that striking,' said Colonel Haike a shade pompously. 'The underground by themselves could never have defeated the German armies. We still had to have D-Day. The regular armies still had to fight across Europe. In my view, the war could have been won without the Resistance. Instead we trained countless of these foreign chaps, we gave them guns and explosives, and what's the result? A legacy of anarchy! Bloody coves end up trained in thought, word and deed to fight the establishment.

Of course, in Occupied Europe, the establishment was Jerry. That was fine. Now, here in Palestine, it's us.' He paused, thoughtful. 'Still, I suppose MO-1(SP) kept a good many unconventional officers out of trouble in the real Army.'

'What's MO-1(SP)?'

Colonel Haike frowned. He had been talking too much. He had never found it easy to mix work and family. Without turning round, he said reluctantly and shortly, 'MO-1(SP)? Cover name in the War Office for these sorts of operations.' He was clearly anxious not to discuss the subject any further.

Edward guessed it was classified material, but he needed to know. 'Axel Romm's an American. Could he have been employed by MO-1(SP)? Could my father have been something to do with it?'

'I don't know.'

'How can I find out?'

'Damned difficult, I'm afraid.' Colonel Haike's back stiffened. 'All the material on these operations is classified. Probably won't be released for fifty years.'

Edward felt he had lost again. The year 1996 sounded like the end of the world.

Abruptly Colonel Haike turned round. 'I realise how much this means to you, Edward, so I'll do my best to find out. I'll have someone in the War Office dig out the report again and look it over. Meanwhile I'll make some inquiries myself about Romm.' He clapped Edward on the shoulder, and said with genuine concern, 'It's all a rotten show. And for your mother. Dear Anne. Diana tells me she's so brave.'

When Edward left, Colonel Haike walked swiftly back to his chair, sat down and paused for a second. Then, his mind made up, he lifted the telephone and dialled.

After a moment a voice answered and Haike began to issue instructions in clipped tones. 'Romm, Axel. United

The Joshua Inheritance

States citizen, a Jew, possibly of Central European extraction. Works for the Consul-General here in Jerusalem. I want you to find out all you can about him. You'll have to contact London. There's a file on him there in MO-1(SP).'

He dropped the phone back in its cradle and drew a service signal pad in front of him. He hesitated for a moment, regretting that there was no telephone link between Palestine and England, and then began to write,

PERSONAL FOR JP FULLERTON COMMA FOREIGN OFFICE STOP FROM COLONEL HAIKE COMMA HQ PALESTINE MIDDLE EAST LAND FORCES STOP ROMM HERE IN JERUSALEM STOP GEORGE'S BOY HAS MET HIM STOP NO INFO GIVEN AS FAR AS EYE CAN TELL STOP EYE WILL TRY TO PREVENT FURTHER CONTACT STOP ANY CHANCE CT MARTIAL CAN BE BROUGHT FORWARD QUERY

Colonel Haike buzzed one of the girls on his staff to take the signal at once and sat back to think. Plainly Romm still wanted nothing to do with the British, least of all Edward Fairfax, but it was annoying that they had met. He felt confident that Edward would have virtually no opportunity to meet Romm again as 6 Airborne was increasingly busy. All the same, it was worrying. Colonel Haike took a deep breath. Foreign Office chaps could be very thick but he hoped Fullerton would realise that the sooner the court martial was settled, the sooner the case would be wrapped up. Reputations were at stake and neither of them wanted the thing dragging on for ever.

In the middle of the following night, the uneasy peace on Lydda airfield vanished in a series of deafening explosions. Out on the pan where the RAF transports were parked, aircraft were brilliantly silhouetted as fuel tanks blew up and ignited tracer ammunition flashed into the sky. In the din, Paul Levi threw caution to the wind and shouted at the top of his voice, 'Come on! Stop gaping at the fireworks! The bloody guards will be on us!'

Reluctantly his sabotage team allowed Paul to chivvy them back through the rolls of barbed wire they had cut at the perimeter fence. Glancing at the burning planes, they settled their rucksacks on their backs, much lighter without the PE charges which they had so successfully laid, and began the long walk back through the cool February night to Rishon kibbutz.

Irgun rules of security were so tight that none of them knew that successful attacks had also been made that night on two other airfields, at Qastina and Kfar Sirkin. Altogether, the Irgun had destroyed twenty-two big Halifaxes, Ansons and Spitfires, amounting to millions of pounds' worth of damage.

Paul's team arrived back just before dawn. In their hideout in the kibbutz, Paul carefully debriefed them on the operation, making sure that they learned from their successes as well as from their mistakes. Then they set about cleaning their weapons. Paul sat on a British Army ammunition box and looked round the little room. It was lined with wooden planks, windowless and claustrophobic. A single electric bulb hung from the low ceiling. There was a door in one corner and a ladder propped up in the opposite corner. The eight young men in his team sat round on other boxes cleaning sub-machine-guns, rifles and a Bren gun, which lay in pieces around them on the mud floor. The parts glinted dully in the yellow light of the bulb and the smell of gun oil thickened the air. To Paul this was the perfume of success.

'We did well, eh?' One young man burst out. His face was dark brown in the poor light and he laughed, a rich mixture of pleasure and relief. 'How many planes d'you think we destroyed? Eight, or nine?'

The Joshua Inheritance

'You did well, Selig,' Paul replied, smiling, pleased that Selig had followed him into the Irgun. It had been an excellent night. They were all in good spirits, though one or two of the younger men still needed time to let the tension seep away before they could trust themselves to laugh out loud. They had performed well.

'Let's say nine!' Selig decided with vicious enthusiasm. After nearly six months in Israel searching for his parents, he had come to accept that they had not survived the camps in Germany. Nor had the rest of his family. Their dream to reach Eretz Israel and run a small farm together was gone and the energy which had sustained him was now directed into the fight for a Jewish Nation State. He was indefatigable.

'What next?' he demanded, polishing the breach mechanism of his SMG. 'What about that bastard in the Paras? The one who shot Mattea Spurstein's little boy during the demonstration in Tel Aviv.'

Paul's face darkened. 'I'd rather find the arrogant young officer who gave the order, but it's not easy to keep a watch on their camp.' He had made a reconnaissance of El Bureij disguised as a fruit seller, a ruse which had been successful before. They regularly logged notes of the convoys going in and out of British camps and normally there was little risk of being found out by the British. They seemed to have no information about where to look for the Irgun or any reliable photographs of Irgun fighters. Soldiers waved cheerfully from the back of their trucks, and laughingly called them 'Dirty wogs,' for driving a hard bargain selling their fruit. However, the problem in El Bureij was the Arabs. Gaza and the whole area was predominantly Muslim and Paul was far more worried that his covert watch would be discovered by the local Arabs who knew their patch too well. Even though the Arabs spent all their waking hours trying to steal from the army camps, he was certain they would inform the British if they spotted Jewish fighters in their area.

He snapped his German MP40 machine-gun shut and gave the casing a last dust over with an oily rag. He looked up and said, 'Don't worry, Selig. We'll get them, one day. But now I've got to go.' He had to make his report on the Lydda airfield operation to Yudelmann in Tel Aviv.

He stood up, put the MP40 in a rack against one wall and crossed to the corner of the room, where he turned. He always liked to leave them feeling good and he could not resist telling them, 'There's another operation coming off soon. So big, it'll shake the world. Keep fit, lads.'

He grinned and began to climb the wooden ladder against the wall in the corner. His legs soon disappeared from view as he rose into the darkness of the shaft above. Already it was cooler. He reached upwards, knocked on the metal trap door above and waited. After a moment he heard scraping and suddenly the trap lifted, allowing a glorious fresh draught of air across his face. A strong hand helped him up the last few rungs. He climbed out and breathed the sharp morning air deeply into his lungs, relishing the delicious tang of the orange trees beyond the kibbutz. Ever since being locked up in Orianenburg, Paul hated being confined and he never liked spending too much time underground.

He thanked the two men and walked out of the corrugated iron woodshed. Without a word, they slid a pile of logs back over the shaft, lowered an old tractor which was pivoted up on its back wheels, and checked the tatty old belt drive from the tractor's power take-off to a circular saw. Finally they scattered handfuls of sawdust from a sack and sat down on the logs to smoke a cigarette.

BOOK 3

JERUSALEM

'The boys who fought did so with pure hearts.'

Golda Meir

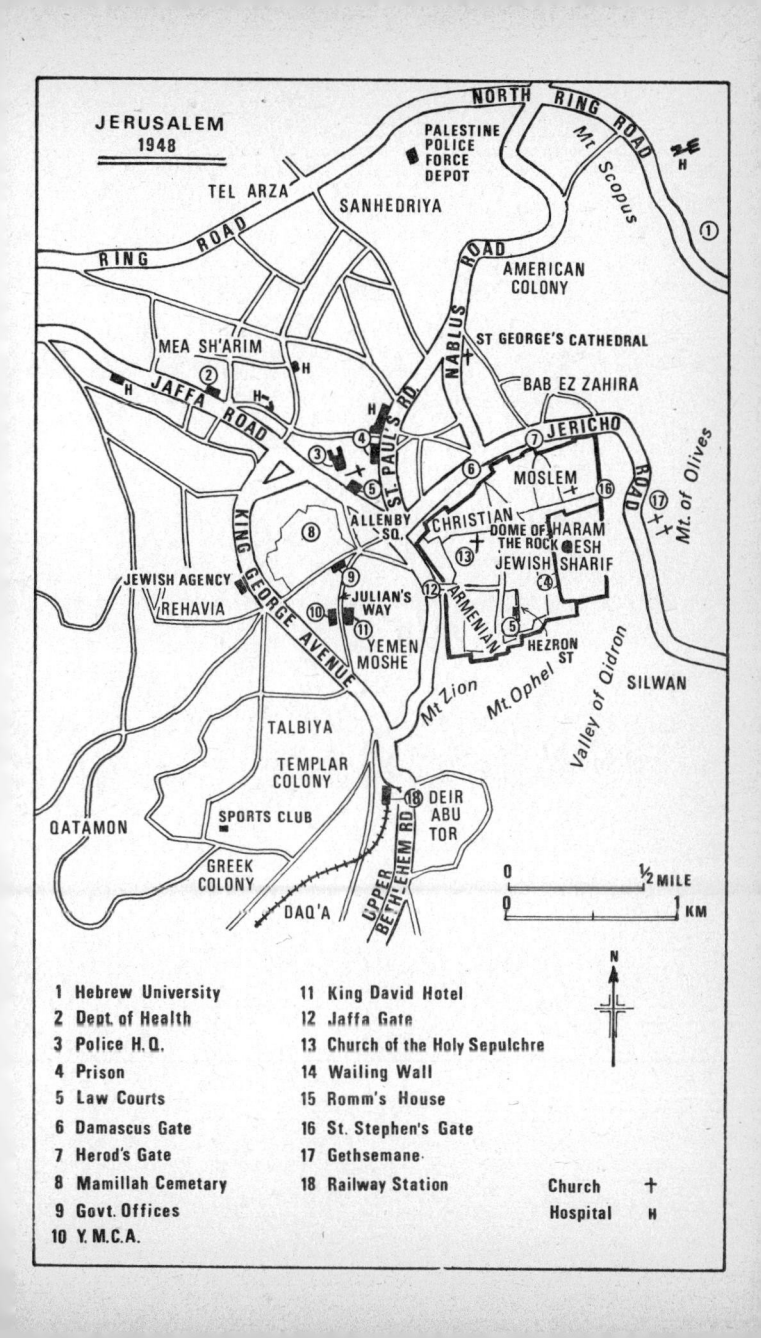

JERUSALEM
1948

Map labels:
- NORTH RING ROAD
- RING ROAD
- TEL ARZA
- SANHEDRIYA
- PALESTINE POLICE FORCE DEPOT
- Mt. Scopus
- NABLUS ROAD
- AMERICAN COLONY
- MEA SH'ARIM
- ST GEORGE'S CATHEDRAL
- JAFFA ROAD
- ST PAUL'S RD
- BAB EZ ZAHIRA
- JERICHO ROAD
- MOSLEM
- ALLENBY SQ.
- CHRISTIAN
- DOME OF THE ROCK
- HARAM ESH SHARIF
- Mt. of Olives
- KING GEORGE AVENUE
- JEWISH AGENCY
- REHAVIA
- JULIAN'S WAY
- ARMENIAN
- JEWISH
- YEMEN MOSHE
- HEZRON ST
- Mt. Zion
- Mt. Ophel
- SILWAN
- Valley of Qidron
- TALBIYA
- TEMPLAR COLONY
- SPORTS CLUB
- DEIR ABU TOR
- QATAMON
- UPPER BETHLEHEM RD
- GREEK COLONY
- DAQ'A

Scale: 0 — ½ MILE / 0 — 1 KM

N (north arrow)

1. Hebrew University
2. Dept. of Health
3. Police H.Q.
4. Prison
5. Law Courts
6. Damascus Gate
7. Herod's Gate
8. Mamillah Cemetary
9. Govt. Offices
10. Y.M.C.A.
11. King David Hotel
12. Jaffa Gate
13. Church of the Holy Sepulchre
14. Wailing Wall
15. Romm's House
16. St. Stephen's Gate
17. Gethsemane
18. Railway Station

Church +
Hospital H

9

COURSE LOGIC

25 March 1946

The regimental sergeant-major stood rigidly to attention in front of the entire battalion in a crisply ironed shirt and shorts, his red beret at precisely the correct angle, his boots somehow free of the dust which blew about the parade ground, and his pace-stick tucked under his arm. He eyed the Paras to left and right, his neck stiff and his jaw tucked in like a horse on the bit.

'Ry-eet, dress!' he bellowed. Eight hundred red berets flipped to the right and the entire battalion shuffled to straighten their lines, chivvied by the company sergeant-majors who stood by each company snapping and growling at individual soldiers like dogs. In moments, the voices died away into silence and the RSM bellowed again, 'Ey-yess, front!'

The heads flipped back to face the front and Edward stood in front of his platoon waiting for Major Rattigan to give the order for his company inspection to begin. He felt grand. The sight of the Paras lined up *en masse* on his left and right was splendid. This had been his first real posting. More than that, Palestine had been a first for everyone but the tiny handful of veterans of the North African campaign who had passed through the country during the war. Their job, now a seemingly endless round of riot control, road blocks and searches, was hardly what Edward had bargained for, but it was a new experience for everyone, even the old hands, and gave the satisfaction that they were all on the same footing, especially in face of an elusive enemy.

After the morning muster parade Major Rattigan called Edward into the Company office, a large box tent in the battalion tent lines, which smelled of hessian. The IO was with him and they were both sitting on collapsible wooden chairs at a table. Edward saluted smartly, more out of respect for Major Rattigan than because regulations demanded it.

Major Rattigan complimented him with, 'Good man, Edward, come in. The IO here says you've done well on your A-lat test?'

Edward nodded. He had continued his interest in Intelligence to wangle another trip to Jerusalem, this time hoping to get away from the IO and see Carole. When the IO noticed his aptitude for language, easily picking up Hebrew and Arabic names and phrases, he arranged for Edward to sit the Army Language Aptitude Test and the brigade education officer had been very impressed with the result.

'As you know,' Major Rattigan continued, 'I like it when my platoon commanders get involved in the Intelligence side of life. Doesn't happen often enough.' Edward noticed how the IO achieved the feat of nodding his head in agreement at the same time as shaking it in despair, presumably at the loneliness of his work. Major Rattigan went on, 'It's good show, what you've been doing. A good show. And the IO was quite right to suggest you sit this test. Languages are vital in Intelligence.' Although Major Rattigan was an enthusiastic supporter of Intelligence, he saw it as a vague and mystical world. Instinct told him it was vitally important but it usually seemed beyond the ken of the ordinary soldier. He asked, 'You speak French, don't you?'

'Yes, sir,' said Edward. He had become quite fluent

The Joshua Inheritance

after a summer in France before the war, working on a base of standard school French.

'Good. Then you should have no trouble with a local lingo, eh?'

Edward was filled with alarm. He had no desire to learn Hebrew, let alone be sent off to some remote academic institution just when time was running short before his father's court martial. He wanted to go to Jerusalem, speak to Carole, and find out what he could about her father as soon as possible. If there was any news which might help, he needed time for a letter to reach London. There was no other way to contact his mother.

'I think it's absolutely right we develop your language potential,' Major Rattigan said with a serious expression on his face. 'You'll be invaluable when you rejoin the Company, dealing with these Jewish chappies again.'

Edward agreed without enthusiasm.

Major Rattigan continued efficiently, 'So we're sending you off to learn Arabic. Alright?'

Edward stared. Arabic? What was the point of learning Arabic when the underground groups were all Jewish?'

'I know what you're thinking, Edward,' the IO smiled. 'But Arabic is a damned useful language, especially here in the Middle East. The Arabs all speak it. The British Army has always found that. You take it from me. Arabic is the language to learn. You can do it at BESAS.'

Edward listened to the IO's logic, his heart sinking. Hebrew or Arabic made no difference. The alphabets were equally complicated and both contradicted his object of meeting Carole. Dully, he asked, 'What's beesass?'

'BESAS is the best school of Arabic there is.' The IO went on, seeing Major Rattigan looking blank, 'The British School of Arabic Studies. It's a civvy organisation with damned good instructors, and the course is ten weeks long.'

Edward groaned inwardly. Long hours slaving over the books in some dusty library was hardly a glittering prize for cultivating the IO. Without enthusiasm, he asked, 'Where?'

'In Jerusalem, of course.'

His spirits rocketed. The Intelligence world was great! Who cared he was learning Arabic when their enemies were all Jews? He would happily learn hieroglyphic Assyrian so long as he could be in Jerusalem.

10

JEDBURGH

April–July 1946

The number four bus stopped just down the street from Homsi Salameh's car showroom in Julian's Way near the King David Hotel. Two Jewish businessmen stepped down into the sunlight, one slim with dark hair and the other barrel chested, both wearing brown suits and clean shirts with ties like any other businessmen in Jerusalem. To the other people getting off, their conversation seemed perfectly normal. They were talking about the Nuremberg war-crime trials which had just started, and expostulating about the Nazi leader, Hermann Goering, who was claiming that Hitler had had no idea about plans for the Final Solution of the Jewish problem.

Once out of hearing of the crowd by the bus stop, Paul Levi asked, 'What's the deal, Yudelmann?'

The older man carried on walking slowly along the pavement of Julian's Way towards the hotel without replying. His eyes flicked round the street. He was suspicious and on edge, and as members of the Irgun they were on dangerous ground. The King David Hotel was the centre of British authority in Palestine, and officers were constantly walking back and forth between it and the YMCA opposite, like worker bees at their hive.

'The British headquarters is in that hotel,' he told Paul, speaking so that only Paul could hear. 'Both the Army headquarters and the Civil Secretariat, for all Palestine and Jordan.'

Paul looked at the hotel properly for the first time. The building was set back about fifty yards from the road, seven storeys high and massively built with rough stone facing to the third floor, above which stone balconies jutted out beneath the parapet on the flat roof. The huge rectangular hotel dominated the west side of Jerusalem, with clear views over the old city to the Mount of Olives and the Garden of Gethsemane on the other side. Its heavy architectural styling gave it an air of enormous solidity, appropriate, Paul thought, to the British administration inside.

Yudelmann whispered, 'That's the target.'

Paul whipped round in amazement. 'The hotel?'

Yudelmann nodded, a grin pushing at the corners of his mouth in spite of the tension he felt. He cautioned Paul not to show his excitement.

Paul stuffed his hands in his pockets to avoid giving away his interest and exhaled a long low breath. He gazed at the hotel with new appreciation. They approached along the front of the building where a balustrade separated the street from a piece of low ground in front of the hotel.

'That's a restaurant,' Yudelmann explained, nodding his head over the balustrade at the basement corner of the south-west wing. 'Called the Regency. It's very popular. British officers use it a lot.'

'What's a restaurant doing in a headquarters?' Paul asked. He could hardly imagine the Gestapo in Germany entertaining the public in a fashionable restaurant in the basement of their headquarters in Berlin.

'The British only occupy three upper floors of the hotel, at this end. All the officers in the headquarters use an entrance on the other side, facing the old city. The actual hotel is still open to the public and everyone uses that restaurant.'

The Joshua Inheritance

'They're mad,' said Paul amazed. 'What about security? They can't just let people wander in and out like that.'

'They do,' said Yudelmann shrugging. 'But we want you to make certain. We want you to watch this place and work out the routine. Find exactly what goes on round this HQ. And work out how to attack it.'

Paul appeared casual, his hands in his pockets, but his mind was a whirl of excitement at the sheer scale of the plan. He tried to stay calm and mentally started making a list of the parameters of his mission. He asked, 'What resources are we going to use?'

'Explosives.'

'I'll need a lot, and it had better be good stuff. Fast,' Paul remarked professionally. Yudelmann noticed his eyes were riveted to the stone structure towering above them, flicking over the main features, trying to assess the construction.

A brief smile lit Yudelmann's broad face. 'I'll give you the best plastic, Nobel 808, which we've pinched from the British. As much as you need. We want to blow this place so the whole world hears the bang. We want the Americans to know we've struck the British at the local point of their oppression in Eretz Israel.' He punched one bulky fist into the palm of his other hand. 'And we want our people still held by the British in camps in Germany to know we're striking at the heart of the hydra which is preventing them coming home.'

They reached the sweeping semi-circular drive lined with dusty junipers which joined the street with the main hotel entrance in the centre of the building. They looked like two men simply enjoying the warm April sun on the corner of the drive. Paul stopped.

'When is this attack to be?'

'Soon,' said Yudelmann.

'Well, let's start work, then,' Paul replied. 'Let's have a look inside this lions' den.' He straightened his tie, nodded his head in the direction of the hotel and Yudelmann noticed a glint of amusement in his dark eyes. 'Coming in for a drink?'

Yudelmann smiled to conceal his apprehension, pulled his tie up as well and followed Paul up the drive. They pushed in through the big glass front doors and wandered together across the marble floor of the hall to the bar on the right. A few officers in service dress were sitting at glass-topped tables, some with women, and they looked up curiously at the two new arrivals. Yudelmann felt decidedly uncomfortable but Paul sauntered up to the bar at one end, leaned on the brass rail and studied the rows of bottles on the wall. He could keep an eye on the whole bar through the mirror behind the bottles and hoped the officers watching them did not notice Yudelmann's nervousness.

The barman approached wiping a glass with a white napkin and Paul asked Yudelmann in a cheery voice in perfect English, 'What's it to be, old chap?'

On 3 April Edward left El Bureij camp in high spirits on his way to Jerusalem. News was coming in of a rare and unique success against the Jewish underground. A lone nine-man section from the Paras' 8 Battalion had captured a party of the Irgun which had attacked the railway at Yibna during the night. The Irgun group, twenty-four strong, had miscalculated. They were caught out just after dawn going home through open scrubland and spotted by a light observation plane. The pilot directed the nine Paras on to their target and, in spite of being outnumbered and outgunned by the Jews, many of whom had Bren machine-guns, the Paras attacked fiercely. The training and fitness of experienced regular troops against irregulars showed at once in this almost unique conventional firefight between the British Army and the Jewish underground. After fourteen of the Irgun were

The Joshua Inheritance

wounded, the rest surrendered to the jubilant Paras who were unscathed.

In Jerusalem, Edward was given a room in the YMCA building again and the next day he went to his first lessons at the British School of Arabic Studies in an old institute dating from the Turkish period which smelled inside of polished wooden floors and dusty books. A cultured Arab who had been a lecturer at Cairo University, Husein Al Kader, was his instructor. He was a small man with pale olive skin who liked to wear lightweight cream suits with white and brown co-respondent shoes hand-made cheaply in the bazaar. During the initial test he perceived at once that the fair-haired young Para officer was capable of fluency. He said, 'I think you will do well, Mr Fairfax. Provided you work hard.'

'I shall do my best,' said Edward, likewise impressed with Al Kader. His calm intelligence was a welcome change from Captain Scarland and he spoke excellent English, better than his own if he cared to admit it.

Al Kader smiled sadly. 'My students are not always as committed as I would wish.'

The six others on the course were a mixture of people wearing a mixture of uniforms: a flight-sergeant in RAF Intelligence; a Naval officer on coastal patrol vessels trying to control illegal Jewish immigration; and two Palestine policemen. Two others, an administrator who worked for the Governor's office and an ambitious man from the Colonial Office, wore suits. Edward was the most junior but he was pleased to find none of the prickly rank consciousness which dictated life elsewhere and guessed this was due to Al Kader's influence. He and the Naval officer were the only career officers but they all got on well and Edward sensed an immediate rapport with one of the policemen, Inspector Angus Maclean. He had a dry sense of humour distilled on the Lothian hills near Edinburgh.

On the first evening, Edward excused himself and slipped away. He had every intention of working hard in the next ten weeks, but he had earlier called Carole Romm at the hospital and she suggested they meet in the railway station. He hurried back to the YMCA to change into his service dress uniform and Sam Browne belt, to look as smart as possible, and took a battered black Austin taxi to the station.

Jerusalem's station was a dusty memorial of faded Ottoman glories. Inside, under the vaulted glass roof, was a scene from the days of Lawrence of Arabia. The rich smell of coal smoke filled the air and a dirty black steam engine stood hissing with the effort of having just climbed all the way up the winding River Soreq valley from Tel Aviv on the coast to Jerusalem nearly three thousand feet up in the hills of Judaea. The doors of the wooden carriages behind were flung open and people were disgorging on to the platform. In a cacophony of noise, Arabs and Jews in their long jellabas pushed along with Europeans in pale suits and panamas escorting their women in printed cotton dresses. These were bright flashes of colour against the dull khaki of numerous British soldiers and officers.

Edward forged his way along the platform peering over people's heads for Carole, afraid he would miss her and wondering why she had chosen the station to meet. His heart beat faster at the thought of seeing her again.

Suddenly she appeared out of the crowd, running towards him and laughing with relief. 'Edward! I'm sorry, really I am.' She gestured round at the seething mass. 'I never realised! This train gets in same time every evening. What a time to make you meet me!' She looked at him happily for a second and then flung her arms round his neck and kissed him. Edward was not surprised. Somehow it seemed the most natural thing in the world. He wrapped his arms round her waist and

The Joshua Inheritance

returned her kiss, gently caressing her back. He could feel the warmth of her body under her cotton dress and he breathed in the smell of her lovely dark hair.

Gradually she broke the kiss and stood looking up at him, still inside his arms, her belly pressed against his Sam Browne belt. 'I can't believe we've got ten weeks together,' she said smiling and watching the wrinkles in the corner of his eyes as he smiled too.

Edward nodded happily. 'I couldn't believe my luck when I was given this Arabic course.'

'Yes,' she said. 'Come on, let's go.' She took him by the hand towards a side entrance of the station.

Behind them in the crowds, Paul Levi was moving the other way along the platform looking into the third-class carriages. He was dressed in a long brown jellaba, Arab headress and sandals. He saw Selig climbing out further down and waved.

Selig was dressed in Arab clothing, as Paul had instructed, and they hugged each other like Arabs. The British were looking for Jews. Selig said, 'Those carriages stink. You feel like an animal, all crushed in with the chickens and goats.' They made their way up the platform to the station entrance like any two poor Arabs visiting friends in Jerusalem when, abruptly, Selig gripped Paul's arm. He whispered hoarsely, 'It's him! The Para officer.' He pointed, stabbing his finger ahead.

Paul knocked down his arm with the flat of his palm and looked worriedly round. No-one had seen. The station was seething with people waving their arms and everyone was too busy with their own affairs to notice a pair of agitated young Arabs. Paul remembered that the safest place to hide was in a dense crowd.

'Look, Paul! Wearing a Sam Browne, with that pretty dark-haired girl in the blue and white dress. Very pretty girl. Her dress has got flowers on it.'

'I know,' said Paul quietly. Edward's red beret was

163

distinctive enough without Selig's tumbling description. 'I saw him earlier. I was waiting for you and saw him meet that girl.'

Selig was overjoyed. 'The Lord is on our side,' he said fervently. 'The young swine has fallen straight into our hands.' He moved very close to Paul and breathed at his side, 'Shall I kill him now?' He nudged Paul who looked down and saw an enormous knife in Selig's hand.

'For God's sake put that thing away!' Paul whispered in alarm and shoved Selig's hand with the knife back among the folds of his jellaba. Selig looked hurt and Paul hissed sarcastically, 'Yeah! Kill him, but it'll be a messy job and you'd better ask those officers ahead of us if they'd mind looking the other way.'

Selig looked crestfallen. He had not really noticed how many British soldiers were in the station. 'I was so absorbed,' he said feebly.

Paul pulled his shemag down to shade his pale face and cautiously glanced round again to see if anyone had seen the flash of the knife blade. His eyes roamed constantly over the faces of the people milling round them as he said in a low voice, 'Relax, Selig. This is clandestine work. We're in a city now, not blowing up aircraft in the dark on big wide open airfields. Let's just follow them. If the opportunity to kill him presents itself, in a quiet spot, then alright.'

Selig recovered at once and they slipped through the bustling crowds after Carole and Edward who were crossing the square outside the station.

'Where are we going?' Edward asked as she headed off, pulling him by the hand.

'We're going to have dinner at a little place I know.'

'I hope it's kosher,' Edward grinned.

'Of course! What d'you expect with a restaurant run by a guy called Solly Mannheim? The Astoria is real cosy. You'll like it.'

'Shall we take a taxi?'

The Joshua Inheritance

Carole smiled in the naughtiest way, 'No. Father and Yaacov have gone on some job away from town for the day in another Consulate limmo and I've got the Ford. We drive to dinner, in style!' She led him towards a side road opposite the station where she had left the car.

Behind, Paul warned Selig in a low voice, 'They're going into that alley. Maybe now you will have your chance.' Still no-one else appeared to be taking any notice of them.

Selig tightened his grip on his knife hidden under the folds of his jellaba shirt.

The talk about her father reminded Edward to ask her something which had been puzzling him and he said, 'Where is your mother?'

Carole stopped by the blue Ford and her dark eyes were serious as she said, 'She was left behind in Germany when we went back to the States.'

Edward frowned at his stupidity. 'I'm sorry. I shouldn't have asked.'

'You weren't to know.' She shrugged her brown shoulders and pursed her lips at the memory. 'We had to leave because we were a Jewish family but she never got away.' At least, she thought, that's what my father always said and I suppose I must believe him. 'I was at nursing college in New York so I don't remember the details, but my father told me when he got out in 1938.'

Edward was at a loss. His own straightforward upbringing in England was embarrassingly dull compared to the upheavals suffered by so many on the Continent. He said, 'What happened? I mean, have you seen her since?'

Carole deliberately put on a careless blank expression. She said, 'Nope. I've no idea. As far as we know she hasn't surfaced since the war, so I suppose she's dead. I must admit, I never really got on with her, so maybe I don't care, but it's odd, someone disappearing and not knowing quite how or where.'

She slipped her handbag off her shoulder and added reflectively, 'I think losing her like that did something to my father. He adored her and he hasn't been the same person since.' She shook her head as if pushing the thought from her mind and rummaged about in her bag. With a touch of exasperation she said, 'I can never find the key'.

Edward was waiting to open the door for her, one arm on the Ford's blue roof, and thinking maybe what she had told him excused her father's behaviour throwing them out of his house, but watching Carole took his mind elsewhere. He followed the curve of her neck along the line of her dark hair to her cheek and the tiny smile wrinkle in the corner of her mouth and quite casually he said, 'You are really very beautiful, Carole.'

'You're absurd,' she said without looking up as she concentrated on finding the key but the little wrinkle deepened as she smiled.

On a whim, Edward reached forward and turned her face in his hand to kiss her. She offered no resistance. Across her shoulder he saw two Arabs shuffling quickly across the square from the station towards the alley, their sandalled feet stirring up the dust on the cobbles. There was something about their manner which looked suspicious. With the rise in political violence had marched an inevitable rise in petty crime, and criminals, who seemed mostly to be Arabs, were taking advantage of the police being overworked and unable to cope.

'Let's go,' he said, reluctantly breaking the kiss. He opened the car door and she said a little breathlessly, 'I'll drive. I know the way.'

Edward saw her into the car and closed the door. He sauntered round to the passenger side. The two Arabs closed with them along the pavement. He opened the passenger door, dropped into his seat and slammed the door. The two Arabs stopped only yards away and stared. Carole started the engine and let out the clutch. The two Arabs watched them go.

Selig cursed viciously under his breath as the powerful Ford pulled away. They had been so near to avenging the dead boy. Paul was less concerned. He made certain he had noted the number plate.

'Don't worry, we'll get back to him,' he reassured Selig. 'There are plenty of good Jewish boys in the police who will find out whose car that was.'

'Shalom, Miss Romm,' said Solly Mannheim cheerfully, rhyming the greeting and slapping his fat hands back and forth to wipe them on his blue and white striped apron. Carole Romm was good for business. People liked restaurants where attractive women came. Besides she was good company. 'It's good to see you again, and you, sir, are a lucky man,' he said to Edward with great seriousness. He winked ostentatiously with a laugh like treacle and shook Edward's hand with both of his as Carole introduced him.

As he ushered them through to a small table in one corner, Solly's laugh rumbled on. He stood for a moment with his arms folded comfortably over his stomach, enjoying the happy expression on her face as she watched Edward settling down beside her. Then he smiled at a private thought and abruptly declared, 'Tonight is a special night. I will fetch my best wine and my best food. You will eat like a king and a queen.'

He left them for the kitchen, shouting instructions to his staff, and Carole said, 'Isn't he just wonderful?'

'Is he always as generous as this?'

'What's the matter?' Carole smiled, taking Edward's hand. She looked closely at him and guessed what was worrying him. 'You're worried about the check? You know, the bill?'

'Well, yes, actually,' Edward said, reluctant to admit

it. His second lieutenant's pay was only eleven shillings a day, hardly a king's wages to pay for a royal supper, although he had managed to save most of it in the past months. There was precious little to spend it on in El Bureij camp.

Carole put his mind at rest. 'Don't worry about it. Solly talks as if this was the Plaza in New York but he makes sure this is one of the cheapest places to eat in Jerusalem.' She went on to explain, 'Solly is an Italian, from the Tirol area in the mountains on the border with Austria, but he's Jewish. He was rounded up by the Nazis in 1942 and sent to a camp. He says he got real skinny, though you wouldn't believe it looking at him now. After the war, he'd lost all his family, there was nothing left for him in Italy, and he was so amazed to find he'd survived that he decided to come here, to Jerusalem. He hates the politics. All he wants to do is feed people who come to the Holy Places with good food and put them up in little rooms he's got upstairs. He doesn't mind if they're Jewish, British, Arab, Greek, even German, or any other race or creed on earth. It's his way of thanking God for surviving.'

'I'm pleased to hear there are some Jews who don't hate the British,' replied Edward, impressed. 'We always seem to be called out to deal with the agitators.'

'There are plenty who don't approve of those methods, I assure you,' said Carole.

Solly came bustling back with his hands full of bread, a carafe of red wine, two glasses and two plates of steaming hot freshly cooked spaghetti. Edward suddenly remembered he was famished. As they ate, he asked the question which was uppermost in his mind. 'Has your father said why he threw us out?'

She put down her wine and said, 'He refused to talk at all at first.' She watched his face closely as she spoke, trying to relate his interest in her father with his interest in her.

Edward leaned forward expectantly. 'What did he say?'

'He said he and your father worked on a special team towards the end of 1944.'

'Why were they together? I mean an American and an Englishman?'

Carole frowned slightly. She had not realised how little Edward knew. 'Plenty of Americans in OSS joined forces with you British and were parachuted behind the lines. They had various missions relating to the Allied armies advancing through France, to Holland and Germany. You know, sabotage, working with local resistance and so on.'

Edward held up his hand in amazement. 'Slow down! You mean my father parachuted? I thought he was a cavalry officer.'

Carole said, 'I didn't know his unit, but he was certainly dropped into France with my father, in September 1944.'

'Into France?' Edward gasped, trying to imagine his father, no longer in smart uniforms or London suits, but disguised in the rough clothes of a French peasant. He remembered their talk in the flat in London. No wonder his father had asked the right questions about his first training jumps. He had done it all himself and for real. Maybe he had been working with local groups, and he recalled Colonel Haike's scathing remarks about the Resistance. There was so much he had to find out. He asked, 'And what's this OSS? Is it anything like MO-1(SP)?'

Carole was impressed and said, 'Sort of. OSS is the American version. The Office of Strategic Services. It was formed in June 1942. Then, at the end of the war, from D-Day on, about a hundred Americans worked with the British in England in small groups. They were called Jedburgh teams.'

'Was Jedburgh the name of the operation?'

'No. Jedburgh was the general name for operations of this sort.'

'Where was the operation?'

'Somewhere in Eastern France, but the whole team was caught by the Nazis.'

'So that's what the problem's all about?' Edward said slowly. At last he had discovered the real cause.

She nodded, 'Yes. He said more men flew out but they were entirely compromised. Everyone was captured. They haven't been seen since. He said the only explanation was that your father had given away the location and time of the drop.'

Edward held his wine glass and stared unseeing at the glittering red reflections, trying to absorb the implications of Carole's words. The operation had been a complete disaster and his father was blamed. Carole searched the strong lines of his face to see how he was taking it. She wanted to know more about the operation too, from Edward's father.

At last, Edward frowned. 'I didn't know my father was captured.'

Carole pursed her lips. 'I don't know, but that's what my father says. He says your father gave them all away to the Germans. He blames the whole disaster on him.' She paused. She wanted to believe her father but she was certain there was more to come out. 'It seems your father and mine were the only two who survived. He said he was so shocked when he found out what your father had done, that he made his own way back to American lines. He doesn't trust the British any more. When he got back, he filed a report to his superiors in OSS. He said it's been passed to the British. Then he clammed up.' She remembered the hurt as her father had suddenly lost his temper with her, apparently furious at the recollection of what had happened in France and he had utterly refused to say any more.

The Joshua Inheritance

Abruptly Edward burst out, 'What bloody nonsense!' It was all impossible. His father was not a traitor.

She had been half expecting the outburst but it hurt all the same. She felt he was blaming her for her father's accusations. 'You think your father's been stitched up?'

'What?'

'You know, framed,' said Carole. She was determined to find a solution to help them both. 'If my father's right and your father's right, then something else must have happened which they don't know about. I don't know what, but maybe someone else is to blame. Maybe someone else wants your father to take the rap?'

Edward had never doubted for a moment his father was innocent of the charges, but it had never occurred to him that someone might be deliberately fixing the blame on him. It was too much. 'I just don't believe it. Everyone was fighting the Germans. They were the enemy, not my father. Anyway, if only the two of them survived, why should your father be right and mine wrong?'

Carole said in a small voice, 'I guess maybe the British prefer to believe my father's report?'

'Why on earth?' Edward burst out again. He stared at her questioningly and suddenly saw the pain in her dark brown eyes. He realised that the choice of whom to believe would hurt one of them. He took her hand over the table and apologised. 'Carole, I'm sorry. I didn't mean to upset you.'

She could see he was badly upset too. 'It's really important to you, isn't it?'

Roughly, Edward drained his wine glass and filled it again from the decanter. He nodded. 'Quite apart from the humiliation, my father is a career officer, like me. This will be the end.'

'And you'll be affected too?'

He shrugged dismissively though he was sure Carole was right. Captain Scarland's attitude was probably only the unpleasant surface of an undercurrent of rumour

171

against him. 'I don't care about myself. What's important is that this court martial will finish him. I am convinced it's unfair. I just don't believe my father's the sort of person who would give away his men and disgrace his country.'

Very gently she squeezed his hand in hers and asked softly, 'You love him, don't you?'

Edward was rather shocked. He replied quickly, 'I'm certainly very fond of him.' Then he paused and added, 'Yes, I suppose I do love him, really. It just sounds odd saying so.'

'Only to an Englishman,' she said. They said nothing for a moment, Edward thinking of his father and Carole reading his thoughts. Her eyes twinkled and she asked, 'Would you say you're fond of me?'

Edward coloured, which she adored. He said, 'Yes, I am fond of you. Of course.' He was not used to such direct honesty about his feelings with women. Unnecessarily, he blundered on, 'But I don't know about the rest.'

'You mean the love bit?'

He glanced at her and laughed. He relaxed, realising that she was teasing him.

At that moment, Solly Mannheim brought *scallopine al limone* and a crisp green salad and they agreed to leave the subject of their fathers' problems. Edward decided to write the following day to his mother, telling her for the first time what little he knew. In one of her letters to him, she had said the impending court martial was tearing his father apart and she would do anything to stop it happening. He hoped what he had learned from Carole would be enough.

While they ate, Carole talked about her time in America and Edward described his childhood in England. They were worlds apart but felt completely at ease with each other and the time passed quickly. They took it for granted that they would spend all their spare time together while Edward was in Jerusalem. After dinner, they argued happily about who should see whom home first, as Carole had the car. She teased him about his English sense of good manners and compromised by driving to the top of the street so he could at least see her drive home without fear of being seen near her house in case her father and Yaacov were back. They kissed and he stood at the corner until she turned under the arch into the house.

Filled with a sense of great well-being, Edward walked back through the old city streets, out by the Jaffa Gate and across the open ground past the King David Hotel to the YMCA. He went over the evening again in every detail. Nothing seemed to matter now that they had met. There was no urgency, and only the Jedburgh business pressed on their enjoyment together. He dreamed of the promise in the uninhibited way she had wrapped her arms round his neck and returned his embrace.

Easter Day in 1946 fell on 21 April, three days before George Fairfax's court martial was due to be heard. Anne Fairfax persuaded her husband to go to the Holy Trinity church in the Brompton Road for the morning service. It was not their usual church, but John Fullerton was a regular and she wanted to speak to him.

After the service Anne and George shook hands with the vicar on the way out and they joined the well-dressed congregation which milled about in the sun on the steps of the church. Most of the men wore morning coats and the women gaudy dresses, determined to put on a brave show in spite of the government's drive on austerity and Britain's grim economic situation. She excused herself, leaving her husband talking to a friend, while she slipped off to find Fullerton. Typically, he was talking to three voluptuous, rouged and expensively dressed middle-aged ladies wearing beautiful wide-brimmed Easter hats.

'Anne, how delightful to see you,' he said as she joined them and he introduced her to the other women.

'I'm sorry if I'm interrupting,' Anne replied.

'Not at all, not at all,' said Fullerton, extracting himself from the three women with practised charm. Flattering overweight society women was a useful way to develop his influence but talking to Anne Fairfax was a real pleasure.

Fullerton linked his arm with Anne's and guided her across the church steps to one side so they could talk without being interrupted.

'What gossip of the rich and famous were you passing on there?' Anne asked with a smile.

He laughed. 'Actually it was all gospel true. I let slip that the government has rejected the report of the Anglo-American Commission on Palestine which was produced yesterday. It's no surprise to anyone really.'

'What difference will that make to Edward?'

He looked bland. 'Oddly enough, none really.' There were a good many other things he would have rather talked about than her son, but he said, 'The Commission spent months looking at everything and then concluded the Zionist arguments are wrong. They say the Jewish refugee problem can't be entirely solved in Palestine. They almost said that Palestine should not be turned into a Jewish state or an Arab state.'

'I thought that's just what the British government wanted?'

Fullerton frowned. 'In a way, but the Commission also recommended that we allow one hundred thousand Jewish refugees into Palestine at once. It's out of the question! I can tell you, Anne, we're all very fed up in the Foreign Office. Most people blame the United States. They've got so much influence nowadays.'

'You mean they've got so much money.'

Fullerton nodded gloomily, thinking of the Marshall Plan to refinance Europe. He cheered at a thought. 'I told those women just now that a Syrian chappie, Faris el-Khoury, spoke to the Commissioners in Washington and told them that since the Americans favoured the Jewish position so strongly, why didn't they give the Jewish refugees a piece of Texas.'

They both laughed and Fullerton said seriously, 'Damned good idea, actually!'

Over Fullerton's shoulder, Anne saw her husband watching them from the church steps. She quickly changed the subject. She had to speak before her husband came over.

She put her hand gently on his arm. 'John Peregrine, I want to talk to you about George's court martial. It comes up on Wednesday, the 24th.'

Fullerton immediately went on the defensive but he concealed his feelings and assumed an expression of grave concern. 'I know, Anne. I'm so sorry. My efforts to help have come to nothing. I do assure you I tried everyone I knew.'

'You've done your best,' said Anne. He had been perfectly sweet meeting her and listening sympathetically while she let her hair down. 'I suppose there's nothing else you can do?'

'Well, no m'dear. Not really,' he hedged, smiling and shaking his head. His experienced social antennae had picked up a delicate nuance in her voice. She was not so much fishing for information as preparing the ground to tell him something herself. If it was to do with George Fairfax it was likely enough to be trouble.

'That's a pity,' she said, her large blue-grey eyes fixed on his. 'Then I'd better tell you something. I've found out quite a lot about what George was doing in the war.'

'I see,' said Fullerton slowly. 'Such as?'

Anne knew Fullerton well enough to realise she had caught her fish, but she had to play him very gently indeed. The bait she had was woefully small to achieve what she wanted. She ignored the question and lied.

'George told me the bare bones of the story when he found out the case would be held in secret.' The scanty information she had would sound better from George rather than third-hand from Edward.

'Really?' Fullerton was surprised and then admitted that it was a mistake to think that George Fairfax would be the sort of man who would stick to the rules.

He was even more shocked when Anne continued by saying, 'If they are determined to ruin the lives of my husband and my son, then I intend to tell everything I know to the newspapers.'

Fullerton stared at her. Her eyes had gone quite grey and she was gazing at him with total conviction. He asked himself why were all the most attractive women he met so damned self-confident?

'And I mean everything,' she repeated firmly.

'Surely not?' Fullerton held authority's deep suspicion of journalism. He knew that even if BBC Radio was still fairly well controlled by official influence, newspaper editors had switched to a quite different and altogether more critical line than the one they had been obliged to follow under censorship laws during the war.

'Everything.'

His tone hardened. 'Such as?'

Anne noticed the edge in his voice. This was the bit that counted. She said clearly, 'I shall tell them about his secret work for MO-1(SP), about working with the Americans in OSS on a Jedburgh operation in East France. I shall tell them he parachuted in with Axel Romm and that the whole team were captured by the Germans, and I shall say Axel Romm has unfairly blamed him for everything in a report he wrote for the Americans.'

She told him everything Edward had written, deliberately keeping to the facts, though they seemed awfully spare. It was tempting to embellish them but she did not want to dilute the impact by making mistakes. Better

The Joshua Inheritance

stick to what little she had and give the impression of a greater knowledge. 'It's quite obvious to me that George is being blamed because no-one wants to upset the Americans just when we need their support so badly in Palestine, and when we're grovelling to them for their dollars.' She looked Fullerton straight in the face and repeated, 'I think our British Press would love a story like that, don't you?'

Fullerton did not reply at once and she desperately hoped she had made her point. Then he whispered urgently, 'Anne, m'dear, it's against the Offical Secrets Act. You might go to prison!' He must stop her. He did not care about George Fairfax, but it was awful to think that Anne should suffer on his behalf. Her point about the Americans was horribly near the mark. The Foreign Office would be terrified of publicity criticising America which would further inflame the bitter disagreements over Palestine and embarrass the negotiations for a huge post-war loan from the American Congress. He was sure the government would react very strongly indeed to stop her at once. It was hard to imagine her in prison clothes, though he guessed she would still look rather beautiful.

She shrugged her slim shoulders and simply said, 'I don't care. I've nothing to lose.'

'You look a little pale,' George Fairfax bellowed, suddenly appearing at their side. He made Fullerton jump.

'George! How nice to see you,' he said with a charming smile. They shook hands and Fullerton rushed on, 'I'm really terribly sorry to hear the news, but I simply must dash.'

'What news?' George Fairfax demanded in a loud voice.

Anne smiled and put out her small hand which he shook rather gently.

'Do forgive me, won't you. Anne, it's been a real pleasure having a little chat. Simply fascinating.'

177

She was sure he squeezed just a bit harder at his last words and watched him slide off into the Easter crowd hoping what she had said was enough.

'What the devil's he talking about?' George Fairfax repeated.

'Oh, just chatting,' Anne said lightly, taking her husband's arm. She felt better. She knew Fullerton well enough to see he was badly shaken. She would have to wait and see whether he would be able to speak to the right people to stop the court martial.

'He's a rum cove and no mistake,' said George Fairfax gruffly. 'Handshake like a fillet of cod.' He wondered why John Fullerton always seemed to buttonhole his wife and was on the point of asking when she looked up at him and asked blithely, 'George, darling, who is Axel Romm?'

11

JEWS AND BRITISH

May 1946

The first three weeks of the Arabic course had slipped past very quickly for Edward. He found the work easier than the others, which particularly irritated Angus Maclean, the police inspector. They had become good friends and Edward spent an increasing amount of time with Angus in the small villa he rented in a quiet residential area of Jerusalem. In spite of appearances, Angus Maclean was an unconventional police officer. He hated army restrictions and leading a normal civilian life from his own place suited his brand of police work. For Edward, Angus's bachelor life style was a pleasant change to the Officers' Mess in the YMCA. When they got back in the evenings after classes, they changed out of their uniforms into casual shirt and trousers and passed a couple of hours together over their homework.

'That's enough for the day,' Angus said, dropping his Arabic vocabulary on the wooden boards of the verandah. He stretched and reached for his gin and tonic. Edward agreed. It had not been easy to get back into the swing of study again after the Easter break. He and Carole had spent most of the weekend together, with Angus and his girlfriend, Liz Warren, who was Colonel Haike's assistant.

They relaxed and enjoyed their drinks. Edward listened to the creak of their wicker chairs and the tinsel sound of ice in their glasses. Outside, the cicadas were noisy in the evening light, hidden somewhere in the enclosed garden beyond the verandah, perhaps under the eucalyptus or bright green acacia trees. For Edward it was the best time of the day. He said, 'This really is a wonderful little place you've got.'

Angus smiled. 'I only put up with you here because you're the best on the course and I need all the help I can get.' He was dark, with short hair and beetling eyebrows, wiry and full of controlled energy. Edward could imagine him in a kilt and knew he was a dedicated and determined policeman. 'I know damn well I'd never do enough homework for that bloody slave driver, Al Kader, if we didn't have these wet towel sessions together. What infuriates me, Edward, is how you learn it all so fast?'

Edward shrugged. He and Angus were much the best on the course and Husein Al Kader seemed pleased with his progress.

Angus put his glass down and rubbed his eyes. 'I'm sure my eyes are going with all this bookwork.'

Distantly, they heard a car in the quiet street outside. Angus checked his watch and said, 'That'll be Liz.' She came over to see him most nights when she finished work in the King David. Liz Warren had lost her husband in the war, killed in Normandy aged twenty-two, and society in 1946 cast a less critical eye over her freedoms and where she spent her nights than it did over other unmarried women. The front door banged and a girl's voice called, 'Anyone in?' Angus shouted a greeting, then a thought occurred to him. 'Look Edward, aren't you meeting Carole tonight? Why not take my car and by the time you're back we'll have supper ready?'

Edward agreed at once. Sometimes they met at the hospital but that evening he was meeting her at the Astoria to avoid being seen by her father picking her up at the house. She was on her own but Solly Mannheim

The Joshua Inheritance

would look after her till Edward arrived. Angus tossed the keys over. Edward said hallo to Liz and slipped out to Angus's small green Austin 7.

He drove slowly down to the old city. At the Astoria Carole was sitting at a table under the awning, talking to Solly. The owner's practised eye spotted Edward at once and he waved his arms expansively as though personally responsible for conjuring Edward out of thin air.

Carole jumped up and gave Edward a big hug. She was wearing a dark blue pleated dress and white shirt with casual slip-on shoes and she was in a wonderful mood. 'Solly and I were talking about his home town in Italy and he has given us some wine for supper, from the Tirol,' she said happily. 'Isn't that kind?'

Edward thanked him and could not help smiling at the expression of coy delight on Solly Mannheim's round face. 'You are good friends,' he said as he pressed two bottles of good red wine into Edward's hands and point blank refused any payment.

When they got back to the villa, Edward found a note on the kitchen table from Angus to say that he and Liz had decided to go out to a dinner-dance and would be back late.

Carole smiled quickly at the thought of the others' love affair and flicked her dark hair back over her shoulders. It was an unconscious gesture but somehow provocative, catching some of the magic character of the villa. Carole had never felt so relaxed. She loved the friendly atmosphere, with the four of them coming and going. Angus kept open house and for all of them the villa was a retreat from the worsening violence on the streets. On the garden side, the french windows always stood open, an invitation to step on to the verandah and relax in the cushions on the sofa and chairs. This was the focus of the house, shaded from the real heat of the sun during the day by a pergola of jasmine, but warm and sheltered from cool evening breezes at night.

In the seclusion of the trees round the garden, the villa was a haven where no demands were made nor duty imposed.

Edward watched her walk on to the verandah, at ease, her long legs little and supple under the blue cotton skirt. He apologised, 'I don't quite know what there is to eat in the kitchen.'

She half turned in the french window and her breasts were silhouetted through the thin cotton of her shirt against the bright green acacias in the garden. 'At least we've got Solly's wine,' she smiled.

Edward nodded and tried not to stare as a rush of excitement flooded his stomach.

Carole could feel the same excitement. 'I'll find the glasses and see what else there is in the larder.' She knew her voice was husky and kissed him lightly on the lips as she passed. She slipped out of his embrace before he could prolong the brief contact.

She found fruit, bread and fresh yoghurt which they took on to the verandah. They settled themselves on the soft cushions on the long sofa under the jasmine and began to eat, washing down the simple supper with Solly's excellent wine. When Edward pulled the cork on the second bottle, Carole leaned over him with her empty glass and instead of filling it at once they kissed, their lips wet with pears and wine. After a long moment, she let the glass slip from her hand to the wooden boards and he put down the bottle to wrap his arms round her and caress her back. She melted on to him, pressing her soft breasts on to his chest and they became utterly self-absorbed, each one lost in the taste of wine and the sweet smell of the other, hidden from the world behind her cascading dark hair in the centre of the secret garden behind the villa.

As naturally as it seemed, his hands slipped under her rumpled shirt and found her warm skin, sliding over the firm contours of her back and under the pleated elastic of her skirt to the soft mounds of her bottom. Her long fingers began to search across his muscled chest, and each inflamed the other with an electric touch which lit the smouldering kisses they had been satisfied with so far.

Carole cupped his face with her hands and instinctively lifted a little so he could pull apart the buttons of her shirt. Without rushing, he opened his own shirt and she began to breathe faster as his fingers skipped under her heavy breasts, her nipples stiffening as they dipped to touch his chest.

Long moments later, intoxicated by their caresses, they moved more boldly, pulling at the restricting clothes which separated them until they lay perfectly naked together, Carole still stretched out on top of Edward, voluptuously moulded to his hard body. The last rays of the sun wrapped them with intimate dappled shadows on the soft cushions of the sofa.

'I love you,' he whispered. She replied huskily, 'Don't speak', kissing him with her lips apart. Their movements quickened. She sat up astride him, leaning back, swinging her head from side to side. Her skin tingled with the feel of her long black hair swaying round her shoulders and her breasts ached as his hands reached up to cup them and fondle her swollen nipples. His fingers swept across her soft belly to the damp heat between her thighs, and her excitement threatened to overcome him too when her first trembling shook her like a storm. He sat up and wrapped his arms round her slender waist, holding her in the shuddering climax of her ecstasy, thrilled by the gentle expression on her face and the feel of her stretched apart on top of him. She opened her eyes and slowly lifted herself to kiss him, crushing his lips, twisting as she did so to move round under him on the cushions where she began to move and cry out again as he lost himself in her embrace and finally melted in her warmth, exhausted.

Much later, after Edward had reluctantly taken Carole home, to avoid her father's suspicion, and they had parted in the street outside her house, uncaring of the world around them, he came back to the little villa. He stood on the verandah sipping the last glass of red wine and hardly daring to believe what had happened. He had never experienced such intense feelings as with Carole and she had returned them in full measure.

He had had a few other women, but the groping explorations with girls at dances, a chase to somewhere quiet, covert bursts of physical release and the satisfaction, a long word for something very soon over, had been very one-sided. The girls, in one case a prostitute in Shepherd's Market, had been quite unmoved. He thought of Diana, who loved the game of dancing and kissing, and wondered why she was so frustratingly cool when he pressed her for more. He guessed she was inhibited, not by her feelings, as she had often said she loved him in her letters, but by her English upbringing. He shrugged. She was a long way away and easy to forget while he could still sense Carole's presence in the villa, hear her laughter and smell her. He half expected to see her appear on the verandah any moment.

He had always loved women – the chase, the dinners and conversation – but until he met Carole and discovered that two people could match each other's desires so instinctively, he had considered that the male world made a quite unwarranted fuss about love-making. There seemed to be nothing more over-rated than an unsatisfactory coupling and nothing more under-rated than a good crap.

He heard the front door and, after a moment, Angus came into the room behind him. He was on his own.

'Where's Liz?' Edward asked.

'I took her home after dinner,' he said and the dull

The Joshua Inheritance

tenor of his voice made Edward frown. 'We were having a lovely time at the restaurant when someone I knew came over and ruined the bloody evening. He said some bloody lunatics have attacked the guard supervising the liberty trucks in Tel Aviv.'

Edward felt suddenly empty and cheated, with a premonition of Angus's next words. This was not the time for bad news to infiltrate his secret world in the villa.

'Bastards fired machine-guns at three tents from houses overlooking the car park and then ran into the tents to finish the job. Poor buggers never had a chance. They killed seven, most of them sitting on their beds. All Paras I'm afraid.'

Edward sat down heavily. It was extraordinary how the deepening intensity of his affair with Carole was matched in equal measure by increasing violence between the Jews and the British. Emotions in the Holy Land seemed distilled by the dry sunshine to the very essence, intoxicating everyone with dangerous extremes of love and death. The murders in Tel Aviv seemed an omen of disaster and he prayed Carole and he could survive the storm which seemed inevitable.

Over the weeks of the course Angus Maclean had come to respect highly Al Kader, their cultured Arabic instructor, and, as a policeman, he wanted to ask his view of the Arab position in the country. Violence had worsened, led by the minority Irgun and Stern groups, but all Jews were agreed that the main issue was immigration. Angus was puzzled to know why the Arabs were sitting on the sidelines, even though Jewish immigration continued to whittle down their majority, from ninety per cent in 1922 to sixty per cent in 1946; and the boats kept bringing more Jews from the refugee camps in Europe.

Al Kader was drinking a small cup of the thick black

Turkish coffee he adored, holding the tiny cup pincered between finger and thumb carefully keeping it away from his pale linen suit.

Angus was in uniform. He stuck his hands in his pockets and started the conversation obliquely, following Arab custom of a preamble to the main question. He said, 'Exams coming up soon, eh? I suppose Edward Fairfax will take first place?'

Al Kader nodded, a slight smile wrinkling the corners of his eyes, 'He's done well, even though he's been burning the candle at both ends.'

Angus returned the smile. 'You mean his nurse? Aye, he seems well hooked there.' In recent weeks, Edward and Carole had been virtually living together in his villa, and the four of them, with Liz Warren, had become close friends. Work and play dovetailed perfectly and life had only been marred by Edward's worry that nothing had yet been decided about his father's court martial. The first hearing was held in secret after Easter but no decision had been made.

'He's a talented young chap and she's certainly a fine-looking lass, but who knows what will happen in the future?' Angus added, hoping to turn the conversation and hear what Al Kader thought would happen in Palestine.

Al Kader said, 'I am pleased. Such things should happen on my course.'

Angus frowned, wondering if the lecturer was suffering from the heat. Al Kader smiled at him, thinking how little the British understood of the Arabs and the Middle East, no matter how much time they spent in Occupation. He said, 'This school may be a calm pond outside the turbulent river of life, but we are learning Arabic here, a language of emotions and love, a language framed by such famous poets as Ibn al-'arabi and Ghazali.' He cocked his head on one side and needled gently with, 'For example, Inspector, I

The Joshua Inheritance

imagine you've heard of Cheikh Nefzaoui's *The Perfumed Garden*? The book of love, or has that been banned in Scotland?'

'Not banned, but I fancy you won't find it in every household. Just now, after the war, Scottish passion is more tuned to pounds, shillings and pence.'

'As always, no?' Al Kader smiled, pleased to be able to show off his knowledge of British characteristics. 'The Arabs too are passionate about money, but their search for profit is ruled by their hearts, through the passion of their language and religion, not from the economics which drive your British Empire.'

'This sounds like the rhetoric of Arab politicians,' said Angus, grinning. He saw a chance to switch the conversation. 'But is rhetoric enough?'

Al Kader shook his head sadly. 'I think not, Inspector Maclean. Arabs prefer to follow charismatic generals, like Salah-ad-Din of old. Nowadays, our politicians do nothing. They hope the British will not let us down. Meanwhile the Jews manipulate both world opinion and the Americans, which comes to the same thing.' He picked up one of the foreign newspapers on the common-room table. 'Look, the *New York Post*, 20 May. A diatribe against your police force written by an American Jew, Ruth Gruber.' He found the piece he was looking for and read out loud, '"The Palestine Police are Nazis. They walk round the streets of Jerusalem and Tel Aviv singing the Nazi Party's Horst Wessel song and giving the Heil Hitler salute."' He stopped reading and dropped it back on the table. 'This is what the Americans believe.'

Angus agreed. 'Journalistic tripe! But what are the Arabs doing about it?'

Al Kader answered with a question: 'Will the British let us down? Will your Foreign Minister, Mr Bevin, really refuse to allow in these one hundred thousand Jews from camps in Europe?'

Angus looked at Al Kader in surprise. 'He's said so enough times, hasn't he?'

Al Kader shook his finger. 'I know. But the British are trying to persuade the American Congress to give them a massive loan. To rebuild your country after the war. Letting in these Jews would please the Americans.'

'You don't seriously think Bevin would compromise his views?'

Al Kader sighed. 'The principles of politicians are like grass in the wind. You realise Jewish violence will get worse if Bevin refuses?'

'We've dealt with uprisings before,' Angus said firmly.

'Oh yes, you crushed the Arabs most effectively nine years ago.'

Angus looked embarrassed.

'But I don't think you can do it again. Empires, Inspector, must be supple to survive and there is too much inflexibility in Palestine.'

Husein Al Kader's eyes glazed, as if he were looking into the future, and he spoke with unnerving clarity. 'The age of empires and colonialism is over. You cannot crush the whole Jewish population as you crushed the Arabs in 1936, because you don't want to copy Hitler, as Ruth Gruber suggests.' He gestured at the *New York Post*. 'Opinions matter now, and the world will stop you. You will be defeated and the Jews will have their way.'

Angus frowned. The idea that small groups of terrorists could defeat the British Empire was hard to swallow but he wanted to know how the Arabs would react and he persisted. 'And what will the Arabs do then?'

Husein Al Kader said with calm conviction, 'There will be no peace in Palestine.'

'And you are a Palestinian?'

Al Kader nodded.

Paul Levi booked a table for lunch in the Regency

The Joshua Inheritance

restaurant in the King David building, directly under the British Army Headquarters. He knew he was pressing his luck but, after weeks observing the hotel, he felt almost certain that there were no hidden dangers. The British were amazingly complacent. There were Military Police guards on the main headquarters entrance at the back of the hotel, facing the old city, but elsewhere there was nothing more than an infrequent Land-Rover patrol on the streets.

Paul walked in shortly after midday, deliberately early. Only a few tables in the Regency were occupied, by a mixture of officers and businessmen, with a few women. A handful of waiters hustled in and out of the kitchens with trays full of dishes. Paul sat down at a table behind one of the large pillars which supported the ceiling and ordered a plate of sesame bread with spicy za'atar sauce while he waited for the Jewish policeman who had agreed to meet him there. He appeared a few minutes later. He was off duty, wearing a badly fitting lightweight suit, and was clearly uncomfortable in the fashionable restaurant. In spite of the fans turning lazily at the ceiling he was sweating.

Without preamble, Paul leaned forward, his elbows on the table and asked in a low voice, 'Where is the Ford registered? You've had long enough.'

The policeman leaned forward too, looked at Paul with sad eyes and said mournfully, 'I've been damned busy trying to stay alive. They've shot up police stations everywhere, at Yibna, Isdud, Ramat Gan, Sukhreir, Sarona for the second time, and Tel Aviv. Me, I'm Jewish, but how can they tell the difference between a Jewish policeman and an Arab policeman? I tell you, it doesn't pay to be a policeman these days.'

Paul took a deep breath and wondered if Yudelmann had been right to put him in touch with this man. He called over the waiter, an Arab neatly dressed in white jacket and black trousers, and they ordered borscht soup and lamb. Leaving the policeman to eat the sesame bread, Paul went to the Gentlemen's. He had another job to do. On the way, he made a careful mental note of the layout of the restaurant, the doors to the kitchen areas at the back, a corridor leading under the hotel to a room beneath the lobby and the exact location of the structural pillars which supported all six floors above. As he stood against the wall in the lavatory, he was amused to think of the British working in their offices over his head, unaware of the plans being made by one insignificant Jew relieving himself in the basement beneath them.

'You were away a long time,' complained the Jewish policeman when Paul returned to the table. The policeman had started eating and lowered his head again to his soup, spooning up the purple beet with relish. Paul watched in disgust. He reflected that everyone has something to trigger co-operation. With the policeman, it was food. He had become quite cheerful.

'This car of yours is not an ordinary car. It doesn't belong on the usual records.'

'What d'you mean?'

The policeman wiped his mouth, leaving bright red stains on the white napkin. 'The car is registered to the American Consulate, in Mamillah Road.'

'But it's not a diplomatic plate.'

'You're telling me? I know it's not a diplomatic plate, but it's a diplomatic car.'

Paul sat back. What was the officer doing in such a car? This was very frustrating. He would have to watch the American Consulate to find out who was driving the car, and follow them to find out where they lived. That meant breaking off from his work on the hotel, just when he was nearly finished.

'Very good soup, that,' said the policeman, eyeing Paul's bowl. 'You're not hungry?' The young man buying him lunch seemed unnecessarily thin and sallow for his own good.

The Joshua Inheritance

Paul focused on the corpulent policeman. 'This car. I wanted to know who drives it and where they live.'

'Why didn't you ask? As I say, it's registered to the Americans. I can't say who drives it, but our constables have often noted it in Hezron Street, in the Jewish quarter. We like to keep a note of special cars, especially this type.'

Paul leaned back and smiled bleakly. That was what he wanted. The information would save a lot of trouble. The waiter removed their soup and brought the lamb and beer. The policeman tucked in, rattling on about his problems. He took no notice of Paul who surreptitiously measured the dimensions of the pillar beside him, using his feet undercover of the tablecloth. More than three foot square. He whistled softly, thinking of the quantity of explosives he would need. The policeman looked up. Before he could speak, Paul asked blandly, 'D'you know who I am?'

The policeman pulled a face, his eyebrows went up, the corners of his mouth arched down. 'I don't want to know.' He wiped sauce off his plate with a piece of bread.

Genuinely puzzled, Paul asked, 'How can you resolve being a policeman and at the same time meet people like me?' Paul knew he could never serve two masters himself.

The policeman chewed for a moment, sipped his beer and replied, 'You're an idealist. You want to change power. Policemen are realists. They support who's in power.' He shrugged again. 'Or sometimes they support who will be in power. Anyway, like you, I'm Jewish.'

That afternoon, Paul dressed in his dirty-brown Arab jellaba and shemag head-dress and went on foot to find the house in Hezron Street. At once, he could see it would not be easy to watch. He wandered round the streets and alleys till he knew the layout of the area, and then chose a place where he could sit on the pavement as a beggar, pulling his Arab shemag around his head to conceal his face as much as possible. He was thin, his skin pale and sick looking, stubbled with beard, but he still felt self-consciously fit for a beggar.

After three hours, he had collected $9^3/_4$d. and his crossed legs were horribly stiff. He was beginning to think there must be other ways to observe the house when he noticed a girl coming up the street towards him. He recognised her at once as the girl with the Para officer at the station. Even in her nurse's uniform and flat hospital shoes, she was strikingly pretty. He guessed she was coming off duty and going home. She was obviously absorbed in thought and she nearly passed him before stopping to drop a penny in his outstretched palm. He felt uncomfortable begging from a beautiful girl he would in other circumstances have wanted to chat to, but it would have been odd to have refused her coin. Jealous of the young English officer, he watched her all the way down the dusty cobbled street and through the wicket gate into her father's house.

Two hours later, at about seven o'clock, Paul had the satisfaction of seeing the blue Ford saloon burble slowly past him, its white-wall tyres smacking wetly on the cobbles, and drive in the double doors of the house. Sitting on the ground, he had no view inside, but he guessed the girl's father was being driven home after work at the Consulate. Confirmation of what the policeman said was heartening, but he wanted to find the Para officer. He wanted to follow the girl from the house. He decided he must go on waiting.

Nothing happened. The street quietened with early evening and Paul was about to give up when the wicket gate opened again and the girl emerged. This time she was dressed up to go out, in a tight jacket and skirt and heeled shoes. Paul caught his breath watching her and forced himself not to stare. The odd thought struck him that all beggars must ogle pretty girls. At least he had the chance of meeting them on equal terms but the jealousy returned as he thought of her going to see the Para officer.

She stopped in front of him, searched for another coin from her handbag and dropped it into his hand. Close to, he was struck by her flawless straight legs but he dared not look her in the eye. As before, he watched her all the way to the top of the street. He was about to move after her, when a hoarse voice spoke up behind him. 'Sit quite still or I will kill you!'

Paul froze. The venomous clarity of the voice left no room for doubt. A great wave of failure washed over him, like a physical blow, reminding him of the moment during the war when he had been seized. He cursed his stupidity. He had been so obsessed with watching the girl, waiting to follow her, so fascinated by her long legs and figure, that he had not heard the man slip up behind him. His British instructor would not have been impressed.

He turned round. A huge, broad-shouldered man in his forties in a brown suit with an open-necked shirt was watching him steadily. He was holding a massive pistol half-hidden inside his jacket. Paul easily recognised the Colt .45 automatic. Not a calibre to argue with.

'Get up and walk slowly towards me,' the man instructed coldly. Paul struggled to his feet, groaning, *'Effendi, plis! Plis!'* and shaking out the folds of his dirty jellaba. His legs were stiff from hours of sitting, just like any other disabled beggar.

The man's eyes never blinked. He gestured towards the wicket gate in the archway of the house. 'Walk!'

Paul shuffled over the cobbles cursing his over-confidence. He should never have stayed so long in the street. He supposed the Americans would check him out and hand him over to the police. At least he was clean. He had no identification on him at all. He would stick to speaking bad English and hang on to his story of being a beggar.

He stepped inside the heavy wooden doors of the house, his mind rapidly working over his options, excuses and escape. He knew the best time to make his break was as soon as possible but the big man shut the solid wooden door swiftly. Paul let his eyes adjust to the cool shadows in the hall.

A voice called from the end of the hall, 'Yaacov! Put him in the dining-room.'

Paul's attention was distracted by the voice. At once Yaacov tripped him and shoved him flat on the marble floor, crushing the breath from his body with his weight and pressing the cold muzzle of the Colt to the nape of his neck. The body search was thorough and indelicate. Then Yaacov stepped swiftly back out of reach and let Paul stagger to his feet, furious at being caught out again.

In the big dining-room, the table had been pushed to one wall and the middle of the room was clear except for one high-backed wooden chair. Yaacov gestured Paul to sit down. Paul hung his head and watched Yaacov's feet from under the edge of his shemag. Neither spoke.

After a moment Yaacov's employer came in, dressed in a grey suit and heavy black shoes. He observed the scruffy cringing young Arab beggar with distaste, taking care to stand out of Yaacov's field of fire. He said, 'No-one begs in this street. It used to be a place where lepers lived and the reputation has lasted. So we spotted you at once. Catching you was easy. There aren't many men who can help staring at my daughter. So, if you aren't a beggar, who are you?'

Paul refused to look up, ashamed to show his face under his shemag. Crossly the man stepped quickly forward and whipped off the head-dress. He flung it in a corner and turned back to inspect his prisoner.

The Joshua Inheritance

His eyes widened. 'Paul Levi! Goddam it. I thought you were dead!'

After a long moment, Paul whispered, 'You survived too!'

As one, the thought occurred to them both that the only other person they knew who had survived was Major George Fairfax.

'What happened?' Paul asked.

Axel Romm nodded at Yaacov. 'You can go, Yaacov. I know this sonofabitch.' He waved and Yaacov silently left them alone, without a flicker of interest to know how his employer knew such filthy peasants in Jerusalem.

Axel Romm went to the sideboard at one end of the dining-room, and poured two large whiskies with precise movements of his small hands. He handed one to Paul. 'Shit, Paul, how in hell's name did you manage to get away from those Nazi bastards? They had the goddam plane surrounded.' He drank and pulled up a chair to listen.

Paul told him: the Gestapo, the painful, pointless interrogation which meant nothing because the whole team had been wiped out, the transport to Natzweiler, then a ghastly train to Orianenburg, the death march west at the end of April and the refugee camp at Poppendorf.

'Christ, man, that was only a year ago! Seems like a different age.'

Paul nodded. The cold weather of Europe and Germany was remote now. He relaxed on his chair, feeling more comfortable even in the dirty brown jellaba, took a long pull on his whisky and asked, 'And you?'

Axel Romm looked serious. 'You know the old adage, "Escape early"? Like you I was pinned down at the landing strip when they attacked. I was stuffed in a truck but I managed to get free.' He grinned, running a hand through his grey hair. 'Let me just say I persuaded the guard to hand over his Schmeisser and jumped. Then it was escape and evasion all the way till I met up with the US Third Army near Saarburg. It helped knowing the region.'

Paul nodded. Trust the American to have all the luck. 'Did you get back to England?'

Axel Romm laughed, an acid sound without humour. 'You gotta be joking! Those Limey arseholes got us into that mess and I had no intention of reporting back. No, I found our guys in the OSS and gave them my report. Needless to say, I didn't pull my punches.' The anger at being surprised in the house still hurt him.

Paul nodded again. Then he asked the question which had been needling him ever since. 'Who betrayed us?' The memories were fresh and bitter.

Axel Romm replied in clipped measured tones, 'George Fairfax was the only man not on the landing zone who knew the location and time. The Gestapo and the SD boys from Department Four were waiting for the whole team with goddam searchlights and mortar paraillum. Fairfax was captured before, in October, due to his own failure to follow the correct procedures to check he wasn't being followed, so who else could it be?'

Paul gulped his whisky and stared at the flat marble floor. That was what the SD officer had told him when he had been interrogated. Hearing Axel Romm's story, it made sense. He muttered, 'Fairfax. What a bastard!' The suspicion he had nurtured ever since that interrogation hardened into hatred for the Englishman who had betrayed them and been the cause of so many deaths. If only he could find him again, to avenge the others. A great conviction settled on him that he was right to fight the British in Palestine. He no longer cared how many he killed.

He looked up and focused again. Romm was standing by him with the whisky decanter and refilled his glass. Feeling a bit light-headed, Paul asked, 'You working here in Mamillah Road?'

The Joshua Inheritance

Romm smiled. 'I should ask you first why the hell you're watching my house?'

A thin smile split Paul's tired face. 'Just checking on your daughter.'

Axel Romm frowned. 'Carole?'

'I want to know the name of the man she's dating,' he said.

'Dating?'

'Yeah. She's seeing a British Para officer. Blond-headed fellow.'

'Goddam it! Fairfax!' Axel Romm roared with anger.

Paul stared in amazement.

Romm nodded furiously. 'Yes, yes. He's the goddam son of the man who betrayed us in France.' He had been so busy working he had hardly noticed she was out so much and it suddenly fell into place. Paul never knew it, but the revelation was doubly painful. He stood up and paced round the dining-room. 'I told Carole not to see him, but she's too much like her mother. Wilful. She doesn't tell me she's seeing him, but she works and I can't stop her.'

'I can,' said Paul with deliberate calm. 'I shall kill him.' He explained about the dead boy in the Tel Aviv riot, Mattea Spurstein's little boy.

'They're a pair of bastards, eh?' Axel Romm said thoughtfully. 'Father and son.' It was a piece of good fortune meeting Paul Levi again. They knew each other well from their training together in England, and that was an important start between secret contacts in the violence which was tearing Palestine apart. However, Paul had changed, toughened by his experiences, and he was plainly involved in some way with the Jewish underground. He might be useful. Very useful. Romm felt that even if he did not wholly trust him, they could work together. He stopped pacing, sipped his whisky as he contemplated the younger man and asked, 'He doesn't know you're here?'

Paul shook his head.

'Then we can help each other. My job in the Consulate is to maintain a brief on Jewish underground movements here. You can give me information.' Paul was about to protest but Axel Romm held up his hand. 'You don't have to deny or explain anything. I understand your motives. I'd do exactly the same in your place. I'm a Jew too, remember, only I have a country already. The United States.'

Paul nodded and Romm went on, 'Let's just arrange meets from time to time. I know you guys are always looking for outlets to the big wide world, for reliable readouts on the Big Power positions or to give statements to the bastards in the Press. I can help you with all that. In turn, I'll tell you more about young Edward Fairfax.'

Paul agreed at once.

When he left the house in Hezron Street, he had a peculiarly jaunty step for a beggar. He had recovered from the blackest depression at being captured, with visions of being locked up in Acre jail. In a day, two problems had been solved. His recce of the Regency restaurant had finalised his plans for the attack on the King David Hotel, and he knew exactly who had killed Mattea Spurstein's boy. Better still, the young officer was the son of the man he most hated. He walked briskly back to the small flat over the garage on the edge of the Arab quarter where Selig and he were staying, and set his mind to preparing the explosives. All he needed was the order to go ahead.

12

KIDNAP AT THE ASTORIA

June 1946

Paul Levi did not see Edward Fairfax cross from the YMCA building into the King David Hotel the following afternoon. He was busy arranging the details for something else, an important side-issue which had delayed the main attack on the hotel.

Edward used the public hotel entrance, pushing through the glass doors. He ran lightly up the broad stairs and down the passage on the right. He was in good humour. His Arabic course had ended that day with the final exams and he had done well. Al Kader had congratulated him and he was looking forward to the end-of-course party with Carole that evening. The only black cloud was that this was his last night in Jerusalem.

On the fourth floor, he knocked on the outside door of the Intelligence offices, put his head in and grinned at Liz Warren who was on duty in charge of Colonel Haike's pool of girls in the secretarial office. Edward said, 'Can I come in?' She smiled back and said, 'Go on through, Edward. But he's not in a very good mood. Something to do with your course, but I told him about it ages ago.'

Edward assumed he was going to be congratulated for doing well. He checked the sleeves of his shirt were rolled up neatly and smartly adjusted the belt of his shorts as he thanked her and walked past into Colonel Haike's office.

'Fairfax!' Colonel Haike shouted bluffly as Edward came in and saluted smartly. 'What the devil have you been doing in Jerusalem? Why didn't you tell me you were here, eh?' He was sitting behind his desk and glaring in a sharp unfriendly manner.

The question took Edward by surprise. He replied politely, 'The British School Arabic course, sir. I thought you knew?'

Colonel Haike scratched his moustache and grunted, 'That's what I'm told, but I've been damned busy. Too much to do with these bloody Jew-boys causing so much trouble.'

Edward was not surprised to hear Colonel Haike's blatant dislike of the Jewish underground. The British seemed constantly doomed to react to attacks as there seemed so little real intelligence to act on in good time. He guessed Colonel Haike was constantly being pressed to provide better information.

Colonel Haike stared bleakly at Edward, irritated that he had missed the chance of cancelling Edward's place on the Arabic course, to stop him being in Jerusalem. As a matter of routine, he had interviewed Husein al Kader the day before about the Palestinian Arab reaction to the violence of the Jewish underground and heard quite by chance that Al Kader's star pupil on the current Arabic course was Edward Fairfax. Colonel Haike wished he had not shown his annoyance. Al Kader had immediately slipped behind a typical Arab mask of polite misunderstanding and he claimed not to have any idea what Edward had been doing with his spare time. Colonel Haike said with feeling, 'Damned silly language to learn when we're all fighting the Jews.'

'Yes sir,' said Edward, 'but the Batallion IO recommended it.' He waited silently to see what happened next.

The Joshua Inheritance

Rather aggressively, Colonel Haike appeared to switch subjects and demanded, 'Kept yourself busy in Jerusalem?' He peered at Edward standing in front of his desk.

'There was a lot of homework to do,' said Edward, not sure where the question might lead. 'Vocabulary and grammar. Never-ending, actually.'

Colonel Haike, not in the slightest interested in grammar or vocabulary, went straight to the point uppermost in his mind. 'Heard anything more of that fellow Axel Romm?'

Edward hesitated, but reminded himself he was leaving Jerusalem the next day. He plunged in and said, 'I've seen his daughter a couple of times. I gather he wrote a report about my father's operation. Is there any chance you can get hold of it?'

Colonel Haike looked surprised. He stood up and walked over to the window. This was the last thing he wanted to hear. Edward Fairfax was meddling. Fullerton had told him by signal that his mother, Anne Fairfax, had threatened to go to the Press. This would be disastrous and Fullerton was right to delay the court martial for the time being. Now Colonel Haike believed her information was supplied by Edward. He had to put a stop to it at once. Standing with his back to the window, hands behind his back, he lifted his head slightly to give himself greater authority and declared bluntly, 'Romm's out of bounds, Edward. As far as we're concerned, he is a dangerous man.'

Edward frowned, genuinely puzzled. 'Is he something to do with the Jewish underground?'

Colonel Haike snorted out a dry laugh. 'Of course not! You know perfectly well that he works for the American Consulate. He has diplomatic status. He's got nothing to do with the bloody terrorists.' The naïvety of Edward's question amused him and he added, 'All the same you never know with the Americans. They're very much at odds with us on this Jewish question. It's no secret they want us to let in thousands of refugees. They don't like the British Empire, and I believe they'd do anything to upset our influence in the Middle East.'

'Why?'

Colonel Haike snorted again. 'So they can take over, of course. Spheres of influence, dear boy. I don't know if they'd actually go so far as to work with terrorists but I wouldn't put it past a toad like Axel Romm. However, the point is, Fairfax, you must stop seeing him. That's an order. Understand?'

Edward nodded. He guessed there must be some confidential reason to do with the Intelligence battle against the Jewish underground. In any case, Romm hated the British and there was nothing more he could find out from him about his father. Which left the report. He asked, 'Is there any possibility of finding that report?'

Colonel Haike replied with complete sincerity, 'Not a damn chance!' He had been appalled to hear from Fullerton that all the files on the people in George Fairfax's operation had disappeared. There was nothing on Romm.

Edward thought perhaps Colonel Haike was not permitted to see the file and diplomatically asked, 'Is it a question of access?'

'Not really,' said Colonel Haike and looked agitated. 'There's nothing to find. The files have been destroyed.' No-one seemed to know why, or even how. Fullerton was still finding out what had happened. Or so he claimed.

The answer was a blow Edward had not expected. It seemed hard to believe that secret documents could simply have disappeared, but Colonel Haike was plainly unwilling or unable to pursue the matter. Edward dropped the subject and squashed his frustration and anger. Every time he began to find out about his father's work during the war his inquiries were lost in a miasma of obstacles, ill-defined and impossible to grapple. In spite

The Joshua Inheritance

of Romm's accusations, he was still sure his father was innocent. He seemed to be a victim of the system, but the system was too massive to penetrate.

Colonel Haike fixed Edward with a hard look on his narrow face and said, 'As I say, this chap Romm is dodgy. He's up to no good here in Jerusalem, I don't trust him and I don't want you to see him again. Is that clear?'

'Yes, sir,' Edward agreed. He suspected he had not been told the whole truth, and began to wonder if Colonel Haike was being as helpful about his father's case as he had thought.

Colonel Haike gave him no chance to relax. He stepped briskly round the room, sat down at his desk, smoothed his dark hair with both hands and announced, 'Good. That's that. Now, Edward, my dear boy, thought you'd like to know Diana is coming out.'

'What?' Edward stared at him in amazement.

'Yes, the dear thing has been badgering me for months. I know how you're both very fond of each other,' he gave another of his sharp, embarrassed laughs.

Edward tried to muster his thoughts. He had simply never thought of Diana in Palestine. When they said goodbye, it never occurred to him that she would come out too. Or that she would even want to. She seemed so much a London person. Trying to control his surprise, he asked weakly, 'When?'

'Quite soon. I've managed to get her on one of the Dakota flights out.'

Edward thought, not even the time of a sea trip to sort things out with Carole.

'I knew you'd be pleased,' said Colonel Haike, rubbing his hands. It had been very difficult fixing a ticket for his daughter and he took the shock on Edward's face for a sign of how impressed he was by such powers of influence. Air flights to Palestine were hard to obtain.

Even quite senior officers had to travel by boat, which took a week to sail out at the best of times and usually dumped their passengers in Egypt, so that the last leg had to be completed in a hot dusty railway carriage along the northern edge of the Sinai desert.

Edward was speechless. He could foresee the inevitable confrontation, as hard as reconciling England's cool green land with Palestine's violence and heat. Diana was beautiful but she was so English and remote. He asked, 'When, er, does she arrive?'

'Not sure, dear boy. I'll let you know.'

Edward left the King David Hotel, his mind buzzing with the problem of how to see Carole when Diana would be expecting to see him too. Colonel Haike had been damned unhelpful that afternoon.

He changed in his room in the YMCA into his smart service dress with Sam Browne belt and went directly to the Astoria to meet Carole. They planned to have a quiet drink together before the end-of-course party in the Institute. He walked quickly through the streets of the Old City and was so absorbed in his thoughts that he almost fell over a beggar sitting on the pavement as he turned into the restaurant. The Arab beggar idly struggled to his feet and wandered out of sight along the pavement begging alms.

Carole was already there, sitting at their usual table in the corner and wearing a beautiful red dress bare at the shoulders. Edward immediately forgot all about Diana and kissed her full on the lips. He brushed his hands over her shoulders and grinned, 'Do we have to go to the party?'

She smiled and gently pushed him away. 'Angus would drag us out to the party if we went to the villa now. Besides, you're the top of the form and they'd miss us if we didn't turn up.'

Edward pulled a face and took her hand. 'What about here? In one of the rooms upstairs?'

The Joshua Inheritance

Carole hesitated as the idea sank in, a wicked smile lighting her eyes. As if on cue, Solly Mannheim appeared. He waved his fat hand to Edward in greeting and rolled out between the tables towards them, making sure his other guests were happy on the way. Frothing goodwill, he said, 'Miss Carole tells me your course is finished and you 'ave to go away. This is very sad.' His round face looked so sorrowful, Edward could not help smiling. 'So, I said to myself, Solly, you will give them some of your best wine tonight.'

'Some more of that excellent red wine you gave us before?' Edward asked, taking Carole's hand and beginning to laugh. 'That would be wonderful!' Carole blushed furiously.

Solly Mannheim smiled at the compliment to his wine without understanding the meaning of their joke. 'No. Tonight I give you *'il re del vino'*, the king of wines. I want to give you champagne!' He half-turned and clapped his fat hands. At once a waiter in a white jacket and bow tie appeared from inside the stone restaurant with a bottle of champagne in an ice bucket on a tray with three glasses.

'*Ecco!* A bottle of Veuve Clicquot champagne, the vintage of 1928, a wonderful year. A superb wine!' Solly declared, his lips moistening with expectation. With theatrical panache, he whipped the slender glasses off the tray and placed them on the table. Then he lifted the bottle with exaggerated care from the bucket and lovingly clothed it in a dazzlingly white napkin. He delicately removed the gold foil and wire, teased the cork from the neck with his chubby fingers till it popped and with practised movements poured swiftly into the glasses.

The ritual of pouring and the veneration with which he lifted his glass to his lips, like consecrated Communion wine, gave the occasion almost religious significance. Carole's eyes glittered with anticipation. She squeezed

Edward's hand and lifted her glass, first to Solly, thanking him, and then to Edward.

They touched glasses. '*Salute!*' Solly whispered in his deep voice. His lips hardly touched the tall-stemmed glass as he sipped and murmured ecstatically, '*Eccellente!*'

'*Salute*,' echoed Edward touching his glass to Carole's. 'To us. To the future,' and they drank with their eyes locked over the top of their glasses.

'For ever,' she said, never taking her eyes off his.

A bustle beyond the awning on the pavement spoiled the moment. Edward saw Carole's eyes widen, the smile at the corner of her lips faded and he twisted round on his chair. Two scruffy Arabs in jellabas were running towards them. Solly Mannheim waved his podgy arms and shouted, 'Go away! No beggars in my restaurant!'

'Be quiet, fat one!' the older of the two beggars hissed and Solly Mannheim stepped back in horror as he caught sight of a revolver in the man's hand. Edward could not see the revolver. He thought the Italian had been struck and leapt to his defence, but the Arab charged on, moved deftly to one side and pulled over the table in Edward's path. Edward stumbled across the falling table in a shower of glass, champagne and ice from the bucket. Carole screamed in alarm. Edward rolled out of the mess on the flagstones, trying to recover and protect her, but the second Arab lunged at him from the other side with a piece of piping, and swiped him across the side of the head. For a brief moment, Edward's mind filled with a haze of screaming and noise. The Arab hit him again and he passed out.

The other guests were screaming and backing off in terror, terrified of the Arab with the gun. Carole glanced at the street. There had to be soldiers nearby. She began to shout for help. Instead, four more filthily dressed Arabs barged in, armed with pistols. One knocked her across a table with a vicious backhand blow and she lost consciousness. Solly Mannheim tried to push his bulk in the way, waving his fat arms to stop them hitting her again. The Arabs left her and he bent down to help her, ignoring the danger from her attacker.

The Arab leader was kneeling over Edward, holding a wad of chloroform firmly over his face. Another dropped a rough linen sheet on the ground between the tables. In moments Edward was rolled up like a sack of dirty washing and flung over the shoulders of the biggest Arab, who set off at a run. The rest backed out of the Astoria waving their pistols at the shocked diners.

On the street again, out of sight of the Astoria, the Arabs hid their weapons under their jellabas and walked. Only a few people were about but no-one paid them any attention. They were just another group of merchants hurrying along with a linen bundle. In less than a minute they reached a battered flat-bed Dodge truck parked in a bend in a narrow street close to the restaurant. The truck was empty.

'Start her up, Selig,' Paul Levi snapped. He walked round to the side of the truck by the stone wall, pulled the hood of his jellaba back and bent to undo the tool box under the chassis. The lid flopped down and he reached inside to remove the bag of spanners. The other 'Arabs' lifted Edward in the linen bundle and shoved him feet first into the tool box, pushing him through into the concealed compartment behind the tools underneath the wooden boards of the flat bed. Paul stuffed the tools back and slammed the box shut. He leaped into the cab shouting, 'Let's go!' Selig let out the clutch and the truck leapt forward. The others disappeared into the streets behind, mingling among the crowds.

Paul grinned across the cab at Selig. Everything had gone well. No-one had seen them put the officer into the truck. Two minutes later, the Dodge truck trundled out of the Jaffa Gate and took the winding road down the Soreq valley towards Tel Aviv.

* * *

Edward awoke in total darkness with a splitting headache, breathing musty, damp air from a sack tied over his head and his nostrils filled with the sharp smell of chloroform. He was lying on the ground. His fingers felt hard, dry earth and he guessed he was indoors somewhere. His whole body hurt and the right side of his face felt stuck with glue. He tried to concentrate and take stock. Slowly he remembered what had happened. The sound of Carole's screams echoed round his head, mocking his pathetic efforts to save her from attack and he forgot his own discomfort in the horror of her being beaten up.

He rolled over on his back to relieve his bruised muscles and a blazing pain in the side of his head lit the darkness behind his eyes, like the cascading ice from the champagne bucket. Through the pain, he realised he was tied, not with rope, but manacled, like a slave, with chains linking his hands and feet. His head ached terribly and he guessed that the sticky feeling on his cheek was where his blood had congealed on the cloth. The chains rattled as he wriggled about on the floor trying to lift the hood from his face and he sucked in deep breaths of fresher air from under the edge of the hood, making low moaning noises.

'You're still alive,' said a voice unsympathetically.

Edward froze. He had not thought his feeble struggles were being observed. He felt at once vulnerable and foolishly embarrassed lying helpless on the floor, sightless and chained. After a moment's silence, he said, 'Who are you?'

'You needn't worry about that, Second Lieutenant Fairfax,' said Paul. 'Just know that you have been kidnapped by the Irgun Zvai Leumi.'

'How d'you know my name?'

'Don't be thick. It's on your identity card.'

Paul had changed from his Arab clothes back into kibbutz work clothes and wiped his hands on his blue work trousers. It was warm in the cell. He pushed his shirt sleeves up and sat down back-to-front on the single chair in the tiny room, leaning over the chair back. The dull light of the bare electric bulb hanging from the ceiling cast a sallow glow on his face. He looked down at his prisoner on the beaten mud floor. It was not ideal keeping the Para officer in one of the rooms in the secret underground complex in Rishon kibbutz, but the British were unlikely to find him. The Army had already begun frantically to search anything remotely Jewish in the whole Yishuv for their captured officers but there was little chance they would find the secret hideout. Paul was more worried that these new kidnapping orders had delayed the attack on the King David Hotel, but at least he had the chance of revenge.

He gazed thoughtfully at Edward's dirtied and ripped service dress uniform and the pale blue Para wings on his right arm. He said casually, 'I should kill you now.'

There was no reply and Paul stood up over the hooded figure lying helpless on the floor at his feet. He felt immensely powerful. Edward Fairfax's personal life was irrelevant. It was only necessary to remember his guilt. Paul thought of Mattea Spurstein's small boy in the riot, his neck broken by the British Army bullet. He kicked out savagely.

The kick exploded on Edward's chest, the shock more terrifying than the actual hurt, driving the air from his lungs in a deep groan. He curled up at once as far as his chains would allow, his breath coming in panicky gasps, like a wounded animal. He began to sweat. Helpless, he waited for the next blow. His ears ached with listening as his attacker walked round him. He could feel the soft footfalls through the earth.

Paul lashed out again with his boot, as hard as he could, in the back. And again, several times. Edward cried out and jack-knifed this way and that in a rattle of chains, gasping for breath beneath the smothering hood as earth smeared his sweat-stained uniform. Paul moved in for the kill, maddened and wanting to go on kicking till his victim stopped moving. He noticed the hooded head twisting and turning, trying hopelessly to tell where the next attack would come from. And he remembered. He had been there. He still dreamed of the terror he had felt when he was first interrogated by that bastard SD officer in Strasbourg, how he too had jerked his head left and right to avoid the next blow. The memory triggered a tiny sliver of sympathy and Paul's rage slipped away. Breathing hard, he sat down again.

Edward found the silence more awful than being kicked. Fear swilled round inside him, as liquid as the sweat pouring across his stomach and back. His body ached and he tried to stop shaking. He hated himself for being terrified. Gradually his breathing calmed but his muscles stayed rigid with expectation. He strained his ears trying to tell how many were in the room with him. He had a sudden terrible vision of a ring of men standing round him, grinning, ready to kick him to death, booting him from side to side.

Paul watched. He knew what was going through his prisoner's mind under the cloth hood.

Edward tried to speak but his mouth was dry. No words emerged. He coughed to find his voice and demanded hoarsely, 'Who are you?'

Paul ignored the question. 'You killed a small boy,' he stated, his voice thick with disgust. 'In Tel Aviv, in November. Good shooting.'

Edward exhaled softly, surprised at the man's command of English. So this was why he had been seized. He said feebly, 'We didn't mean to kill him.' The weeks in Jerusalem with Carole had softened the hard skin which had formed over his feelings about the boy.

Paul heard the lack of conviction in Edward's voice. He snapped, 'You gave the order!'

The Joshua Inheritance

Edward hesitatingly said, 'Yes, but I didn't mean to kill the boy.'

'You meant to kill someone else?'

Edward stopped. He knew it was impossible to justify himself in cold argument. The riot had been chaos, hot and wild, for hours, and his platoon had been nearly overrun.

Paul stabbed another question into the silence, 'How d'you feel, a trained soldier, killing civilians? You Paras with your blood-clot berets have got quite good at it recently.'

Edward closed his eyes. His uncertainty about the boy's death faded under Paul's attack. 'I suppose you think it's perfectly alright to kill soldiers, or policemen.'

'You're trained and armed.'

Edward snorted. 'What about those Paras you killed in Tel Aviv, in April, two months ago? They were just looking after the liberty trucks for the lads. They were on a bloody night out!'

'That wasn't us, the Irgun,' Paul said forcefully. 'That was the Stern gang.'

'What's the bloody difference?' Edward demanded angrily into his hood, forgetting he was lying helpless on the floor.

'Timing,' said Paul frankly. He had criticised the attack himself. There had been celebrations in Rishon, but many moderate Jews in Palestine had been shocked, just as they had been when the Stern gang assassinated Lord Moyne in Cairo two years before in 1944. Support for the underground would have been weakened had the British not been so stupid with their response. The Army had demanded a huge fine from the city of Tel Aviv and threatened to blow up public buildings as reprisal. He said only, 'The attack permitted you British to claim your poor Paras were defenceless.'

'They were murdered sitting on their camp beds!'

Edward said, appalled at his captor's attitude. 'Seven of them!'

Paul told him harshly, 'Killing a few British soldiers is nothing compared to the deaths of so many Jews in the camps.'

Edward inwardly groaned at the worn phrase. He said, 'How long will the Jewish people go on saying that? How long will you go on using the Nazi death camps as an excuse for more killing?'

'It's not an excuse. It's a fact!' Paul shouted, his dark eyes blazing in his pale face as he glared at Edward on the floor. 'Every death is a fact. Six million terrible facts. You weren't there, you couldn't even begin to know what they did to my people!'

To Paul's surprise, Edward reacted fiercely, bitter that he had missed all the action, shouting back, 'I wasn't there, but the soldiers you're killing were there. And their friends died fighting the Germans to free your people from the camps.'

'Only at the end.'

Edward replied uncertainly, 'I don't understand. D'you mean we should have had D-Day earlier?'

Paul shook his head at the figure on the floor of the little room. 'All you hear is the British version of the truth, just like the Nazis were taken in by the propaganda of Josef Goebbels. I don't suppose anyone told you that, in 1940, the Nazis wanted the Jews to emigrate here rather than kill them in concentration camps. It was only because the British refused to let them into Palestine, that they ended up in the ovens.'

'I don't believe it.'

Paul went on relentlessly, 'In December 1941, the Nazis in Romania allowed nearly eight hundred Jews to leave on a boat called the *Struma*. She sailed through the Black Sea till she was stopped by the Turks in the Bosphorus. They sat at anchor for weeks, under the blazing sun, with no food or facilities, while the British argued with the Turks about regulations. The British said they were illegal immigrants, and refused to let them sail round to Palestine. Of course, the *Struma* was sent back, into the Black Sea and the Nazis torpedoed it. It sank. Husbands, wives, brothers, mothers with babies. Eight hundred people drowned.' Paul paused before adding bitterly, 'Oh yes, I forgot. Two Jews survived and the British were so ashamed, they allowed them into Palestine. Of course, they still called them illegal immigrants, because that's what the petty British regulations said they were, but the apparatchiks in your damned Foreign Office allowed it as "an act of clemency".'

Edward tried to imagine the explosions and children screaming as the boat sank, but he felt obliged to defend the British position. Weakly, he said, 'I suppose the government was trying to follow the immigration rules in the Mandate given us by the League of Nations'. He desperately hoped he would not have to defend the Mandate in detail, as he would be seriously out of his depth, but Paul snorted, dismissed the Mandate with a wave of his hand which Edward could not see and said, 'Bureaucracy. Meetings, minutes and resolutions are the luxuries of established nations. For us, it's more a question of spirit and commitment.'

'In other words, you turn the facts to suit your case,' Edward replied into the stuffy hood. 'Making eight hundred sound like six million. You know bloody well you can't blame the British for murdering all those poor people in the camps.'

Paul rose in his chair and shouted angrily, 'Eight hundred is more than seven miserable Paras!' He calmed slightly, sitting down again and added meaningfully, 'In any case, you'll be pleased to hear that we in the Irgun are concentrating on smaller numbers now.'

There was a long silence. Edward said, 'Meaning me?' The words seemed to clog in the black hessian sack over his head.

'Yes,' said Paul with harsh satisfaction. 'And your single, pathetic life doesn't depend on me, or anyone else in the Irgun.'

'Who then?' Edward asked, as the real implications of Paul's casual remark slipped into his consciousness like a stiletto. His body felt heavy lying on the earth floor, like lead, as if he were already suffering rigor mortis.

'General Barker.'

'That's ridiculous,' said Edward, thinking he was being made fun of as a new tack to humiliate him. 'Bubbles Barker is the GOC.' Lieutenant-General Sir Evelyn Barker had taken over as General Officer Commanding all British servicemen on 9 May that year.

Paul laughed unpleasantly. 'What a nickname for such a bastard! This "Bubbles" has condemned two of our men to death. They're prisoners of war in Acre jail. The Irgun can't tolerate that. So we've retaliated by capturing some British officers.'

'Kidnapped them off the streets, you mean, like me.'

Paul ignored him. 'It's quite simple. If "Bubbles" decides not to hang our two men, you'll be released. If he goes ahead and they hang, you die.' Paul had wanted to kill Edward Fairfax at once, but Yudelmann insisted he must keep him alive, as a bargaining counter for the lives of the two Irgun men. Paul added sarcastically, 'It's all up to good old "Bubbles".'

Edward lay still. He had known there was more to it than just the boy in Tel Aviv, things beyond his control. Cold rivers of sweat dribbled down his sides. The dusty cloth over his mouth made him choke. He remembered. 'Are those two in Acre the men who were captured in March, after an attack on Sarafand Army Camp?'

'Yes. Two soldiers like you, but unlike you they were fighting for an honest cause.'

Edward grunted. 'I don't suppose the King's Own Hussars thought they were honest, planting a bomb in the parade ground to blow them up while they're doing a bit of drill.'

Paul glared at Edward's hooded face. He shouted, 'What's honest about hanging prisoners of war? It's completely against the Geneva Convention.'

Edward countered, 'Your men were wearing British uniforms. That's also against the Geneva Convention. They weren't fighting like real troops. They sneaked into Sarafand Camp dressed up as Paras. Real soldiers don't behave like that. You bloody terrorists want it both ways.'

'A habit I must have picked up from the British,' Paul retorted angrily. 'You trained lots of people during the war to fight the Germans in occupied countries and you weren't bothered about dressing up in all sorts of uniforms.'

Edward remembered what Colonel Haike had said about training the Resistance. He wondered if he would ever see his father again.

Paul went on, 'You condemned Hitler because he ordered the Germans to shoot all your Commandos, and we in the Irgun will condemn the British if they hang ours. What's the difference?'

Edward rolled painfully over on his other side, pulling his chains across his body, to show his back to the voice. There seemed little he could do to influence his fate. He said, 'And I suppose it will make you feel better if you kill me?'

'It certainly will,' stated Paul unequivocally.

There was something in the man's voice which suggested there was more still to explain. Edward hardly dared to ask. The simple word slipped through his lips into the hood, 'Why?'

Paul looked down at his prisoner curled up on the mud floor. He reflected that General Barker was a forceful soldier who hated compromise. The two Irgun men would certainly hang and Edward Fairfax would inevitably die. Paul decided to tell him why he, Paul Levi, was going to kill him.

He stepped over to Edward who cringed expecting another kicking. Paul bent down, undid the knot at Edward's neck which held the hood, and sat down again.

'You can take it off. It doesn't matter much whether you see us. You won't last. Your "Bubbles" will see to that.'

Surprised, Edward listened through the darkness of the hood and then carefully peeled it off, expecting a beating every second, just for trying. Nothing happened. He dropped the hood on the mud floor and his chains rattled as he sat up. He glanced swiftly round. The room was bare. The walls and ceiling were lined with rough planks and he could see no windows. He guessed they were holding him in some sort of shed. There was a solid-looking wooden door in one corner. He switched his full attention to the man facing him on the chair. He took in Paul's shirt, stained under the arms, and blue trousers, his arms folded over the chair back, his workmanlike hands and his eyes which glittered through the shadows cast across his face by the yellow bulb hanging over the mop of thick black hair.

Edward whispered, 'You're the man who picked up the boy in that riot?'

Paul nodded as he leaned over the chair back and spoke with great intensity. 'I'm a Jew. I believe in revenge and I'm going to kill you because of that boy. And for what your father did to me and the others.'

Edward stared and whispered, 'Who are you?'

'I thought I was the only one to survive, apart from your father, that is.'

Edward made an inspired guess. 'Till you found Axel Romm in Jerusalem?'

Paul was surprised. 'How d'you know that?' Axel

The Joshua Inheritance

Romm had not mentioned that Edward Fairfax knew anything about the operation.

Edward shrugged, knowing he had scored a point but having no idea how to build on it.

Paul frowned. He would ask Romm about that. He brushed the interruption aside and went on speaking relentlessly. 'Let me tell you in detail why you deserve to die. I trained with your father and Axel Romm and went with a group of others to join them in eastern France, near the German border. There were ten of us. We were a reinforcement by plane, a Hudson. That was a twin-engined aircraft supplied to the British by the Americans for these sorts of secret operations.'

'What were you going to do?' Edward put in.

'Be quiet,' snapped Paul, cross at the interruption. He began to explain, recalling every vivid detail of the disaster as he talked, 'We flew through the night towards that landing strip in the hills. There were no lights on the ground at all. The whole of Europe was blacked out. Sometimes we saw searchlights waving in the distance, to our east. I suppose British bombers were attacking everywhere at that time in the war. Our pilots were incredible, finding the way to that tiny strip of grass. At about forty miles out, they picked up the Eureka beacon. That was a sort of radar which directed us on the right bearing. We flew on in utter darkness down the invisible funnel given us by the Eureka. Then the pilot told us, "ten minutes to go". We readied our rucksacks and weapons. We were Commandos, in helmets and uniform, our faces blacked, but I could see the others' eyes. We were all frightened to death and trying not to show it. What d'you expect? We were so goddam vulnerable up there and most of us had not been on ops before. I was at the door at the back, ready to open it the second we landed, so I had earphones. About ten miles out, I suddenly heard the man on the ground using the S-phone. His job was to talk down the pilots on the final run-in. I couldn't make out the voice but he used the right codes. We were almost there. None of us Commandos liked being in the plane. We had trained our guts out for this and we wanted to get out as soon as possible, into the bushes where we were in our element. I opened the door. I shouldn't have done it till we landed but I was impatient. It saved my life. I could see the trees and hillsides of the mountains only a few hundred feet away, level with the plane. It was incredible. In total darkness, the pilots were flying the valley countours they had memorised before leaving base. The S-phone crackled and the voice said we were only a mile out. The plane flew towards a dark ridge ahead and juddered as the undercarriage went down. The wind rushed passed my open door and we dropped further. I thought we'd catch the trees as we topped the ridge. We sank towards the long grass, so low I nearly jumped. Then I spotted the landing strip lights. Little piles of burning wood along the sides of the open grass strip. It was a miracle the pilots had seen them at all and as quickly as I'd seen them they disappeared as we touched down, bouncing on the rough turf. The pilots turned the plane as fast as they could and began taxiing back to the take-off point. As they did, I jumped out and fell in the wet grass.'

Paul stopped and focused on Edward. He said quietly, 'That's when everything went wrong. The sky lit up like day, with mortars throwing up para-illum flares, searchlights from trees on the edge of the open area and more tracer than I've ever seen before. The place was swarming with SS and the team in the plane never had a chance. The Hudson was still half full of fuel and burst into flames at once. Only two of us survived. Axel Romm and me. He escaped, I didn't. At least, not till the Russians came.'

Paul paused. Edward said nothing, trying to absorb what he had heard and make sense of it. Paul stated, 'Your father betrayed us. He was the only other person

The Joshua Inheritance

who knew about the landing that night. And he made certain he wasn't there.'

'Couldn't it have been someone else?'

'No!' Paul shouted. The goddam SD officer had confirmed it. 'Your father betrayed us!' He stood up abruptly and Edward thought he was going to be attacked, but Paul checked his watch. He stretched and crossed to the wooden door in the corner.

'Wait!' Edward shouted. 'Please!' He had just remembered where he had seen Paul before, in the refugee camp in Poppendorf. He tried to stand up to follow and was pulled up short, stumbling and falling again on his hands and knees. His chains were attached to a ring set in a concrete block in the middle of the floor.

Paul laughed. He pulled the door and was gone. Edward heard a bolt shoot on the other side.

Paul walked along a narrow corridor where the earth was shored up with wooden props but no plank lining, like a coal mine. He passed through two more small rooms, like the one Edward was locked in, crossed the briefing room where they kept the racks of weapons and the planning table, and began to climb the ladder which led up to the old tractor in the wood yard.

Edward slumped back on the floor, sitting cross-legged. He had learned more in the last few minutes than in months of waiting for Colonel Haike to come up with information, but the Irgun leader had raised endless questions as well. Edward still refused to believe his father was guilty, so who else could have been? And why? He knew so little about how these clandestine operations worked, but there had to be an explanation for the Germans having time to set up such a complicated ambush, with searchlights and heavy machine-guns. They must have had prior knowledge. How? Who from? There was still so much to know.

He was desperate to get out.

* * *

Axel Romm watched his daughter come towards him across the patio. She was no longer the adolescent teenager he had left behind in New York when he crossed the Atlantic to fight the war in Europe. She was a woman now, lovely and strong willed, but she was still his family. All he had left. He said, 'You've been lucky, Carole. Those Arabs might have seized you too.'

Carole looked at him in surprise. 'They weren't Arabs. They were Jews.' She could still feel the bruise on the side of her face where she had been hit when she went to help Edward.

'No,' he said firmly, shaking his grey head. 'They were Arabs.'

Carole shook her head, 'I heard them talking to each other in Yiddish.'

'You must be mistaken. You're not familiar with either language.'

'Don't patronise me, please.' Her father always managed to treat her like a child. 'I hear enough of each in the hospital. The interns and nurses are Jewish, and the porters are mostly Arabs.' She wondered why her father should insist the attackers had been Arabs, but she could not catch his expression in the shadows of the patio. He moved away, sipping the glass of wine he had brought through from dinner, and watched her from the shadows under the jasmine on the walls.

He said, 'Maybe now that officer has gone, you'll spend more time at home?'

Carole stared. 'Is that all you can say? He's been kidnapped, beaten up and you talk as if he's on vacation! It's been a whole week!' Worry and upset churned in her stomach as she was reminded of what might be happening to Edward. Every day, with ghoulish relish, the newspapers rehearsed the arguments for General Barker opting to hang the two Irgun men in Acre jail, and juggled the chances of whether the Irgun would kill their kidnap victims. Every day, she hoped to read

The Joshua Inheritance

that Edward had been discovered in one of the endless searches, but not one of the officers had been found. She had not slept, and had eaten little. Tiredly she added, 'And by the way, Father, his name is Edward. Edward Fairfax.'

'Yeah,' said Axel Romm impatiently. 'He's not the only one. Five other Limeys were taken, from the British officers' club in Tel Aviv, but I ain't surprised, considering the British say they're going to hang two of the Irgun.'

Carole clenched her fists angrily and snapped, 'You don't care what happens to Edward, do you?' She loved her father but he was forcing her to take sides and making no concessions.

He did not reply.

Carole shook her head. 'You're wrong blaming Edward for something which happened in the war, something you won't even talk about. And you don't seem to care how deeply I feel about him.'

Axel Romm winced hearing his daughter talk like that about Edward Fairfax. He had decided never to have anything more to do with George Fairfax or his family. 'I'm sorry, Carole. I'd explain if I could, but you wouldn't understand. Just accept from me that you must not see him again.'

'I won't, will I? Not if they kill him,' she cried out, suddenly bursting into tears.

'I'm sure they'll release him.'

'How d'you know?' Carole sobbed. 'It's not up to them. It's up to the bloody system. Some goddam general. Of course he's going to hang those two in Acre jail.' Even if they released the two men, she had no confidence. She had seen the hard, starved expressions on their faces when they grabbed Edward. They would have no compunction keeping him in terrible squalor, or beating him, day after day. Feeling sick, she wondered if they were even feeding him. She left her father in the patio and walked into the sitting-room where she slumped into a wicker chair, put her head in her hands and let the tears run down her cheeks.

Axel Romm followed her inside. He stood behind her chair, put his hand on her shoulder and said soothingly, 'It's okay, Carole. I'm sure.'

She looked up. She knew him so well and there was something reassuring in his voice, in the tone he had used to her when she was a little girl and he promised her a treat. She asked, 'How can you be so sure?'

'Just take it from me,' he said firmly. 'It's my business to follow these affairs and these groups. I have to report on their activities all the time to the Consul, and I know.'

She watched his face closely. Was there something defensive in his voice. It struck her as odd that she was actually thinking of distrusting her father.

Romm felt the hard set of her shoulders and turned away from her, cross that she had not allowed him to comfort her.

'How do you know?' she insisted, watching his grey head and his slim back as he filled his glass again from the wine decanter on a side table. Intuitively, she said, 'You knew it would happen, didn't you? You knew they would take him!'

'That's nonsense,' he snapped and turned round with his wine. Carole's face was wet with tears which glistened on her cheeks and lips. 'You're upset. That's natural. But you'll get over him.'

'No!' Carole cried, hardly believing that she was having to fight her father at such a time. 'This is 1946, not 1919. I'm over twenty-one. You can't tell me what to do any longer. I'm not a little girl, I'm a woman. Things have changed in the last five years while you've been at war. Women have changed. They've been working in factories, ships, offices and even fighting in the front line. We don't need men to tell us what to do any more. I thought you'd have realised that from my mother!'

The remark was like a physical blow. Her father lost his temper and shouted back, 'You're my child. You'll do what I say until you marry. Understand?' He stabbed his finger at her and a thick shank of grey hair fell over his forehead. 'If it wasn't for the war, your mother would be here to tell you herself.'

'You have to forget the war, Father,' she replied sadly, shocked. Something had changed him in the war. Maybe it was losing her mother but he was closed and hard now. She said, 'I don't want to hear your bitterness about the war. That was your war, your disaster. Five years of world misery was the fault of your generation, not mine, not Edward's. We aren't responsible for what happened. We're the victims and you want us to go on being the victims.' She wiped her eyes with her damp hankerchief. Neither her father nor, it seemed, Edward's father cared how much trouble they caused. 'As long as you refuse to talk, to explain what happened between you and George Fairfax, you have no right to tell me what to do with my life. You have no right to visit your bile on me.'

High spots of colour appeared on Axel Romm's face. He pursed his lips and shouted angrily, 'It's none of your goddamed business, Carole! You're my daughter and you'll do as I say. And don't be so goddamed rude to your father!'

Carole shrugged her slim shoulders, and looked away at some photographs on a table by the wall, ignoring him. Then, she stood up slowly, still stiff from the bruises she had from falling over the tables in the Astoria, and walked painfully to her bedroom. She decided Edward was right trying to find out about the wartime operation, to settle the matter once and for all, so they could both build a new future, but she would have to find a different way. She began to think how.

Her father watched her go, furious. She was distraught, he told himself; but he had no doubt she would come round to his way of thinking when she got over young Fairfax.

13

CORDON AND SEARCH

29 June 1946

Edward was pretending to sleep, with his arm across his eyes to shut out the light from the bulb which was never turned off. He was alone for the first time since the day of his arrival. Every minute of the endless days, a relay of guards sat with him in the tiny cell. When they brought him food, always the same mess of semolina rice and vegetables on a tin plate, someone watched him; even when he asked them to push over the bucket so he could relieve himself, they watched. Now he was alone. He listened carefully, feeling the sweat on his arm softening the stubble on his cheeks, and wondered why.

He glanced at his watch. He was grateful they had not taken it, but he had to ignore the awful thought that the Irgun leader was being lenient because he expected to kill his prisoner in the end. Day after day, he had wound it faithfully and with infinite care so as not to damage it by overwinding. The passage of time was his only link with reality in the world outside. The hands said five o'clock. His secret scratches on the concrete slab in the floor told him eleven full days. That made it five o'clock in the morning, Saturday 29 June.

He listened for noises in the corridor outside till his ears ached, but the guard seemed to have gone. His heart beat faster. He had to take the chance. Moving slowly, he gathered the chains into his hands to stop them rattling, and stood up. No-one came. He crouched over the concrete slab. He had spent hours surreptitiously examining the ring in this slab under the eyes of the guard. He thought the slab would move, if he used the chains to lift it up. He placed his feet on each side, wrapped the chains around his wrists and heaved. Nothing. He strained again, ignoring the pain of the chains pressing deep into his hands. Suddenly the concrete lifted, he lurched off balance and was staring down a deep black hole into the ground between his legs. The swinging concrete slab smashed into his ankle and he staggered, almost falling into the hole. He hung doggedly on to the heavy weight, shuffled forward out of danger and dumped the slab to catch his breath.

Still no-one outside. He grasped the slab again and staggered to the wall, thinking that at least he could use the concrete to break through the planks and escape. He peered through a crack and saw earth, dull red in the light of the bulb behind him. He shuffled to another wall and saw more earth. It was then he realised he was underground. His expectations of escape were shattered, his confidence badly shaken. He leaned against the wood, shifting his grip on the slab and looked round the room, thinking hard. Above the stinking slop bucket in one corner was the square grill in the ceiling he had seen day after day. It was obviously a ventilation flue, but he had never realised its true importance. It was the only conduit of fresh air into the cell. The occasional noises he heard from outside the room must have come from that grill.

He heard soft footfalls along the corridor. Someone was coming. Hurriedly, he shuffled back to the hole, dropped the slab back in place, and slumped down on top as the door opened.

Two men came in. As usual, they were armed with sub-machine-guns and wore shemags round their heads to hide their faces. They surprised him by talking.

The Joshua Inheritance

Normally his guards were silent or at best monosyllabic. More than that, they were speaking Arabic and to his delight Edward found he could understand. He guessed they were Sephardim Jews from Egypt, or perhaps Iraq.

Rapidly the taller one said, 'You cover him. I'll go round the back and stick this chloroform over his nose before he gives us any trouble.'

'Be quick! The soldiers are almost here,' the other said with a note of panic in his voice.

Edward gave no sign of having understood them and groaned, pretending to wake up. They were careless, in a hurry. The taller man stepped across the cell and pulled the filthy prisoner off the floor by the scruff of his shirt. Edward sucked in a deep breath, desperately hoping they did not see, and a thick wad of chloroformed cloth was stuffed over his nose and mouth. Stubbornly, Edward concentrated on gradually releasing his breath, for ages it seemed, and he fought to ignore the acrid vapour in his nose and eyes. He gagged, his struggles slowed, he went limp and the man let him collapse on the floor.

The guards watched him for a moment. The taller one said, 'He's out. I'll leave you now. I've got to get up top to help the others.'

He left at once, ignoring the scared look on the other guard's face. He was glad he was not the one having to stay underground. Even if he was not killed at once when the soldiers found him guarding the British officer he would face a military court and a hanging.

Five miles from Rishon under a black starry sky, a long column of Army trucks stopped on the roadside, their engines running. Exhaust fumes clouded the clean night air and one or two men coughed in the darkness under the tarpaulins covering the back of the vehicles. Scrubby hillsides rose in shadow on either side of the narrow road where the first paleness of dawn could be seen over the ridges to the east.

Paras ran up the column to a group of Land-Rovers near the front. They wore full patrol equipment with '44 pattern webbing pouches, boots and puttees and carried Stens. At the back of one Land-Rover Major Rattigan sat on the tail-board smoking a cigarette, his angular face in shadow under his helmet, waiting for his Company sergeant-major to tell him everyone had arrived. As usual, Aubrey was last. He shoved in next between Sergeant Hodgson and Roger Haike whose gunners were driving the trucks. Major Rattigan looked round the darkened faces of his men and said, 'This is another cordon and search op, called Operation Agatha. Bloody silly name but it's big. Really big. Every damned Army unit in the country is going to search every damned kibbutz, house, office and factory. In short, anything remotely kosher.'

'About bloody time too,' Captain Scarland muttered and for once Aubrey found himself agreeing with him.

Major Rattigan pulled on his cigarette and added, 'If someone doesn't find Edward Fairfax and the other kidnapped officers today, then I'm afraid we must expect the worst.'

There was a rumble of assent. Edward was popular, and losing one of their officers had really hurt. The Paras wanted to get their own back.

'Why did we need to come all the way out here before telling us what we were doing?' Aubrey asked.

'Quiet!' Captain Scarland hissed glaring darkly at Aubrey who took no notice of him.

'Fair question actually,' said Major Rattigan mildly. 'I've two minutes to explain. The whole operation has been set up in the greatest secrecy. We all know that the local wogs round the camp know everything that goes on in El Bureij and the staff were terrified their plans would be found out. They decided we should deploy like

The Joshua Inheritance

this before giving final orders.' He told them that Field Marshal Montgomery, the Chief of the Imperial General Staff, had visited Palestine and wanted a stronger line taken. He had returned to London recommending total rejection of the Anglo-American Committee's idea to allow in one hundred thousand Jewish immigrants until all the illegal groups were eliminated. Ernest Bevin and the Cabinet agreed and Operation Agatha was set up. Major Rattigan said candidly, 'I think the good Field Marshal is expecting the moon, but Op Agatha will certainly show the people of Palestine we can be tough. Some of you chaps were with us in the war and will recognise the principles are exactly the same as we used for a big push at the Germans. First, deception, with this convoy to maintain operational security, then a full co-ordinated move to seize all objectives. Only difference is that here all the objectives are civilian. Telephone exchanges, radio stations, post offices, bus stations, railways, offices, houses and so on.'

Aubrey observed, 'Sounds like a coup d'état.' It was odd to think that the British Army, with its history of non-involvement in politics, would ever engage in such an operation, or know how to.

Major Rattigan agreed, a slight smile on his hard features. 'More or less. Hate to think what the Labour Party would say if they noticed what we're doing. By dawn we'll have the whole country under Army control and have paralysed all Jewish influence in Palestine.'

'Our target is to search Rishon Kibbutz, ten minutes away,' he said and swiftly detailed everyone's tasks for the operation. They had done plenty of cordon and search operations in the past and the orders did not take long. He paused at the end and spoke with great emphasis, 'Bloody well search every nook and cranny. The buggers will fight us, and we'll have to force our way in, but don't let them tire you out. If someone doesn't find Fairfax today, I fear the bloody Irgun won't release him at all.'

The Paras nodded grimly. General Barker enjoyed a tough reputation and no-one expected him to commute the hangings in Acre jail. They now ran back up the line of trucks to brief their men and five minutes later the convoy moved off through the grey pre-dawn light to Rishon.

The kibbutzniks resisted Major Rattigan's Paras every step of the way. Another company of Paras cordoned the kibbutz through the fields and citrus plantations around, while Major Rattigan's platoons tried to force their way in. Sergeant Hodgson, standing in for Edward, led the platoon towards the main gate where a crowd of men and women screamed and pelted them with clods of earth and stones.

Major Rattigan did not hesitate. He ordered the platoons to use tear gas. The din of shouting was punctuated by the pop of exploding tear gas canisters but the kibbutzniks had an answer. They threw wet sandbags over the spewing canisters and the gas was neutralised. The Paras tried again. They brought up water cannon and the powerful jets turned the balance. The section commanders shoved forward, bullying and pushing the Jewish settlers back. The Paras were veterans of vicious pub brawls in Aldershot and with months of internal security duties in Palestine behind them, they slowly but surely forced their way into the kibbutz without resort to firearms. After an hour, they had arrested forty-seven of the most violent kibbutzniks who were handed over to the Palestine police. The rest retreated at speed across the open middle of the kibbutz to the school-house and medical centre where they barricaded themselves in, shouting defiance.

Underground, Edward could hear the din of battle, filtered and muted through the grill in the ceiling. He pretended to be unconscious. He had recovered from the chloroform, and his breathing out had prevented most of the worst effects though he had a splitting headache. He lay on his front, his head turned so he could watch the guard. He was certain the kibbutz was being searched. He wondered which unit was doing it and where the ventilation shaft came out. There was no point shouting till he was certain someone could hear him. He forced himself to be patient.

By eleven o'clock in the morning, nearly four hours after the start, the Paras had fought the kibbutzniks to a standstill. The school-house and medical centre were occupied and another ninety-three people had been arrested, including a number of women who had flung boiling water over Corporal Jacobs, seriously scalding him. Major Rattigan ordered his men to rest for half an hour before starting the search and the quartermaster-sergeant brought round urns of hot tea to all the platoons on the back of a Land-Rover.

In the secret room under the wood yard, Edward's guard stood up. He stared at the ventilation grille and tried to guess why everything had gone quiet above ground. He held his nose against the appalling smell coming from Edward's slop bucket. He could feel the sweat trickling down his face and neck under his shemag. He was scared to death. He was convinced the Paras would kill him out of hand if they found him with their officer drugged and tied like a chicken.

The Paras started a thorough search of every building in Rishon, starting with the medical centre and the school. Roger Haike, whose gunners were guarding the prisoners, went into the kibbutz to watch. He was curious to see what all the fuss was about. He found Aubrey searching the wood yard alongside Sergeant Hodgson's platoon.

'Found anything, Hall-Drake?'

Aubrey had a large gash across his head from a stone

and he was in an evil temper. He said 'Go away, Haike. I'm busy.'

'I say, old chap. That's no way to talk to a fellow,' said Roger pleasantly. They were equal in rank and he had no intention of being bossed about. Besides, he had enjoyed the drama of the battle through his binoculars, standing on the top of the cab of his truck. 'I think you chaps did a splendid job.' He wandered over to an old tractor and saw-bench.

Private Brogan was searching a pile of wood beyond the tractor, with Sergeant Hodgson.

Roger gestured at the tractor and said to no-one in particular, 'These kibbutznik chappies have all the gear, don't they.'

'Haven't you got anything better to do?' Hall-Drake asked, exasperated. He stared at the tractor, trying to remember the principles of a search. Think like a kibbutznik, he told himself. Where would I hide my weapons? They must be easily available – after all, the Arabs had begun attacking the kibbutzes of late – but well enough concealed to survive a full-scale search.

'I don't know why you're bothering here,' Roger interrupted importantly. 'My chaps are holding ninety of these bloody terrorists and interrogation is what it's all about now. Not pratting about with all this old wood.' He flicked sawdust off his boots and pulled a packet of Players Capstan cigarettes out of one of his webbing pouches. 'Would you like a smoke, old chap?'

Aubrey snapped, 'Don't be an idiot. The place'll go up in flames.' He began to fiddle with the tractor. There was something out of place.

Deliberately, Roger put one foot on the tractor's front axle and tapped out a cigarette for himself. He put it between his lips, struck a match and cupped his hands as he lit the end.

Aubrey looked up crossly. 'Are you mad? This is a bloody wood yard!'

The Joshua Inheritance

At once, Private Brogan knelt down out of sight behind the pile of logs, grinning, as if he were searching there, delighted with the impending row.

Sergeant Hodgson's face tightened. His patience was exhausted after the fight to get into the kibbutz and he could see Captain Scarland striding in their direction across the sandy kibbutz yard. He did not want his platoon involved. He stepped across to Brogan.

Brogan was so absorbed by the argument between the two officers that he never noticed the dull glint of the metal grille under the pile of logs at his feet. In the cell beneath, Edward and the guard were gripped by the blurred sound of angry voices filtering down the ventilation shaft.

Over by the tractor, Aubrey shouted, 'Put your bloody cigarette out!'

Roger Haike looked down his nose, took a deep pull and exhaled a cloud of smoke. 'I don't really care if this place burns to the ground, Hall-Drake, old chap. Serve the bloody Jewish wogs right, eh?'

Aubrey lost his temper. His hand flashed up and knocked the cigarette to the ground. Roger fell back astonished as Aubrey crushed the butt-end with his boot and took another step forward.

'Jesus, mother of God! There's going to be a fight!' Private Brogan exclaimed in amazement, his face buried in the wood pile.

His words carried clearly to Edward and the guard. Edward had no idea who was up there, but the words were plainly those of a British soldier. He took his chance and shouted at the top of his voice.

In the same instant, Sergeant Hodgson reached Brogan and bellowed, 'Get on wiv the frigging search! I ain't in the 'abit of telling you what to do twice over!

Edward never heard him as the guard's Sten smashed on down on his head, stifling his second breath before he could shout again. The guard frantic with fear, went on hitting him, using his Sten gun barrel like a club. Locked in place by his chains, Edward was helpless. He collapsed on the floor under the swinging blows and passed out.

Roger Haike backed quickly out of range of another swipe from Hall-Drake's large hands and recovered his voice. 'You bloody rude swine!'

Captain Scarland ducked into the wood yard. 'What's the matter with you, Haike? We're all sweating our bollocks off and you're the only man with a pale face.' He glared from one to the other, shrugged and stated, 'I've persuaded Major Rattigan we've done enough in this bloody place. What about you, Hall-Drake? What? Too bad. You've had plenty of time and anyway we've got to go. Damned if I know where these bastards are keeping that young idiot Fairfax.'

Hall-Drake glared at them both, kicked the tractor wheel and stamped off.

Captain Scarland noticed Sergeant Hodgson and Brogan on the other side of the wood pile and called over, 'Pack up and move the men out, Sergeant Hodgson. We've had this bloody place up to the gills.'

The kibbutz was badly damaged. The Paras had vented their frustration tearing down walls and ceilings and ripping up the floors, adding to the mess caused during the earlier fighting, but without finding anything at all.

Elsewhere in Palestine the British had had more success. They had found mountains of documents, illegal arms under the Great Synagogue in Tel Aviv, and a huge find of 300 rifles, 94 mortars, 800 lbs of plastic explosive and nearly half a million rounds of ammunition in another underground complex at Meshek Yagur, a kibbutz near Haifa. However, they had not found a single one of the kidnapped officers.

Then, to everyone's surprise, two days later General Barker commuted the sentence of death over

The Joshua Inheritance

the two Irgun men in Acre jail. Now, it was up to the Irgun.

In a foul temper, Paul left the kibbutzniks in Rishon to clear up the mess and drove the Dodge truck to Tel Aviv, to see what Yudelmann wanted him to do with his prisoner.

Edward lay on his back in his cell and turned his aching head very slowly from the light above him. Even the dull yellow light burned painfully on his swollen, puffed eyes. His face was purple and black with bruises and his whole body resented the slightest movement after the beating he suffered from the guard. He could hardly breathe. He supposed he had several broken ribs, his shoulder hurt terribly and one arm was useless. He guessed it was broken. None of that mattered. His depression at failing to escape was worse. He kept telling himself that if he had shouted earlier, he might have been heard. Or, if he had attacked the guard first, he could have escaped. Regrets stacked up till they were driven away in stabbing pain around his chest whenever he shifted position.

The guard cradled his Sten on the chair and watched him, just his eyes showing from behind the black and white shemag. Edward groaned and lay still. At once his regrets began to pile up again. Even if the two Irgun men were not hanged, the young Irgun leader had left him in no doubt that he would be killed anyway. A crushing sense of failure and despair settled on him. He had no idea even what the day was any more. His watch, his last link with the outside world, had been smashed. Grimly, he supposed nothing worse could happen till they killed him. He made himself think of Carole.

He woke from a fitful sleep with a start. Voices in the corridor. Looking sideways across the floor because it was too painful to sit up, he saw the door burst open. The young Irgun leader strode in, his pale face cold and unfriendly.

'It's over,' Paul told the dishevelled figure on the floor. Edward's uniform was torn, bloodied and stained and he had a two-week growth of beard which was caked with dirt and scabs. Paul glanced at the slop bucket in the corner and nearly gagged.

Edward tried to answer, to show them he did not care what they did to him, but his throat was dry and no words came out. His stomach suddenly felt terribly light and he had a horrible desire to urinate. He licked his lips and tried to control his emotion. It was childish, he knew, but he felt like crying.

Paul Levi spoke rapidly in Yiddish to the guard and another two men behind him. They could see he was in no mood for mistakes and listened carefully. Edward saw one had a bottle and guessed what they were planning. Ignoring the agony of his chest, he sucked in a long slow breath and was ready when Paul dropped on one knee with the wad of chloroform-soaked cotton wool. Paul's leg battered his rib-cage and he nearly lost the precious air in his lungs but he hung on. His eyes ran and the fiery liquid stung his mouth. He forced himself to relax, pretending to pass out, fighting the agony of his grinding ribs.

Finally Paul stood up. He unlocked Edward's chains and waved at the other guards. Edward tried to keep his face relaxed and his eyes closed. He was terrified they would kick him, even by mistake, because his reaction would give him away. He nearly fainted with the effort of forcing down the pain as they lifted him over someone's shoulders and was thankful when they reached the dark corridor. Unseen, he could release the agony, alternately staring wide-eyed into the shadows, stretching the stubbled skin on his cheeks, and then screwing his puffed eyes up tight.

They carried him down the corridor and Edward bit his lip till he tasted blood, to stop himself screaming as they banged his body carelessly on the wooden props.

The Joshua Inheritance

He was pushed and pulled up the ladder to the wood yard and left on the ground. The pain receded and the smell of fresh air was pure nectar. Carefully he opened an eye. Between the roof over the woodpile and the ridge of the medical centre across the yard, he could see stars. He began to feel he might survive.

Paul had parked the Dodge truck next to the tractor. Under his instructions the other guards lifted Edward in a narrow box, like a coffin, and slammed the lid. Then they lifted it and slid it through the tool box under the chassis as before.

Paul climbed in and shouted roughly in English, 'Come on Selig, get this old heap going. We've got work to do.' Selig started the engine without a word. Minutes later, the truck was trundling out on to the dusty road beyond the kibbutz.

Edward lay in total darkness, squashed inside the narrow box, but he could hear everything being said in the cab. Disorientated by the way he had been manhandled, and swamped with savage waves of pain as the truck bounced and heaved over the uneven road, it was some time before he worked out that he must be hidden directly under the back of the cab.

'Where'll we dump the bastard?' Selig asked.

'I'll tell you when I'm ready,' Paul replied curtly.

'What was the point of keeping him all this time if this is what it's come to?'

'Just drive. It doesn't matter any more.'

There was silence for a long time after that. Edward got cramp but was quite unable to move his leg. He thought his muscles would tear themselves apart. He wanted to shout for help but the thought there was still a chance of survival stopped him. He screwed his face up and tears of pain streamed down his cheeks.

The truck stopped. He heard the cab doors slam and then noises at his feet, as they opened the compartment. His box was pulled out and dropped on the ground. He nearly fainted with the agony, but hung on once again. If they were going to kill him, he intended to be conscious to the end.

A voice said, 'Let me shoot him now.'

There was a long pause. Edward lay bathed in sweat staring up into the darkness of the wood over his face, as if he could see the two men he instinctively knew were standing over his box, like undertakers.

Finally, the Irgun leader grunted, 'Not this time. It's not my decision. We can't. Forget it. We've got to get back to Jerusalem. The other operation's been delayed too long.'

Edward heard their boots scuff on the ground. 'At least we saved Ashbel and Simchon, and they never found him under the tractor.' The rest of the sentence was lost as the cab door slammed. The ancient diesel engine revved and Edward heard the truck grind away. Silence descended. He let out his breath in a long harsh gasp and passed out.

Much later, the warmth of the sun on the wood and faint sounds outside the box woke him. He listened and finally plucked up the courage to shove off the lid. It would not budge. Fighting the pain, he pushed with his good shoulder. The lid sprang off and fell to one side. Edward struggled to sit up.

He was on a triangle of rough land between two streets of low concrete houses with flat roofs. Shop-owners were opening the shutters and dragging out trays of fruit and vegetables on to the dusty roadside. Two rabbis in long black coats and gaiters passed by chatting, and women in skirts and printed headscarves bustled along with bags and baskets, up early for the market. No-one took the slightest notice of the bizarre box which had been dumped in their midst. No-one came over to help when he shouted.

* * *

The Joshua Inheritance

Angus MacLean's polished shoes squeaked on the linoleum as he walked down the hospital corridor. He was wearing his Inspector's uniform, a sandy tropical service dress with black Sam Browne belt. An Arab worker was swabbing the floor from a bucket and the reassuring tang of ammonia filled the air. He asked the starched matron walking beside him, 'How is he?'

'Lucky,' she replied, pulling her strong features into an expression of manly grit to emphasise the deliberate understatement. She stopped at the door of a room, checked the time on a watch pinned over her bosom, smoothed her spotless white hospital uniform and told him crisply, 'I'll leave you here, Inspector. I'm very busy. Some soldiers were brought in an hour ago. Burns and blast. Another bomb attack on a road convoy, I'm afraid. It never stops does it?' She strode off, and Angus pushed through the door.

'Angus! Good to see you,' Edward exclaimed. He tried to sit up and missed the expression of horror on Angus's face.

'I came as soon as I heard you'd been brought in here. What the hell have they done to you?'

'Could be worse,' Edward said through the side of his mouth. One cheek was still thickly bruised and he had lost two teeth. 'Could have killed me.'

Angus was too much a realist to disagree. No-one believed the two Irgun men would be let off, and he had not expected to see Edward again. 'What's the damage?'

'Head, ribs, collar-bone and arm,' Edward said, trying to grin. The surgeon could do no more than bandage his chest to hold the three broken ribs. He had let the collar-bone mend on its own and supported the broken arm in a sling. Edward moved his plastered arm slightly and grimaced. 'Worst thing was this had begun to mend before they let me go. The surgeon had to break it and reset it.'

'Och, you poor beggar.'

'Anyway, what's the news?' Edward asked.

'I saw Solly Mannheim and took a statement from him. He was distraught, especially when I teased him that people wouldn't come to his restaurant if his guests were beaten up and kidnapped. You must go and see him.'

Edward nodded. The first thing he wanted to do was to see Carole again and he obstinately wanted to take her to the Astoria. 'They're bound to give me some sick leave,' he said smiling lopsidedly. 'Can I come and stay?'

Angus laughed. 'Of course. Tell me, how did you get out? And that's a professional question.' Edward nodded and told him all he could remember, especially the last conversations he had overheard in the truck. 'Trouble is, I expect every kibbutz has a wood yard and tractor in it.'

'We'll check,' Angus said. 'At least it's something to work on.'

'Angus, I'm sure the man I heard before I was beaten up was part of a search team.'

'He was.' Angus explained about Operation Agatha. 'One of a hundred thousand soldiers who searched the whole damned country that Saturday. Wasn't very popular with the Jews who complained about being arrested on a Sabbath. Got a point, mind you. Short of interviewing every soldier in the Mandate, I doubt we'll identify the place. All the same, when you've recovered and they let you out of this antiseptic box, you can come to my office and we'll go through the paperwork. God knows, I could do with some help sifting the mountain of documents we seized. Of course most of it's incomprehensible.'

'In code, you mean?'

Angus laughed. 'You might say so, but no, it's in Hebrew. You and I did the wrong language. We can't trust the Jewish policemen any more to give us a proper translation. These are sad days, Edward, and getting worse.'

The Joshua Inheritance

Edward wriggled into a more comfortable position in bed, wincing with pain as he jolted his ribs. He asked, 'What about the operation in Jerusalem? Have you heard any talk from your sources about that?' Edward knew he might be asking Angus to break security by telling him but felt he had earned the right to know.

Angus nodded. 'The Irgun are planning something big here, but the question is, what?'

'I'm sure it's something really important,' said Edward out of the side of his mouth. Too much talking was painful. 'Just a feeling. The way they spoke.'

'Probably the police headquarters,' Angus said morosely. 'They hate the police more than you military wallahs.'

'Didn't get that impression when I opened my box and shouted for help,' said Edward sourly. 'Not a single person came to help. Just wandered past, going about their daily chores, as if I didn't exist.'

'So much for the Good Samaritan,' Angus said. 'The ordinary Jews don't want to know anything about the violence.'

The door opened and the matron put her head round, her starched cap neatly pinned on her bobbed hair. A smile creased her stern features. She announced, 'More visitors, Mr Fairfax.' She wagged a finger. 'I'm sure you'll be pleased to see them.' She wagged a finger. 'But don't you get overtired. You're in no condition for parties.'

Edward smiled lopsidedly, hoping it was Aubrey Hall-Drake with a bottle of whisky. Matron ducked out of view, the door swung open and Diana Haike appeared.

'Darling Edward! You poor thing, you look awful!' She looked stunning, and knew it. She had done her fair hair to frame her oval face and wore a smart suit, pin-striped like a man's city suit, in a lightweight pale grey material.

'Introductions, if you please,' said Angus Maclean with a wide smile, glad he had chosen to look his best in uniform for his visit.

Somehow Edward found his voice. He introduced them but Diana brushed past Angus with hardly a nod. She sat down on Edward's bed, at his side. 'You dear thing,' she cried putting a hand up to his face.

'When did you arrive?' Edward asked, flinching under his bandages at her touch. He suddenly felt trapped. He had forgotten she was coming out, and had been thinking of nothing else but seeing Carole again.

Diana looked at his tortured face and said, 'Don't talk now, darling. It must be agony. There'll be plenty of time later.'

Edward made silent appeal to Angus who remarked dryly, 'Aye. You'll enjoy that. He's got plenty to tell you.' He only had a second to enjoy the appeal in Edward's eyes when a voice behind him at the door said, 'I'd like to hear that too.'

Edward's eyes widened more. 'Father!' Was he dreaming?

'Dear boy!' George Fairfax boomed. He was in a tropical service dress of lightweight cream barathea, major's crowns on his shoulders and carrying his hat under his arm. He marched across the room to his son. 'I've just been talking to Matron. You have been in the wars, eh?' Affectionately, he gripped Edward's leg through the bedclothes.

'He has indeed,' murmured Angus and introduced himself, delighted by the turnout of events. The unexpected always shed new and interesting light on people, which was one reason why he enjoyed being a policeman. He had achieved his greatest successes engineering situations like this one. He could see perfectly well the meeting had turned into a family affair but his professional curiosity made him

The Joshua Inheritance

stay on. Something told him they were less a family and more like three pieces from odd jigsaws.

George Fairfax looked carefully at his son. 'How're you feeling, dear boy?'

Diana gently held one of Edward's hands in hers.

'Better for being here,' said Edward conventionally, not knowing where to begin. He felt overpowered by the sudden appearance of both Diana and his father. They were hemming him in, one on either side of his bed, and embarrassing him with questions and their worried expressions. He knew they were concerned but they irritated him, putting him at a disadvantage on his own ground. He was the one who had been in Palestine nearly a full year, and they were the newcomers. He ached all over and was in no mood to waste time on superficial chit-chat. Bluntly, he asked, 'What's happened about the court martial, Father?'

George Fairfax coughed, glanced at Inspector Maclean, and said, 'It's been dropped.'

Edward waited a moment, hoping his father would go on and explain, but he did not elaborate. Annoyed, he breathed out, 'Why?'

George Fairfax shrugged slightly. 'I don't know, dear boy. I think your mother managed to pull a few strings. Something to do with that smoothie John Fullerton in the Foreign Office. Anyway, they dropped it very suddenly about two weeks ago, about the time you were kidnapped.' George still did not know why. They had had their chance to crucify him for the mistakes of Joshua and for some reason they had let it slip, leaving the case open.

'Thank goodness,' said Edward. He wondered if the little bits of information he had written to his mother had helped.

'Cleared of charges?' Angus Maclean put in quietly. Edward had mentioned the case briefly to him.

'Well, no. Not exactly,' said George Fairfax. The

question was irritating but he hesitated to tell an Inspector of Palestine Police to mind his own business.

Edward looked gratefully at Angus. He would not have thought to ask the question, but it seemed crucial. The blunt approach was having more success getting his father to talk than he could ever remember. He supposed his father was feeling sympathetic, seeing him bruised and bandaged. He gasped, 'Well, what then?'

With obvious reluctance his father said, 'They've suspended the case indefinitely.' He knew it sounded like an admission of guilt, but there was nothing he could do. Crossly, he pre-empted the inevitable question he expected from either his son, whose rudeness he put down to being unwell, or the blunt Scots Inspector, and added, 'They wouldn't give any reasons. Just told me the case was suspended. Then we heard you had been kidnapped and they let me come out here with Diana. We came by plane but I'll have to go back by boat. Not a journey I'm looking forward to. In a month or so.'

'You going back as well?' Edward asked Diana. At least he could see Carole after that.

'No,' she said smiling happily. Idly, she brushed a hand through her hair and explained, 'Daddy's letting me stay at his villa. As long as I like. There are servants and everything. Isn't that sweet of him?'

'Aye, he'll be delighted with that,' said Angus, grinning broadly at Edward, and then excused himself. He shook hands with Edward's father and Diana, and slipped out, leaving the door ajar, promising to keep in touch with Edward.

'How the devil d'you meet him?' George Fairfax asked as Angus's footsteps faded away down the corridor.

Edward replied, 'We learned Arabic together. He's a very competent policeman.'

'I'm sure,' said his father condescendingly. He looked at his wristwatch, pulled a face and put on his hat.

The Joshua Inheritance

He wanted to get away. 'I must get on, dear boy. I'm working with Diana's father while I'm here, and there's masses to do, settling in and so on.'

'You'll be in the King David Hotel?' Edward asked. He did not feel ready to confront his father about what he had heard from the Irgun leader during his kidnap, but he had every intention of doing so when he had recovered. The court martial might have been dropped, temporarily, but the stigma was still attached. To them both. He was damned if he would allow his father to run away from it any longer, even if the case was suspended.

George Fairfax nodded vaguely.

'We're all together. Isn't it splendid?' Diana said happily. She squeezed Edward's hand again, 'Except your mother, of course.'

'Matron tells me you need rest,' George Fairfax told his son, 'but I expect you two want to chat?'

'Oh yes,' said Diana. 'I'm looking forward to hearing all the news.' Edward had written less in recent months and his letters had become more factual, giving away nothing of his feelings. She assumed this was due to his being busy and so far away. That was why she had pestered her father to come out. She smiled. 'I want to hear everything you've been up to.'

Edward gave her a peculiar look which she imagined was another brave effort to control the pain of his injuries. He forced a smile. It seemed the whole world was working against him.

Diana wanted to look after him. She said, 'You can come to the villa while you recuperate. It's a lovely place. Daddy called it a hiring, I think. Isn't that right, Uncle George?'

Edward's father nodded. 'That's it. The Army rents the place from the civilian owners on behalf of the occupant. Your father's done himself proud.' He nearly added that there was nothing unusual about that.

Edward managed to gasp out, 'What's this "Uncle George" business?' He had never thought of his father, a distant, often quite abrasive person, as being Uncle George to anyone.

'Yes. Your father's been really sweet about it. Major Fairfax was so formal, and Major George sounded silly,' Diana explained. She smiled from Edward to his father. It had been Anne's idea and George Fairfax had not really objected, just as long as Diana never poked her nose into his work affairs.

'Yes, dear boy,' he said bluffly. 'It'll be Uncle George until you two decide to get on with it. After all, you've known each other long enough, eh?'

Edward felt dizzy. He said, 'What d'you mean?'

Diana looked earnestly at Edward's bandaged face with her wide blue eyes and said, 'You know, darling. Get engaged and so on?' She gently squeezed her long fingers on his hand and added, 'Well, we're almost there, aren't we? Your letters are so sweet and kind.'

George Fairfax grunted good-humouredly. 'Bloody wedding bells next. Time I went.' He wagged his finger at Diana like a schoolmaster. 'And don't you tire him out, young woman!' He opened the door and backed out, waving goodbye to Edward. Edward heard him bump into someone in the corridor and his gruff voice apologising. A female voice answered. One of the nurses, presumably.

Diana looked at him fondly. She leaned forward towards his bandaged head and delicately found a part of his forehead which was free of crêpe and kissed it. Her lips were incredibly soft, like a breath on his skin and he found her touch rather exciting. The smell of her was cool too, and clean, like the sterile hospital room. But he felt distant. His skin, under the muslin, was caked with blood, his ribs throbbed with pain and he felt hot and unwell. In a detached but lustful way, he watched her breasts moving under her white shirt as she leaned forward over him, and could think of nothing else to say but, 'Thank you.'

'There,' she said, talking as if to a child, and sat down on the bed again. 'I expect you want to hear all about my trip out?' He hardly nodded, feeling suddenly very tired.

'I was bullied unmercifully at Blackbushe by some RAF people called Movements Officers. They said I had too much luggage, and I said they were silly to call themselves Movements Officers when all they wanted to do was stop me leaving. Fortunately, Uncle George turned up in the nick of time, waved a piece of paper at them and we set off in this rackety old crate called a Dakota.'

Forgetting that Edward had parachuted from a Dakota, she told him, 'It's so steep walking up the aisle between the seats! Of course it levelled off in the air but it was terribly noisy. Uncle George fixed our seats at the back because he said the noise is less behind the propellers.' Edward's eyes closed but she was looking at the sky through the window, remembering every detail. 'Oh dear! We had to refuel in Rome, and Athens, and in Cyprus. D'you know that there is a whole division of British soldiers in Athens? Your father says they're staying on to prevent another Communist attempt to seize power.'

She shifted to look at him and the movement woke him up. He nodded soporifically and said, 'We've got troops everywhere.'

'Yes, these poor countries seem to depend on us so much, don't you think? Like Palestine here. They'd all be in such a mess if the British Empire wasn't there to give them an example of the proper way to do things.'

Edward murmured, 'Yes.' He was too sleepy to tell Diana that the men who had kidnapped him took a different view.

Diana realised he needed to sleep. She kissed him

again on the forehead and the touch brought him wide awake. 'I must leave,' she told him and promised, 'I'll come back tomorrow and finish my story.' She walked to the door of the room and blew him a kiss before disappearing. He waved his hand and let it fall back on the sheet. He felt drained. He listened to her neat footsteps fading along the corridor.

As soon as Diana turned the corner out of sight, a young nurse walked briskly up the corridor to Edward's room and banged through the door without knocking.

Instinctively, he turned quickly to see who had come in and gasped through a flood of pain, 'Carole! God, I'm pleased to see you.'

Her anger evaporated seeing his agony. She pulled a tight little smile and said, 'I'm lucky to get in here at all, past Matron. She's busy at the moment with the convoy casualties. I can't spend long.'

Edward complained, 'But you've only just arrived!' He noticed she was rather brusque and asked, 'What's the matter?'

She stood leaning against his bed, as if she were his nurse, not his lover. He took her hand to pull her down and sit on the bed. To his surprise, she refused. 'I was here earlier, when you had those other visitors. Your father bumped into me on his way out.'

'So you met him?'

'Not really. I didn't introduce myself, if that's what you mean.'

'Just as well,' said Edward. He wondered how his father would have reacted to meeting Axel Romm's daughter within a day of arriving in Jerusalem. He would tell him later.

'I thought you'd say that.'

Something dull and bitter in Carole's voice made Edward look at her more closely. 'What d'you mean?'

To Edward's surprise, tears began to fill her eyes. Carole gazed at him, feeling her control slipping and hating the tears. Her emotions were torn. She was furious at what she had heard, and at the same time utterly depressed. She wanted to go on loving him, especially because he was hurt, but she had to know the truth. She wanted to end the torture of suspicion in her mind, but all of a sudden she had no courage to ask the question which might give her the answer she dreaded. She said obliquely, 'You were all talking, when I arrived.'

Edward frowned, trying to understand why she thought the time of her arrival was so important. 'You mean when Angus was here? Or when Father and Diana arrived?'

'Yes, when Diana arrived,' she said bitterly. She pulled away from his hand and walked to the window so that he could not see her tears. She had been furious watching Diana leave. Now she had lost the impetus. He was hurt enough. She felt empty. In half an hour, her world had fallen apart. She wanted him to explain what she had overheard but jealousy and the fear of losing him had sown vicious seeds of suspicion in her mind which appeared all too obvious. She stared miserably at the tall cypress trees in the hospital garden. She said, 'I heard everything. All your plans with your precious Diana.'

Edward forgot all the pain in his chest. 'Carole, darling, I promise it wasn't like that at all.'

'I suppose you want me to believe this Diana's just a friend of the family.' Blurred through her tears, she watched a British Army ambulance driving away from Casualty.

Edward hesitated. Of course the two had never met before. 'She is, actually. We've known each other since we were children.'

'Childhood sweethearts, I guess,' she interrupted, without looking round. 'Getting married in the end.'

'No! Nothing like that!'

'Weren't you sweethearts, then? In England?'

Edward hesitated again, caught between the truth and desperately wanting to explain what had been said that afternoon. He had been as shocked as Carole.

For Carole the hesitation was enough. She turned round, filled with hurt, knowing the tears were coming. 'Then what about all your letters to her? So sweet and kind!' she cried, mimicking Diana's voice. 'You must have been writing to her while we were together in Jerusalem.' She felt sick at the image of Edward sitting down to write to this English girl on the verandah of Angus's little villa which had become so special to her over the last months.

'I wrote nothing. They weren't special, just news,' he pleaded. He felt pain building in his chest, not from his broken ribs, but deeper inside, from the fear that he would lose Carole. His helplessness grew at the thought it was no fault of his own. It was a misunderstanding, and not his words, but the nightmare darkened.

'Not special?' Carole repeated. 'Then how come she turns up here talking of engagement?' She turned her back on him disdainfully.

Edward shook his head, 'No-one's mentioned engagement before, I promise.'

He watched her wipe the wetness on her cheek with the back of her hand and brush a wisp of dark hair back under her nurse's cap. He felt a desperate longing for her. He pushed the bedclothes back, eased his legs out of bed and sat on the edge, his mouth open, trying to take shallows breaths to control the burst of agony in his chest.

'Your father seemed to know all about it,' she said accusingly. She swung round to face him, so cross and full of her own hurt that she refused to be affected by his pathetic efforts to struggle off the bed. She wound herself up into a fury.

'The whole affair must have suited you all very well. You have a nice time with me till your precious Diana

The Joshua Inheritance

comes out here. It doesn't matter because I'm a Yank. I don't count. And then you go back to marry your nice little girl from a nice British family. You forget, I've spent enough time in England to know what you English bastards call "the done thing". Well, I can tell you the goddam thing is well and truly done now.'

Edward managed to find the breath to gasp, 'Carole, please! Stop this!' He wanted to tell her that he loved her precisely because she was so different, so refreshingly different to Diana and all the other British girls he had met, because she was optimistic and positive compared to the stifling restrictions of British life, but he could not draw the air from his aching lungs.

'It's clear to me now! You just wanted to find out what you could from me about my father. All you worried about was your father's goddam court case.' This was particularly galling when she had made up her mind to help him all she could after her last argument with Axel Romm on the patio.

Edward found enough breath to say, 'That's absurd!' Their time together had not been like that. One hand on his side, he tried to push himself off the bed.

Carole shouted, 'Absurd? Well how do you account for my overhearing you talking about your wedding, all three of you? How, for godsakes?'

He stood up and began to walk unsteadily towards her. 'Please, Carole, there's been a terrible mistake.' He wanted to hold her in her arms but she dodged him easily, furious.

'You're damned right there's been a mistake! And I'm not going to make the same goddam mistake again.'

Holding his side with one hand, he reached out with the other. 'Carole, wait, please!'

She ignored him and walked purposefully towards the door. 'Get back into bed,' she snapped. 'You can have your sweet-as-pie Diana come look after you, just like you always planned.'

Edward clutched the windowsill for support, peering after her sideways from under the bandage round his head, his striped pyjamas crumpled and loose.

She pulled open the door and walked out. 'She's all yours,' she said and slammed the door behind her.

14

THE KING DAVID

22 July 1946

Nearly three weeks later, on the morning of Monday 22 July, Paul Levi made sure he was up early, like most others starting a week's work in Jerusalem. He watched his men load heavy milk churns on to the back of Selig's Dodge truck in the garage yard in the new Jewish quarter of Ohel Moshe. The men, dressed in Arab jellabas and dirty-brown jackets, grunted with the strain but there was no milk inside the churns to slop or spill. They were heavy and needed great care because each was stuffed with a mixture of plastic explosive and TNT. The Irgun leadership had given the word to press home the attack on the King David Hotel.

As Selig stood in the back of the truck where he was helping to pull the churns aboard he noticed that Paul seemed unaffected by the tension which loosened his own stomach. He asked, 'Why're you so goddam cheerful?'

Paul's smile broadened momentarily. Every time he thought of what they had to do the adrenalin rushed, and he was in a savagely good mood. The kidnappings had upset the continuity of their observations on the British headquarters and he had thought it best to make some final checks, watching it again. Disguised as a street shoe-polish man, he had sat outside the hotel in Julian's Way and seen the one man he wanted to kill more than any other. Over four days, he had watched Major George Fairfax coming and going into the Hotel from the YMCA opposite. He was certain he was working there, and there could be no better person to blow up with his milk churns. All he said to Selig, however, was, 'We're going to make this explosion carry to every newspaper in the world.'

Selig asked, 'You happy with the link-up of these cans?' He patted one. The sound was dull, quite unlike the pleasing hollow ring it would have given if it had been full of milk.

'Of course!' Paul was fiercely decisive. 'The ring main and initiator are ready.' He pulled aside the folds of his baggy jellaba where a canvas bag hung concealed. 'Nothing can go wrong.' His confidence was reassuring.

Selig reflected that the bag seemed insignificantly small though it was the key to massive destruction.

Paul read his mind. 'Don't worry. There's five hundred pounds of explosive in these seven churns. The blast should reach the roof and there won't be much left in all their filing cabinets on the way.' Which was part of the objective. All the Jewish underground groups, the Haganah, the Irgun and Stern gang, were worried how much information the British had seized in Operation Agatha.

Selig had seen Paul blow up railway lines, and the Iraq–British oil pipeline but this bomb was in a different league. He had none of Paul's training and found such an explosion hard to visualise. He would stick to what he knew: mechanics. He climbed into the cab and started up the engine. Then he jumped out, opened the bonnet and made some last-minute adjustments, listening with a critical ear to the steady growl of the diesel.

Paul watched him. They were almost ready to move. Mentally, he went over the sequence of events in the plan. He hoped the young woman they had picked to telephone the bomb warning would get the timing right.

The Joshua Inheritance

Although the headquarters was virtually unprotected as far as he could tell, but if she gave the warning too early, the British might catch them still laying the bomb.

He checked his watch. 11.05. The hours had flown by that morning while he made the final preparations on the churns. There was something inexorable about time once a decision to attack had been made, relentlessly taking them towards the moment of truth, for the Jews or the British, when time ran out on the fuse. They must leave. The Dodge had to be driving down the ramp to the Regency restaurant in the basement of the hotel at midday precisely. He slipped his watch back into his pocket. Arab workmen did not wear wristwatches.

The other 'Arabs' shoved the last milk churn aboard, all of them conscious of the electric tension between them. Breathing hard, one remarked, 'I hope it'll be easier to get them out.'

Paul grinned, 'You'll hardly notice the weight.' Guards or no guards, the fear of being caught would lend them superhuman strength. A sickening rush of excitement twisted his stomach. He wanted to get on with it. They all did.

No-one smiled at his light-hearted bravado. They climbed into the pick-up, adjusting their Arab headdresses and settling down around the seven churns. They checked their revolvers and Sten guns with deliberate movements of hands and fingers, trying to suppress their feelings, and hid them under their clothes. Everyone was keenly aware they were sitting beside five hundred pounds of high explosive. Their faces were tight with apprehension, like men who had not eaten for days. As Paul nodded the signal to go, there was an audible sigh of relief.

The delapidated wood gates of the yard were opened by one man who was staying behind. Selig gently let the truck slip out of the courtyard into Bezalel Street, into the mainstream of the busy Monday morning traffic in Jerusalem.

'These files are a bloody waste of time,' commented Edward, morosely waving his hand at the pile of papers on Angus Maclean's desk in Police Headquarters, half a mile from the King David Hotel.

'You young whippersnapper! That's no way to talk about the work of His Britannic Majesty's Palestine Police.' Angus shoved his chair back, the chair legs screeching on the wooden floor, and stood up to stretch under the ceiling fan. The end of July was uncomfortably hot. Even wearing summer uniforms of shirt and shorts they were tired after sifting through files on the Jewish underground all morning. He lifted his shirt where it had stuck to his back and let the cooler air filter down his neck.

Edward leaned back on his chair. 'There's nothing here on the Jews. It's all stuff about the Arabs and they aren't our problem just now.'

Angus nodded. It was true. The police had realised the threat from the Jews too late, at the end of the war. He wiped his face with a hankerchief and wished the fan was not so slow. A few sheets on top of the pile of papers fluttered in time with the turning blades.

Edward had spent a couple of weeks recuperating in hospital. Diana had visited him every day, but talk of marriage was the last thing he wanted after his kidnapping. He had stayed in Angus's villa and tried to contact Carole, and failed. He supposed she was hiding behind her father's order not to see him, refusing to take messages or answer his letters. So, after seeing Diana once or twice he went back to the 'Sandpit' in El Bureij, thankful for the simplicity of life there and Aubrey's undemanding good company, and immersed himself in work once again. At Angus's special request, he had come up to Jerusalem to try to identify the kibbutz where he had been held prisoner. The first few hours that morning had not been encouraging.

'If only you had decent photos. I'll never forget their faces.'

The strained expression on Edward's face made Angus realise he had suffered more than just kidnap and a thorough beating. He had suffered the humiliation of capture. His self-confidence was badly damaged and, as biblical as the Jews themselves, he wanted his revenge. Edward had been pinning his hopes on finding out something useful in the police files.

Angus said, 'I'm sorry. We might as well pack it in here. We're getting nowhere. I'll give you a lift to the King David.'

They walked out of the spacious colonial-style police headquarters along passages lined with office doors, down broad wooden stairs into the sunlit courtyard at the back and climbed into a police Land-Rover. Angus drove past the police guard at the gate into the Jaffa Road through a narrow channel left in the maze of barbed wire which was laid from pavement to pavement across the streets outside. The area included the police HQ, the central prison and the post office, and was called the Russian compound, after a Russian Orthodox church in the centre; but after endless attacks on the police by the Irgun, its new nickname was 'Bevingrad'.

They cleared the coils of wire and turned left into Princess Mary Avenue past the big cemetery on Mamillah Road. Angus said cheerfully, 'At least we've got Paul Levi's name from my contacts in London.'

Edward nodded. Angus had not been impressed when Edward said Colonel Haike was unable to find the files on his father's operation, and had used unofficial contacts among friends of his in Special Branch in London. From what Paul had told Edward in the cell, Special Branch files on foreign nationals had identified the names and identities of the foreign members of the team. The signal from London revealed that Paul Levi was a Pole and the third man on the operation, and confirmed what Carole had said, that Axel Romm was attached from the OSS. Special Branch knew nothing about the operation itself but had added that the name was Operation Joshua.

'Joshua's an odd name for an operation, don't you think?' Angus said.

'Why?' Edward shrugged. He was used to the Army's bizarre and often childish choice of names.

'Maybe not, then,' said Angus allowing the point. 'Just thought it sounded rather Old Testament, that's all.'

The Land-Rover crossed Mamillah Road into Julian's Way, looping round a wobbling donkey and cart with a very old man sitting on the worn boards. Ahead the vast stone bulk of the King David Hotel and the YMCA tower behind it loomed above the surrounding houses. 'I'd be willing to bet Levi was the demolition man on that operation.' He glanced across at Edward who looked puzzled and he explained, 'Those sort of covert operations behind German lines had three key men. The leader, who was your father, a signals man, and a demolitions man. It's pure guesswork but if, say, Romm was signals, that makes Levi the dems man. It would make him very useful to the Irgun.'

'And account for his comment about another big operation.'

Angus nodded grimly. 'Ironic that we trained him.'

'That's what Colonel Haike said.'

'He may be right. There were several dozen Jews, trained in Palestine in covert anti-Nazi groups, working in Jerusalem and elsewhere, and thirty-two worked in Germany for SOE. Another 32,000 Jews fought in the British Army during the war. No doubt a good percentage are now putting their training to use against us.'

'What's SOE?'

The Joshua Inheritance

Angus wondered if he should answer. Strictly according to regulations, he should not have allowed Edward to see the police files. Edward was not security cleared, but his interest was no mere curiosity. He had a genuine desire to clear his father's name.

Angus said, 'SOE was the Special Operations Executive. It organised clandestine operations in countries occupied by the Nazis. Your father was the commander of one of the last of their "Jedburgh" ops. They were closed down last January.'

'Colonel Haike called it MO-1(SP).'

'That's the SOE cover title used in the War Office.'

They reached the King David and Angus turned the Land-Rover down the ramp to the main headquarters entrance at the back, adding thoughtfully, 'I'm surprised Haike didn't know more about the operation.'

'Why?'

'He was in intelligence in London. I think he was actually involved in MO-1(SP) work. He should know.'

Edward considered. If what Angus had said was correct, Colonel Haike had not been telling the whole truth. Was that because Edward was a junior officer who was not supposed to know, or because Colonel Haike had something to hide? His depression increased. It was difficult enough finding a way through the secrecy surrounding his father's operation without supposing that Diana's father was deliberately trying to fob him off. Briefly he thought going straight to Colonel Haike and confronting him. Then he ruled it out. He was more interested in seeing his father. They had not had a chance to talk properly and he had arranged to meet him that morning in the King David where Colonel Haike had given him a temporary office on the same floor.

The Land-Rover drew up at the entrance. Two Military Policemen stamped their gleaming boots to attention and saluted the two officers. With their eyes almost hidden beneath the peaks of their red-cap hats, wearing crisply ironed shirts and shorts, and armed with revolvers tucked away in spotless white holsters, they were the image of British colonial authority.

Edward stepped out and Angus waved goodbye, promising to keep in touch if he heard anything. His professional instinct told him that the extra dimension of Major George Fairfax's wartime operation might give him the lead he needed to find the Irgun terrorists who had kidnapped Edward. He drove off and cut round to the front of the hotel, past the Regency café and restaurant on the ground floor under the headquarters in the south wing of the hotel. As he passed the unguarded restaurant entrance an old flat-bed truck, loaded with milk churns and Arab workmen, trundled down the slope. Angus paid it no attention. The restaurant was closed at that time of morning, taking deliveries and preparing the tables for lunch. There was nothing untoward about the flat-bed delivering milk. Besides, his mind was busy on the next step of his investigations. He accelerated up the ramp to Julian's Way, parked, and walked along the curving drive to the hotel's main entrance. Inside, in the bar, Carole Romm was waiting to see him.

In the large office at the end of the hotel on the fourth floor, the girls in the Intelligence typing pool surreptitiously watched Colonel Haike's office door and tried to hear what was going on inside. Edward walked in.

'Edward! Good to see you back,' said Liz Warren.

'Your father's with the Colonel. Bit of a barney, I'm afraid.' She frowned. Colonel Haike had become increasingly critical of late, and she did not approve of officers losing their tempers in front of the typing staff who worked damned hard. However, life must have its order. She snapped at the nearest girl and the buzz of typewriters picked up again.

They could hear raised voices. The sharper tone of

The Joshua Inheritance

Colonel Haike's voice was cut off by the gruff tones of Edward's father; the heavy wooden door of the office banged open and George Fairfax stormed out, his face suffused with colour. He spotted Edward at once and snapped, 'Come with me!'

Edward gave Liz a look of surprise and followed. She smiled encouragingly at him and turned back to the typists. With the faintest expression of female complicity, witnesses to another example of male aggression, she let an unmistakeable note of authority into her voice. 'Right girls. The show's over. Back to work.'

Edward followed his father to the office he had been given at the back of the headquarters wing. The room was small, but had a magnificent view over the Old City. His father was furious. He stamped over to the window and stared aggressively at the ancient city walls shimmering in the heat a mile away and the hypnotic focus of attention of the golden Dome of the Rock.

'I want to stay on here,' he announced. 'But that stupid bigot Haike won't agree.'

Edward was too surprised to speak and his father went on, 'In the short time I've been working in this department, it's plain as a pikestaff there are various things people with my experience can do about all this terrorism.'

'You mean your war experience?'

His father threw him a curious look from the window and Edward sensed his opportunity. 'Your work in SOE?'

'Who the hell told you about that?' Major Fairfax's tone was very much the field officer ticking off a junior subaltern.

Edward always felt a slight sense of panic when his father was cross, as if he had been caught stealing apples. Now he was acutely conscious of treading on dangerous ground. He was trespassing on official secrets to which he had no right, risking Angus Maclean's confidence let alone making trouble for himself with Colonel Haike. He switched tack and said bluntly, 'Axel Romm told me.'

His father stared at him for a long moment. Then he said very quietly, 'What's this about Axel Romm?'

Edward frowned. He had assumed his father would have heard about Axel Romm being in Jerusalem from Colonel Haike. He put Angus's guesswork to the test. 'He was on your operation, wasn't he? Your radio operator?'

'Romm's here in Jerusalem?' So that was how Anne had heard of him. In letters from Edward.

Edward nodded and before he could stop himself, he told his father everything he had found out about the operation from Axel Romm and Paul Levi. He had to confide in someone. He justified his confession by supposing that once his father saw how much he knew, he would open up with the rest.

His father did not. After a moment he merely said, 'Levi, I can understand. I suppose he belongs here, but Romm in Jerusalem is all we need.'

'What d'you mean?'

George Fairfax hesitated but Romm was American, on the other side now. 'After working together in the war, we would normally expect excellent co-operation with the Yanks, person to person, whatever their politicians ordered them to do. Not so with Romm. The Washington administration is anti-British enough without that bastard working here. He's a pettifogging little shit who tells tales in school.'

Edward hazarded a guess. 'That report he wrote about you is all wrong, isn't it?'

His father looked up sharply. He wondered how Edward had found out so much when the system tried to be so careful about its secrets, but he ignored the question and asked, 'Did Levi mention any others who'd survived?'

The Joshua Inheritance

Edward shook his head. 'All the rest were killed in the plane.'

George Fairfax exhaled a long breath. 'So that's it then,' he said and sat down heavily behind his desk. His long search around the camps after the German surrender had been pointless, and being away for so long had merely sealed Romm's accusations against him. He shrugged. 'You seem to know the whole sorry tale. There's no more to find out.'

'But why did it go wrong?' Edward exclaimed. His father could not just give up. To his amazement, his father seemed to deflate inside his uniform and said, 'I don't know, dear boy. Forget it. It was just something that happened in the war. You weren't in it and it's nothing to do with you.'

Edward retorted with feeling. 'I'm fed up with being reminded I wasn't in the bloody war, and don't tell me I'm not affected. I'm convinced Paul Levi kidnapped me because of Operation Joshua!'

'Why?' his father asked in a tired voice, surprised Edward had even got Levi's name right.

It was Edward's turn to be dismissive. Briefly, he told his father about the boy in the riot. 'He wants revenge. On me now as well as you. In his mind, we're linked.' He added bitterly, 'I had plenty of time in that bloody cell to think about what he told me.'

George Fairfax grunted, 'How typical of the young! You're convinced, Levi is convinced, but I spent longer than you sitting in a cell, a Gestapo cell, trying to work out what went wrong. I was in the bloody cell when that plane landed and I still don't understand.' He waved a hand vaguely and let it flop back on the desk. The feeling of guilt which had haunted him and driven him searching through the camps came flooding back. He could not shake off the suspicion that he had drawn the SD on to them by his own carelessness. He sighed and closed his mind against it. It was the only way. The loss of all those men was too much to dwell on. Almost in a whisper he said to Edward, 'I just don't know how the Germans could have known where the plane was coming in. It wasn't possible.'

Edward had never seen his father so deflated and he hated it. He leaned forward on the desk and asked quietly, 'Maybe it would help to go over what happened again?'

For George Fairfax, this was the very last question Edward should have asked. Everyone had asked it. Endlessly, the SD officer had come back to his cell in Strasbourg asking it, the British debriefing officers in London had asked it over and over again, and every night he tortured himself asking it. No-one had provided the answer he so desperately wanted to hear – that the disaster was not his fault. He had had enough. The court martial was in abeyance and his mind was closed to the whole thing. He stood up without a word, turned round and looked out of the window again, his broad back a statement of obstinate silence.

Edward could not believe it. He waited, staring at the back of his father's dark head. His sympathy evaporated and finally, when his father still said nothing, he lost his temper. He slammed his fist on to the desk between them and shouted, 'I need to know. I don't want any more flannel about the bloody Official Secrets Act. I want to find that bastard Levi before he finds me!'

He took a deep breath and stopped. He suddenly felt terribly empty. He had come looking for his father's support. He also thought he could help. He wanted to clear his father's name. And his. Instead they had argued. Everyone seemed ranged against him. His father had rebuffed him, Colonel Haike had spun him along with bland assurances and a pretence of ignorance, neither Paul Levi nor Axel Romm could be trusted, and Carole had left him. His father confirmed that Edward had more or less found out what had happened, but Edward

The Joshua Inheritance

wanted to know how the Germans had broken into the operation. His father refused to say and underneath all Edward's frustration lurked the nasty suspicion that his father's guilt might be the answer.

Thoroughly confused he grabbed his beret off the desk and turned to go. He yanked open the door.

His father looked over his shoulder and said blandly, 'You going, dear boy?'

'Yes,' Edward snapped. 'I'm going downstairs, to the hotel bar, for a drink.'

George Fairfax said, 'Look out for Diana. I thought it would be nice to ask her for lunch with us today.'

Edward stopped in the doorway. He was not sure whether to be pleased or angry. Diana was attractive and good fun, but he was still furious about the conversation in the hospital which had made Carole walk out. 'What makes you think I want to see her? I might be seeing someone else.'

His father cheered up. 'Found a dusky number, eh? Splendid show. Good for the loins, but don't for God's sake get serious, dear boy. Diana's a beautiful girl. Charming. I know she can be a bit sticky, like her hatchet-faced father, but she knows what she wants. She'd make a first-class general's wife.'

Edward was speechless. He looked at his father a moment, then left, slamming the door. He went down the broad stairs in the centre of the south wing to the bar.

In the basement beneath them, Paul Levi pulled the tangle of detonating cord from the dirty old bag under his jellaba and began to connect it to the seven milk churns stacked around the pillars in the centre of the Regency restaurant. These big structural columns supported the entire building above his head. His heart raced. In cool argument he could justify his actions, with theories of anti-British imperialism and the right for his people's self-determination, but in practice the rush of excitement through his veins was pure anarchy, and he loved it.

The others in the team were nervously keeping watch. Two were hidden in the darkness of the restaurant entrance staring at the sunbaked approach ramp outside, and two more were in the passage which led through the basement to the hotel itself, past the Ladies' and Gentlemen's lavatories and the hotel's hairdressers. The Arab waiters and kitchen staff, who had at first protested loudly at the excess delivery of milk, were in the kitchens, cowed into terrified silence by a .45 Thompson SMG held with grim purpose by another of the team.

Paul was nearly finished when he heard a commotion in the passage. Distinctly, he heard an English voice an officer's shouting at one of his 'Arabs', 'I say! You bloody Arab wog, what the devil d'you think you're doing?'

In the bar Angus had had no success with Carole. She was convinced that Edward was behind their meeting and was reluctant to answer any of Angus's questions. When Angus asked her to describe the kidnapping in the Astoria all over again, she lost her patience, stood up and refused point blank. Then she walked out. Angus watched her go, cross at the way he had mishandled the interview. He realised he should have taken more account of her affair with Edward.

A voice behind made him twist round. 'I thought you were supposed to be working?' Edward had come in the side door and Angus hoped he had not seen Carole. He did not want the blame for another row. He said offhandedly, 'My meeting was rather shorter than it should have been. Anyway, I didn't expect you down here so soon.'

Edward started to explain about the argument with his father but Angus interrupted with 'Did you hear those shots?'

The Joshua Inheritance

Edward shook his head, absorbed with his own problems. 'Probably some damned jallopy back-firing,' he muttered and ordered two large pink gins from the waiter.

Angus allowed himself to be persuaded, and was left with a distinct feeling of unease.

Paul Levi decided he dare not chase after the British officer. Paul's guards had ordered him to join the Arab staff in the kitchens, but he refused. In the ensuing fight, one of the guards shot him in the stomach but somehow he had managed to stagger down the passage. He might raise the alarm any second.

Paul swore at the two guards and ran back to the dining-room, to the milk churns. He had connected them with a trail of detonating cord which ran across the white-clothed tables like a vast spider's web from pillar to pillar. Selig put his head round the door and shouted that another British officer, a lieutenant, had looked into the passage through a narrow grille in the wall of the Regency passage but vanished as soon as he saw two of the 'Arabs' in blue and white jellabas with SMGs.

Paul waved him away. He had to make sure the ring-main circuit was right. There would be no second chance. He absorbed himself in his hands and fingers, working as fast as he could, clipping each churn to the detonating cord and, when he had finished, checking the whole circuit again. He connected the initiator timing device, then shouted for everyone to withdraw.

In the same instant there was a din of shooting in the corridor. One of the team shouted in Hebrew that he was under attack by the British Military Police. Selig shouted at him to pull back.

'Let the Arabs in the kitchens go,' Paul shouted. Their hostages needed no second warning. They left the front door of the restaurant like greyhounds released from the trap and making as much noise. Paul pulled the final pin which started the timer. He glanced round the empty dining-room at the churns and detonating cord, at the beautifully laid tables waiting for guests who would never come. Then he ran outside to catch up with Selig.

'Where the hell is the diversionary bomb?' Paul shouted to Selig as they ran out of the Regency entrance. 'We want the goddam thing now!'

In the blazing sun outside Paul saw they could not use the Dodge truck. Faces were peering down at them from the balustrade overlooking the restaurant and puzzled soldiers, acting on their own initiative, were unslinging their Sten SMGs. Sporadic shots began to snap round their heads. 'The truck is too slow,' Paul shouted. 'Make for the taxi!' The seven ran round the corner of the south end of the hotel to the second option for their getaway, a black six-seater Plymouth taxi stolen from Tel Aviv which was parked on the north-eastern side of the hotel, on the road running past the French Consulate.

At the same time, a dark-haired girl in the Irgun slipped into a telephone box to make the warning calls, first to the hotel's own telephone exchange, then to the French Consulate and lastly to the offices of the *Palestine Post*.

Carole was almost at the French Consulate when she heard the shooting. She stopped at once and moved uncertainly into a doorway. In moments she saw half a dozen Arabs in jellabas, some with head-dresses, run round the end of the hotel and sprint madly across the open ground towards her. Soldiers behind them fired their Stens. The bullets cracked overhead and ricocheted off the walls near the Consulate. Terrified, she pressed herself into the doorway. The Arabs had almost reached the road when one staggered and fell to his knees. As the others passed him, he seemed to recover and ran on.

She peered along the wall of the building and saw

The Joshua Inheritance

their objective. An Arab was waiting in a big black taxi parked beyond the Consulate, with the doors open, and he was shouting and waving his arms for them to hurry. She recognised the language. Hebrew. They were Jews. Fearfully she looked back towards the King David Hotel.

Paul Levi cursed and struggled as he pulled Selig the last few yards across the road and shoved him into the taxi. The six others inside pulled him in.

'Go, go!' Paul shouted at the driver and flung himself through the back door. The car lurched forward and gathered speed. They could all hear bullets thumping through the air around them and plucking at the metal bodywork.

'Eight men is against British taxi regulation,' Selig gasped, grimacing with pain. Paul could see he was badly hit, in the stomach and chest and he was bleeding heavily. They had no dressings so he stuffed his own sweaty shemag in the wounds. He worked desperately. Selig had come too far from Europe to die in a dirty old taxi.

They heard an explosion from the other side of the hotel. The diversionary bomb, concealed in an Arab hawker's barrow at the south end of the hotel, destroyed Homsi Salameh's car showroom and lashed pedestrians and a passing Number Four bus with vicious shards of glass.

'Typical!' Paul shouted, feeling the shemag growing soggy under his bloody hands. The taxi was out of danger but he shouted, 'Goddamed diversion was too late'. Too late to save Selig.

The driver swung round under the Old City walls away from Bevingrad and the Police HQ and asked hoarsely, 'When will the churns go off?'

'Soon,' Paul muttered glancing back at the hotel which he could still see over the rooftops. 'Soon.'

At the hotel main entrance, Diana Haike stepped out of her father's staff car wearing a cotton dress in bold pastel flower patterns and walked elegantly towards the big entrance doors. As the explosion went off in the street, she felt the blast push at her back and propel her inside. She was surprised she was not more frightened.

More excited than afraid, Diana walked back outside and looked across the balustrade down the street. More than a dozen Arabs and others were screaming with shock, their faces and long white jellabas covered in blood. One or two were lying on the ground. She glanced up at the windows of the hotel and saw a lot of faces looking down from the headquarters and Secretariat offices. She fancied she saw her father, and Edward's father, and waved, but they were looking the other way, at the damage caused by the bomb.

As soldiers began running to help the injured and bring them up the road towards the hotel, the wartime air-raid sirens, triggered by the sound of the bomb, began to wail all over the city. The mournful noise droned on in the background, rising and falling like some awful toneless requiem.

A Military Policeman joined Diana and began to herd people back inside the hotel, talking in a deep reassuring bass voice. 'Come along now, ladies and gentlemen! You'll be safer inside while we clear the street. It's all under control. The bomb chappies are on their way.'

Diana allowed herself to be ushered inside the lobby and immediately found Edward who was trying to get outside.

'Diana! Are you alright?'

Thrilled by the blatant concern in his blue eyes, she reached up and give him a kiss on his cheek, her lips hot with the excitement. He looked so smart in his pressed shirt and khaki shorts. She smiled bravely. 'Of course. It was only a little explosion, but I must go and tidy up downstairs.'

She slipped off down the marble stairs to the Ladies' powder room in the basement and Edward went back into the bar. Angus had disappeared. Edward guessed he was doing something about the bomb or seeing Liz Warren upstairs. He wandered over to the window. The sunlight was blinding outside, turning buildings and the street alike to a white glare. The tall cypresses beyond the balustrade on the street were motionless in the heat. All traffic had stopped and only the Army medics moved about among the injured. Inside the bar under the cool fans, the scene appeared remote. Even the wailing siren was muted.

Diana came back into the bar at a fast walk, trying hard to control her panic. She grabbed Edward's arm and whispered, 'There's a man in the powder room! In the basement.'

Edward smiled. 'Whatever next?'

Diana held her voice to a low whisper and hissed, 'For God's sake, he's wounded! Unconscious. Blood all over the place!'

Edward stared and pulled her away so the barman could not overhear. 'Explain,' he said bluntly and she told him the man was lying on the floor of the Ladies', naked from the waist up and there was blood all over his stomach. He was an officer, and a sergeant in the Military Police was looking after him. 'He ordered one of the hotel porters to take me to the Men's room instead, but, Edward, the last thing I wanted to do at that point was to powder my nose. What the hell's going on?'

'I don't know,' said Edward hiding his surprise at her unusually direct language. 'I'll try to find Angus Maclean.' He led her by the hand from the bar into the hall which was crowded with people injured outside. Army medics were patching up the bloodiest victims and other soldiers appeared with white enamel mugs of tea. He found an internal telephone and dialled Liz Warren's extension in the Intelligence department.

A girl in the exchange came on the line and said

something about Arabs running amok in the Regency restaurant and then cut him off.

Cross, he dialled again. This time he got through to the typing pool and asked for Lieutenant Warren. Liz answered. Speaking quickly and cupping his hand over the mouthpiece to cut out the din of the crowd in the hall, Edward asked for Angus. He came straight on the line. Edward told him about the wounded officer in the basement and Angus Maclean said at once, 'I'm coming down.'

Diana looked round at the injured people crying and moaning in the lobby and announced, 'I'm going to help out here while you see Angus.' Without further ado, she dropped her handbag in a corner, tucked her blonde hair in a twist at the back of her neck and knelt down to comfort a fat Arab lady who had been badly cut by glass splinters.

Angus Maclean came down the stairs three at a time. He told Edward that another senior Palestine policeman, Richard Catling, was in the hotel and that police were searching the area for other devices.

'So why was this officer shot downstairs?' Edward insisted.

'I don't know,' Angus said, his dark eyebrows drawing together in a deep frown. 'We've already found another bomb in another barrow at the other end of the hotel. It's being defused by the explosives chaps. Maybe the attackers were using the low ground round the Regency restaurant as a cover for laying the barrow bomb and shot that poor devil when he came through the restaurant behind them?'

Edward was about to speak when the air-raid siren wailed a different tuneless note signifying the all-clear. They relaxed. The emergency seemed to be over. He checked his watch at half-past twelve.

Suddenly, a frantic group of Arab kitchen staff appeared in the lobby all jabbering at once. Angus

The Joshua Inheritance

tried to calm them, waving his arms for silence and he and Edward tried to understand what they were saying.

'Not Arabs,' shouted one waiter, gesticulating wildly. 'Not Arabs! Jews! With guns!' His hands flashed through a frantic mime of shooting which seemed tragically childish when he added that the Regency was filled with milk churns and cards in three languages which read, 'Mines, do not touch!'

Edward and Angus both recognised the awful truth at the same instant. All the people in the Secretariat and headquarters were busy back at work after the earlier alert, dozens of them on the floors directly above the restaurant, staff officers, civil servants, colonial staff and secretaries. Diana's father, Edward's father, Liz Warren.

'I'll go up,' Maclean shouted and started along the passage for the stairs.

For a second Edward hesitated, looking round for Diana. She stared at him from the other side of the lobby trying to read his expression, not having understood a word of the Arabic. There was no time to explain. He had to warn his father. He turned to follow Angus.

A deafening roar stopped everything in the hotel. The marble slabs in the lobby rippled, sending jets of dust from the cracks between, and a solid wall of air tossed Edward down the corridor in a dense cloud of sooty black plaster and pieces of brick. He lay motionless in the darkness while the terrifying noise of rending stone and concrete battered his ears, built up to a deep crescendo of noise and finally died away as the trembling hotel settled and came to rest. In the silence, in the dust and smoke billowing up the passage from the stairs, in the patter of falling debris, people began to scream.

In the black Plymouth they cheered. The blast was deafening even at that distance. Everyone in Jerusalem heard the sound and turned to watch the huge black pall of smoke rising over the big hotel which could be seen all over the city. The Irgun had triumphed. Paul's team managed to thump him on the back in congratulation and he smiled. This was a real bomb, one that would be talked about all over the world and set alight the fight for Eretz Israel. He looked down at Selig beside him, but he had not heard the explosion. He was dead.

Edward slowly recovered his wits, lying on his back on the floor, covered with dust. Painfully, he raised his head. Dimly, he could see figures through the smoke filling the hall. People were beginning to get up, enshrouded in black dust like zombies in a haunted churchyard, and crunch across the rubble which covered the floor to help others. He stirred, amazed to find he had nothing broken, wiped some dust off his face and dragged himself dazedly to his feet. He must find Diana.

He passed the side door to the bar. The room was wrecked. The glass shelves had vanished, slivers of mirrored glass glittered everywhere and the floor was covered with fragments of bottles, smashed tables and chairs. One woman was sitting on the floor covered in dust, staring at the blood pumping from her arm and screaming. An officer, himself bleeding from cuts on his face, knelt to help.

Edward stumbled across the murk in the lobby, checking everyone, some lying motionless, some beginning to sit and help each other to stand, some mute with shock, others screaming hysterically. Others injured outside were streaming in through the main entrance over a pile of broken glass, while frantic-looking Army medics and soldiers, called to deal with the earlier explosion, were arriving to find an underworld of screaming, bloodied victims of the far greater outrage.

Someone grabbed his arm, pulled him round and Diana fell into his arms. She was sobbing and clutched him tight, tears streaking her cheeks, her fair hair matted

The Joshua Inheritance

with dirt. He closed his eyes, unable to think clearly, just terribly relieved she had survived, and they clung to each other, not thinking at all but soaking up the comfort of each other's vital warmth.

He began to gather his thoughts. He had to leave Diana somewhere safe and find his father. And Angus, and the others. He pulled her away, saying, 'Let's get outside, find some fresh air.' The acrid plaster dust hanging in the lobby caught his throat and stung his eyes.

Diana nodded and allowed Edward to lead her outside. In the doorway, they fell against the wall as two grim-faced soldiers ran inside with a stretcher. They shoved out through the broken glass doors into the heat of midday and staggered to the left, to rest on the balustrade along the drive.

At first Edward could see very little. A billowing black cloud of dust hung over the street and hotel obscuring the blue sky and the solid shape of the building. Then a mocking breeze wafted up the street and revealed the devastation in glimpses through the reeking cloud. Edward was aghast. The whole south-west corner had vanished. Six floors had been chopped out of the hotel like a huge slice of cake, and had collapsed on to the Regency restaurant below in a mountain of rubble which spilled out over the car park. The stairs between the two south wings hung like tired banana leaves pinned diagonally up the surviving wall. Above them, a section of the flat roof was hinged from the top of the wall, flapping in the eddying smoke. Twenty-eight rooms full of people, desks and filing cabinets, were crushed beneath the chunks of stone and masonry.

The wail of ambulances and shouts of nurses and medics mingled with the screams of the wounded. Edward dragged his eyes away from the destruction and took Diana to a medic who led her away to an ambulance. He had to find his father. He looked over the balustrade again, unbelieving. Already soldiers were beginning to scrabble in the wreckage for survivors. He stared at the shattered stairs and realised he had only escaped running into the epicentre of the explosion by a fraction of time. His legs began to shake with the shock.

Then he spotted Angus Maclean climbing up the pile of rubble, stumbling and stopping at every step to tear desperately at the lumps of concrete with his hands. Edward's ears were still ringing from the blast but he could see Angus shouting, his mouth working open and shut as he peered in the dark crevices between the broken blocks of stone and brick. He did not need to hear the name. Liz Warren's office had been directly above the bomb. With all the girls in the typing pool. He thought of Colonel Haike beside her, and his father. God, he hoped he was still in his office on the other side.

Trembling violently, he went back inside the hotel.

15

NO FLOWERS

27 July 1946

'I am the resurrection and the life,' intoned the chaplain as six soldiers marched slowly into the cemetery of the English church carrying a coffin draped with the Union Jack, their arms linked, sweating in the July heat, like some huge multi-coloured insect with twelve khaki legs. A wreath, wilting in the mid-morning sun, lay with the dead man's peaked hat on the flag.

Edward walked behind wearing his service dress uniform, red beret, polished Sam Browne belt and brown shoes. He could feel the sweat beginning to trickle under his arms. The sun beat down on the mass of white gravestones and great dusty-blue eucalyptus trees stood round the walls lolling their heads in the heat. The chirping sound of cicadas hidden in the spiky weeds sprouting from the path mocked the solemnity of the occasion.

'He that believeth in me,' droned the chaplain, in black stole and white surplice, as he walked along the path ahead of the small cortège, 'though he were dead, yet shall he live.'

To Edward, it seemed a travesty of fortune that his father was dead, that he had been in Colonel Haike's department and not safely in his own office on the other side of the hotel. Colonel Haike was walking just behind him, his brown face still pale from his astonishment that the simple urge to leave his office and relieve himself in the lavatory had saved him from plunging to his death under tons of masonry along with his friends, his secretary, and all the girls in his typing pool.

Diana Haike walked by her father holding his arm, wearing a jet-black cotton dress, a black silk hat tilted stylishly on her blonde hair and long black gloves. From time to time she smiled at Edward, to make him feel better, her blue eyes glittering behind the veil hanging from her hat and she clutched a startling-white handkerchief in her gloved hands.

Edward smiled back. He was pleased she was there. She seemed to represent home, in England, and his mother who could not be there. He turned to the only other two, Angus Maclean and Aubrey Hall-Drake, who walked slowly along beside him also in their smartest uniforms, and whispered, 'Not many bothered to come.'

'I suppose people have had their fill of funerals this week,' replied Angus in an empty voice. They had all helped him through Liz Warren's funeral the day before, which had been well attended. She had been lively and popular with everyone and Angus was distraught without her. A great many others had suffered too, and by no means only the British. Arabs and Jewish civilians were among the 91 dead and 110 injured in hospital.

Edward shook his head, his face grim. 'No, talk about that bloody court martial has kept them away.'

'I say, I don't think that's true really,' said Aubrey in a helpful tone. He had come up to Jerusalem to help Edward with the funeral and noticed at once that Edward was seriously depressed. His boyishness had gone, his face was thinner, brown and hard. The loss of his father was a terrible shock, especially after seeing him last in a furious argument, and it came so soon after the humiliation of his kidnapping. Edward had by no means lost his sense of humour, but in the previous

The Joshua Inheritance

four weeks he had come to see the world through different eyes.

Edward grunted cynically. 'Disgrace has a nasty smell. Captain Scarland down in El Bureij can talk of nothing else.'

'Only because that toady Roger Haike keeps him briefed.'

Edward agreed. Aubrey was right to blame Roger. But what concerned him more was that Roger could only have heard about George Fairfax from his father.

The chaplain stopped at the empty grave. With precise and well-practised military movements, the carrying party put the coffin down on wooden struts which crossed the mouth of the grave, they removed the flag and hat, took the strain on the ropes, slid out the pieces of wood and began to lower the box into the ground. The chaplain looked round at the little group, to check they were all paying attention, and read from his worn leather prayer book: 'Man that is born of woman hath but a short time to live and is full of misery.'

How appropriate, thought Edward, staring at the top of his father's casket as it disappeared out of the blazing sun into the shadows of the dry yellow earth. Palestine was full of misery. Nothing had gone right since he arrived, neither in a personal way, nor, it seemed, for the British as a whole. That week, the Americans and British had been on the brink of making an agreement to let in all the one hundred thousand Jewish refugees from camps in Europe and to partition the country between Arabs and Jews. Then the plan was leaked and the Jewish Agency utterly rejected it. The Jewish leaders objected to the proposed land allocation, which was certainly not large but contained most of the best citrus-growing land, including scope for expansion, and gave them the only Mediterranean deep-water port. They called it a ghetto. The Arabs were two-thirds of the population and had to give up their land to the Jewish one-third, but, whatever they felt about that and the chance of peace, President Truman dropped the plan, to appease Jewish pressure groups in the United States. The attempt to find a solution in Palestine was back to square one, and the British Army back to controlling the increasing violence.

The chaplain moved with efficient speed through the service. He said, 'We therefore commit his body to the ground, earth to earth, dust to dust.' He threw a handful of earth on the coffin, inviting Edward to do the same.

Edward refused. It seemed such a stupid gesture, meaningless when the gravediggers were about to shovel in clodfuls to fill up the hole, and symbolic of godless pre-Christian animism. What significance was there in a few granules of dust? The chaplain looked rather shocked, but Edward shook his head again and straightened his back. There was nothing dustlike about his father's body inside that coffin. He had been obliged to identify it in the morgue. The sight would stay with him for a long time. His father had been badly crushed and his body horribly bloated after lying in the rubble for two days in the heat before the search teams found him. The only satisfaction, if it could be called that, was that he had obviously died at once. His injuries showed no sign of bruising.

The chaplain hurried through the rest of the service and Edward thanked him formally afterwards. He knew the poor man had been exceptionally busy. The corporal in charge of the bearers marched up to Edward, punched his heels to attention and handed over his father's hat. Edward took the hat and noticed the familiar sweat stains on the leather band inside which he remembered so well when he had played with the hat as a boy. Distantly, he saluted and watched the corporal march the other bearers away down the path to the cemetery gates.

'Tragic, tragic,' muttered Colonel Haike distantly as he excused himself. He allowed Diana to lead him after the

The Joshua Inheritance

bearer party to his staff car which was waiting outside in the road, its black metal gleaming in the sun. They all followed them out of the cemetery gates and stood in the dusty road outside.

'Not as tragic as it should have been,' said Angus bitterly as they watched the big car accelerate up the street, stirring whirls of pale dust in the gutter.

'What d'you mean?' Aubrey asked, surprised. He pulled out his silver cigarette case and offered it round. Angus refused, but Edward decided he needed one.

'You'd have thought a disaster like this would at least bring public support our way but not a bit of it,' Angus complained watching them light up. 'General Barker's vitriolic letter about retaliation by hitting the Jews in their pockets where it hurts them most has the whole world complaining about us, not about the bastards who blew us up.' The General had pardoned the two Irgun fighters in Acre jail – which saved Edward's life – but he was so incensed by the devastation of the bombing that he immediately stormed back to his office and wrote a furious letter. His remarks linking the entire Jewish population with the attackers infuriated even those Jews who, like people everywhere just after the war, thoroughly disapproved of terrorism. It was foolish to have put pen to paper in the heat of the moment; but disastrous when it was leaked at once to the newspapers.

Edward took a long heady pull on the sweet Turkish cigarette as Aubrey put in, 'We've got to do something about the situation. Can't let these buggers get away with everything, eh?'

Angus snorted agreement but he said, 'Our intelligence was bad enough before, but that bomb has really screwed us up. It destroyed all the files in the secure registries in the headquarters.' He had heard that MI6 had lost everything they had on the underground movements.

There was a silence for a moment while Edward and

Aubrey digested this extraordinary bad news. Crickets burred in the dusty grass along the bottom of the cemetery wall and a car passed on the street. Aubrey exhaled clouds of smoke from his Turkish cigarette. Then Edward dropped his cigarette, stamped it out and turned to Angus with his face set hard. He said, 'I want to do something to right the balance. I don't care what it is. Anything. I've had enough of being on the receiving end.' He wanted to find Paul Levi, the demolitionist. He had a score to settle.

Angus gave him a sharp look. 'Anything?'

'Don't be such a bloody policeman,' Edward snapped, thinking Angus disapproved of taking the law into his own hands.

Angus shook his head, looking directly at Edward. 'I'm not. I assure you. You're not the only one who's wants to fight back.'

'Damn right,' said Aubrey and breathed out another cloud of tobacco smoke.

Edward noticed Angus looking very directly at him and suddenly the idea that there might be some way of fighting back filled him with a burst of hope, like a warming ray of sunshine through dark rain clouds. 'I don't care what it is, Angus. Just make sure I'm on it.'

'Nothing is even planned,' Angus warned. He held up his hand to restrain Edward's optimism. 'Yet.'

BOOK 4

FUEL TO THE FIRE

Thou shalt be for fuel to the fire; thy blood shall be in the midst of the land; thou shalt be no more remembered: for I the Lord have spoken it.

The Book of the Prophet Ezekiel, 21:32

16

SPECIAL SQUADS

February–March 1947

Edward stared through the windscreen of the truck and allowed himself to be jolted about on the canvas seat. Beside him, in battledress, Private Sean Brogan fought with the steering wheel as the truck bounced on the uneven road. Ahead, the column of sandy-coloured lorries snaked round the bends between the olive groves on either side as the convoy made its way towards Lydda, east of Tel Aviv.

Edward paid no attention to the countryside. Nothing had changed since his father's funeral six months ago. Angus Maclean's exciting suggestion of hitting back at the terrorists had not materialised. The violence had worsened, with attacks on police stations, railway lines cut, trains blown up, oil pipe lines destroyed, roads mined to blow up Army trucks in convoys, grenades thrown into cafés used by soldiers who had now to go about in groups, even off-duty, and they were always armed. The Jewish underground had refined its techniques, killing Army explosives men with booby-trapped explosive devices, just a few of the 212 people who had been killed in 1946. Only 26 had been members of the Jewish underground.

Edward had not been involved in any of these dramas, and he was still sharply conscious that he had had no chance to even the score for his father's death or for his own humiliating kidnap. Nor did it help when Angus said the King David Hotel investigation was not going well. For Edward, life had continued with a seemingly endless round of cordon and search operations on Jewish houses, villages, and kibbutzes where the occupants were always unpleasantly antagonistic even if the riots of the early days were now rare. Intelligence was always lacking. They found a dribble of arms caches but the underground fighters eluded their grasp. Nearly all of the people they arrested were no more than sympathisers, and they would be released within days.

This convoy was at least a change in routine, but he was furious with Captain Scarland for deliberately putting himself in charge when he heard Edward's platoon was to be the convoy protection party. Major George Fairfax's disgrace lived on. In so many words Captain Scarland implied that Edward came from 'dodgy stock' and needed supervising. Edward's resentment and constant sniping from Roger Haike grew in equal measure with the frustration of daily routine. Sometimes it gnawed dangerously close to the limits of his self-control.

Brogan deliberately interrupted his thoughts, 'Terrible news that the women have gone home, don't you think?' He never thought brooding helped at all.

'Yes,' said Edward monosyllabically. At the end of January, the Army had decided the situation in Palestine was too dangerous for wives and families and all service dependants had been sent home, by order of Operation Polly. Another silly name for a military operation, Edward reflected, but perhaps more apposite than some. All the women had gathered with their suitcases at Jerusalem railway station with children clutching teddy bears and toys, and he had said goodbye to Diana. She cried and flung her arms round his neck and he was himself quite upset to see her go. She had been exceptionally supportive after his father's funeral.

The Joshua Inheritance

She leaned out of the carriage window and they had waved at each other till the train pulled out and she disappeared from view amid clouds of steam and a forest of other arms waving to husbands left behind. He pitied her. Her letters from London said that was everything was frozen in the worst winter England had suffered in decades.

'Well, it's bad news if you're married,' Brogan continued in his soft southern Irish brogue, determined to break through Edward's depression. Normally, he would not have bothered to bridge the gap between himself and the officers but he and the others liked their young platoon commander. 'But, if you're not, which I ain't, then it's not any sort of news at all.'

Edward looked at him puzzled and Brogan grinned, manhandling the wide steering wheel with savage pleasure, his sleeves rolled up to reveal a livid Irish tricolour tattooed on his muscled forearm, encaptioned, 'Ireland, the Free!' Brogan said, 'There's always plenty of spare about, who aren't fussy as to politics and know what they want. If you know what I mean.'

Edward thought of Carole and wondered if she fitted this description. He had not seen her since before the King David Hotel bomb. She had ignored all his attempts to make contact and he had stopped trying. He wondered what she was doing. Still at the hospital he supposed. Maybe, now that Diana was gone, he should try again. He smiled at the idea.

Brogan cheered up and looked left and right at the olives on the terraced hillsides. There would be some fine places to ambush the vulnerable line of trucks. He hated convoys. They made him feel trapped, like a bird driven on to the guns.

Abruptly they heard a muffled crump ahead. The trucks in front slowed to a halt, concertina'd nose to tail. Brogan swore. 'Bastards 'ave mined us. And I don't like being all squashed up. Sitting ducks we'll be.'

'Come on,' shouted Edward snapping alert and springing out of the cab with his Sten. The convoy was entirely his responsibility, had Captain Scarland not intervened, and someone in his platoon might have been hurt. Shouting for the soldier at the back to keep his eyes peeled for the enemy, Edward and Brogan ran up the road. As they passed each vehicle, Edward shouted to the Paras to take up positions of defence in the ditches in case they were attacked. They found the damaged truck near the front of the column.

The mine had blown up right under the engine block, driving great chunks of metal up through the floor of the cab and killing the two men inside instantly. The front wheels had been blown off and the forward part of the vehicle had slumped on to the road, like an Arab fallen on his face praying to Mecca in the East.

'Nowt we can do about the poor beggars, sir,' said Sergeant Hodgson matter-of-factly. He gestured at the tangled remains of the cab with an unused first-aid shell-dressing in his hand. Edward looked in. From the waist up, the two men were bloodied, their faces swollen but relatively intact, lolled forward on the wreckage of the steering wheel and dash-board. Below, they were shredded, their flesh mangled and torn completely away from the leg bones. The driver's stomach hung out of the bottom of his shirt over his belt which was all that remained of his battledress trousers. Edward turned away, disgusted but feeling remote. He supposed the reaction would set in later, as it had after the King David bombing when, to his own private shame, he had been more tortured by the fear that one day his own body might end up with its flesh peeled back by blast than by dutiful feelings of remorse for the dead and injured, his father included.

Sergeant Hodgson also seemed detached. Professionally, he had seen a good many dead people in four years of war. He stuffed the clean shell-dressing in his battledress pocket and said quietly, 'The driver was a gunner, one of Lieutenant Haike's lot. The other is Corporal Jacobs.' Corporal Jacobs had been with the platoon a long time.

Brogan swore fiercely and looked into the cab too. Joe Jacobs had been a close friend since recruit days. He cursed out loud, 'Bloody typical bad luck of the English! And him Jewish too!'

Edward had not recognised the dead man next to the driver and was badly shaken. He looked back into the cab. Under the puffed cheeks, which were spotted with blood and pieces of flesh, he finally recognised Corporal Jacobs. What a way to end life. He swung back to Sergeant Hodgson and demanded, 'Where's Captain Scarland?'

Sergeant Hodgson replied quickly, 'He ran up here from the front vehicle immediately after the explosion saying he's seen a wire which he thinks they used to detonate the mine. Now he's disappeared into the bloody bundoo.' He jerked his head towards the olive plantation beyond the ditch.

'On his own?' Edward asked, amazed.

Sergeant Hodgson nodded. His expression indicated he did not think very much of this.

At once Edward ordered Sergeant Hodgson to continue securing the convoy against further attack and to summon assistance on the radio for the damaged vehicle and the dead men. Then he said, 'Brogan and I will go and find Captain Scarland. If we're not back in twenty minutes, send a section after us.'

'You'll hear firing if there's trouble,' Brogan promised. He was seething with the frustration of constantly being helpless on the receiving end. 'I hope Captain Scarland has found the bastards.'

Edward followed Sergeant Hodgson's direction a few metres back down the road and saw the wire where it came out of the ditch. He noticed the flex was standard issue 'D10' twin-flex, no doubt stolen from an Army camp. The blast must have disturbed the light camouflage of dust and sand which had been brushed over it, enough for Captain Scarland to spot it when he ran up after the ambush was set off.

'Might be the captain is right for once,' Brogan muttered, gripping his Sten gun. Edward looked into the olives but the green leaves of the low branches obscured everything more than a few rows back. The adrenalin started to pump. He wondered what they would find in the trees. After a moment's hesitation, thinking he perhaps ought to have taken more men, he set off following the line of the wire uphill among the gnarled trunks of the old olives. Brogan kept a tactical ten yards behind him, aggressively alert for danger and ready at an instant to open fire. This was the sort of work he enjoyed.

Once they had found the beginning, the wire was easy to follow, laid on the baked ground between the trees and disguised with only a sprinkling of earth. Edward picked out Captain Scarland's boot prints in the dust and noticed another set of prints, also boots. Thinking all the local people wore sandals, even when working in the vineyards, he pointed them out to Brogan who provided a scathing contradiction. 'Bastard Irgun think they're soldiers, see? I'd like to tell 'em there's more to being a soldier than wearing the bloody boots.'

Edward grinned. He looked back. The road was not visible but he could still see glimpses of the trucks through the olive trees. The grove rose up a slight hill and after nearly two hundred yards they reached the top of the rise and the end of the wire. 'This is it,' said Brogan lying down and peering towards the road. 'Yer can just see the place to blow it.' Edward lay down and, framed in the distance by grey-green olive leaves, he could see the damaged truck where Corporal Jacobs lay eviscerated. He stood up and moved away from Brogan. It would not do to be caught out close together. They could both be killed in one burst of fire.

Brogan gestured for silence. Edward stopped moving. They could hear shouting, further away from the road at the back of the olive grove. At once they moved towards the noises, crouching and holding their Sten guns ready. Both of them, each for their different reasons, were determined not to lose the chance of finding the men responsible for the attack on the convoy.

Ahead Edward could see a low stone wall running through the plantation. Beyond was a rough stone hut, its thatch roof rotted in. Further away, the trees stopped and open dry scrubby hillside stretched away into the heat haze burning the valley hills.

'You bloody bastards, stand up!'

Captain Scarland's voice reached them clearly now. A frantic outburst in some other language followed which he tried to drown with more swearing in English.

Warily, Edward and Brogan approached, giving the stone hut a wide berth until Edward could see Captain Scarland standing over two men in filthy jellabas with dirty suit jackets over the top. They were cowering on the ground against the wall outside the hut.

Captain Scarland was kicking his two prisoners when he caught sight of Edward's shadow appearing round the trunk of an orange tree. He whipped up his revolver and nearly opened fire. 'Fairfax! Bloody fool creeping up like that!' he shouted. 'Could have shot you.'

Further away, Brogan knelt down, his eyes roving round the trees for trouble, and Captain Scarland spotted him too. If he felt any embarrassment at being caught unawares by them both, he did not show it. Instead, he announced, 'These are the bastards who blew that truck.' He kicked the man nearest them who moaned pathetically and tried to protect his face with swarthy hands. 'Buggers won't stand up. Guilty as sin, look at them!'

'How d'you know?' Edward asked, kneeling down like Brogan beside the corner of the stone hut, alert for trouble. They were vulnerable to attack, a long way from the road where the rest of the troops were. Even if Captain Scarland did not seem to care, Edward had no intention of being taken by surprise, not for a second time.

Captain Scarland looked down scathingly at Edward and snapped, 'I got to the end of the detonating wire and caught them hiding in this hut. Had to drag them out to get a proper look but there's no doubt about it. And don't worry, Fairfax, there's no-one else about.'

Edward ignored the sneering remark. How would Captain Scarland know? He had failed to see them approaching. Edward moved swiftly to the hut and took a good look inside. Light filtered through the broken roof and the place smelled atrociously of sheep and goats. The two men at Captain Scarland's feet followed Edward's actions with wide terrified eyes and Captain Scarland kicked them both. To stop him, Edward said, 'At least we've something to show for the whole thing, taking these two back. The Intelligence boys can really get their teeth into them. Maybe find out who they work with.'

'Stuff the Int boys,' Captain Scarland declared. 'I'm going to shoot these bastards myself.'

Edward stared at him.

'Here and now,' Captain Scarland confirmed. 'Only trouble is they won't stand up. Can't shoot the beggars sitting down. Not right.'

Edward blinked. There was nothing in his training or experience to help him with this situation. Killing them would be easy. Why not? His own kidnapping, his father's death, the ambushing of Corporal Jacobs and the gunner were all fuel to a boiling frustration which might be instantly appeased by killing these two terrorists. Excuses could be found later. There were no witnesses. Anyway, none who would tell. But he was still gripped by the cold professional detachment he had felt looking at Corporal Jacobs's corpse. His fury was under control.

The two men at Captain Scarland's feet were both filthy, their black curly hair was matted and their skin and clothes grimed with dirt. One was older, maybe in his thirties, and the other was younger, almost a boy. They looked guilty, totally unappealing, and they had been found close to the detonating wire with no apparent excuse. Any normal person, even someone not involved, would be expected to run away as soon as the bomb went off. Edward glanced at Brogan, unsure. Brogan shrugged. He was close enough to hear every word. He loathed Captain Scarland but these men had killed his friend. And the driver. Probably a good many other soldiers too. In Brogan's book, if they lived by the sword, they should expect to die by it. Like he did. Like soldiers.

'What's the matter, Fairfax? Squeamish?' Captain Scarland sneered. He jutted out his jaw and decided, 'If the bastards won't stand up like men and be shot, I'll blow their black woolly heads off where they sit.' He cocked his revolver.

Immediately the older man launched into a torrent of pleading, wringing his hands and holding his arms across to protect the younger one.

'Stop!' Edward shouted, stepping forwards, uncertain what to do to prevent Scarland pulling the trigger and feeling as though a great chasm was opening in front of him. The two peasants subsided into whimpers, chanting as if in prayer.

Captain Scarland ignored him. He took aim at the man's head.

'They're not Jews!' Edward yelled. 'They're speaking Arabic!'

At the last moment, he had recognised Muslim prayers in the fatalistic whispers of the two peasants.

Captain Scarland hesitated a moment, looking at Edward. He said, 'Jews speak Arabic too'. There was a distant look in his eyes. Then he turned back to the older man and raised his hand with the revolver.

A final glance at the men released Edward's uncertainty. He swung the barrel of his Sten brutally fast down on Captain Scarland's wrist, smashing the bone, and the revolver went off. Captain Scarland screamed and dropped it and, before he could react, Edward stepped forward and punched him hard in the chest with the butt of his Sten, knocking him to the ground. Swiftly, he kicked the revolver out of reach. The two peasants cringed by the stone wall, miraculously unhurt, their eyes wide in terror.

'They're Arabs, you idiot! Arabs!' Edward yelled glaring down at Captain Scarland. 'Not Jews at all.' He held his Sten ready, hefting it with both hands, and the vicious light of attack faded in Captain Scarland's eyes. His face was suffused with blood, his expression black with hate and pain. He clutched his wrist and swore, 'I'll break you for this, Fairfax. Smash your miserable career. God, I promise you!'

Edward shouted back, 'They're Arabs! The men who laid that wire wore boots. These two are barefoot and there aren't any boots inside this hut. They're bloody goatherds!'

At this, Brogan walked over.

Captain Scarland struggled to his feet, his battledress covered in earth and shouted, 'You're under arrest, Fairfax! I'll make your bloody father's court martial look like chickenfeed, by God I will. Brogan, arrest this officer!'

Brogan ignored him. He peered at the two goatherds and nodded. 'I think you're right, Mr Fairfax. These two certainly aren't wearing the kind of boots which laid that wire. Barefoot, they are. Arabs you say?'

Keeping a wary eye on Captain Scarland, Edward

The Joshua Inheritance

spoke to the two men in Arabic. '*Laysh inta hinna?*' What was their excuse for being there?

The older of the two men answered immediately, his eyes rolling and showing the whites. The few words tumbled out. The nearness of death had seared away the layers of habitual Arab dissimulation and he said, '*Ashan ihna muhibayn.*' He looked apologetic and shrugged slightly.

For a moment, Edward puzzled over the last word, then he remembered and laughed. The relief that he had done the right thing was like a drug pumped into every vein at once, washing away the tension like a cool sea wave. When Captain Scarland recovered from his surprise at seeing Edward laugh, he shouted again, 'Brogan, arrest this officer!'

Edward snapped, 'Bring charges if you like but these two aren't Jews. You were going to murder two innocent men!'

'You saw what happened, Brogan! Arrest him,' shouted Captain Scarland again. Blood was dripping off his hand and staining the khaki serge of his battledress jacket. 'That's an order!'

Brogan looked him square in the eye and said, 'It's true, I did hear a shot, but I don't remember seeing a thing. Not a frigging thing.' Brogan's tough features were set, his blue eyes obstinately steady.

Before Captain Scarland could draw breath at the shock of this, Sergeant Hodgson came running through the trees with a group of Edward's platoon fanned out behind him, their Sten guns held in front of them, ready for a fight.

'I heard firing and came at once. You alright, sir?' He peered at Captain Scarland but Edward gave him no chance for explanations. He said loudly so they could all hear, 'Captain Scarland has hurt himself. Something to do with these two Arabs, so we'll have to take them back with us. Otherwise no sign of the bombers, apart from the wire, that is.' He added pointedly, 'I'll show you their footprints on the way back down to the road.' He turned to Captain Scarland and said with exaggerated politeness, 'Need any help down the hill to the road?'

Captain Scarland shouted rudely, 'You report to the Company offices the minute we get back to camp!'

'If you like,' Edward agreed blandly and could not help adding, 'but that looks a nasty wound. I'd go and see the Medical Officer first, if I were you.' Brogan had to turn away as Captain Scarland stamped off through the olive trees livid with rage and pain, clutching his bleeding wrist to his chest.

When the convoy finally started up again, with a recovery vehicle towing the damaged truck, Edward sat in silence in the cab while Brogan drove, concentrating on the road ahead, keeping exactly the right distance from the truck in front. He realised that Edward was in serious trouble. Captain Scarland was bound to deny trying to shoot the two Arabs and that left a straightforward attack on a superior officer. A court martial offence. If found guilty, Edward faced certain dismissal or even a jail sentence.

Edward reflected dejectedly that things had finally reached the bottom. Nothing seemed to have gone right since he had been commissioned, some eighteen months before. And now this. He was badly worried, but he was sure he had acted properly. He was certain the two Arabs were innocent. In conversation on the way down the hill, they said they had heard the explosion on the road and seen three men run away through the trees. That at least might help the Intelligence staff. Taken by surprise the Arabs had no time to move and had lain terrified in the hut till Captain Scarland found them. Thinking of what might have happened had they not gone looking for him made Edward seethe with fury. He wanted revenge on the Irgun more than most, but that would have been cold-blooded murder. He sighed

The Joshua Inheritance

and said to Brogan, 'What will you say if Scarland presses charges?'

'I'll tell them you stopped him shooting the two Arabs,' Brogan stated cheerfully. He had been sublimely uninterested in the fate of the two Arabs but he was delighted with Captain Scarland's broken wrist.

By the time they reached Lydda camp it was dark. Captain Scarland climbed painfully out of his truck and marched off at once to find Major Rattigan. Edward absorbed himself sorting out the last of the convoy duties, trying to forget the impending disaster, when one of the Paras came running to say the Adjutant required both him and Brogan at Battalion Headquarters. Edward was sunk in depression. He supposed he would be placed under close arrest. He noticed a large black Austin saloon parked in the shadows outside RHQ. Inside, the lights were blazing in all the rooms, including the Colonel's office. He stepped on to the wooden verandah which ran the length of the hut, feeling as if he were mounting the scaffold.

Major Rattigan put his head round the Adjutant's door when he heard their hollow steps on the wooden floor and snapped, 'You two wait in the Orderly Room. I'll call you when I've finished talking to Captain Scarland.'

Edward looked at Brogan who shrugged slightly. They found chairs behind a couple of desks in the Orderly Room and sat down. Edward was thankful that none of the clerks was about at that time of the evening. The desks were cleared of paperwork, pens and pencils neatly tidied in rows in glass trays. The waiting was unbearable. He could hear voices inside the Adjutant's office but it was impossible to make out what was being said. He stood up, unable to sit still any more, and walked over to the window. A few soldiers were moving among the tents on the other side of the dusty avenue, dark forms just visible in the dull electric lights, and he could hear the distant throb of the big diesel generator which provided electricity for the camp. When he turned back, he saw that Brogan had silently moved his chair to a place close to the door and was listening intently, his head cocked on one side. He put his finger to his mouth and grinned. This small gesture raised Edward's morale enormously but there was no time for Brogan to pass on what he had heard. The Adjutant's door suddenly opened and Captain Scarland walked out. His hard face was pale and he was holding his arm at an odd angle, but he put on an expression of sinister satisfaction when he caught sight of Edward. 'You're both for it!' he said. 'And good riddance. Now, Brogan, get in there and make your report.'

'Rightaway, sir!' Brogan retorted with obedient cheerfulness, as if being asked to take a week's leave. Captain Scarland glared at him. Bustling with military efficiency, Brogan knocked loudly on the door with his bunched fist and marched into the office as if he were on the parade ground. The door banged shut and Edward could hear Brogan's boots crashing to attention on the wooden floor inside. Captain Scarland sneered at Edward and left.

The minutes dragged. Edward had finally decided he had to tell the truth when the Adjutant's door flew open again. Edward hesitated, expecting Brogan to emerge at a swift pace, but a voice inside shouted, 'Come in, Fairfax!'

Edward walked in and saluted smartly. Brogan was nowhere to be seen and Edward guessed he had been sent out through the Colonel's office, through the connecting door. That was not a good omen. The Adjutant, Captain 'Phileas' Fogg, was sitting behind his desk with a serious expression on his face while Major Rattigan was sitting to one side on a collapsible chair with his legs crossed, unsmiling. Without preamble, he said, 'Right, Fairfax, tell us what happened.'

Edward told them. They sat and listened without

The Joshua Inheritance

interrupting, Captain Fogg making notes on a pad in front of him. When he had finished, he felt empty and committed to his fate, like falling through space to earth in the eternal moment between leaping from an aeroplane and waiting for the parachute to open. There was a long silence. Captain Fogg looked at Major Rattigan who nodded imperceptibly and said finally, 'This is a bad show. Very bad. I don't like officers fighting. Not good at all for discipline. Especially not between a junior subaltern and Company second-in-command. You realise your story is a total contradiction of what Captain Scarland has told us?'

Edward nodded. He was still falling.

Captain Fogg continued gloomily, 'Brogan's account doesn't really help, so it's still your word against Captain Scarland.'

'What about the Arabs?' Edward asked trying to keep the desperation out of his voice.

Captain Fogg looked at Major Rattigan who sat forward and said, 'Arabs and Jews are not reliable witnesses in this sort of affair.'

Edward had fallen. He was lost.

Major Rattigan stood up walked to the window and looked out. He hated these situations, and he blamed Captain Scarland. As the more senior officer, he should have avoided the problem. However, the damage had been done, too much damage to let the matter go. He glanced at the black Austin parked in the shadows outside. He said, 'You'll have to go, Edward. You and Brogan. Best thing, frankly. Let the dust settle.'

The blow was almost physical. Edward opened his mouth to protest but closed it again in astonishment when Major Rattigan turned round with a smile on his face and said, 'It's damn bad show, old chap. But the timing at least is perfect. A friend of yours turned up here this afternoon. An inspector of police called Maclean. About the same time as you were having your barney with Scarland. He says you're wanted for special police duties because you speak Arabic. Brogan too, for different reasons. He had quite impressive authority for his demand, from the Inspector-General of Palestine Police, no less. And I must say it fits in very nicely, both of the guilty parties being whisked off by the police.' His smile broadened for a moment.

Edward nodded mechanically. He could not quite take it all in; but he knew his fall had stopped, that a parachute had miraculously opened. Obviously Rattigan meant that the camp grapevine would quickly rattle with the story of their departure in a police car. Instant punishment for the charges brought by Captain Scarland. But Edward was still young enough to worry about the justice of the situation. He said, 'Trouble is, sir, I don't believe I'm guilty, and all this sounds a bit like running away, doesn't it, sir?'

Major Rattigan snorted good-humouredly, 'Leave it to me. The IO has already begun interrogating the two Arabs. I expect they'll support your story, or you wouldn't have brought them in, eh? They might spend a few days in jail but that's better than being shot in the head. What's important is to avoid a big fuss. Morale here is bad enough, with us all cast as Aunt Sally for the Jews, without fighting among ourselves as well.'

The interview was over. Captain Fogg stood up and opened the door to the Colonel's office. He said, 'You'll find them waiting at the end of the building.' Edward remembered the black saloon. He hesitated and said, 'What about my kit?'

'It's already packed. In the car. Aubrey did it for you,' said Major Rattigan. He stuck out his hand and added, 'Good luck, old chap. No idea what they want you for, but if you're doing it with Brogan, you'll be alright. He's a good man. Lots of experience.' They shook hands. Rattigan could see Edward was thoroughly bemused by the rapid turn of events but

The Joshua Inheritance

Private Brogan, MM, could be trusted. On operations, at any rate.

Edward nodded, trying to understand what Major Rattigan meant, but the Adjutant was ushering him through the Colonel's office and events were moving too fast for him to appreciate the full measure of the volte-face in his fortunes. He felt like a piece of flotsam tossed helplessly from wave to wave, and supposed that this was normal in the Army. All he could think was that, even if interpreting Arabic did not sound very exciting, it was a tremendous improvement on a court martial. With a feeling of extraordinary unreality, he walked on to the verandah outside and the door closed behind him. The night was cool and starlit. A voice called him from the shadows at the end of the HQ hut where the black Austin was parked. The rear passenger door was open. He climbed in and the car pulled away at once.

The driver headed for the camp gates and the other man in the front turned round. 'Thanks for providing such a good cover story.' Angus Maclean's face was in shadow but Edward could see he was grinning. Edward swore softly, 'If I'd known you had this planned, I would've shot Scarland.' Brogan laughed softly from the darkness of the back seat next to Edward.

Conversation stopped as the car passed through the armed guard at the gates. On the main road, the driver turned towards Jerusalem and accelerated into the dark hills ahead. Edward's curiosity could stand it no longer. 'What's this all about, Angus?'

Angus turned round, leaned over the padded leather seat and replied, 'You wanted an opportunity to get back at the terrorists. This is it. I'll give you a proper brief when we get to Jerusalem, but suffice it to say you're in exalted company. You'll have to run to keep up. I only got you in because you speak half-decent Arabic. And because I think you've the right motivation. The rest, like Brogan here, certainly have. They all spent months behind enemy lines in France during the war. They behaved like a bunch of terrorists then, upsetting the Germans after D-Day, and the idea is they'll know how to catch the terrorists working against us here.'

Brogan declared happily, 'This is music to my ears!'

'You'll be working with one of the two groups we're setting up, called Special Squads. The whole thing is the idea of the Assistant Inspector-General of Police, Colonel Bernard Fergusson. He's our boss. It's taken long enough to get the idea accepted and now, of course, the politicians have given us no time for the sort of preparation we'd like. They don't want to know how the squads will work. They don't want embarrassments, but they want instant results.'

'Typical,' Brogan grinned from the darkness. Edward looked at him thinking how relaxed he seemed, in his element. Brogan had never seemed comfortable in the platoon, seemingly always in trouble. After his experience of fighting with raiding parties through Occupied France, Regimental life was far too restrictive. Edward found himself instantly fascinated by the prospect of clandestine operations but very conscious of his lack of experience. He resolved to watch the others, like Brogan, and learn.

After Angus finished talking there was a short silence. The driver swung the powerful car easily round the curves and bends as they climbed up the Soreq Valley to Jerusalem and Edward looked out at the endless dark olive trees flashing past, their old trunks and glaucous leaves silvered in the moonlight. Edward's spirits rose. This was his chance. He thought of all the things which had happened to him since arriving in Palestine, of Paul Levi, and of his father. It was time to settle a few scores.

His thoughts were interrupted by Brogan speaking softly from the shadows of his corner. 'Well now, Mr Edward Fairfax, before we get too involved in all this secret stuff, I'd like to clear up a little something that happened by that stone hut with Captain Scarland, may the Blessed Saints take care of him soon. Just what did that Arab fellah say which made you laugh?' Knowing very well the effects of a violent surge of adrenalin, Brogan had been impressed.

Edward switched his thoughts back, and said, 'The Arab told me that he and the boy were lovers.'

'Shirt lifters?'

Edward grinned. 'Right. Friends of Dorothy. They were hard at it when the bomb went off and couldn't run away for fear of being seen by the Irgun guys.'

Brogan stared out of the darkness for a moment, his imagination at work, and then roared with laughter. When Edward explained, Angus joined in and the atmosphere was set. These were friends and Edward knew that life was on the up. Death and laughter were a magic drug; with sex thrown in, intoxicating.

They reached Jerusalem just after midnight. Angus Maclean dropped Brogan and Edward off at their new quarters in a secluded street off the Nablus Road, in the quarter on the north side of the Old City walls known as the American Colony. The area offered the distinct advantage of being largely populated by Arabs, and the special squad, with all its equipment and cars, was comfortably lodged in an unobtrusive rambling house which had belonged years before to a senior Turkish administrator who enjoyed his privacy. The stuccoed two-storey house was hidden from prying eyes behind large Jerusalem pines and a high garden wall.

The other members of the six-strong squad were already there and Brogan was immediately at home. When they walked across the colourful mosaic of the big hall, there was a noisy impromptu reunion as he found some old friends from his days in France. Edward felt very much a newcomer. His head buzzed as he tried to absorb everything and not look too like a gaping novice.

When Brogan introduced him all round, Edward learned they had all been part of a special forces unit called 2 Special Air Service which had operated ahead of the advancing Allied armies in France in landrover groups, harassing German headquarters and lines of communications. All but one were decorated. Erskine Meynell was their squad leader, a young major of twenty-six who had the DSO and MC. Ranks were adhered to, but Edward was immediately struck by the easy-going relationship between them all, crossing the boundaries from major to private, which appeared more like a powerful bond than a weakening of the usual Army formalities. Nor did it reduce Meynell's unquestioned position as leader. He was a small, wiry, extremely fit man with dark hair and constant energy. But his impeccable manners and charm were, as Edward was to discover, reserved only for his friends.

The house was still furnished as it had been when its Turkish owner fled as the British took Jerusalem thirty years before in December 1917. The rooms were filled with elegant Empire chairs and tables though all the fabrics and curtains were faded by the sun. The parquet floors were bare and no doubt the Turkish carpets Edward had expected to see were now decorating the home of some British officer in England. There were plenty of bedrooms upstairs for everyone and he was given one to himself with a soft divan bed which made him think of Carole.

Angus was right. There was no spare time. The following day, Bernard Fergusson came to the house with Angus in civilian clothes in an unmarked car to brief them. The squad gathered in the dining-room and made notes at the polished mahogany table. Their job was simple. Find the terrorists and eliminate them.

Edward wondered what exactly eliminate meant but

The Joshua Inheritance

dared not ask and was anyway quickly absorbed in their training. Major Meynell led his squad through a tough week-long schedule of physical training and shooting. They were given civilian cars, an Austin saloon, a Citroën and a Bedford van which they used to drive into the hills behind Jerusalem where, in two days, they shot their way through more ammunition than Edward had seen used by Major Rattigan's whole company in a year. He was introduced to the Colt .45, the Luger, the Walther P38 and Browning pistols, the Thompson sub-machine-gun and the new Sterling 9mm parabellum SMG which was being developed to replace the Sten. Edward's wrist ached with the endless recoils. Brogan was his instructor and professed himself pleased with Edward's performance. In the evenings, they gathered in the colonial splendour of the dining-room which was used as an instruction room and studied maps and innumerable police photographs of suspects. Other NCOs in the squad went through procedures they would need, how to make rendezvous together in the streets and countryside, meeting local contacts, and how to use the new radios which Angus Maclean brought on the second day. These radios could be used in cars or carried in bags for communicating between members of the squad over short distances. By the time they finished late at night each day Edward was exhausted. He collapsed on to his bed and slept as though dead till they were woken for physical training on the mosaics in the spacious hall at half-past six each morning.

Edward saw Carole, however, sooner than he expected, but not in any circumstances he could have imagined. At the end of the week, Major Meynell called them into the dining-room after lunch and, when they had settled down round the table, briefed them on their first job. To Edward's surprise, they were after Paul Levi. Angus Maclean, caught his eye and smiled briefly.

Erskine Meynell said, 'This bastard Levi was one of

those responsible for the King David outrage and we've got a line on him. The intelligence chaps tell us he visits a house here in Jerusalem. We're going to put a stop to it.' He looked round at the men. Everyone was grim-faced and determined, their sleeves rolled up, elbows on the table, leaning forward and listening intently. For the first time since coming to Palestine, Edward felt he was part of something really effective. Erskine Meynell acknowledged Edward with a wave of his hand and continued, 'Mr Fairfax knows Levi and the house in Hezron Street, so he and Brogan will watch the house from the back, on the patio side, from another house Inspector Maclean has managed to rent for us.' Quickly and efficiently, he detailed the others, including himself, to stay on the streets, waiting in cars to follow Levi once Edward identified him and alerted the squad by radio.

'The optimum is that we follow him to where he lives. That way we'll find more of his cronies. But don't underestimate him. The rat was trained by us.'

A hard-looking sergeant who had been with Major Meynell in France grunted at that and asked, 'When we find this Levi, what do we do?'

Erskine Meynell grinned, his dark features lighting up. His eyes twinkled fiercely and he looked round the small group. 'We'll see. These bloody terrorists have had it all their own way but I want you all to understand that, as far as we are concerned, the boot is now on the other foot.'

The squad spent the rest of that afternoon preparing their equipment. They ate an early supper of curried chicken and rice and tried to catch a few hours' sleep during the night. In the small hours, they dressed in Arab clothes, dirty jellabas and old suit jackets against the February cold, and set out in the cars. The place Angus had rented turned out to be a stone house just off Yehudim Street overlooking the domed stone roofs of the Jewish quarter. Brogan and Edward were dropped

The Joshua Inheritance

off from the Bedford van shortly before dawn. In the murky half light, they climbed the wooden stairs to a little stone room on the top floor under the beams of the flat wooden roof. Soon the pale overcast light of dawn lit the white stone domes and tangle of rooftops in the Jewish quarter and Edward could see there was a clear view into the back of Axel Romm's house. He looked down at the windows around the patio and wondered whether Carole was somewhere inside.

'Don't stand so close to the window,' said Brogan conversationally. Edward hardly noticed this was not the usual way for privates to speak to officers. Instead, he listened carefully as Brogan explained they would watch the house in the shadows away from the window so there was no chance that the weak winter sunshine falling through the shutters would light up their faces, make them visible and compromise them to anyone who glanced up at the window. Edward nodded, then Brogan asked, 'How d'you know so much about this Levi?'

Edward took a deep breath. As the two of them had to get on together on their own, there was no reason for him not to explain a bit more. Brogan listened while he unpacked their radio and set it up. Edward worked too, as he talked about his kidnap and his father's operation in the war, laying out their tins of food which Brogan said they would have to eat cold to avoid the smell of cooking. Finally he checked over his pistol, a Browning automatic, and the new design Sterling sub-machine-gun they had for extra protection. Brogan had advised the choice. He preferred more bullets in the thirteen-round Browning magazine over the harder-hitting seven rounds in the Colt .45 and pointed out that both the Browning and the Sterling used the same 9mm parabellum ammunition.

'What the hell is this Yank doing seeing the fellah in the Irgun?' Brogan asked, dropping his blanket roll on the cold stone floor.

'He's Jewish,' Edward replied, still staring at the shuttered windows of Romm's house. 'And he hates the British.'

Brogan remarked cheerfully, 'This is going to be just like me old home in Sligo, then. Everyone hates the British there, only of course we're all Catholic, you understand.' In Arab clothes Brogan's muscled bulk made him look like one of the Forty Thieves, his strong brown face and blue eyes suggesting a Circassian, undoubtedly a descendant of the hardy crusaders who fought and died for fortune in the arid Holy Land centuries before, two thousand miles from the soft green pastures of Ireland. Seeing Edward grinning, Brogan added, 'Maybe you'd like to take the first watch? I've no doubt you're dying to see the bastard again and we'll pray to all the saints that he turns up soon. This is going to be a cold wait.'

Edward agreed and they settled down to watch the patio behind Romm's house, taking two-hour stints each. On watch, one of them sat on a table they brought up from the floor below while the other dozed on the floor or ate from the tins of corned beef. Edward identified Romm first, taking a breath of fresh air in the patio after breakfast before going to the Consulate. When Yaacov came out to fetch him, Brogan took a long look through the binoculars and remarked. 'That Yaacov's an ugly sod.' Edward smiled, thinking Brogan was hardly one to criticise.

Morning stretched into afternoon and there was no sign of Carole or of Paul Levi. Angus had not been able to provide any clue about how often Levi visited the house but he expected the Irgun to make numerous political contacts with the Americans.

Earlier, in February, a tripartite conference in London had broken down when the Arabs rejected the partition of Palestine, the Jews walked out, and the British resolved to hand the dispute to the United Nations.

The Joshua Inheritance

They blamed the Americans for treating the problem as a domestic vote-catcher and flatly refused President Truman's request to let in one hundred thousand or more European Jewish refugees who were still in displaced-persons camps in Germany. However, Britain was struggling through economic ruin and an appalling winter, saddled with an Empire which no longer paid the bills and the British government was desperate for American cash-aid. Finally he recognised that, however important the Arabs were to Britain's interests, a solution in Palestine was not possible without America's co-operation. In Palestine, the Jews were faced with a two-thirds Arab majority and needed the support of the powerful American-Jewish lobby to support their case for a Jewish National Home. Axel Romm's meetings with Paul were a rich source of information and had become more important than ever.

Late in the afternoon, Brogan whistled under his breath and remarked, 'Jesus, who's the pretty nurse?' Edward was half asleep and jerked awake. He scrambled to his feet and took the binoculars from Brogan. Carole was moving about behind the patio windows inside the house. Edward guessed she had just returned from duty at the hospital. She looked tired and seeing her triggered all sorts of confusing memories. But 'Romm's daughter, Carole,' was all he said. Brogan gave him a sharp look and asked no more questions. The hours passed until the call of the Arab muezzin echoed over Jerusalem's roofs to signal the last call to prayer in the fading sun and night fell.

Brogan was on watch again and cursed the bad light. 'I can't see a sodding thing any longer. We'll have to get closer.'

Wondering if they were going to get any sleep at all, Edward agreed. He passed a message on the radio using a simple word code they had prepared in their safe house, which said they were moving position, and then followed Brogan downstairs. He brought the radio in its canvas bag slung round his shoulders. On the floor below, they had found a shuttered window which gave access on to the roofs between them and Romm's patio. Moving very quietly in their newly issued rubber-soled suede shoes, they dropped out of the window and crept softly across the flat stone roofs, keeping in the shadows of the rounded domes which were a common feature of the old houses in that part of Jerusalem. As they closed up to a parapet overlooking the patio, they crouched down and sank to the stone behind it. Above, the sky was dark and a fresh wind threatened rain. Edward noticed Brogan grinning up at his worried face so when the rain began to fall, he remarked, 'Just like Salisbury Plain,' and wrapped his jellaba closer round him. Brogan chuckled. The young officer was doing fine.

No-one used the patio and there seemed to be little sign of life behind the shutters. They saw Romm and Yaacov come back at ten and Carole appear just before midnight. They heard raised voices somewhere inside and then all the lights went out. Edward suggested Carole might be on night duty and Romm had gone to bed. The rain stopped at one o'clock, just when they had decided to give up watching and they crept damply back to their empty stone room above the rooftops. Brogan fixed up a booby trap on the stairs below, to warn them if anyone tried to surprise them. He locked the door of their room at the top of the house, they wrapped themselves in their dry blankets and went straight to sleep.

At dawn, less than five hours later, they started the whole routine again; and they doggedly continued watching and moving up close under cover of darkness for six days. One night it snowed. Brogan brushed the snow as they crossed the roofs to disguise their footprints and Edward thought they would freeze to death behind the parapet. Luckily it rained again the following night. By this time, he knew every roof, minaret and church tower in the quarter and could guess the time of day by the calling muezzins, Christian bells and the murmur of prayers from the Jewish Western Wall which carried to them sometimes when the wind was in the right direction. In the empty house, they crept round using water on the ground floor and a day lavatory and, once during the week, Major Meynell turned up with more food and took away the old tins in a sack. He was pleased with Edward and Brogan, but the others were finding it hard too, trying to avoid being noticed on the streets. They knew that Romm and Levi were SOE-trained and there was an element of Regimental pride in their determination not to be caught out by them. As he stuffed old tins in a sack, he asked, 'D'you hear that explosion a few days ago?'

Edward and Brogan nodded. They had thought nothing of it. Everyone in Jerusalem had become accustomed to the occasional shot and explosion in the last months. Erskine Meynell said grimly, 'A group of the Irgun attacked the Goldsmith Officers' Club and blew a big hole in one corner. They killed thirteen and sixteen were injured. Everyone's furious and the whole of Tel Aviv is sealed off now. It's called Operation Elephant and bloody well named. They've surrounded 300,000 people.'

Edward snorted, 'I don't suppose they'll find much.'

Major Meynell gave his young officer a sharp look and asked why not. Without hesitation, Edward told him that huge blanket-area searches were fruitless, costly and frustrating. He thought of Aubrey, Major Rattigan and the Paras sweating it out in Tel Aviv. 'What we're doing is more effective,' he said firmly. 'Pinpoint work. That's what we've lacked before.'

'If we find Levi,' Brogan put in.

Major Meynell agreed. 'If he's stuck in Tel Aviv now, we've got a long wait till they lift the curfew there, but I'm sorry lads, we can't stop what we're doing till "Op"

Elephant is over, just in case he makes a surprise visit.' Before leaving, he agreed a code word to indicate the curfew was over.

Edward and Brogan settled back into their routine and the stubble on their cheeks grew. To start with, Edward found the relentless pace of watch-and-sleep exhausting, but by the end of the first week he had adapted and learned how to cat-nap for almost the full two hours while Brogan was on duty watch. Also, watching Carole from time to time through the binoculars had changed his feelings for her. At first it was very strange, like peeping through the curtains of her bathroom, but seeing her regularly soon healed the raw disappointment of missing her and he became convinced that she had no idea what her father was doing. He decided she ought to know, if he got the chance to see her. Brogan observed this mental and physical toughening with some satisfaction. Even though he had none of the others' wartime background, Edward had come from his platoon and had not let them down. So far.

The days dragged past. Edward persuaded Brogan to talk about the war. He had fought in Africa, Sicily and France and only the natural way he talked about the fighting, as though he was discussing a fine day's walking on the Chiltern Hills followed by a good night's drinking, stopped Edward feeling thoroughly inferior. Instead he learned a good deal about the way his father had operated. Much of Brogan's SAS experience in France behind enemy lines had parallels with SOE techniques.

Operation Elephant was lifted on 14 March, the sixteenth day of their watch. The following day, a Sabbath, at the end of a hot afternoon when the sun glittered off the white stone rooftops and dazzled their eyes, Brogan, who was on watch, announced that Romm was in the patio. He made another entry in their log book, and said, 'I suppose if this Levi was the demolition man, Romm must've been the radio operator?'

Edward, lying on the floor cleaning his Browning, nodded.

Brogan was thinking out loud. 'I was the radio operator in France, so I suppose me and him have got something in common, though you wouldn't think so now, him being a terrorist. All the same, it's not an easy job, radio operator. If you didn't send your message quick enough, bloody Jerries could find you in minutes and you'd have to move like hell then.' Edward frowned, not understanding, and Brogan went on, 'They had direction finders to pick up our Morse signals. Huge receiving stations in France and Germany which got a fix on you. Jesus, I got nervous sometimes.'

'Were you ever caught?'

'No, thank Christ. But a few were in your father's lot, in SOE. I heard that in Holland a whole circuit of agents was arrested and the Krauts used their radios to get the RAF to drop stuff to them. What a bloody cheek!' Brogan laughed softly. The idea appealed to him.

'Couldn't the base station, in England, tell if a radio was being used by someone else?'

'That's what they said, but I never thought so myself. It's true each person has a way of tapping the key, individual like, but they made so many allowances, for bad atmospheric conditions, natural mistakes, and being under stress, of course, that a good operator could pass himself off as someone else. I've done it myself, for a mate in another patrol, and no-one noticed. I was using his security checks, see?'

'No,' said Edward, enjoying Brogan's instant exposé of signals procedure.

'Ah well,' said Brogan without looking round. He continued to stare through the binos, his broad back immovably hunched on the table and went on talking, just for something to do. 'Every operator had to remember a couple of security checks which he fitted into his messages. He used one all the time, to identify himself, like. Then there was another in case he got caught, so he could let England know, such as using the same word again at the end of the message. Say you used "SAM" as your personal code. You might have used it again at the end slipping two letters in the alphabet to disguise it, making it "UCO", and then added two more letters at random to make up the necessary five letters for a group, say "MUCOX", or "BUCON". Of course the Krauts aren't thick, and they twigged that, so the poor bloody operator had to remember another check, a bluff, so, when the Gestapo tweaked his balls for the first check, he could tell them and keep the second to himself. He might, for example, deliberately make the seventh letter of every text wrong.' Brogan chortled at the complexity of it all. 'In theory, that was you, all safe and sound and no mistakes made at base in England. Of course, it didn't always work out as planned. The best security of all was not letting the Germans get their greasy paws on the codes in the first place. No codes, no false messages.'

Brogan nodded at his own wisdom, gazing through the binos; and Edward, from some instinct he could not explain, thought that what he had just heard was important. Suddenly, though, Brogan sat forward on the table and hissed, 'It's him! I'm sure of it, but the bloody sun is right in my eyes.'

Edward snapped his Browning together, stuffed it in his belt and took the binoculars. He stared through the half-open shutters into Romm's patio, adjusting his position to lessen the sun's glare. Axel Romm was standing near the fountain, talking to a slightly built young man in a brown suit with a shock of dark hair. He nodded. He had never expected to see Paul Levi again and a deep sense of satisfaction flooded through him.

The Joshua Inheritance

'Yes, Sean. That's Paul Levi. Give the code word.'

Brogan noticed Edward's use of his Christian name. They had spent a long time cheek by jowl and rank had never impressed him. All the same, they both knew there were barriers still between officers and other ranks so he merely said, 'It's a pleasure. The boys will be delighted.'

Speaking into the mike in a low voice, he described what Paul was wearing in clear. Major Erskine Meynell knew the Army signals security men would have cardiac arrests to hear the Army transmitting vital information uncoded, but his team needed these vital details instantly. They had no time to fiddle about with decoding papers in their cars when they had to move at once and risk being seen in broad daylight in the streets. By the time the radio message was picked up by anyone, they would be gone.

When Paul left Romm's house an hour later, an Orthodox Jew in a badly fitting black suit, black leather shoes and wide-brimmed Homburg hat wandered after him. Major Erskine Meynell, very dark and slightly built, considered his disguise as a Jew the safest, and, besides, it was the one which gave him the most satisfaction. Behind him, one of the team cruised along in the Citroën, ready to pick him up if Levi jumped into a car. Several streets away the last two in the squad started the Austin's engine and listened intently to their radio.

Edward and Brogan were extremely busy. They had kept everything in a state of readiness to move, but it was a hectic few minutes packing their few things in the blanket rolls and checking there was no rubbish left to be found. Edward made a final check, Brogan sent a code word on the radio and they pattered quickly down to the ground floor and waited inside the old wooden door.

Two streets away the men in the Austin heard the signal, replied and moved off. Two minutes later they were moving slowly down a dusty alley on the edge of the Armenian quarter running next to the Jewish quarter and saw two Arabs walking ahead of them carrying blanket rolls. They pulled up beside them and offered a lift which was gratefully accepted.

When they were moving again, the Austin's driver, a solidly built Welshman from Cardiff, exclaimed, 'By God, you two boyos stink! I've never smelled anything like it!'

Edward took the remark as a compliment and Brogan told the driver, 'The trouble with you, Taff, you're a bloody Welsh git and you've no love of the natural things in life. Just get us to the van and tell us if we've still got the bastard in our sights.'

Taff chuckled. 'We have.'

Paul Levi was walking purposefully along the pavement towards the Jaffa Gate where he would be picked up by the man who had replaced Selig as driver. He was in a good mood and, when he saw a man selling pretzels from a battered wooden stand, gave in to a sudden urge to buy one. It reminded him of happier days in Poland. He was sure those better times were coming again, but out of habit he glanced up and down the street as the man handed him the pretzel. It always paid to be on the lookout for police in civilian clothes. His eyes swept round the people going home in the early evening and he paid no attention to the dark figure of an Orthodox Jew standing at the top of the street deep in thought in a book. The pretzels smelled delicious and he was hungry. They had not eaten very well in hiding during the last two weeks in Tel Aviv while the British Army rumbled round the streets and searched houses and gardens inside out near their hiding place.

He munched the pretzel contentedly and walked on. Things were going well. His contacts with Romm were proving useful, giving the Irgun the chance to reach out from the constrictions of the underground to the outside world where they hoped one day to take a

The Joshua Inheritance

prominent place in a new Jewish State. He had passed on several messages from the Irgun leadership and received updates of the American position which he would take back. Menachem Begin had also survived being found during the curfew of Tel Aviv and, after the Goldsmiths Officers' Club attack on 1 March, wanted to make it clear that there was never any decision by the Irgun to kill the British. He simply wanted to remove the British from Eretz Israel and inevitably there would be casualties, but that was only to be expected in a military operation. This, he said, was the essential difference between his fight for the liberation of his country and what the British called terrorism.

'What about the King David Hotel?' Romm had asked. Paul was less pernickity about killing British soldiers than the leadership but he was embarrassed by the civilian death toll at the King David and replied that the British had been given plenty of warning by telephone call to leave the building. The American appeared to accept this explanation, and even told him that word on the diplomatic grapevine said the French Consulate confirmed they had been warned too. But Romm did not add that the French had not received the warning until five minutes after the explosion destroyed the hotel. He valued his contact with the Irgun too much to upset Paul Levi.

However, Paul was surprised when Romm told him the British had decided to pass the whole Palestine problem to the United Nations. He had not expected the British Empire to give in without a greater struggle. Britain, he deduced, must have ulterior motives. The United Nations would hand the Mandate back to Britain but without the obligation to set up a Jewish State. The struggle had to go on.

He finished his pretzel, smacked the crumbs off his hands and looked up past the old stone buildings into the clear ultramarine sky. It was like looking out of a deep chasm, and the clear blue air, deepening as the sun faded, carried a freshness of summer warmth like a prophecy of triumph. This sky, he thought, would soon shed the same glorious light on all his people as free men in their own State, a state rightfully theirs since Joshua had crossed the Jordan and beseiged the city of Jericho.

He found his new driver waiting for him near the Jaffa Gate in the old blue Chevrolet they had borrowed from a Tel Aviv taxi-driver who was an Irgun sympathiser. Paul climbed into the passenger seat and the driver pulled away. As they passed under the huge gate, Paul thought of all the victorious soldiers who had passed through Jerusalem's massive walls to rule the most famous city in the world. Soon, he thought, soon, Jerusalem would be ruled once again by its people, by the Jews.

In the street behind, the dark-suited Orthodox Jew gratefully accepted a lift from a stocky businessman in a grubby suit and shirt with no tie driving a Citroën. He shut the door and the Citroën accelerated after the blue Chevrolet ahead. He asked, 'Have Fairfax and Brogan reached the van yet?'

'No, sir. But they've been picked up by Taff in the Austin.'

'Good.' Major Meynell nodded, his eyes on the car in front. He was thankful the traffic was light. He did not want to lose the Chevrolet. He could imagine what Brogan would say after spending more than two weeks in a cold stone room watching for their target. Nor would Edward, on his first special operation, be impressed. All the same, he knew everything they did was breaking new ground. None of them had trained for this sort of work. Their experience was fighting Germans behind enemy lines, not chasing terrorists through the streets of a Middle Eastern capital. The thought that, as soldiers, they were being asked to behave like policemen, and rather unusual ones at that, left him feeling uneasy, but he kept such reflections to himself. It did not pay to introduce uncertainty, especially once committed to an operation. He must trust to his reconnaissance and planning.

The Chevrolet was leaving Jerusalem. They followed it along the Jaffa road past Police HQ, the Egged bus station, and through the new Jewish areas of Maskeret, Mahane Yehuda and Givat Ram. On the radio Meynell was relieved to hear the code word which indicated Brogan was in the Bedford box van with Edward Fairfax. Now the whole team was behind him, ready to react as he dictated. He wriggled out of the black jacket, pulled a thick blue and white check jellaba over his head and, instead of the Homburg, he finished his transformation with a white Arab shemag and black cords.

Paul Levi relaxed into his seat and watched the narrow main road sucked under the big Chevrolet as they picked up speed on the edge of the city. He was thinking of the men and women who had sacrificed themselves for the cause. There were four Irgun men under sentence of death in Acre jail and no doubt the man who had been caught a day ago with a hand grenade in his pocket would be sent there as well. He was not hopeful they would be released. There was talk this time that there would be hangings. As events on the world stage dragged politicians nearer some sort of solution, the British appeared set on vicious relief for their frustration.

As soon as they cleared Romena, on the outskirts of Jerusalem, the driver began to look nervously through the windscreen to the left and right, up the steep hillsides on both sides of them. The road from Jerusalem to the coast plunged into a narrow defile of the Soreq valley offering plenty of good ambush places among the rocks, scrub and olive trees. Worse, the area was Arab and recently more cars than ever had been attacked because the Arabs were beginning to suspect that the great powers would ignore their interests.

Paul sensed the nervousness of his driver, and both were so absorbed trying to spot trouble in the scrub gulleys and bends under the rocky bluffs above them that they did not notice the Citroën closing up behind them.

Major Meynell decided that, since Levi had left the city, he would pick him up before he lost him. Over the radio he heard that the Austin and Bedford van were not far behind, hidden by the twisting road in the bottom of the valley. He ordered them to close up and stand by.

'We're going to get the bastard,' grinned Brogan savagely, hearing the message crackling out from the radio in its canvas bag on the floor of the cab. He pressed his foot on the accelerator and the old van swung dangerously round a bend after the Austin. Edward now felt he was really living and Brogan's erratic driving only added to the thrill of the chase. After so long cooped up waiting for Levi to appear, the speed and expectation of danger was like a drug. For the first time, they had the upper hand on his enemy, all the surprise and the advantage, and, like cavalry officers charging at the Battle of Waterloo, they were committed to the fight and could not be turned. Without thinking, Edward pulled his new Sterling SMG on to his lap and checked that the thirty-round magazine was tight in place. Brogan nodded his approval.

Paul hardly noticed the Citroën as it hooted its horn to overtake. He was more concerned that his driver slow down and keep them out of the ditch between the edge of the road and the rocks rising away to the hilltops.

'Mind out!' he shouted. The Citroën had cut in too soon, giving them no room. Too late, Paul realised the Citroën was braking, that another car had closed up behind them, that they were being ambushed.

'Drive round,' he screamed, but his driver seemed to freeze in terror, shoving his foot on the brake. The big Chevrolet skidded off the tarmac into the ditch and ground to a halt on its belly, two wheels firmly wedged

The Joshua Inheritance

in the ditch. As Paul fell against his door with the driver on top of him, there was a screech of tyres on the road and he saw the black saloon behind pull up in a cloud of dust beside them.

'Get out!' he yelled at the driver, struggling to shove him away. Glancing through the back window he could see a medium-sized van stopping behind with two heavily bearded Arabs in the front. All of a sudden, the road seemed to be filled with hard-faced Arabs carrying pistols and sub-machine-guns and shouting for them to get out of the car.

As the two clambered out, the driver panicked. Convinced he was facing brutal Arab torture and death, he ran, ducking past Taff as he came round the back of the Austin. He sprinted towards the van, half-thinking to cut round the back and make his escape over the bank into the valley below the road. Edward saw him coming and heard the shouted orders to open fire. It was unnecessary. After the days and weeks waiting for Levi under the tight discipline of their watch routine, he was in complete control, functioning on every detail of his job with terrible simplicity. He knew the others could not shoot in his direction for fear of hitting him, he knew the Jewish driver had to be stopped, so he levelled his Sterling, waited till the man was halfway across the road and then pulled the trigger. The long burst hit the driver square in the chest and his momentum lifted and spun him headlong the rest of the way over the tarmac till he crumpled in the dust by a milestone. Edward observed they were eight miles from Jerusalem and went to check the body.

The others gave Paul Levi no such chance to escape. Three men jumped on him as he climbed out second from the Chevrolet and dragged him into the back of the van. Taff handcuffed his wrists and ankles and sat on him with his Browning rammed into the soft flesh beneath his chin.

They all piled back into the cars and set off through the deepening dusk. Mayor Meynell led them off the main road on a route he had reconnoitred into the remote dry scrubby hills behind the Soreq valley. This area was criss-crossed with cart tracks and contained only a few Arab villages and rough grazing land for their sheep and goats. The track he chose was rough and hardly suitable for cars and Brogan swore richly trying to keep the van straight. Meynell stopped once, to position the Austin out of sight behind a stone wall in an olive grove where two men could act as lookout in case they had been followed. Then he stopped again several hundred yards further on in low ground by a small stream-bed where he placed the Citroën and van facing ready to escape on to the high ground upstream if they had to leave in a hurry.

'Nice quiet place, this,' remarked Brogan as he dropped out of the cab. He had discarded his shemag. In his jellaba with the sleeves rolled up, he looked like an Old Testament prophet about to perform an heroic task. He walked round to the back of the van and without ceremony helped Taff pull their prisoner by the legs on to the ground like a sack of meat.

Paul tried to ignore the bruises on his face and stop himself shaking, knowing it was nothing more than the shock of being seized. Memories of being captured as he tried to run away from the blazing Hudson flooded back. Then, several German soldiers had crushed him into the cold wet grass. Now, he was lying in the dry dusty earth of his homeland. He told himself that should give him courage, but the feelings of utter failure were identical. Worse now because he knew what was in store. The first time, he had been able to cope, through training and ignorance. Now he had experience, he knew the pain that was to come and it terrified him. He tried to divorce himself from reality, but Major Meynell did not intend to give him the chance, any chance.

Conversationally he said, 'Break his arm, Taff.'

Taff nodded and Edward's shock at the order vanished as Meynell deliberately added, 'Don't let's forget. This was the chap who blew up the King David'. The rage returned. Levi was the man responsible for reducing his father to a shapeless bloody mess. There was so much they could do to him before he looked anything like the object Edward had sickeningly identified in the hospital morgue. Edward moved without feeling to sit on Paul's legs. Brogan held the prisoner's wriggling body by the head. There was a moment's total silence except for a few distant crickets, grey dusk filled the ravine and one or two faint stars had appeared in the deep-violet-blue sky arching over the darkened high ground above them. Taff knelt down, seized one of the arms handcuffed behind Levi's back in his big hand, held the forearm and wrist twisted over his bent knee and suddenly rammed his bodyweight down.

Paul tried not to scream but the sound throttled him, pumping from his lungs like liquid terror, echoing round the arid gully. The agony ripped up his arm and seemed to tear his shoulder from its socket. Detachedly, as though his mind was floating a few feet above the grim fate of its body, he complained to himself that the bastards were giving him no time. The rest of him was lost in uncontrollable twitching and tortured stomach cramps. When the big Welshman dropped him again, he screamed and screamed as his broken arm flopped on to his back, wrenched by the other handcuffed to it.

Major Meynell crouched down beside Paul's head and asked, 'What are you going to tell me about the Irgun Zvai Leumi?'

Paul stared at the soft suede shoes in front of his face. Stupidly, inconsequentially, he wondered where they came from. He twitched spasmodically, unable to stop himself, and streaks of pain shot up and down his arm and across his chest from his shoulder. He felt as if he were being electrocuted. He dared not refuse to answer, but he had to. He shook his head, unable to control himself enough to speak, to open his mouth and not scream.

Someone lifted his broken arm and the scream came anyway.

Meynell repeated his question, Paul shook his head, gurgling, and waited to float away in agony when someone pulled his arm again. No-one did. At least, not when he expected it. He waited, terrified. Then it came.

In twenty minutes Paul's resistance folded, not because of the racking pain which tore him end to end each time Meynell shook him by the hand of his broken arm, but because his energy evaporated in the awful waiting for the pain to start, in the knowing it would start, because his interrogator mercilessly told him it would, but never knowing exactly when.

Night fell. It was cold and the stars blazed as Paul talked freely about the underground but his eyes were tight shut against the world and the blackness was nothing but dark failure in his heart. The pain had stopped. Or at least subsided and he refused to open his eyes to admit the reality of his guilt, even when Major Meynell stopped asking questions, apparently satisfied at the long list of names and addresses he had collected from his prisoner. The other men left him alone and he lay on the hard earth as if dead, face down in the dust, his front caked with sand and sweat, his back and his mottled, swollen arm covered with dew settling out of the open night sky.

He was dimly aware of soft footfalls and torchlights as they read his answers in their notebooks. One of them crouched down beside him again and his mind fell away in terror and self-contempt. He prayed they would not make him betray any more. He knew he would, just to stop the agony. He braced himself but the quiet voice which spoke reached out

The Joshua Inheritance

to him from a dark place beyond his present misery.

'Why don't you tell me about Operation Joshua?'

Paul groaned. So that was behind his failure, for the second time he cursed having anything to do with the British.

Edward looked down and realised the wretched prisoner had not recognised his voice or bearded face. Perhaps it was as well. Detachment. And besides, he no longer cared what happened to Paul Levi. He had watched Major Meynell's dispassionate and cruel interrogation without any feeling of nausea or sympathy which surprised him. Edward did not think he had suddenly changed into a devil, merely that Paul Levi had committed himself beyond the help of the usual course of law, especially with people whose lives and families he had destroyed. Simply, his luck had changed. He had fallen into the hands of enemies as lacking in compunction as himself. In a very short time Edward had discovered that life could be most unpleasant and, having been kidnapped himself, he had the scant satisfaction of having seen both sides of the coin.

Brogan watched him, leaning against the van, his ears open for the noises of danger beyond the darkened gully. Taff sat on the running-board of the Citroën, a Sterling over his knees, smoking a cigarette, cupping the glowing tip in his hands when he inhaled. Major Meynell was reading his notes with a torch, happy for Edward to ask the prisoner a few questions of his own. He was pleased with the young officer's hard dedication.

Edward leaned forward and whispered harshly into Paul's ear, 'Major George Fairfax was in a German prison when you landed in the Hudson, so how could he have betrayed you?'

'He knew where we were going to land. He told the Germans.'

Edward detected a ring of obstinacy through the

croaking defeated voice. He repeated, 'He was in jail. Maybe he knew your Hudson was coming, but not when.' He put his fingers lightly on Paul's back, just near his broken arm, exactly as Major Meynell had done during his interrogation.

'I'm trying to remember!' Paul gasped, terrified by the shock of that light touch. He dragged his mind back to England, to their training sessions with Fairfax, Romm and the others before the operation, and their briefings, and said desperately, 'Fairfax told us he would send for us.'

'What d'you mean?'

'They were going to set up in the area, in a safe house, then Fairfax was going to signal us to join them when he had done the recces for the landing strip.'

'Where was it?' Edward leaned down near the ground to hear Paul's reply.

'In some hills called Mittlere Vogesen on the map,' Paul said quickly. He closed his eyes again, his cheek cool on the ground and tried to remember their last briefing before taking off. 'I think we landed near a village called Salm, but we didn't need any more information. Fairfax and Romm were supposed to take us from there. All we had was an emergency rendezvous at a grid reference on a wood corner and a bearing to go and find the American army if we didn't make the RV.'

The names meant nothing to Edward, but he nodded and made a note on a piece of paper. He asked, 'Who else was involved?'

'They're all dead, except Axel Romm and me.'

Edward paused at that. Paul's deliberate omission of his father's name was striking. So, he must know he had died in the King David Hotel bomb. Ice cold, he planted his hand firmly palm down on Paul's back, right by the tortured arm and hissed, 'No, you shit! I mean in England. Who briefed you there?'

Paul began to tremble. His words tumbled out. 'Some

smooth fellow in a suit came down to see us a lot, but we never knew any names. I promise!'

There was no need for them to know names and security was tight. The story seemed likely but Edward did not take his hand away.

'What was the object of Joshua?'

Paul hesitated and then whispered reluctantly into the cold earth by his face, 'I don't know.'

Edward's hand flicked hard and gripped the arm. Paul screamed and his back arched till Edward let go when he collapsed on the dirt, his nose and mouth slapping back on the sand which was damp with his own snot.

'Come on,' Edward insisted venomously. 'What was it?'

'God, please! I don't know! We weren't told. Fairfax was going to tell us after we landed. For God's sake, we never knew what the bloody operation was all about!'

Edward looked down at the dark, panting form at his feet and asked one more question. 'How could Fairfax know that final message was sent bringing you out if he was in a prison cell at the time?'

'He knew. I'm sure. How else did the Germans know exactly when to come?'

'Liar!' Edward snapped angrily and yanked the broken arm in frustration. He could not work it out, but he was sure his father was innocent.

Paul screamed hoarsely, his throat dry with screaming, and tried to wriggle out of the way, like an earthworm, but Edward was finished with him. He stood up.

'Time to go,' Major Meynell announced. 'Got to hand this bugger to the proper authorities. He'll join his friends in Acre jail.'

He smiled broadly and reached for the radio to warn the two in the Austin. So far, he thought, the Special Squad seemed to have made a good impression on the Irgun.

* * *

Paul Levi was handed to Angus Maclean at a rendezvous arranged by Major Meynell over the radio on the way back into Jerusalem. Blandly, he told Angus that Paul must have broken his arm in the chase after which he was handcuffed and brought in. On the way, he had been good enough to give a great deal of information about the Irgun. Angus asked no questions, and Paul was formally arrested and handed over to a police doctor. While his broken arm was examined with unceremonious and agonising efficiency in his cell, the Special Squad threw a party in the secluded villa in the American Colony during which considerable quantities of beer were consumed.

They lounged about in open-necked khaki shirts and battledress trousers, incongruous on the rich colonial easy chairs in the drawing-room, bathed in a feeling of a job well done. After two weeks through wet and shine in the same filthy Arab clothes, Edward felt much refreshed after a good soak in an enormous cast-iron bath. He changed into a khaki shirt, trousers and suede shoes, but Meynell advised the two of them to keep their beards for the time being.

Brogan distributed another round of beer bottles, shouted for attention and announced, 'Here's to a new member of the team!' He drank copiously from his glass and wiped beer froth from his thick black beard as the others responded and drank Edward's health.

Major Meynell agreed. He had been impressed with Edward's behaviour during the long and difficult watch and his quick thinking during the ambush.

'You done well, lad,' said Taff approvingly.

'Thank you,' said Edward. He drank his beer enjoying the thought that he had never expected a corporal, however experienced, to address him as 'lad'. Nor had he expected to sit about in a smart drawing-room belonging to people he had never met, in shirt and trousers and a heavy beard drinking beer and celebrating. Not at all like the Officers Mess dance. Surprisingly, it seemed perfectly natural in the circumstances of their job. Roger Haike would not have approved. Nor would his father. He frowned, reminded that he wanted to see Colonel Haike again.

Taff went on cheerfully, 'Good work. That driver might've got clean away if you 'adn't shot him.'

Edward nodded, smiling. It seemed an odd thing to do, to smile, having just shot someone and then to sit about discussing it in self-satisfied tones, drinking beer. But Taff was right. There was actually no pleasure in the act of killing, but there was self-satisfaction in accurate shooting and a good feeling that, by the terms of his work as a soldier on the team, he had acted correctly and efficiently, and the others accepted him for it.

Major Meynell came over and said, 'Good show, Edward. By the way, I don't think Levi realised you were listening when he admitted kidnapping you, but I expect you're pleased he's told us where you were held? It sounds like there's quite a place under the ground at Rishon.'

'Yes sir,' Edward replied. Even if Major Meynell used his Christian name, he was still the officer in charge. He thought for a moment of asking if he could go to Rishon during the inevitable raid and see his cell again. But the idea was a weakness, placing ridiculous importance on reliving miseries of the past. He rejected it, but the thought gave birth to a plan to do just that for his father. Before too much beer muzzed his thoughts, he resolved he would visit the place where his father's operation went so disastrously wrong. Maybe there he would find out more of what happened.

In the early hours, Edward dragged himself upstairs, blurred by drink. Fully clothed, he collapsed on to his bed and a confused image floated across his mind, of the dead driver crumpled by the milestone, and the tattoo on his outstretched arm. Number 495663, Edward remembered, and passed out.

7

A LITTLE HOLIDAY IN THEIR HEARTS

4 May 1947

Paul Levi was sitting on the stone floor of his cell in Acre jail cradling his left arm. The break had been set and plastered but was not healing. His whole arm ached and throbbed and he kept adjusting his position to ease the pain. Around him sat other members of the Irgun who were prisoners in the old castle.

Outside in blazing sun, the citadel rose in solid castellated tiers over the old port of Acre with its flat roofs and narrow cobbled streets as it had for centuries, guarding the spit of land which hooked into the sparkling sea and provided a natural port for the galleons of Crusaders and Saracens who fought each other to the death for Christianity and Islam. Now, a still-older religion was at war with both, its young men incarcerated for wanting to possess the Holy Land.

Paul glanced round the crowd with him. They took his nervousness for their own, waiting for the explosion they all expected, but Paul's expression was a curtain over the secret guilt he carried for being an informer. The pain of his broken arm was a constant reminder.

In spite of the cool stone walls, they all sweated. Someone looked at his watch. It said 4.15 in the afternoon. The Arab prisoners had been routinely locked up in their cells at four o'clock and through the narrow barred windows they could hear their Jewish friends

The Joshua Inheritance

deliberately playing noisy games in the prison yard. Time dragged terribly.

Outside, in the salty, seaside heat of late afternoon, Solomon sweated too as he pressed his lorry through the Arab crowds and street vendors in the winding lanes which cluttered the market Suq al-Abyad behind the prison. The truck cleared the Suq and Solomon stopped at a chosen point beneath the walls of the fort. He looked up. The ancient stone walls looked massively impregnable. Above, on the promenade, Arab guards patrolled, part of a force of 132 Arabs led by British officers and NCOs.

Solomon and the man with him had no time to think what would happen to them if the guards looked over. Dressed and equipped as telephone men, they pulled ladders off their truck, set them against the wall, dragged two huge twenty-kilo packs of plastic explosive up the ladders and fixed them to a ledge beneath two windows in the fortress wall. They lit the fuse cord, retired down the ladders as fast as they could and ran down the narrow lane to shelter by the corner of a house. Inside, the 29 Jews chosen to escape counted the hanging seconds. Paul wondered if the attempt had been abandoned and if they should change back from their civilian clothes into the rough prison shirt and trousers the British made them wear. Then, maybe, the British would execute him after all.

At 4.22 the Citadel shook with a massive explosion. Huge pieces of stone were hurled into the air and clattered down all over the prison and the houses outside. Solomon and his friend moved forward uncertainly into the dense cloud of smoke and dust filling the lane and obscuring the Citadel wall. Closer, they could see a great hole. The castle prison was breached.

Paul and the others were shaken and a little deafened by the blast which echoed through the cave-like cells inside. The Arab prisoners began shrieking while the

Jews went into action at once. Two prisoners rushed from their cells with explosive charges which had been smuggled in and blew two connecting steel doors, each time retreating down the corridors as the fuses ran out to avoid the blasts. In three minutes they were scrambling up the mound of rubble in the room behind the breached wall and met Solomon peering in as he perched on the ladder outside. They shouted the password, '*Banu!*'

Solomon shouted back, '*Anu!*' It was the signal for escape.

Above, the Arab guards were in total confusion. The second explosions inside had only added to the chaos, and home-made grenades were being flung at them by Jewish stay-behind prisoners who had been ordered to create further diversion. Outside the walls, still more diversionary parties of Irgun attackers were mortaring the guards' quarters. On the outskirts of Acre, roads had been mined and ambush groups waited to hamper any British who came to help.

Inside Paul followed the others down the grey stone corridors, past the smashed steel doors, till he reached the last room. With a thrill he saw the gaping hole in the wall and struggled up the rubble, slipping and knocking his plastered arm, uncaring now of the pain. Hands helped him out and down the ladders to the road. In moments he was pulled over the backboard of the truck as it moved off and accelerated into the narrow Arab streets. Already Arabs were gathering, shouting and beginning to throw stones and missiles. As they gathered speed along the cobbled lane to the medieval gate in the al-Jazzar town wall, Solomon saw an Arab beginning to close the great wooden doors. He shouted a warning. Desperate measures were needed or they would be caught inside the Arab quarter and certainly lynched before the British guards could collect their wits and find them. The man beside him hurled a grenade on to the road ahead and the crowds scattered. The truck roared out through the great doors, still open, to freedom.

18

EXODUS

July–August 1947

Edward agreed to meet Aubrey in the Astoria restaurant on 18 July. He had seen Solly Mannheim when he left hospital after his kidnap the year before, but had not used the place since, so it was with a feeling of nostalgia that he walked off the cobbled street and sat out under the blue and white awning at the table where Carole used to wait for him during his Arabic course. He had deliberately chosen the Astoria in the hope of seeing her again.

Without being asked, Solly Mannheim eased between the tables with a glass of 'Eagle' beer. He showed no surprise at Edward's thick beard, suit and tie.

'Thanks,' said Edward, sipping the cool refreshing beer. The middle of July was sticky-hot as usual. Solly folded his hands over the apron round his stomach and watched him, thinking Edward looked almost Jewish with his sandy beard.

Edward noticed his gaze. He grinned boyishly and lied, 'I've been in the desert for weeks, on the Transjordanian border. I've got a forty-eight-hour-pass, but I'll have to get all this cut before I go back to camp, or I'll be for it.'

Solly shrugged again. He doubted any of what Edward had said, but then again there were so many British servicemen doing all sorts of things, anything was

The Joshua Inheritance

possible. In the end, he did not much care. Like so many of the Jews, he hated the extremists' violence.

Edward wiped his mouth with a napkin. 'How're things Solly?'

'Business isn't good' he pulled a face and spread his hands.

Trying to sound as casual as possible, Edward asked, 'Carole come here any more?'

'No-one comes,' said Solly. 'I'd tell you if she does, but she doesn't. I don't know why. Just to run a business is all I want, but no-one comes any more.' For more than a year, even off-duty servicemen had been carrying pistols and rifles at all times and they went about in groups. The Arabs and Jews were polarising into their own localities and social groups, not so many people visited the Holy Places in Jerusalem because of the tension and violence, and Solly Mannheim's trade had suffered badly. Only a couple of other tables were occupied.

Edward noticed Aubrey Hall-Drake walking down the street. He looked neat in his summer uniform of shirt and long lightweight trousers. He refused to wear shorts. He always said they reminded him of hateful early days at school. The dark red Parachute Regiment lanyard circled his shoulder and a .38 Smith and Wesson revolver hung in a canvas holster from his webbing belt. He stopped, smoothed his black hair and peered under the awning at the people on the tables. Edward waved and Aubrey looked astonished. He stepped over and declared loudly, 'What a revolting beard, old chap!' Grinning, they shook hands, pleased to see each other, and sat down. Solly brought another beer and wandered off to his kitchens. Perhaps the two Englishmen would order food.

Aubrey dropped his red beret on the table and said, 'Why'd you have to choose a place in the Jewish area? Gives me the creeps walking here on my own. Real feeling of hostility.'

'Oh, don't worry. We're well covered.'

'What d'you mean, covered?'

Edward ignored the question and said, 'Besides, I can hardly go into the King David wearing this beard, can I? Someone might see me.'

'Never mind the beard, it's the suit that bothers me.' Aubrey smiled. He had the distinct feeling they were being observed but Edward appeared relaxed and at ease, so he added, 'Rather too much silver thread for my liking. Local purchase, was it, from a tailor with a sense of humour? Or was it issued?'

Edward smiled. He wanted to avoid any further questions about his work on the Special Squad and coolly asked why Aubrey had wanted to meet.

Aubrey knew Edward was prevaricating but he admired the easy way he had turned the conversation. Edward had changed. He was more confident in himself.

'To tell you about that trouble with Captain Scarland.'

'Well?' Edward asked, sitting forward and immediately interested. Captain Scarland had vindictively insisted on pressing charges.

Aubrey deliberately played a game of his own, and said, 'Major Rattigan's been posted back home, lucky devil.'

'Not before sorting out Scarland, I hope?'

'No,' said Aubrey. He lit one of his Turkish cigarettes and offered one to Edward who refused.

'Come on, Aubrey! What happened?'

Aubrey smiled through a cloud of smoke, sipped his beer and said, 'The evidence of those two wogs was quite clear. They spent a week in jail, of course, but Major Rattigan advised Captain Scarland not to make a fuss. The whole thing's been brushed under the carpet.' He paused, enjoying the expression of relief on Edward's face, and then went on bitterly, 'Trouble is, Scarland has now taken over the Company. We spend all our time on those bloody cordon and searches, and the stupid man is obsessed. We've got no time off, not even a day out

The Joshua Inheritance

to shoot a few snipe or duck, and there's nothing else to do in this awful country. We can't go out of camp without being armed to the teeth and all one reads in the newspapers is junk about this UN Special Committee on Palestine. Poor devils have been sent here on a rat's job, to sort out the unsortable. God knows why anyone thinks it's special. It's the nineteenth committee to come here and it certainly won't be the last. I tell you, Edward, you're lucky to have something useful to do. I've had enough, and I'm off.'

Edward was sorry. They had become good friends, sharing the 'Sandpit' in El Bureij and the frustrations of the early days in Palestine. He asked, 'Where to?'

'I'm going to sea.'

Edward laughed out loud. 'You! Don't be absurd. You were sea sick on the boat coming over.' Still laughing he waved at Solly to bring another two beers.

Aubrey looked hurt and said, 'Only because they made us wear those smelly canvas life-jackets all the time, telling us the Med was still full of Jerry mines. This time, I'm going to be in charge. I've volunteered for guard duties on these ships taking illegal immigrants to Cyprus. Sounds a cushy number. I'm going up to Haifa later today to take some illegals off an old tub called *Exodus*. Four and a half thousand of them, all exhausted after a running battle with the Royal Navy. It's obviously a big propaganda event for this bloody UN Special Committee. The Jews broadcast the whole fight on their illegal Kol-Israel radio. I must say, it made rather exciting listening, like a pirate ship battling it out with the Navy fender all through the night. Still, I expect they'll quieten down in the displaced persons camps in Cyprus. I'm looking forward to the trip. I thought the sea breezes would do me good.'

'Nonsense,' Edward laughed. 'You just want to get your grubby little hands on these Lebanese and Egyptian girls who go to Cyprus for their holidays.'

Aubrey grinned. Cyprus was well known as a good place to spend leave. 'What about you, Edward? How's all this civvy-clothes thing going?' He waved his cigarette vaguely in Edward's direction. 'Interesting?'

Edward nodded. He trusted Aubrey and decided it would be churlish not to say what he could. 'We caught that sod Paul Levi the other day.'

Aubrey was impressed.

'Then he escaped from Acre jail in the breakout,' said Edward bitterly. The memory still made him furious. 'D'you realise twenty-nine got away? Makes you sick after all the effort to catch them. And 214 Arabs found the hole in the wall and buggered off too.' He pulled his wallet out of his inside pocket and extracted a black and white photograph which he tossed across the table at Aubrey.

Aubrey leaned forward and inspected it. 'So this is Levi? He looks young.'

'Same age as us,' Edward said. Angus Maclean had taken it when Levi was handed over and cleaned up after his interrogation in the gully and Paul's eyes betrayed the pain and humiliation of his torture.

'Funny,' Aubrey sighed studying Paul's smooth, broad forehead and thick dark hair, 'I would have expected someone who blows up so many people to have been older. Seems sort of irresponsible in someone young.'

'As if they don't know what they're destroying?'

'Yes, I think that's it. You ought to suffer a little first before you inflict it on other people.'

Edward shook his head. 'There are plenty of teenagers in the terrorist groups. Like that boy we killed in the riot.'

'Well, you don't have to worry about him on the files,' said Aubrey. He picked up the photo and asked, 'Can I keep this? This is a rather better photograph than the usual police mugshots, and you never know, I might spot him.'

The Joshua Inheritance

'Help yourself,' said Edward. The chances were remote, judging by the long days Brogan and he had spent waiting to catch Levi, but anything was worth trying and there were plenty of copies in Angus's files. He felt better for Aubrey's company and suggested lunch.

'Sorry old chap. I've got to catch the train. To Haifa.' He grinned. 'For my little rest trip to Cyprus.'

'I'll give you a lift,' said Edward standing up and leaving the money for the beers on the table.

Aubrey laughed. 'I suppose you'll tell me next you've got your own private car?'

Edward grinned through his beard. He gave a discreet wave and Brogan started up the squad Austin which was parked across the street.

'Anne, dear,' said John Fullerton,' you really don't need to wear black any more.' He himself was wearing a dark pin-stripe suit, having come straight from working late at the Foreign Office to take Anne Fairfax out to dinner. He went over to the drinks table to pour her a dry sherry and himself a large whisky. 'After all, it's more than a year now.'

'I know,' she replied uncertainly, looking at the calendar – 29 July. 'Only a week more.' Her blue eyes watered at the memory. 'Isn't it odd that we know exactly when George died on the 22nd? At 12.37. Just before his lunch.'

'Yes, dear,' said Fullerton without having the slightest idea what she was talking about. He knew all the King David's electric clocks had stopped together showing the same time, but he did not understand her thoughts that, in spite of that peculiar precision of his death, a whole year had passed and she had not been able to visit his grave. She said, 'It seems like yesterday.'

'Tragic business,' said Fullerton, sipping his whisky and looking at her carefully. She had suffered the shock of losing her husband well, supported by endless letters from Edward who for some reason had taken to writing more regularly. And he had been pleased to help too. She had been easy to help. A pleasure, but he wished she would stop wearing black. The colour suited her sad expression and fair hair, in fact she looked very well in black, but he wanted to make her forget George Fairfax.

Anne shook herself out of her reverie, telling herself that that phase of her life was over, and she was lucky to be young enough to start again. She looked up at Fullerton and said, 'Dear John, you're right. I'll take off my widow's weeds tomorrow, I promise. I suppose, if I'm being honest, I got so used to being alone during the war when George was away, that this last year has been no different, and quite honestly I've only worn black to be, well, official, I suppose. People rather expect one to do it, don't they?'

'Not any more, dear. Not after a year, anyway.'

She smiled at him. 'You've been marvellous, John, sorting everything out for me. I don't know what I'd have done without you, really.'

He smiled with pleasure. 'Good health, then,' he said, lifting his glass and was delighted when she returned his smile and sipped her sherry.

'Things aren't any better out there, are they?' She doubted she would ever be allowed to visit her husband's grave, the way the situation in Palestine seemed to be developing. The British seemed less and less capable of controlling the violence of the Jews, and the Arab countries around Palestine were increasingly belligerent.

Fullerton walked over to the mantelpiece and stood with his back to the empty fireplace. He shook his head. 'Worse, I'm afraid. I don't like the look of this *Exodus* business at all. All the illegals were transferred to our three ships without too much trouble. Everyone on board expected them to go to Cyprus, but this time we

The Joshua Inheritance

knew where they came from, and under international law, we're entitled to send them back. So, you'll read in tomorrow's papers that they have arrived in France, at a place called Port-de-Bouc on the south coast, near Marseilles. That's where they all came from originally and Ernie Bevin has told the French in no uncertain terms that they must take them all back.'

Anne laughed. 'I don't imagine the French like being ordered about by Mr Bevin.'

Fullerton looked glum and agreed. There was an atmosphere of impending disaster in the Foreign Office already. 'The French are being typically awkward, but I must say Ernie Bevin's hardly the epitome of tact. There's a French minister called François Mitterand who says that France will take no measures to force them on to French soil. Of course he knows damned well that the Jewish subversives are filling them up with a lot of Zionist propaganda to stay on board. I can't see how we'll get them to land unless we throw them overboard and make them swim ashore. It's all very embarrassing.'

'And none of you men in the Foreign Office like being embarrassed.'

Fullerton bridled but softened when he saw that Anne was teasing him. But there was no end to it all in the signals coming from HQ Middle East. That morning three convicted Irgun terrorists had been hanged in Acre jail, but the Irgun were holding hostage two sergeants who had been working in SIME, MI5's cover name for their secret Intelligence network in the Middle East. For two weeks the Army had searched everywhere in suspect Jewish areas for the two sergeants without success.

'Nothing's happened to Edward, has it?' Anne asked worriedly, misunderstanding Fullerton's expression.

'No,' he said cheering up. He changed the subject. 'Any news from him?'

'Yes, I got a letter today. As a matter of fact, I wanted to talk to you about that.'

Anne picked up an airmail letter from the little mahogany table beside her chair and flicked through the two pages before finding the part she wanted. 'I don't really understand all this Army jargon, but he says he wants me to ask you about George's work in the war.'

Fullerton's spirits sank and he rubbed his long nose to conceal his annoyance. He said, 'Of course, dear Anne. Delighted to help if I possibly can.'

'He says there is still a lot of unpleasant talk about George's court martial. He doesn't give details but says the case is affecting him and he wants to clear it all up, and he thinks he can. That would be really wonderful, wouldn't it?'

'Yes, dear.'

Anne smiled at him again and went on, 'He says he needs to find out about what he calls "the orders, briefings and signal messages" of George's operation. Is that right? All sounds very technical. He says he's especially keen about these signal messages.'

I bet he is, thought Fullerton angrily, but he put on a bland smile and said with all truthfulness, 'I'm afraid most of all that sort of paperwork was destroyed after the war.'

'Officially?' Anne asked, puzzled.

Fullerton shook his head. 'Normally, of course, a lot is weeded out, leaving the core as a record, but in January 1945 there was a terrible fire in Baker Street where the files were held and they were nearly all destroyed.' She looked so disappointed that he added, 'I'll see what I can do. I promise.'

And he made a promise to himself to contact Colonel Haike at once to put a stop to Edward's meddling, even if it meant posting him back to England. As far as he was concerned, Operation Joshua had died

The Joshua Inheritance

with George Fairfax and that was the way he wanted to keep it.

Jerusalem's hillsides baked in another hot August afternoon and its people moved slowly on the dry streets seeking shade against the old stone buildings. Nervously, Paul turned into the narrow dusty alley leading to Romm's house, constantly looking up and down, like a bird sure the cat is about. He felt vulnerable. He guessed by now every British serviceman had his photograph and this time it was a good one.

His left arm still hurt – it was taking a very long time to heal. On the run, it was a serious drawback, the plaster showing up like a white beacon. He had resewn the seam of his jacket arm, allowing extra material, but it looked peculiarly large and there was nothing he could do about the stiffness. Every time he passed a road check, he felt sick, expecting to be arrested. He reached the stone house and knocked on the wicket gate under the arch. He waited impatiently staring at the dirty wooden doors shut tight against the outside world, willing Yaacov to come soon, before he was noticed. He heard noises inside and the little gate opened.

'Carole!' He could just see her slim shape in the shadows, in a skirt and blouse. Presumably she was off-duty.

'Paul! What are you doing here?'

'I've got to see your father.' He glanced up the street, desperately wanting to slip past her out of the glare into the safety of the shadows inside. 'Is he here?'

'Yes,' she replied, hesitating, not sure whether Paul should come in when her father was at home, busy with diplomatic papers to do with the UNSCOP committee.

'It's important,' said Paul urgently.

She noticed the underlying tone of panic in his voice. 'Alright, you'd better come in.'

He slipped inside at once and followed her through the

cool rooms of the house to the patio at the back where Axel Romm was working in his shirt sleeves at a wooden table under an umbrella against the heat of the sun. The table was covered with papers.

'Paul's here,' Carole announced evenly, leading him into the sunlight.

Her father frowned and said gruffly, 'The hell you are, Paul! What in God's name are you doing here? We made no plan to meet, and you Irgun guys aren't exactly popular after hanging those two sergeants.'

Paul said, 'Nothing to do with me.' He lifted his arm slightly.

Axel Romm modified his tone but said, 'Yeah, okay, but goddam it! Why, your people even booby-trapped the bodies. Put a bomb in the ground under their feet. A Limey captain called Galetti cut them down from the eucalyptus tree and nearly blew himself to bits. Goddam outrageous!' Romm had no doubts about his support for the Jewish national home but the execution and mining of the two soldiers was hard to reconcile with the work of the UN committee. It had shocked all sections of Palestine's community.

'I'm sorry,' said Paul automatically. He did not want Romm to throw him back on the street, but he could see no difference between the British hanging Irgun prisoners-of-war and the Irgun hanging British prisoners-of-war. Except the British had hanged three while the Irgun had hanged only two sergeants. He guessed Romm's sharp reaction was more personal than moral. The two sergeants had been working for MI5, undercover, like Romm, and he guessed their deaths brought home the unpleasant end-risk of secret work. Paul's arm ached. He felt irritatingly inferior standing in front of Romm, as if having to make an official report to a senior officer, but he repeated, 'I'm sorry, but I wanted to see you before I left.'

'Leaving? What d'you mean?' Carole asked surprised.

The Joshua Inheritance

She did not want him to go at all. Ignoring her father's look, which told her to leave the two of them alone, she deliberately sat down on one of the chairs, crossed her long legs and waited for Paul to explain. She had got to know Paul well in the last months when he had been visiting her father with information about the Irgun.

Her father gave her a hard look and said, 'Yeah, what's this leaving?' He valued his contacts to the Irgun through Paul, which had considerably improved his prestige in the Consulate. The Consul was impressed and Romm wanted to keep it that way. Paul and he knew each other well, so Romm was able to apply a degree of judgement to what Paul said about the Irgun which would be denied him with another man he did not know.

'My cover here is blown,' said Paul quietly. There was nothing to boast about that. It was a fact and the private guilt of being an informer ruined any feeling of achievement he might have had at his work for the cause. When Yudelmann told him he should leave for his own good, he had been immensely relieved.

'I'm not surprised,' said Carole. She knew he was involved in the underground, but not of his involvement in the bombings, and she could see his plastered arm was a handicap. She said, 'Is it alright? Mending, I mean?' She thought it quite likely the police surgeons had been efficient but rudimentary. Even some doctors found it hard to be impartial sometimes.

'That's the other reason for going,' Paul admitted. 'I can't get it fixed here, so I'm going to Europe to have it done properly in a hospital.'

'Without fear of being arrested?'

Paul nodded.

'So what did you want to tell me?' Romm demanded. He had work to do, and little time to spend on Paul Levi. There was no point if he was going. The Irgun would send someone else if they wanted to. And he was sure they did.

Carole noticed her father's curt tone with a sense of embarrassment but Paul ignored it. He knew Romm too well. He lifted his broken, plastered arm and said, 'The men who gave me this wanted to know about Operation Joshua.' Without saying what he had been forced to reveal about the Jewish underground, he explained what he had said about 'Joshua' afterwards.

Carole was shocked. The implication of Paul's description made her feel sick. She pointed at his arm. 'You mean that was done deliberately?'

'There is nothing soft about the British, in spite of all we hear about fair play and that goddam stupid game of cricket,' said her father. 'Why did they want to know about the op?'

Paul shrugged. He had no idea. 'They knew I'd been on the operation. They wanted to know about Major Fairfax. I can tell you they didn't believe what I said.'

'Who were these guys?' Romm wanted to know.

'Some special group. I don't know who exactly. They didn't use names or ranks but they knew what they were doing, I promise you.'

'I can see that,' Romm said glancing at the plaster peeping out at Paul's wrist. He stood up and began pacing about the patio. 'Carole, get him a drink or something,' he instructed his daughter and when Carole had left them alone, he said to Paul, 'When are you going?'

'Tomorrow. Through the Lebanon and Turkey.' He did not want to risk going through Egypt in company with more Englishmen.

Romm gave him a piercing look. 'You're not involved in this farce with the *Exodus*?' American sources told him the Jews intended to make the maximum propaganda impact with the refugees still incarcerated on the three British ships at Port-de-Bouc and that the French had no intention of complying with the British instructions to take them ashore. Further, he had leaned Jews were

The Joshua Inheritance

receiving support from sympathisers on shore and might be planning other tricks.

Paul replied, 'I'm going to get my arm fixed, in Switzerland. Anyway, what more can we do? The British are doing it all for us. They're really behaving like Nazis. The whole world's Press is having a field day recording every detail of their stupidity.'

Romm nodded. It was true. He said, 'Okay, but if you hear any further nonsense about Operation Joshua, you goddam let me know. Yeah?'

Almost four weeks later, at the end of August, Edward was sitting with the others in the rather upright red and white striped easy chairs in the drawing-room of their secluded safe house. They were waiting for Major Meynell to come back from Police HQ. There had been a fuss that morning when Angus Maclean arrived to say that Bernard Fergusson wanted to see him at once. All plans were suspended till he returned.

Brogan wandered in with a steaming hot enamel mug of tea which he gave to Taff who was reading the *Mid-East Mail*, the British Forces' newspaper. 'Just as I told you, Sean,' said Taff sourly. 'Not two weeks since we gave 'em independence in India and the little brown bastards are at it. Says 'ere that more than ten thousand 'ave been murdered in Punjab. There's a lot of work in killing ten thousand people.'

Brogan observed, 'And what would be the point of it all? And them as just got what they wanted? The end of the Imperial British Raj.'

'It's religion, boyo. Poison of the people,' said Taff, knowledgeably misquoting Karl Marx's criticism of Hegel, his lilting voice deep like a prophet and his black eyes flashing at the thought of disaster. 'Fanatics, they are! They're all the same, these religious lunatics. Muslims and Hindus in Pakistan and India, Jews and Arabs 'ere. Baptists in the valleys at 'ome, Protestants and Roman Catholics in the Irish bogs. All murdering each other.'

Brogan grinned. 'You leave the bogs out of it, you homicidal Welsh druid. Just tell me that's a fine brew of tea.'

Taff scowled and pursed his lips carefully against the dirty piece of black masking tape which Brogan had stuck on to insulate the hot edge of the enamel mug. He sipped loudly and grudgingly admitted, 'Passable enough, to sweeten the terrible state of the world.'

'So it should,' Brogan retorted. 'I put your usual five sugars in it.'

On the way back to the kitchen, he asked Edward, 'Want a brew, Mr Fairfax? I've just made a pot of the best, in the kitchen. Even that miserable Welshman likes it.'

'Thanks, Sean,' said Edward. Brogan gave him a funny look and went out to the kitchen.

They heard Brogan's rubber-soled shoes squeaking over the polished red-cedar floor in the hall and he reappeared with another mug which he handed to Edward. Then he sat down on a chair nearby and sipped his own tea, watching Edward staring across the room. He nodded at the signal Edward was holding and said, 'Bad news, is it?'

Edward focused on Brogan and shrugged. 'I don't know. It's from Mr Hall-Drake. He's on one of those boats with the *Exodus* refugees. You read it.'

'Are you sure? I'll not be after intruding.'

'Read it,' Edward insisted.

Brogan briefly studied the incomprehensible routing codes at the top. The signal came from the SS *Empire Rival*, via the Royal Navy in Gibraltar, to the HQ Palestine in the King David Hotel in Jerusalem and finally to the Palestine Police HQ in the 'Russian' compound.

He read, '"EXCLUSIVE FOR INSPECTOR A MACLEAN PALESTINE POLICE STOP   PLEASE PASS ASAP TO 2ND LT E FAIRFAX STOP   FINALLY PERSUADED CAPTAIN TO LET

The Joshua Inheritance

ME SEND THIS STOP THINK EYE SAW SUBJECT OF PHOTO YOU GAVE ME AT SOLLY'S STOP HE CAME ABOARD WHILE THIS AWFUL TUB WAITING OFF PORT-DE-BOUC IN HOT SUN STOP HE IS PRETENDING TO BE A DOCTOR TO QUOTE ASSIST REFUGEES UNQUOTE STOP ACTUALLY PROBABLY PLANNING TO BLOW US UP EXCLAM STOP EYE HAVE TOLD SHIPS CAPTAIN BUT LITTLE CHANCE OF CATCHING HIM AS WE DARE NOT GO INTO AREAS OF SHIP OCCUPIED BY JEWISH ILLEGALS BRACKETS BUT CANNOT ADMIT THAT IN PUBLIC ENDBRACKETS STOP AS YOU KNOW WE ARE ON WAY TO HAMBURG WHICH IS BAD NEWS FOR REFUGEES WHO WILL END UP BACK BEHIND WIRE IN CAMPS IN GERMANY AGAIN BUT GOOD NEWS FOR ME AS WE HAVE BEEN PROMISED LEAVE IN ENGLAND AFTER THIS AWFUL TRIP STOP NOT AT ALL THE HOLIDAY I PLANNED EXCLAM STOP ALL BEST REGARDS AUBREY STOP"'

'The photo was of Paul Levi,' Edward explained.

Brogan looked serious. 'So the little bastard's gone back to stir them up in Europe.'

'I'm thinking I should go back there too.'

'For Paul Levi?'

'Not exactly,' said Edward. He was still not certain what he should do but increasingly he felt he must find the place in Alsace where his father's operation went so badly wrong.

They heard the front door open and slam and Major Meynell's voice shouting in the hall, 'Get all the boys in the dining-room and I'll put them in the picture.' He sounded angry.

They quickly gathered with their mugs of tea and sat round the mahogany table. Major Meynell drummed his fingers on the polished surface and waited for everyone to settle. He wore the summer uniform of his old cavalry regiment, which he always put on when he had to go to the police and Army headquarters to avoid attracting notice in an SAS uniform or one of his civilian disguises. The talking died away and he wasted no time.

'The other Special Squad is run by Major Roy Farran. Some of you will know him.' There was a grunt of approval from two or three around the dining-room table and Edward remembered Brogan telling him that Farran was another Special Air Service commander with a brilliant record fighting across France in 1944. 'There's been trouble. Some time ago, in June actually, the squad was accused of murdering a Jewish lad called Rubovitz. The lad disappeared and when Roy realised he was going to be charged with murder, so did he. To Syria. Colonel Fergusson went there and persuaded him to come back.' Major Meynell paused, looking round the serious faces watching him, and continued, 'To cut a long story short, he's got to face a court. I don't know exactly when, but they've decided to put on what I can only describe as a show trial, just to prove that the administration is even-handed.'

'Did he kill 'im, though?' Taff asked with keen professional interest.

'I don't know,' answered Major Meynell. Privately he suspected it was quite likely. 'The point is that HQ want to show that the Army is not above the law.'

Thoughtfully, Brogan posed a question. 'If we're supposed to stay inside the law, how do we fight the criminals and terrorists who are outside the law?'

'That's what I asked,' said Major Meynell, frowning. 'They've stuck us out on a limb to find these sods and give them some of their own medicine, and now that things have gone wrong, they're dropping us in the shit. I find it particularly galling so soon after those two poor sergeants in 'Slime' being hung up in a eucalyptus grove. You'd think they would want us to hit back at the criminals who did that, but it looks very much as though they'll make Roy Farran take the can and then wash their hands of us.'

'There's British for you,' interjected Taff gloomily. Edward grinned in spite of his surprise and annoyance.

The Joshua Inheritance

Their own squad had perhaps been lucky, or at least careful, with Paul Levi and other jobs since, and they had certainly begun to make an impact on the underground.

Major Meynell ignored the interruptions. He knew the team would be angry and frustrated. Finally, he warned them, 'As a result, the squads are under scrutiny and I've got to warn you that we're likely to be folded up quite soon. I'm sorry, lads, it's bloody wrong, but there's nothing I can do.'

'When, sir?' Edward asked. The thought of returning to his company under Captain Scarland was deeply depressing. Even Aubrey's fate on the *Empire Rival* was preferable.

'I don't know, Edward. Maybe in a week or so, maybe even sooner. Our boss, Colonel Fergusson, is under a lot of pressure right now.'

The meeting ended. One or two pulled faces but they stood up and wandered out. Until they were told to disband, Army life went on. There were jobs to do, cleaning weapons, maintaining the vehicles and preparing their next operation.

Brogan summed up their feelings with the comment, 'Have you noticed, lads, the Army's always late to start the thing at all, then, if it's a disaster, they'll paint a picture of it and call it glorious, but, if it's roaring success, they'll stop it at once and charge you for doing it in the first place.'

'And hang you if you're a Sein Feiner,' Major Meynell laughed at him. Brogan grinned behind his thick black beard but they were all depressed.

In the hall, Edward pulled Brogan to one side and without explanation led him out of the front door, down the steps and round the side of the house into the walled yard where the vehicles were parked. They stood behind the Austin.

'What's all the secrecy for?' Brogan demanded good-humouredly, scratching his beard.

Edward said earnestly, 'I want to raid Romm's house, and I can't do it on my own. I need your help.'

'Just like that?' Brogan asked, raising his eyebrows. 'I've done a few night excursions meself, private enterprise so to speak, beyond the call of duty, but d'you realise the risk you're taking if you're caught? There'll be no genial Major Rattigan to get you out of trouble this time.'

Edward nodded. 'What we've just heard from Major Meynell has decided me. I've got to get at Romm again, find out what I can from him before the squad is disbanded. My father's dead, Levi is gone, and Romm is the only one who hasn't talked about it. Besides, Captain Scarland will be impossible whatever I do. He'll never stop causing trouble and he won't exactly be keen to let me off to Jerusalem when I want.'

'Nor me,' agreed Brogan feelingly. Without hesitation, he made up his mind and said, 'Right. I'm with you. When shall we do it?' He instinctively liked Edward's commitment to clear his father's name.

Edward grinned with relief. 'Thanks, Sean. We'll go tonight.' Major Meynell's summons to Police HQ had upset the squad's plans that day.

Brogan nodded. He approved of Edward's decision to act at once and set about the necessary preparations.

Edward told Major Meynell that they wanted to go out for a drink later and was allowed to borrow the Citroën, while Brogan let it be known to the NCOs that he was actually planning to show their young officer to a brothel in the Beqaa district between Allenby Barracks and the railway station. All curiosity in what they were doing died after that and they left after dark wearing casual shirt and slacks and soft-soled shoes. They drove out of town beyond the North Ring Road on to Mount Scopus where they stopped in the shadows of some Jerusalem pines to slip on grey Arab jellabas and dirty-white shemags. As he settled the thick black cords on his head, Edward looked across at the lights of Jerusalem in the dark below them and wondered who might be in Romm's house.

Brogan drove, and they dropped off the high ground into the winding streets of the city, discussing their plan as they went. They had spent so long watching Romm's house before, that there was no need for a reconnaissance. They entered the walls of the Old City through the Damascus Gate and crossed from north to south between the Arab and Christian quarters. They parked in the Armenian quarter near St James's Cathedral several winding streets away from their target and walked. Edward felt the tension mounting, though he knew their beards and Arab dress made them look unlike anything remotely military and the grey robes melded into the darkness under the stone buildings rising above them. Edward imagined that robbers creeping through the cobbled lanes of Jerusalem had looked the same for centuries, since Christ's time.

Keeping to the shadows of the old stone buildings, they arrived at the door of the house which they had used to watch the Romms before. Edward whispered, 'Have you got the key?' He was anxious to get out of sight as soon as possible. A patrol of soldiers with Lee Enfield rifles turned into the other end of the narrow street.

'Of course,' answered Brogan hoarsely, fishing about under his jellaba, with a wary eye on the soldiers as well. 'If I can just find the thing under this frigging Jellaba. God knows how the Arabs do any work in these clothes.'

Just as he was thinking he must have lost it, his fingers closed on the key which he had taken from the squad admin office that evening. He swiftly opened the door and they both slid inside. Brogan closed the door quietly and they waited, listening in case the empty house had been reoccupied. Silence fell heavily on their ears, like dust, and Edward decided they were alone. 'Come on,' he said and led the way up the stone stairs to the room at the top which they knew so well.

The empty house was grey in the dark and smelled the same as he remembered it, of damp plaster and stale from lack of use. In the familiar little room at the top of the stairs they looked out of the window through the peeling wooden shutters on to the Romms' patio below, a dark square surrounded by the domed stone roofs around. Edward breathed his relief. There were no lights on in the house at all. Maybe everyone was away. He tugged at Brogan's arm to start immediately. Brogan shook his head, his finger to his lips and insisted they wait for an hour. He advised softly, 'A good poacher never blunders straight in. Absorb the atmosphere of the place and listen for all the little sounds and tricks of the night. Remember, we're moving on to their ground. This way the darkness will be on our side.'

The hour passed very slowly. Edward checked his watch from time to time, willing the minute hand to move faster. Nothing moved in the Romms' house and it was past one o'clock by the time they decided it was safe to move. By this time, they were thoroughly accustomed to the dark. They slipped quickly downstairs and dropped through the window on to the roofs outside. Following the route they had taken so many times before between the gently sloping domes, they were soon peering over the stone parapet overlooking the patio. There was a way down using the wooden frame supporting the jasmine in one corner.

'You stay here,' Edward said. 'I won't be long.' He was conscious of the danger of being caught and wanted to give Brogan the chance to get away.

'That's not what we agreed,' Brogan stated flatly. 'We both go or we don't go at all. What happens if you get into trouble and I'm sat up here?'

Chastened by the logic of this, Edward nodded and said, 'Ready?'

'Take these,' said Brogan and pressed something soft into Edward's hand. He looked down and saw a pair of thin brown leather gloves.

'Pilots' issue,' said Brogan without saying how he came by them. 'Very useful things, gloves. Stops the hands sweating.'

'And leaving fingerprints,' Edward smiled, pulling them on.

Brogan's teeth showed in a grin under his beard and he patted Edward on the back to go. Edward swung his leg over the parapet and let himself gently down into the patio through the jasmine, almost choking on the heady aroma of the little white flowers. Brogan watched from the cover of the parapet until Edward crossed the patio to the house and waved. Brogan clambered down the jasmine and joined him and they waited by the wall, listening for noises inside the house.

They heard nothing, so Brogan pulled a short jemmy out of the belt under his robes and stepped forward to the french windows. The wood was sun-bleached and warped and gave way in moments. There was a slight report as the lock snapped over the catch and Brogan eased the door wide open. Edward slipped inside and stood with his back to the wall. According to their plan, Brogan would stay near the door to guard their retreat, so from that point Edward was on his own in the house. He was surprised not to feel more nervous. He was risking everything if they were caught, including a spell in prison, but the feeling that Romm had put himself beyond the pale, not just with his father but by meeting Paul Levi too, gave Edward the confidence that he was acting properly, on the side of right. Breaking and entering in the name of justice at least, even if not the law, he reflected as he looked carefully round dark shadows of the sitting-room. He realised he was enjoying himself.

He racked his brains to think of something Romm had

kept which would throw light on his father and Operation Joshua. He trod carefully over the Persian carpets on the stone floor to a side table where he could see a series of photographs. They seemed to be nothing more than family portraits and he noticed several of Carole. He slipped one in his pocket and walked silently on his rubber-soled suedes into the room next door which he guessed was Romm's study. Books lined the wall opposite the french windows on to the patio, valuable Persian miniatures hung facing each other on the other two, the floor was covered with various rich silk Turkey carpets and a large knee-hole desk dominated the centre of the room. He took out a small torch and switched it on. He had cut down the beam with masking tape but there was enough light to read by and he began working through the drawers of the desk, swiftly rifling through papers looking for something connected with the war, with France, or just checking dates to find those which might tally with Operation Joshua. He tried to minimise the noise he made, shutting the drawers quietly with his thumb against the wood to stop them banging and he stopped altogether from time to time to listen for noises elsewhere in the house. Once, he was worried not hearing Brogan at all and padded over to look through the windows into the patio where he saw Brogan's dark Arab shape pressed against the wall by the door.

He returned to the desk and time passed quickly. In the bottom drawer on one side, he found a file in German. Edward spoke no German at all but he was intrigued, even though the dates on the letters were pre-war from the twenties, and those from a hotel among them suggested this was the record of a holiday in Germany. As he flicked through, a couple of photographs fell out. One was of a very beautiful girl in a half-turned sitting pose typically favoured by photographers of the period and it was signed in ink with

The Joshua Inheritance

a flourish. She looked like Carole and Edward recognised her in the other photograph he picked up. It was an informal snap of a group of three people, all smiling. Axel Romm was beside her, and they were looking at the third man who was a policeman in uniform. Edward wondered why they were filed away and for want of anything better stuffed them inside his shirt with a few of the letters taken at random. He was just shutting the file when a voice burst the silence in the darkened study.

'Don't move!' Yaacov's dark bulk suddenly loomed through the study door and moved fast to one side by the bookshelves. He flicked a switch and the room blazed with light.

Edward fell behind the desk, more from fright than instinctive training, stunned by the sight of a big Colt .45 thrust forwards in Yaacov's large fist.

'Stand up! Or I will shoot!' Yaacov shouted. Edward thought he could hear noises elsewhere in the house and was struck by the horror of being exposed in front of Carole. He pulled out his own automatic and crawled round the back of the desk, whining in Arabic, 'Don't shoot, effendi, I am a poor Arab with a large family. Don't shoot!' He hoped the sight and sound of a wretched bearded Arab might weaken Yaacov's guard and give him a chance.

He need not have worried about his next move. An explosion of sound shattered all remaining hope of secrecy, Yaacov screamed and crumpled to the floor, pulling books from the shelves, and firing his own Colt as he fell. Brogan had shot him twice in the side of the chest through the doorway. Yaacov's bullets crashed harmlessly into the desk but galvanised Edward to his feet.

'Time to frig off!' Brogan hissed superfluously, leaning round the study door, his black beard and shemag evilly lit in the glare of light. There were shouts deeper in the house and Edward thought he could hear Carole. He sprinted after Brogan through the patio door, where Brogan stayed watching into the house, his pistol held ready, while Edward scrambled up the jasmine and over the parapet on to the roofs.

'Move!' Edward gasped, out of breath when he had fallen on to the roof and twisted round to cover Brogan's retreat. As Brogan crossed the patio, the lights went on everywhere and Edward saw Axel Romm run into the drawing-room holding a short M1 carbine. One glance at the open door and the stocky Arab figure running across his patio was enough and he opened fire, shattering the glass panes and smashing the statue on the fountain. From the parapet, Edward pulled the trigger, aiming carefully with his pistol resting on the stone, and he had the immense satisfaction of seeing Romm's carbine swing wildly, his shots spraying the room and stop altogether as he ducked away for cover inside the house.

'Jesus!' Brogan panted, pulling himself over the parapet. 'Stealing things was never like this in Sligo!'

Edward grabbed a handful of his jellaba and shirt and hauled him over the parapet as if pulling him across the gunwales of a boat and they set off at a crouching run across the flat stone rooftops. Once back inside the empty house, they stopped in the hallway for a moment to catch their breath and listened for street noises outside.

'Go!' Edward whispered urgently. Romm was bound to telephone for help and they had to get away before a patrol arrived to investigate the racket of shooting. Brogan opened the door and slipped away through the shadows towards the city walls. As Edward turned to shut the door, he glanced up the street and saw movement in the darkness at the top of the street.

'Halt!' The unmistakeable tones of a British soldier echoed from the stone walls. Brogan had reached the corner and was waving frantically at Edward who was struggling with the lock.

The Joshua Inheritance

Beyond, the soldiers had started running. 'Halt, or we fire!' The words had hardly died away, when the street reverberated with the sound of gunfire as two soldiers opened fire with their Lee Enfield rifles.

Edward pulled the key from the lock, lifted his Arab jellaba from his legs and ran. He ducked and weaved towards the safety of the alley as several more shots ricocheted off the stone walls above him.

'There's no manners any more,' Brogan remarked pulling Edward round the corner and they sprinted together into the Armenian quarter, stripping off their Arab clothes as they ran. By the time they reached the Citroën, they were Europeans. Brogan stuffed the Arab jellabas under the back seat, Edward took the wheel, started the engine and they drove off. In moments, they were at the Jaffa gates.

A British patrol blocked the road.

Edward slowed to a halt, his heart beating like a drum and a lance-corporal approached the car, his rifle cradled in the crook of his arm. He said politely, 'Excuse me, sir, can I see your papers?' He could afford to be polite. He was covered by a tracked Bren-gun carrier behind him in the shadows by the balconied houses just inside the gate and the gunner was watching the civilian car nervously.

Edward had seen the Bren-gun but coolly handed over the police authority which Angus Maclean had issued to everyone on the squad. The lance-corporal studied the paper without having the slightest idea what it meant. It was nothing like a usual Army identity card, but he could see the pass was issued by the Palestine Police and more than sufficient. He said, 'Can't be too careful, sir. We're looking for a gang of A-rabs, sir. They've been throwing bombs and machine-gunning a diplomat fellah in the Jewish quarter.'

'What a terrible show,' Edward drawled in an exaggerated English accent, his face etched with concern. 'Sorry I can't help.' The feeling that they were getting away with it gave him a real kick and he grinned when Brogan poked his leg and whispered, 'For Christ's sake, cut it out!'

The lance-corporal thanked them, returned their passes, saluted and waved the Citroën through the Jaffa gate.

After a moment Brogan admitted, 'I'm pleased to be outside those frigging walls. Things were fine till the Army turned up.'

'Hardly,' said Edward. He felt rather flat now that they were out of immediate danger. It would only be a matter of time before they post-mortemed Yaacov's dead body and traced the bullets and scattered empty cases to an Army source, and then doubtless to the Special Squad. He envisaged himself standing trial alongside Major Roy Farran. 'Romm will have his American forensic guys trace those bullets and we'll be for it.'

To his surprise, Brogan's bearded face split open and he gave a great belly laugh. 'Why in the name of Mary and all the saints d'you think I gave you a fine German Luger to carry tonight, and some fine German bullets to go with it? The Afrika Korps left plenty to go round. All what I call highly non-attributable.'

A smile spread across Edward's face, wrinkling his beard as he recognised the implications.

Brogan nodded, 'I'll take the Lugers, wipe 'em clean and make 'em disappear for good.'

'How d'you know about this sort of thing?' Edward laughed.

'There's all manner of things a young lad picks up in Ireland,' laughed Brogan. 'Remember, the Irish got their independence from the British Empire before this rabble here thought of it. But tell me, was tonight worth it?'

Edward shrugged and told him about the German letters and photographs 'I hope so. There's certainly a German link and I've decided I must get back there sometime. Though God knows when.'

'Ah well, if Major Farran's case blows up in his face, as our own good Major Meynell expects, we'll all be out of a job.'

Edward turned the Citroën up the hill towards the squad's house and grunted, 'And then we'll be back to Captain Scarland.'

Brogan groaned.

A week later, Angus Maclean came to the house and Major Meynell called them all into the dining-room again. They listened to Angus in silence.

'So that's it,' he said finally in a depressed tone of voice, looking at the men sitting round the table. 'The squads are finished. As of today.' He lifted a hand and let it flop back. There was nothing more to explain. He had enjoyed his liaison work with them. 'I'm sorry, lads. They won't support us any more. Not with Roy Farran's case coming up in the full glare of publicity.'

The men looked at each other and Major Meynell voiced their thoughts, saying, 'Pity. Just when we were making some headway against the underground, but what's going to happen to Roy?'

'They'll crucify him,' announced Taff solemnly from his seat at the end of the table.

Angus smiled a little. He had grown used to the Welshman's gloom and there was more hope than that. 'Bernard Fergusson is going to support him all the way. I think it's most unlikely the case can be pursued, for lack of evidence.'

'I hope so,' Major Meynell said firmly. 'It wouldn't be the first time a British soldier has been sacrificed on the altar of appeasing local opinion.'

'I suppose we'll all go back to our units?' Edward asked, glancing at Brogan. Neither of them wanted to see Captain Scarland again.

Major Meynell answered his question, keeping the good news till last. 'No. They're so embarrassed by

Roy Farran's case that they want us out of the way, immediately. They don't want newshounds sniffing us out when his court case comes up. So, we're all being sent home, willy nilly. By plane.'

Everyone laughed and one or two banged their fists on the table to show their pleasure and appreciation.

Angus added, 'You, Edward, have to leave as soon as possible. Apparently, your friend Colonel Haike has been making a frightful fuss. He was appalled to find you were working with Major Meynell and wants you home at once.'

Taff and Brogan grinned, telling Edward he had been caught out too late for a young chap and he must be sure to shave his beard properly. Spirits were up again. The prospect of going back to England was an excellent and unexpected tonic after the news of the squad's disbandment.

'Typical Army,' Brogan smiled. 'I'll bet you they think sending us home is a punishment.'

Edward was not listening. He was planning what he would do with his leave.

19

FULL CIRCLE

September 1947

On 8 September the SS *Empire Rival* followed its two sister ships slowly up the cold grey waters of the River Elbe towards Hamburg. There was a sharp breeze and the sky was overcast. Paul Levi leaned morosely over the lower-deck rail and his depression deepened as he watched the flat countryside slide past. As they approached the city, the yellow harvest fields and thin poplars swaying over the waterway gave way to blackened ruins of buildings destroyed by a wartime of Allied bombing. The shells of houses and warehouses stood stark on the bank alongside twisted cranes and shattered railway sheds. He asked himself if it was the Jewish fate to return to damnation. He had quit Germany two years before and vowed never to return. All the refugees behind him in the claustrophobic bunks and corridors of the ship had made the same vow. Crammed on *Exodus*, they had made the long and difficult journey to the shores of Palestine, three had been killed when the Royal Navy fought their way aboard, and the British had turned the rest back from the very shores of the Promised Land, all the way back to the country which had murdered six million of their people.

The ship slipped through the oily waters into Hamburg docks and her hull reverberated beneath his feet as it berthed against the rope fenders hanging off the quayside. Thick hawsers dropped to workmen in blue overalls who dragged the heavy ropes to bollards fore and aft.

The dock was criss-crossed with railway lines gleaming wetly in the cobbles and the small khaki figures of British soldiers stood about and stared up. Armed with rifles, they were waiting to escort the refugees. Behind them, the perimeter of the area was bounded by dense rolls of barbed wire. Beyond the wire, past the roofless ruin of a brick warehouse, stood the trains. Steel mesh had been welded over the windows of every carriage to stop the refugees escaping.

'Things haven't changed much here,' remarked a fat middle-aged Polish woman in a shapeless felt coat beside him. Her voice was flat and tired. 'Same thing when I went to the camp before, two years ago.'

When they were run by the Nazis, reflected Paul. He watched the dockers prepare to hoist a gangway up to the ship's side.

On the top deck, Aubrey Hall-Drake and the other soldiers were dressed and ready for a fight, wearing steel helmets and carrying batons. The other two ships had docked earlier and reported that the Jews were refusing to disembark. The soldiers were not looking forward to having to drag the wretched refugees off the boat. They had all been aboard the *Empire Rival* for over seven weeks, from Haifa, to Port-de-Bouc in France, to Gibraltar and through the sickening swells of the Bay of Biscay to Hamburg, followed and humiliated by the world's Press all the way, spat on and abused by the refugees. They were fed up.

Aubrey scanned the faces of the Jews he could see from his vantage point above, looking for Levi. The trouble was that Levi had had three weeks since coming aboard to disguise himself.

'It's hopeless,' he said aloud to himself. 'Never bloody see him among that lot.'

The Joshua Inheritance

'I agree,' said Major Gray, coming up behind him. He was the officer commanding the guard force and looked exhausted. 'But frankly, Aubrey, he's the last person I'm thinking about right now. The Captain and I want to off-load these people as quickly and painlessly as possible. God knows, I don't want a fight, but if we have to have one, let's get on with it. The sooner they can be shoved on those trains over there, the sooner they become someone else's problem.' He looked down on the heads of the motley crowd of refugees on the lower deck and added glumly, 'I must admit, it doesn't look good. There's a full-scale battle going on with the other two boats.' He jerked his thumb along the docks towards the other berths where the SS *Ocean Vigour* and SS *Runymede Park* were docked. 'They've had to call in about eight hundred of our lads from a unit stationed in Hamburg and an equal number of German policemen. It's a rum do, British soldiers and Jerry policemen fighting side-by-side to force Jews off the boats and take 'em off to camps. Probably find some of those Jerry coppers arrested some of these poor sods during the war. Now they're doing it all over again and we're helping. Of course, the bloody journalists are having a field day with the other two ships. I can just see the headlines: "British soldiers fighting to put Jews behind barbed wire again. Scenes reminiscent of the Nazis."'

Without taking his eyes off the crowds of refugees below, Aubrey agreed. 'God knows what possessed Bevin to make us bring them all the way back to Hamburg.'

'Lunacy,' said Major Gray emphatically and went off to supervise the disembarkation.

To their amazement, the refugees began to file off the *Empire Rival* without any fuss and Aubrey immediately asked Major Gray for permission to check the identities of the men as they went down the gangway. Both of them wanted to find Paul Levi but Major Gray refused.

The last thing he wanted was to upset the Jews and start a riot.

Aubrey stood near the top of the gangway and peered at everyone as the crowds moved slowly along the deck to leave the ship. The trouble was they all had the same tired and exhausted look. They had fed themselves well with food taken on at Port-de-Bouc but, finding themselves back where they started and the prospect of endless homelessness, their faces were dull with resignation.

Paul climbed the steel stairs to the disembarkation deck with a growing sense of calamity. He had taken a huge risk joining the Haganah team coming on the boat. He admitted to himself that he would not have done it before his torture and interrogation but he was driven to vindicate himself by an act which would prove his commitment to the cause. However, he did not want to be caught. To avoid being identified, he had removed the plaster from his arm, which felt horribly weak and vulnerable, and tucked himself behind a family near the end of the long queue of refugees. He tried to drain the determined gleam from his eye, to look as defeated as the rest, but the adrenalin had started to sicken him long before he reached the deck and saw the grim helmeted soldiers staring at him. He was terrified, but utterly determined to carry out his final plan, if necessary. From the remains of what he had brought on board at Port-de-Bouc he had made a small home-made grenade which he clutched in his pocket. If they stopped him, he would kill one more soldier, and himself. His guilty betrayal of his people demanded it.

The soldiers watched silently, their faces expressionless under their steel helmets, riot batons ready. One by one the Jews tramped off the deck and down the gangway to the dockside. The soldiers watched silently, hardly daring to hope that all fourteen hundred refugees would leave without causing trouble. Aubrey began to

The Joshua Inheritance

find it impossible to concentrate on the details of the faces passing him on to the gangway. After a while, they all looked the same. He was also distracted by the glimmering of suspicion that there had to be a good reason for the Jews to leave without a fight. By the time a thousand had filed passed him, he had given up trying to spot Paul Levi. Then he overheard one of the soldiers saying he had heard banging below decks and decided to report his suspicions to Major Gray. He ordered Aubrey to take a squad below decks to investigate as soon as the last Jew was off the boat.

The team descended into the bowels of the ship and their suspicions were confirmed. In an area which the British soldiers had dared not enter during the voyage, they found an inspection cover had been damaged. After some effort, the steel trap was lifted and Aubrey shone a torch into the salty black bilges below. A bomb disposal Sergeant climbed down the steel ladder and called up that he had found a seven-gallon cooking-oil tin.

After a pause, during which Aubrey watched the Sergeant's torch flick round the darkness beneath, he heard the man's voice echo round the steel room, 'It's a bomb alright, sir. There's a couple of wires sticking out. If sea water slops over them, the contact is made and this thing would blow a big hole in the ship's side. Just as good as a limpet mine. No wonder they came off the ship like lambs.'

The train full of refugees rumbled slowly through Hamburg with guards at either end of each carriage. Paul sat near a window cradling his throbbing arm and staring out through the steel mesh welded over the dirty glass windows. However much he disliked the Germans, he was shocked by the scale of the devastation that had been caused by the Allied bombing. Even after two years, mountains of rubble remained to be cleared and whole areas of houses were levelled ruins. Once or twice he saw groups of men rebuilding, but when the train took them close to the river, a vista of broken buildings extended into the grey distance as far as he could see. These depressing scenes continued until the train struck off into the countryside to the north-east and even the thought of what would happen to the *Empire Rival* when it put to sea again failed to cheer him up.

In the late afternoon, the train reached Lübeck and he panicked. He imagined he was spiralling backwards in a time warp to the misery of his life two years before when he had trudged into Lübeck from Orianenburg. He supposed no-one could make the journey now that the East Germans had closed the border with the West. Remorselessly, the train slowly trundled through the bombed town and on to the coast. Smoke from the engine drifted past the windows and seemed to be trying to obscure the empty rolling dunes. Finally they jolted to a halt at a low concrete platform in the sand. A rusty notice on the side of the track declared, 'Poppendorf'.

Trying to ignore the British soldiers shouting at them, Paul climbed down with the others. Clutching bags and boxes tied with string, they trudged towards the watch towers rising above the dunes half a mile away, chivvied by soldiers and watched by officers in Jeeps. Paul did not need to look. He shut his mind to it all, bowed his head and listened to the sound of the grains of sand crunching under his boots and swirling across the road round his feet, grains as numerous as the people who had been swept away by the winds of war. But why, he wondered, was it necessary for his people to come back and experience it all again?

In Hamburg docks, the guard force on the *Empire Rival* ate supper in the galley, conscious of the strange silence on the ship. The refugees were gone, leaving their accommodation below decks filthy. The soldiers felt dirty, tired, and drained. Even the prospect of leave could hardly raise their spirits. Most, including

The Joshua Inheritance

Aubrey, felt let down but could not explain exactly who was to blame. Some, like Aubrey, had been to Hamburg before, fighting at the end of the war, and had never imagined they would return, guarding Jews being sent back to camps. Aubrey took advantage of this feeling and managed to persuade Major Gray to let him begin his leave at once. For the last time, he returned the guard's salute on deck and walked down the rope-lined gangway on to the dockside clutching his kit-bag and a suitcase full of civilian clothes which had been part of his long-dead plans to holiday in Cyprus chasing Egyptian and Lebanese girls. In the breast pocket of his battledress were his leave authority, a complicated railway travel warrant and a telegram from Edward. A Land-Rover and duty driver waited for him on the wharf and drove him through the ruins of Hamburg's streets to the Hotel Vierjahreszeiten. The hotel was damaged but struggling to recover its world-wide reputation of excellence. After seven weeks on board with the refugees, Aubrey reckoned he deserved a deep hot bath and a good dinner.

In Jerusalem, Angus had not been exaggerating the embarrassment in HQ about the Special Squads. It almost amounted to panic. The squad was disbanded, its connections with the Palestine police severed and only two days later, Edward, Brogan and Taff were the first of the group to leave the country. As Angus drove them in a small convoy of three Land-Rovers from Jerusalem on the familiar Tel Aviv road to Lydda airfield, Edward allowed the memories of the last two years to filter back. They passed the spot where the squad had ambushed Paul Levi and half an hour later the place where Carole had called out to him at the road block. He wondered what she was doing. He unbuttoned his shirt pocket and pulled out the photograph of her which he had taken from Romm's house.

'Your wife, sir?' asked the driver glancing over and

admiring the pretty dark-haired girl in the soft-focus black and white photograph.

'No,' Edward replied monosyllabically, deliberately crushing the driver's chirpy interest. Edward pulled out the other two photographs he had taken and looked at the girl in them. He had examined the photographs plenty of times and there was no doubt this was Carole's mother. He was amazed how alike they appeared and wondered what had made Carole so reluctant to talk about her mother. She was attractive, both in the formal pose, where her name was clearly signed 'Lisa', and in the snapshot with Axel Romm and the policeman. He turned that one over again, and read, *'Mit Ulric vor seinem Wachen in Maursmünster.'* He wondered where Maursmünster was, and why Romm should have kept the photograph, one perhaps of a holiday in Germany, and why had he felt it important to file it?

At Lydda, Angus said goodbye, briefly, because he was a Scot and disliked displays of feelings. He waved as he drove off in his Land-Rover and left them to a long hot wait in the airfield buildings before they climbed aboard a RAF twin-engined Dakota transport. After that, events speeded up. The plane taxied out, surged up the runway and lifted steeply into the transparent blue September sky. Edward twisted round in his canvas para seat and looked through a small round window at the land below. Like an architect's model, ordered citrus plantations rolled towards the sea down gentle sloping valleys dotted with whitewashed villages and newer settlements occupied by the Jewish immigrants. He thought he could make out the Rishon kibbutz, between Lydda and the coast, and, as the plane crossed Tel Aviv at five thousand feet, he picked out the pale green sycamore trees in Colony Square and the street where he had encountered Paul Levi in the riot. The RAF airloadmaster signalled them to unbuckle their seat belts and, by the time Edward looked back, Tel Aviv was fading into the haze as they flew north, hugging the coast. They passed Acre and Edward spotted the hole in the Crusader fort prison wall which the Irgun had blown for Paul Levi to escape. He pointed it out to Brogan and Taff, shouting in their ears to overcome the sound of the prop engines as they all peered through the small window. Finally, at Haifa, he looked down on the curving jetty which hugged the old port where he had disembarked to the sound of a brass band two years before. Palestine was over, his time had come full circle.

Then, the Dakota headed out across the Mediterranean towards Cyprus on the first stage of their long haul back to England.

Aubrey and a delighted Diana met him at Blackbushe and Edward enjoyed the drive up to London. He listened while Diana complained about the appalling conditions of the previous winter and Aubrey described his trip back with the refugees. Edward refused to be depressed with talk of Britain's troubles or even by the failure to pick up Paul Levi. He was just back after two years abroad and the countryside was green, not brown, oaks and elms bowed over the road and horses plodded the fields in late summer harvest. He was in good spirits, among friends, and besides he had a job to do. He told Aubrey about the photographs he had taken from Romm's house, without saying where he had come by them, and asked, 'Did you get my signal on the boat?'

Aubrey nodded, flicking ash from the inevitable cigarette into the slipstream. 'Thank God I was staying somewhere civilised in Hamburg to offset the struggle I had with all your questions in those government offices. If things are difficult here, just remember that Germany is in total chaos. The Commission is doing well setting the country back on its feet, but even finding telephone numbers and addresses is hard work.' He drew on his Turkish cigarette again and added, 'I could find nothing about this fellow Ulric, not having a surname, and it took me two days to locate Maursmünster. It's a smallish town near Strassburg.' He used the German pronunciation.

'What took you so long?' Edward laughed but he was enormously grateful for Aubrey's help.

Aubrey looked at him and said, 'I was looking on maps of Germany, but Maursmünster isn't in Germany at all. It's in Alsace. In the bit of France which the Germans claim is theirs. That's presumably why Ulric the policeman appears in German uniform in a French town.'

'Alsace is the area where Operation Joshua took place,' said Edward, suddenly interested. He lapsed into silence, trying to reconcile Paul Levi's insistence that his father had given away the location of the landing strip to the SD while being in prison at the time. Maybe his father had been tortured and forced to give it away, which would certainly explain his reluctance to defend himself or even talk about it later, but Edward felt certain his father had not betrayed his team. There had to be other links missing in the story to explain the anomalies.

Aubrey parked off High Street Kensington and they all got out. He patted the shiny red Morgan on its long bonnet and said, 'Delighted to let you have the car, old chap. Here's the key, but treat her carefully. Roads on the continent are pretty bad and I want her back in one piece. I'll take Diana back home by taxi and wish you good luck.' They shook hands and Edward thanked him profusely for letting him borrow the car. Aubrey shrugged. He knew how much Edward wanted to understand what had happened to his father, even if he could never clear his name. He was happy to help. He said, 'I'm glad I'm not going. Tooling about in Germany in its present awful state is hardly my idea of a holiday, which I badly need after that awful time on the boat.' He smiled at a recollection. 'Quite by chance, I bumped into rather an agreeable young English girl staying in the Hotel Vierjahreszeiten in Hamburg who

The Joshua Inheritance

was on her way home. We'd known each other before Palestine. Happily, she was returning to London where she lives and I shan't need the car.'

'I suppose she's a nurse?' Edward asked off-handedly.

Aubrey's smile broadened, 'Yes, a charming little fanny.'

'Don't be dirty, Aubrey,' said Diana but she smiled. She could see why Aubrey had such success with his girlfriends.

Aubrey laughed out loud. 'Not fanny as in person, Diana, but FANY, as in First Aid Nursing Yeomanry. A lot of very nice girls who volunteered for duty. They never seem to know much about nursing but frankly, it doesn't seem to matter.'

The title rang a bell in Edward's mind, but Diana said crossly, 'Aubrey's told me what he's been up to, Edward, and I wish I was coming with you.'

Edward knew she was upset that he was going off without her on his first leave back home in two years, but he had to go to Germany on his own. After his father's experience and death and his own troubles with Paul Levi and Axel Romm, he had to make one last cathartic attempt to understand what had happened on Operation Joshua, if for no other reason than to lay the ghost to rest in his own mind. Enthusiastically, he promised to give her a really special dinner out that evening. 'We'll go to the Savoy and blow the cost!' He turned to Aubrey. 'Will you join us, with your nurse in the FANYs?'

Aubrey put up his hands in horror, 'Two's company and all that. I'd hate to spoil a good evening "à deux".' He smiled, 'Yours or mine.'

Diana was thankful. Mollified by the idea of having Edward to herself, she set her mind on giving him an evening that would make him come back from Germany very quickly indeed. She could see no point in wasting time on the past. She wanted Edward to think of the future. He promised to pick her up at

7.30, she kissed him lightly on the cheek, linked her arm through Aubrey's and they went off to find a taxi.

Edward knew she would look stunning that evening and he was in a cheerful mood when he rattled up in the old lift with his bags to his mother's flat and knocked on the door. He felt in control of his destiny again.

John Fullerton opened the door wearing his usual London office uniform of a dark grey pin-stripe suit. He looked a little startled when he saw Edward standing in the hall and was relieved when Anne Fairfax bustled past him exclaiming, 'My darling! You're back! Come in, come in at once.' She hugged Edward and fondly held his face in her hands to look at him properly. She had not realised how good it would be to see him again. She noticed immediately how he had grown up. He wore his battledress with the comfort of long use, and the gauche uncertainty of his first days in the Army was replaced with a natural self-confidence and the light of experience in his eyes. She wondered if he had suffered much during his kidnap. Later, she told herself, she must ask him all those questions later. Instead, she said, 'How brown you are! Not like us in England. I know it's trite to talk about the weather, but we've really had the most dreadful time in the last six months. I can't tell you how cold it's been. Isn't that right, John?'

Edward looked at Fullerton, thinking how much at ease his mother seemed with him. Her question was almost the sort of banality one might expect between husband and wife. Fullerton, however, looked unusually uncomfortable and tried to make an excuse to leave but Anne would not let him, insisting he help bring Edward's bags from the landing outside and stack them in the hall. Then she led them into the drawing-room where she asked Fullerton to open a bottle of wine, to celebrate Edward's return and hear about his trip. Edward noticed Fullerton had no need to ask where anything was as he fetched a bottle from the cabinet

The Joshua Inheritance

and poured the wine into his mother's 'special occasion' crystal glasses. They drank his health and sat down in the comfortable armchairs around the fireplace. Somewhat to Fullerton's surprise, Edward gestured for him to sit in his father's chair and Edward deliberately sat down facing the fireplace, between them both. He enjoyed the guarded look on Fullerton's face. His mother did not notice. She glanced at the clock on the mantelpiece next to Edward's photograph there, as she had done so many times in the last two years. It was a long time alone, she reflected, and there was so much to talk about. She said, 'I got your telegram but I never expected you to be back so soon.'

'I'm surprised Fullerton didn't tell you,' said Edward, purposely using just his surname – Fullerton's experience with prevarication, he had decided, demanded a direct approach.

Anne was puzzled and said gently, 'Really, Edward dear. That's rather abrupt.' She recognised the signs of obstinacy which had so often caused trouble for his father. Fullerton waved his hand as if he did not mind.

Edward sipped his wine and asked smoothly, 'Mother. When I sent you that information about Axel Romm and Father's operation just before his court martial, whom did you speak to?'

Anne unconsciously tidied her hair with one hand, recalling the events of two years before, when she had threatened to go to the newspapers with the story and said slowly, 'Why, Colonel Haike was in Jerusalem so I asked John Peregrine here for his help. I think he was instrumental in putting off the case.' She smiled at him.

'Maybe, but the charges have never been dropped, have they? The smell lingers on.'

'I think you can rest assured it's all over now, dear boy,' said Fullerton in a kindly voice. 'Your father is gone and the business is closed.' He flicked an invisible speck of dust off his dark pin-stripe sleeve and crossed his legs.

'That's just the problem,' Edward disagreed in a hard voice. 'It's not over. The case was never closed. My father is still considered guilty.' An image of the hot cemetery in Jerusalem and the tiny group of people watching his father's coffin lowered into the yellow earth came into his mind and he turned to his mother again, 'Just recently you also asked him to find out about the signals and messages?'

She nodded. 'But I'm afraid dear John Peregrine has not been able to turn up anything at all. Apparently all the files were burned.'

'How convenient,' said Edward sarcastically.

Fullerton ignored the remark. It was true. Convenient, but true. The fire in Baker Street had wiped out most of SOE's files, but Edward was trespassing on security ground he had no business to know about and Fullerton had no desire at all to rake over the Joshua case. He drank his wine, put down the glass and got to his feet in front of the mantelpiece, saying, 'Anne dear, I really think I ought to be going. You know, leave you two together to catch up on all the news.'

Anne smiled at him but Edward stood up too and blocked his way. He had planned this meeting and had no intention of letting Fullerton off the hook.

With exaggerated politeness, he filled Fullerton's glass again, handed it back and said evenly, 'I'm not surprised you've come up with nothing. Just before he died, Father told me that Colonel Haike was closely involved in Operation Joshua. In spite of knowing this, nothing happened for a year until suddenly Colonel Haike wanted me out of Palestine last month. I think that's very odd. There was no reason, except that he wanted to stop me digging up more information about Operation Joshua from Paul Levi and Axel Romm in Palestine, and the only way he could have found out those details was through my letters home.'

Fullerton sipped his wine to conceal his growing

annoyance and watched Edward over the glass. Edward looked him straight in the eye and went on, 'You see, I deliberately asked my mother to find out about the signals and messages, to see what would happen.'

When Edward had last seen Colonel Haike in the King David Hotel, the Colonel had been furious. Edward guessed it was because the Special Squads had been attached to the Palestine police, under Bernard Fergusson, quite outside Colonel Haike's jurisdiction. He had been unable to contact Edward at all. Finally, he had admitted trying to find Edward in his battalion at a time which coincided precisely with the letter to his mother. Edward stared at Fullerton, his hands casually in the pockets of his battledress which clashed so strongly against the other's formal pin-stripe suit, and smiled. 'The important aspect is the timing, which is explained by you, Mother, asking Fullerton here for his help. Or is there someone else you talked to about all this?'

Anne shook her head. The whole matter was too embarrassing to discuss with her friends and there was no-one else. She realised Fullerton must have contacted Colonel Haike. She put down her glass, put her hands in her lap and tried to compose herself. Edward's words implied that Fullerton had been less than honest with her, having always claimed he was never actually involved in Operation Joshua. She looked at him with her grey eyes and asked in a quiet voice, 'Is this true, John?'

Fullerton realised he had been caught out, but he avoided the implication and said, 'Nothing to do with me, dearest Anne. Perhaps Edward was in a spot of trouble out there?' The suggestion was lightly put, designed to throw her off the subject, so he could recover his position with her later, once Edward was gone again. He guessed that Edward knew he had heard something about the Special Squads, and why Edward had had to come home, and he decided the conversation had gone far enough. He made another attempt to leave, putting his glass behind him on the mantelshelf, out of Edward's way, but before he could excuse himself, Edward said in an offhand way, 'I've got some leave now and I thought I'd go abroad.'

His mother was amazed and saddened. 'You've only just got home, dear. Surely you don't want to go rushing off so soon?'

Edward apologised. He knew she would be hurt, but he wanted Fullerton's reaction. He moved round the back of his chair, leaned on it and watched Fullerton carefully. He said, 'I'm going to a place called Maursmünster. Ever heard of it?'

Anne was distraught. 'You're going to Germany?'

'No, dear, it's alright,' said Fullerton automatically, trying to allay her fears. 'It's not in Germany. It's in France.'

Edward said nothing. He just looked at Fullerton and in the silence Fullerton realised he had been caught out, again.

'You've got a remarkable grip on small-town geography in France,' said Edward, his voice venomously quiet. 'But then you know perfectly well where Maursmünster is because that's where Operation Joshua took place. During the war, you all called it by it's French name, Marmoutier, because it's in Alsace, but the German maps my father's team had on the ground used the German name.'

Fullerton said nothing. His normally pale face showed high spots of colour on each side of his prominent nose.

Anne said, 'Marmoutier? That's a place George mentioned once, ages ago, when he first came back after the end of the war.' The reason for Edward's trip struck her, and why Fullerton had known about the place. Feeling terribly let down, she asked, 'John Peregrine, what's this all about? You know how much I've suffered from this awful business. What happened there? Tell me!'

The Joshua Inheritance

Fullerton refused to look her in the eye. He glanced about the tidy little sitting-room, at the family photographs on the piano in the corner, while the clock solemnly ticked over a few seconds in time. Edward thought he might lose his temper, or quietly admit defeat and explain everything, but he had been away and did not fully understand. Fullerton had indeed admitted a failure, but with Anne. His glance was one of regret for the times he had enjoyed her company in the place, but not a look of defeat. Sadly, he said, 'I'm sorry for both of you, particularly you, dearest Anne, but the matter is closed.' He reflected bitterly that George Fairfax, whom he had always thought a rude and vulgar man, had embarrassed him twice, in life on Operation Joshua and in death in denying him Anne. His lips pursed, tightening his aquiline features and he declared in an official tone of voice, 'I can tell you nothing.'

He moved determinedly past Edward to the door and said forcefully, 'I strongly advise you to leave matters as they are. Forget going to Alsace.'

'At least tell me what was the object of Operation Joshua?' Edward demanded desperately in a last attempt to get Fullerton to talk. He had the feeling that he had mishandled the advantage he had created. The older man had used his experience of hiding behind the rules of secrecy to cover his mistakes.

Fullerton shrugged. The outburst was no surprise but he felt confident again. The files were ashes and nothing could arise from them to embarrass him. He said casually, 'The Joshua team was sent to make a breakout of people being held in Natzweiler concentration camp.'

'Why?' Edward asked.

Fullerton answered disdainfully, 'The camp contained the usual complement of Jews but a number of British agents were being held too. We knew that four women agents had been killed there in July 1944 and we wanted to prevent our other agents being murdered. They were too important to lose. The idea was to co-ordinate a rescue with the advancing Allied armies. We wanted to time the strike before the SS could move the inmates into Germany but not too soon or we'd have given them the opportunity to round them all up again.' He shrugged. 'When Joshua was betrayed, it was too late to mount a new operation.' There was no harm mentioning the purpose. The official position was clear, protected by the Official Secrets Act as much as the fire in Baker Street, and he was sure there was no chance of new evidence. He said, 'I can't say more. Joshua is over. Closed. I'm sorry for you both, but don't make matters worse. Forget Alsace. Forget Joshua,' he said finally and left.

In silence broken only by the clock, Edward and Anne listened to the front door open and slam shut and then the sound of the old lift jerking into life in the hallway. Edward hit the chair back in frustration and turned to his mother. He could see she was on the verge of tears and he suddenly realised he had fatally damaged the one friendship she depended on after his father's death. He stepped over and gave her a gentle kiss on the forehead.

'What does he mean?' she asked in a small voice. 'You can't be hurt, can you? I couldn't stand it. Not any more.'

'I don't know,' said Edward. 'But I'm going to find out.' He was no nearer explaining why Fullerton and Colonel Haike had worked against his father, but he was now certain of their involvement and more than ever determined to find out the truth.

Anne looked up at him from her chair and took his hands in hers, 'For God's sake be careful, Edward. John Peregrine is a powerful man. Of course, I've known for ages he was not just Foreign Office. He must be in MI6 to know all about this business.'

'I agree,' Edward said. He had long suspected it, and what he had learned during his time with the Special

The Joshua Inheritance

Squad, from Major Meynell and Brogan, had confirmed his suspicions.

She squeezed his hands tightly. 'Be careful, they could make a lot of trouble for you.'

Edward looked down at her. She was absolutely right. Colonel Haike had stonewalled his every effort and if Fullerton really had been able to arrange an instant posting back to England, maybe he could stop him leaving now. With Britain in financial straits, there could be few people crossing the Channel and it would be easy to order the customs to look out for him. He made up his mind. He dropped on his knee in front of his mother and carefully explained what he wanted her to do, to take care of Diana and pretend he had decided to stay in London. At least for a few days. She agreed. Her son was all she had left, and she trusted him. He kissed her again and went off to change.

While his mother prepared a quick meal, Edward changed into a casual shirt and pullover and comfortable trousers. Then he drove straight to Dover with the Morgan's hood up as autumn was in the air. In his pocket, he carried all the papers and French francs Aubrey had obtained for him, with his Army leave pass and passport. Aubrey had booked him on a morning ferry, but he hoped there was a night crossing he could take. He was banking on there being plenty of room. Fullerton would not expect him to leave that night, nor by car.

At Dover, the customs and passport authorities were meticulously polite. They asked to see his ticket, his passport and his petrol coupons.

Edward felt they were playing with him, allowing the game to run its full course before asking him to come inside the police station to wait for Fullerton to arrive. He peered out of the Morgan's low window at the official studying his leave pass and felt a ludicrous urge to be light-hearted. He quipped, 'More paperwork to get out of England than you need to get into the Soviet Union nowadays, I bet?'

The middle-aged, grey-haired customs policeman looked serious. 'You been to Russia, then?' The Soviets were a rising menace in the East over the question of Berlin and there was even talk of war. He looked suspiciously past Edward into the back of the car.

'No,' said Edward quickly, chastened and immediately regretting his attempt at humour.

The man gave him a tight look, screwing up his eyes without speaking and continued slowly to scrutinise his car registration papers. Finally, they let him through, on to the midnight ferry.

The French authorities were not in the slightest interested. At two in the morning, a bored-looking gendarme with a blue kepi waved Edward straight past the temporary Nissen hut which served as the French *Douanes* among the ruins of the port and Edward was out of Calais by 2.15 in the morning, exhausted from lack of sleep but elated at his success in reaching France.

He made slow progress in the dark. Aubrey had been right. The roads through France were terrible. Five years of war and neglect left them potholed and missing cobbles in places which always seemed to catch the Morgan's wheels before he could spot them in the headlights, jolting every bone and muscle of his body. Cutting south-east along endless straight roads lined with poplars, Edward saw less and less evidence of the late war, though the sad ruins of Arras and Cambrai had still not recovered from the devastating shelling of the 1914–18 war. At dawn, he stopped to stretch his legs and wake himself up. Shortly after eight that morning, he reached Sedan, on the River Meuse.

He sat in a small café and gulped down hot coffee and consumed two feet of fresh French bread and jam, watching the flat swirling waters of the river and wondering what life must have been like for the people in the town under German occupation. His father had known. He had lived and worked in Occupied France. And been captured.

After breakfast, he continued at a steady pace in the sunshine with the hood down, enjoying the Morgan's power and light handling, and really beginning to feel on holiday. He stopped again for lunch at Nancy where he found a fine-looking restaurant. He was hungry again and plunged into the menu from top to bottom while he studied maps of Alsace on the table beside him which Aubrey had obtained from the British Army HQ map section in Hamburg. After lunch, he set out again and his plans to drive on to Strasbourg that night were destroyed by a sudden overpowering urge to sleep off all the travelling he had done, and give his exhausted body a chance to digest the litre of red wine he had sunk with his meal. He could hardly keep his eyes open and stopped only half an hour later on the road to Strasbourg, in a quiet French town called Lunéville where he found an inn called the 'Cheval Blanc'.

He went immediately to his room, which for some bizarre Gallic reason sported three double beds and made him regret being alone, chose the one in the middle and fell straight to sleep.

20

FUNKSPIEL

September 1947

Edward was up early and drove east in crisp morning sunshine from a cloudless blue sky with the Morgan's top down. The Vosges mountains ahead were purple in the haze and the day promised to be hot. The roads were narrow and bumpy, the French villages sleepy and neglected, but every detail fascinated him. This was the area of Operation Joshua. Only a few years before, his father had been alive, working in these places during the Nazi Occupation. He passed men in blue overalls and black berets slowly bicycling to work, and farmhands on horse-drawn carts were already coming back from the fields with the first harvest load of the day. He peered at them all, wondering if they had been in the French Resistance, and found it easy to imagine German soldiers under the plane trees in the dusty squares of the bigger market towns.

The Vosges mountains loomed on his right side hiding the place where he hoped to find the site of the Hudson crash above tree-covered slopes in the foothills. He reached Saverne at the top end of the range just after 9.30 and stopped opposite the Mairie to check his maps. On the German wartime map which Aubrey had found for him, Saverne was Zabern, and Marmoutier, or Maursmüster, was only three miles away to the south. He could not help, even enjoyed, the feeling of

The Joshua Inheritance

apprehension at what he might find out. He pushed the idea of failure out of his mind. Too much had happened to his father, and to him, to tolerate the idea. He dropped the German map on the passenger seat and set off for Marmoutier.

He easily identified the 'Maursmüster Polizei wache' the police station, as the Germans called it, from the background in the photograph he had stolen from Axel Romm's house. The faded stone building behind Romm and Carole's mother and the smartly uniformed German policeman in the photo had been renamed 'La Gendarmerie'. Edward parked the red sports car outside, ran up the steps and walked in.

The reception room smelled of stale paper and was almost bare except for a chair and several yellowed official notices about rationing and how to find missing persons not returned from volunteer service in Hitler's Germany after the war. He pressed a bell on the counter which divided the room and waited. No-one came. Plainly, police emergencies were not expected in Marmoutier. Edward doubted much had enlivened the place when it was Maursmünster during the war, except of course Operation Joshua. He banged the bell again and was rewarded by the sound of someone proceeding down the corridor. A comfortably built, middle-aged gendarme appeared in blue trousers, braces and shirt sleeves. He stopped in the doorway, as though reluctant to admit there was any real need to go into reception and asked uninterestedly, '*Bonjour M'sieur, qu'est-ce qu'il y a? Sergeant Lescaut à votre service.*'

'*Je vous demande pardon, Sergeant Lescaut, mais étiez-vous ici pendant la guerre?*' Edward asked, embarrassed by his French but determined to be polite in the best way he knew.

The gendarme's bland expression narrowed suspiciously at Edward's use of the French language and he demanded bluntly, '*Pourquoi?*' In post-war France, one did not readily confess to what one had been doing during the Occupation, and certainly not to total strangers, let alone to Englishmen.

Edward put the photograph on the counter and asked, *'Regardez ces types, s'il vous plaît. Peut-être vous les reconnaîtrez, ou non?'*

Sergeant Lescaut adopted an expression of great sacrifice and stepped over to the counter, took a brief look at the photograph and placed one fat forefinger on the uniformed German policeman. *'Ceci, je le connais. Il s'appellait Ulric Denkmann.'*

Edward felt a thrill of achievement. This was an excellent start. From Lescaut he learned that Ulric Denkmann had been born in Marmoutier and was deeply unpopular as a collaborator. He had risen to be chief of the German SD in Strasbourg, the very organisation responsible for catching his father and the others on Operation Joshua. Edward had been right to come. The next step would be to find Denkmann, but the sergeant had spoken of him in the past tense.

'Ah oui. Denkmann est mort. Il était tué par la Résistance.'

Denkmann had been shot. Considering what he had been, it was hardly surprising. Edward asked, when had this happened?

Sergeant Lescount was not sure. *'Je n'en peux pas être précis, mais c'était juste avant la libération de la ville. Je crois à la fin du Novembre 1944 ou le commencement du Décembre.'* The end of November or beginning of December was close enough for government work, Edward reflected. Lescaut's finger shifted across the photograph to Carole's mother and Axel Romm and he shrugged his broad shoulders not recognising them. *'Desolé, monsieur.'*

Edward walked out of the gendarmerie and stood in the sun on the steps. He had learned Ulric's surname, and that he had been killed by the Resistance in revenge during liberation by the American Army at the end of November or start of December 1944. A bizarre thought struck him. As the SD chief, Denkmann would have been the man who interrogated his father, but why were Denkmann and the two Romms together and so relaxed?

It had been an impressive start, but Edward had no idea what to do next. After a moment's thought, he decided to drive south, into the hills above Marmoutier and find the wreckage of the Hudson. Paul Levi had said it was in the 'Mittlere Vogesen', which was the German for the Vosges, near a village called Salm. There could not be many places flat enough to land a twin-engined Hudson at night. He had plenty of time and was determined to find the landing strip. He checked the German wartime map and found Salm about an hour's drive south in the heart of the mountains.

He pushed the sports car hard up the narrow hairpin bends into the hills south of Marmoutier through thick pine forests which shaded the road from the hot mid-morning sun and was grateful for the breeze whipping round the car's open top. He inhaled the rich smell of the pines and hot grass along the roadside, so different and fresh compared to the arid heat of Palestine. On the top, the road twisted and turned across the broad spine ridge running south. He passed meadows and solid-looking stone farm buildings tucked under the forests. Occasionally hazy views opened up between the dark pines and he glimpsed the flat Rhine lowlands far away and two thousand feet below towards Strasbourg in the east. Beyond that was Germany.

Salm was a cluster of stone houses high up in the mountains squatting on the side of a sunny bowl of open upland pasture ringed by trees. Brown cows with bells round their necks grazed heads down in the lush grass and the sound of birds carried from the edge of the woods. Edward pulled up beside a house with a chipped enamel sign fixed to the stone wall advertising 'Vigor' soap and which suggested there were other victuals for sale inside.

The cool darkness inside was blinding after the bright sun. He blinked and made out a fat woman with grey hair in a blue cotton dress busy among shelves behind a pile of hessian sacks. She had all the good humour of someone who lives close to nature and knows enough of the callousness of town life to enjoy her good fortune. She greeted him cheerfully with, '*B'jour m'sieu. Qu'est-ce que je peux vous faire? Du fromage? Du lait? Ou bien, simplement un petit blanc?*'

Edward grinned and chose the glass of white wine. She gave him a wood and wickerwork chair to take outside and he sat down by the door and leaned back in the sun against the hot stone wall of the shop. She brought him a cool glass of wine gleaming with condensation, like a fat yellow jewel. He thanked her and sipped the wine. It tasted delicious, cold and thick, like nectar.

The woman smiled appreciatively, her fat arms folded across her chest. She asked, '*Eh bien, m'sieu, qu'est-ce vous faites dans ce coin ici?*'

For a moment Edward thought perhaps he should not admit he was trying to find the Hudson, and then dismissed the idea as absurd. In the warm peace of Salm, the obsessive secrecy demanded by suited diplomats and soldier bureaucrats like Fullerton and Colonel Haike smacked of tight-lipped self-interest. Everyone wanted to conceal their part in Joshua and none of them gave a thought to the victims of the operation. He told the woman he wanted to find the wreckage of an aeroplane which had landed at the end of the war on the hills behind. She narrowed her eyes and asked, '*Qu'est-ce que c'était la date de l'atterisage?*'

Edward recalled the date perfectly, 8 November 1944. Paul Levi had told him while he was in Rishon. He told her, and asked if she knew where the plane had landed.

The Joshua Inheritance

Sad memories smoothed the good humour from the woman's red cheeks as she answered. She remembered the time, the only time during the war, when the road through Salm and the valley had been filled with Germans. SS troops and SD, from Strasbourg. They had set up their headquarters in Salm for the operation and deployed into the hills above in great numbers.

Edward looked down the narrow road and across the warm fields, to imagine the black uniformed and helmeted soldiers bustling round their trucks and the guttural shouted orders before they marched into the forest behind. He wanted to know what time they arrived. *'En plein jour,'* said the woman in disgust. The Germans had helped themselves to her store throughout the day and cleaned the place out without paying a sou.

Edward realised Ulric Denkmann must have felt very confident to have arrived in broad daylight to set up the ambush for the Hudson. Plainly, he had not cared who saw the deployment of his men and that argued his complete control over Operation Joshua on the ground. This was the first real proof of treachery. But whose?

Then, in the middle of the night, she said, they had been woken by a roaring sound like trucks revving their engines. Edward puzzled at this but she was sure that was what she had heard. At dawn, she said, the SS had come down, got in their waiting trucks and driven off.

'Avez-vous vu des prisoniers?'

'Non, m'sieu. Seulement des cadavres,' the woman answered solemnly, pulling her mouth down at the sides. Only bodies. A sad time, she added, and stared over the sunny grass at the cows chewing the cud in her meadows. There had been much shooting and killing. She waved her hands as if to ward off the lunacy of men who could defile the tranquillity of her valley.

Edward fetched his map from the red sports car and asked the woman to show him where the wreck was. Like quicksilver her mood changed and she laughed, a rich throaty laugh, shaking all over. She had no idea how to read a map, nor had she ever been up to the place herself. Grinning coyly, she squeezed her stomach and declared she had not walked into the hills for years. Her husband could help, but he was out in the fields, with the cows, till nightfall. However, seeing the disappointment on the young Englishman's face, she told him what she could remember her husband said at the time. Edward listened carefully, trying to link her directions to Aubrey's map. He was too close and too impatient to wait for precise directions from the woman's husband. He wanted to start searching at once. It was nearly lunchtime so he bought some of her cheese and bread and a bottle of white wine. As he paid, a thought struck him and he showed her the photograph of Denkmann and the two Romms.

To Edward's surprise, her face lit up, she pointed at Axel Romm whom, she had occasionally seen, she said, before the war.

'*Avec la femme?*'

She frowned. She could not remember seeing the pretty woman in the photograph. She apologised. The time she had seen the man before the war seemed so long ago.

Edward thanked her and drove back down the narrow road to the hairpin bend where she said he could leave the car and walk up the track to the area of the wreckage. He parked the Morgan off the road, in the shade of some tall pines. There was no worry about it being stolen. He took the German map and his food in a light shoulder bag and started to walk up a well-defined track which followed a stream tumbling from the hills above. No doubt farmers drove cattle that way to the top pastures for the summer and down again as winter approached. It was hard to imagine winter cold in the heat of the middle of the day, but the weather would have been quite different when the SS tramped up the same path to ambush the Hudson in early November.

* * *

The Joshua Inheritance

In the gendarmerie in Marmoutier, Sergeant Lescaut wandered out of the reception room, down the bare boards of a corridor into the squad room. He was frowning, and scratched his chest, shifting his braces about to get underneath.

'*C'est dingue, ça,*' he said to a young gendarme in full uniform sitting at a broad desk and slowly typing out a report, using one finger on an ancient upright typewriter. His blue kepi sat on the desk beside him.

'*C'est quoi?*'

Sergeant Lescaut shut his eyes a moment and took a deep breath. He repeated, 'how odd it was that, for the third time that day, he had been asked about the war, and about Ulric Denkmann and his wife.' '*Tu ne le trouves pas extraordinaire, non?*'

The gendarme, too young to have done anything in the war, was fed up with hearing other men and women boasting of their exploits in the Resistance, most of which sounded too colourful to be true. Frankly he could not care less if a hundred people asked about Denkmann in a day. Without taking his eyes off the sheet in his typewriter, the gendarme pressed a key and watched it strike the paper. Then he said, '*Oui.*'

After more than an hour's walking, Edward wiped the sweat off his forehead with his handkerchief and stopped to look back at the view. The valley and road leading up to Salm was long out of sight. He could see no more than several hundred yards of the track he had followed and the stream had shrunk to a clear trickle fed from the rough pasture which spread across the steeply sloping hillside between clumps of pines and scrubby bush. There was nowhere here to land an aircraft of any sort. The sun was very hot indeed and he wondered when he would reach the flat plateau which the woman had described. He walked on, pushing himself. He sensed he was close to finding out the truth of Operation Joshua and, as far as he knew, no-one else with an interest in Joshua had visited the place since the night of the disaster itself.

He topped a ridge, walked through the shade of some pines and emerged on to a flatter piece of ground. He recalled Paul Levi's description in Rishon and knew at once he had arrived. He was on one side of a wide expanse of rough grassland which extended more or less northwards for some distance in a broad undulating bowl and sloped gently upwards at the other three sides towards higher ground where outcrops of rock burst through the turf at the tops of the mountains circling round. He estimated the flatter ground was at least half a mile long and four hundred yards wide – plenty of room for a Hudson to land, even at night, while the lie of hills and forests all round would confuse anyone who heard the plane go over. He smiled. It was a perfect place.

He imagined his father had stood in that exact spot with the same idea and he decided to eat his lunch there, to absorb the atmosphere. He sat down on a slight rise, stuffed pieces of soft cheese into flaky chunks of bread and washed it down with white wine. As he ate he scanned the grassy landing area for the Hudson. Although the ground appeared flat, there were gentle rises and dips across the area and the plane could easily be hidden from where he was sitting. And provide plenty of cover for the ambushing SS troops, especially lying on the ground in the dark. He approached the problem differently, trying to guess the likely wind direction and landing procedure. Brogan had said the plane would have landed into wind and taxied straight round to the take-off point again before unloading its passengers. So, as the Hudson had to be at one end or the other, Edward assumed it was out of view further away.

Feeling refreshed after his picnic and suddenly impatient, he stood up and walked briskly across the open area in full sun, his shoes bristling through the long grass.

The Joshua Inheritance

Near the top end of the wide bowl, he breasted a slight rise and found the Hudson.

Encased in long, waving meadow grass, the cigar-shaped plane lay flat on its belly, its wings and twin engines lifeless on the ground, its double tailplane snapped in two across the fuselage. Edward guessed the wheels had either collapsed during the fire which had left little but a blackened shell, or been shot off as there seemed to be no part which had not been punctured with bullets. The glass of the cockpit, the little square windows down the fuselage and the bubble over the dorsal gun turret were opaque with the effects of heat and starred with bulletholes. The ambush had left the plane's occupants no chance at all. Paul Levi had indeed been lucky to be first out of the door.

He walked down the slope and wandered around the wreckage. It looked like some sort of boat floating in the thick pasture, a coracle perhaps with the ribs of the fuselage sticking out. He tried to imagine the scene at night, as Paul Levi had described it, the Commandos aboard the approaching plane trying to control a sickening feeling of tension as they felt the Hudson drop out of the sky towards the black ground below, the glorious jarring as the wheels touched down safely and their worry that the din of the powerful Pratt and Witney engines would wake all Alsace before they could tumble out and race for the trees a hundred yards away.

There had been no shelter for them. The night sky had suddenly lit up with rocket flares and mortars and tracer laced across the ground, ripping into the Hudson from end to end. Edward suddenly realised that what the woman had taken for roaring truck engines was the cacophony of machine-gun fire muted by distance over the hills to Salm. He spotted an empty flare cartridge in the long grass and noticed several more. The area must have been lit like day. The Hudson had disintegrated very quickly, killing everyone inside. Paul Levi had escaped by jumping out before the shooting started and been caught when he stumbled into three SS on his way to cover in the trees. Edward peered through the door of the plane, and saw a fragment of camouflage clothing, torn and burned, but there were no bodies. After the carnage, the SS had removed everything. There was no smell of cordite or fuel or burning, which puzzled him till he realised two years of rain and weather had bleached the tragedy. At least the physical evidence was cleansed, even if the stench of disaster still hung around the name and reputations of the people who survived.

He walked a few yards off and nearly fell into an overgrown hole in the deep turf. Thanking his good luck not to have twisted his ankle so far up in the hills, he observed that the hole was actually an old slit trench. A quick search in the bottom and the long grass around the top produced several empty cases which he recognised as 7.92mm cartridges from a German MG42 machine-gun. The Paras had found several in caches in Palestine. He imagined a SS trooper firing at the Hudson from the slit trench and nodded his professional appreciation of how Denkmann had been able to make the ambush so effective, by digging slit trenches on the open ground where they had expected the aircraft to land so they could fire at close range for maximum effect.

But how had the SS known where to wait? Who had talked the plane down, and marked the spot where the Hudson had taxied back to, and finally been attacked? Brogan had explained the details of Paul's description. Secret night landings were controlled by someone on a special radio called an S-phone, with which the man waiting all alone on the ground could talk to the pilots approaching unseen in the night sky above. Edward wondered who had used the S-phone. He sat down on the gentle slope facing the wreckage, his arms wrapped round his knees, and tried to work out how Denkmann had managed the ambush. George Fairfax or Axel Romm must have betrayed the plan. One of them must have been lying, but which?

A black Peugeot 301 saloon was grinding up the steep road to the hairpin below Salm where Edward had left the red Morgan. The man crouched by the Morgan, looked up and listened to the noise of the approaching car. Then he ran over to the pine trees on the far side of the track. From the shadows, he watched the black car grow bigger, winding back and forth up the long slope and finally swinging round the hairpin on its way up to the village above. The driver was in shadow on the left side of the car and it was impossible to see anything of his features except a glimpse of pale skin as he turned suddenly to look at the red sports car as he swept past.

The man in the pine trees waited until the sound of the Peugeot faded and disappeared. He listened to the silence. There were birds in the pines round him, insects whirred in the hot grass among buttercups and thistles, and just below the track water rippled across the black stones in the stream-bed. These are the sounds of peace, he said to himself with a crooked smile as he looked thoughtfully at the little wires in his hand, and then he walked across the layby again in the hot sun, to the Morgan.

Edward had no idea how long he had been sitting, gazing at the wrecked Hudson and thinking, when he heard a soft voice behind him, 'I thought I'd find you here.'

He whipped round looking up the slope and saw Carole Romm watching him. Slowly he stood up.

She shaded her eyes from the bright sun with one hand, pushing her dark hair from her brown face and peered at him, smiling slightly at the expression of complete astonishment on his face. Edward stared, trying to come to terms with her sudden appearance and read the candid look in her dark eyes. She was wearing a pale yellow sleeveless shirt, which left her brown arms bare, and a cool knee-length blue and white spotted cotton skirt. She came down the slope and he noticed she had come well prepared with good walking shoes and short socks rolled down at her slim ankles. She stopped a few steps past him, fascinated by the wrecked Hudson.

He asked, 'What on earth are you doing here?' His surprise overcame all the bitterness he felt towards her after she refused to see him in Jerusalem. Palestine was too far away and the events of the past two years too remote from the delicious warmth beating down on them in the Vosges mountains.

Without taking her eyes off the wreck, she said, 'I knew you'd come here after we worked out that it was you who burgled my father's desk. Father said there were camera shots and papers missing. Arab thieves aren't interested in that sort of thing.'

Edward said nothing, unwilling to admit anything, thinking of Yaacov, but she read his mind and told him, 'Yes, Yaacov died, in hospital, but not before he was able to tell us his attackers spoke English. Rather good English actually. It had to be you.'

She looked at him gravely. Her brown eyes seemed bigger than ever. She said, 'Arabs rob houses, but not with guns, and they can't fight their way out like you did. You nearly killed my father.'

Edward shrugged. 'He was trying to kill us.' The lack of accusation in Carole's voice was encouraging, but he frankly did not care about Axel Romm, not after the damning report he had written about his father, still less after his meetings with Paul Levi. He asked her again, 'You haven't said why you came.'

In a low, awed voice she asked, 'Is that really the wrecked Hudson? It looks so quiet, peaceful really, just sitting there in the grass.'

It passed through Edward's mind that he had not

The Joshua Inheritance

expected her to know the aircraft type but he nodded and took her round, explaining his reconstruction of the landing and the violent ambush. He asked again, 'Why did you come? Not just because you thought I would be here?'

She looked at him sideways, against the sun, thinking how little he understood of her feelings. She half-smiled and half-answered, 'I had to come for the same reasons you're here. My father was one half of this Operation Joshua, the other was your father. I had to find out what happened as much as you.'

'I never thought you had any doubt?' He stepped close to her and took her arm. He could smell the warm scent of her skin.

'I knew something was wrong from the very beginning,' she replied firmly, finding she liked his hand on her arm.

Edward frowned, 'From the beginning?'

Carole moved away from him and said quietly, 'I was a FANY signals operator in the SOE receiving station in England, in Buckinghamshire.' She looked up at him. 'Don't you remember, when we met in Whitehall, I was wearing my FANY uniform?'

Edward stared. He remembered their meeting very well, but he had been more interested in her face and figure than the insignia of her uniform.

'I thought you were a nurse?'

'I am. That's how I came to volunteer for the FANYs in the first place. When we came over from the States, my father suggested it, and when they realised I spoke fluent French, I was used in the French section. It was too late in the war to send me into France. As it was, Operation Joshua was one of the last.'

'Pity it ever took place,' said Edward bitterly. He felt left out. He seemed to be the only one who had not been directly involved in some way. He sat down on the grass again. 'What did you know about it?'

She sat down beside him and sighed. 'A lot. I was the person responsible for the coding and decoding of the signals and messages. They, that is your father and mine, parachuted into this area in September 1944 and found a safe house. Maybe in Marmoutier. I don't know. But from the first week of October I knew something had gone wrong.'

'You mean the security checks were missing from the signals?'

It was Carole's turn to look surprised. 'How did you know about those?' She knew perfectly well that platoon commanders in battalions, even in the Airborne, have no reason to know anything about the signals procedures of clandestine radio operators.

'Never mind,' said Edward brusquely, pleased with her reaction, but he did not explain himself. Brogan and his work on the Special Squad were best not revealed. However, he told her that he knew security checks were supposed to be used by an operator who had been captured, to let his base station know if he was in enemy hands.

Carole nodded and explained, 'I noticed the bluff check and the true check were missing at once but no-one did anything about it.' Her voice was bitter. 'That was Colonel Haike's fault. He was responsible for reading the messages but he never took any action.'

'For God's sake, why not?' Edward asked amazed. It was clear now why Colonel Haike had been so keen to hush the matter up and why he wanted to appear helpful. He needed to know what Edward managed to find out.

She shrugged her slim shoulders. 'His attitude was common. Some of the staff simply said the operators were under such pressure that mistakes were inevitable. That must have been true. They were terrified of being caught by the SS, they worked in cramped conditions, and simple encoding mistakes while adding and subtracting off the one-time pad were common. Of

The Joshua Inheritance

course, mistakes were made at base in England too, sending and receiving, encoding and decoding. Colonel Haike made it quite clear to me that a couple of security checks could not be depended on among all the other errors.'

'So how did you know there was a problem?'

'Because my father was a perfectionist. His signals procedure was a bit slow but superb. I knew at once when he left out the first bluff check and then immediately when he left out the second true check. That meant he was in trouble.' She shrugged again. 'I was personally involved, I suppose, but I knew he had been captured.'

Edward frowned. 'I thought he denied it?'

She nodded. 'That's why I had to come here, to see for myself what had happened. Now I see that the SS took all day to set up their ambush, it's clear that not just your father but both of them were caught, probably by the German direction-finding units. They were damned efficient.'

Edward recalled Brogan's explanation and asked, 'So the Germans forced him to send their own messages and arranged for the Hudson to fly in?'

She nodded. 'Or used their own radio operators once they had the codes from him. The Germans called it "Funkspiel" a radio game. Odd name for something which ends up like that.' She gestured at the shattered plane where the crew and ten men had died.

Edward let the truth sink in. After two years, he had found out that his father did not betray Joshua. He was surprised to feel no relief, just a great emptiness. Romm had blamed him, perhaps genuinely believing he had been guilty of getting both of them captured. Then his absence trying to find the men in camps had supported the accusations and convinced Colonel Haike and Fullerton who had anyway been keen to cover their own mistakes.

After a moment, he asked quietly, 'Why didn't you tell me all this before?'

She had expected the question and answered without hesitation, never taking her eyes off the wrecked plane. 'We were both trying to do the same thing, each to understand our fathers and what they had done. We wanted them to be heroes, just as they were when we were children. We wanted to prove they had done nothing to feel guilty about.' She turned to look at him and took his hand. 'Forgive me, Edward, but I always thought your father's problem was linked directly to the people in London, like Colonel Haike and Fullerton who were trying to cover their own tracks. The threat to him was in England, not through what happened here in France. That was my father's problem. So I never told you what I knew. Anyway, just like you, I could not believe my father was wrong.'

She paused, recalling the bitter argument with her father after Edward had been kidnapped, when she had realised he was in touch with the men who had seized him, and had perhaps even let slip the vital information of their meetings in Solly Mannheim's restaurant. She had seen a frightening gap in his honesty with her which made her wonder about his version of Operation Joshua. She had decided then to tell Edward, but when she came to the hospital and found Diana with him it was already too late.

They gazed at the plane, each deep in thought, until Edward became aware of someone else watching too. He looked round.

Paul Levi was crouched in the long grass staring at him, a small automatic in his hand. His white shirt sleeves were rolled up and his dark trousers creased with weeks of wear.

Carole turned round and scrambled to her feet. She saw the pistol and cried out, 'Paul! There's no need for that.'

The Joshua Inheritance

Paul laughed unpleasantly and showed his left forearm. 'Or this?' The flesh was mottled dark and yellow round the lump where the break had healed badly and throbbed constantly. He said, 'This time, there's no-one to tell me to let you go.'

Edward stood up slowly, watching the pistol in Paul's hand. He felt cold, suddenly quite unconscious of the sun beating down on his back and his mind flashed across the chances of escape.

Carole tried to defuse the situation. 'When you left me to go on ahead on the track, I thought you had gone back to the car for your camera?'

'Yeah, I did nip back, but I couldn't find it, Carole. Probably left it in the hotel.'

Edward was amazed. He stared at her. 'You knew he was coming here?'

'We came together,' Paul said looking pleased with himself. He wiped the sweat from his high forehead and pushed his dark hair away from his face with his left hand. His right hand, holding the pistol, never moved from Edward.

Carole was sure she had seen the camera on the back seat of the Citroën they had hired from a garage in Strasbourg but before she could say so, Edward shouted at her, 'Why didn't you tell me you'd come with this shit?'

'Because we got involved talking about Joshua,' she shouted back desperately and waved her hand at the wreckage. 'What d'you expect me to feel when I see this for the first time?'

'I don't believe you,' Edward shouted back. She was still standing quite close to him, almost in line with Paul's pistol as well, and he knew her too well to miss the flicker of guilt cross her face. The facts were staring him in the face. 'How long have you been together, you and Paul? Is that why you never got in touch? Never answered my letters or calls?'

'No!' Carole shouted. She had refused to be used, to come running back after what she overheard in the hospital; but she had still waited to find out about Joshua, for the sake of her father. 'Paul promised to show me the Hudson and sent me a telegram when he got to Germany. That's all I wanted of him, I promise!'

'Nonsense!' Edward cursed his stupidity. 'I should have guessed. You were seeing him all the time this criminal was coming to see your father. Bloody cosy for you all, I must say.' The idea of Carole with Paul made him mad. He nearly launched himself at Paul, who grinned and lifted his pistol. Edward checked his rush and glared helplessly. The grass was rough. He would have no chance of covering the short distance between them without being shot first.

'He's not a criminal!' Carole shouted. 'You'd do exactly the same as him if you'd been born a Jew in his place!'

Edward swore at the idea. 'What? Blow up the King David, killing all those people, women and children? Remember? My father was among them. This bastard killed my father.'

Carole was silenced, astonished. Paul shrugged and announced casually, 'I knew your father was in that building. I watched him come and go to his office. He deserved to die.'

Carole stared at him and whispered, 'Is Edward right? You set the bomb?'

Paul shouted, 'So what? I kidnapped this sod too and more's the pity I never killed him then.' He waved his pistol at Edward. 'The swine is no better. Look!' He lifted his left arm again, the damage lurid on his pale skin in the blazing sun. 'I suppose you thought I never knew who was asking me all those questions about Joshua. You may have changed, Fairfax, with your beard and Arab clothes, but I knew.'

Edward saw the shock on Carole's face as she stared at him in horror. She stepped away from him, and

The Joshua Inheritance

whispered, 'You're both the same, both as brutal as each other.'

'He has no excuse,' snapped Paul. 'With the power of the British Empire behind him. I have nothing.'

'You're a criminal, like all the others who bomb and ambush us,' Edward replied angrily.

'We are soldiers,' Paul corrected proudly. 'But we refuse to fight according to the British book of rules. How else could we make you leave Palestine and create our own country, Israel?'

'You haven't done it yet,' shouted Edward unconvinced.

Paul laughed. 'We have, you'll see. Soon the British will be gone and our enemy will be the Arabs.'

Carole burst out, 'For God's sake, that's enough. Hasn't there been enough bitterness and killing?'

'Not quite yet,' said Paul grimly, pointing the pistol at Edward. Like an executioner he said, 'For the boy in the riot and my arm.'

'You'll be caught,' said Edward desperately, his eyes flicking between the muzzle of the pistol and Paul's eyes.

'No I won't. This Walther's non-attrib, as your British instructors say. It came off the ship I was on. No-one can link it to me.'

Edward remembered Brogan's non-attributable Lugers. He also recalled Aubrey's story of the boat. 'Non-attributable like the bomb you left on board, to blow up and drown everyone when they put to sea?'

Paul grinned and thought of the car down on the road. He liked explosives. 'They deserved that too, taking all those people back to Nazi concentration camps in Germany. All the British deserve to die for those boats!' He aimed his pistol. Carole watched transfixed while Edward's mind filled with useless ideas to break and run, hoping Paul's aim was poor, that the pistol was inaccurate over short ranges, that he might find cover round the Hudson and reach the pine trees a hundred yards away, but he was as helpless as the men who had died in the plane. He shouted, 'What about the British who fought to release your people? What about you on this bloody operation?' He waved his arm at the empty Hudson. 'Joshua! Don't you realise you were going to rescue Jews from Natzweiler, not ten miles over there?' He flung his arm eastwards.

Paul shouted, 'Liar!' and stepped forward thrusting his arm out to shoot, but he glanced at Carole to see if Edward was right and never saw the thin slit-trench hidden under the long grass in front of him. His foot slipped into it and he stumbled. Edward leaped on him, grabbing at his pistol and swinging his other hand in a brutal arc on to Paul's neck.

The blow missed, striking Paul's shoulder and a desperate struggle began. Edward squeezed his fist over the hand which held the pistol and grappled with Paul's neck, while Paul tried to roll away and pull his leg out of the narrow trench, his left arm useless. Locked together on the ground, Edward's mind cleared. After the initial fury of his reaction he had a fraction of time to think, though not to lose the terror of survival which gave no quarter on either side. Before Carole could intervene she saw Edward's hand release Paul's neck, and watched fascinated as it swung in a wide arc to seize Paul's damaged left arm by the wrist, and then savagely drag it backwards close to his body, under the armpit. The sharp snap of the breaking bone was drowned by the screams which were lost time and again in the expanse of blue above the hot grass meadow. The fight was over.

Edward pulled the pistol out of Paul's hand, pushed him away and stood up panting hard. He did nothing to stop Carole kneel down and try to help Paul. His screams lessened, but his chest heaved and his body shook as she made him lie back on the grass to ease his shock. The break had split the skin and bone was visible. Blood poured from the wound and she yelled at Edward, 'Give me your shirt. I've got to stop it bleeding or he'll die.'

'Sod him,' said Edward coldly. 'I'm going to blow his frigging head off anyway. Get away from him.'

Carole looked him straight in the face and refused point blank. 'There's been enough killing,' she shouted at him. 'Give me your shirt!'

For a moment, Edward stared at Paul, hating him. He had slumped down on the grass on his back and had gone very pale, incongruously pale in the hot sun. His screams had died away completely and he appeared to have passed out. Blood pumped out of the smashed forearm bright red on the grass.

'Come on!'

Edward looked at Carole. Maybe she was right. He reached into his pocket and dropped his handkerchief on Paul's chest. 'Use this. If the bastard dies, he deserves to, but I'll not harm him any more.' He flicked the pistol round to hold it by the barrel, turned, and flung it as far as he could into the long grass.

Carole watched the pistol arcing through the air, looked at Edward, and then she began binding the handkerchief as a tourniquet around Paul's arm to stop the bleeding. He began to scream and moan again, and she tried to ignore the pain she was causing him, soothing him with soft words.

'You can keep him,' said Edward coldly, mimicking her words to him in the hospital in Jerusalem. He turned away and began to walk back across the open meadow towards the track down to his car. It was time to go. His father was cleared, even if he could never prove it. Carole had explained the signals and it all made sense.

Funkspiel. She was right to say the word was a mockery of the death it caused.

21

THE CEMETERY AT MARMOUTIER

September 1947

Edward walked down the track quickly with the sun hot on his back but he paid no attention to the fine views of the hills around. Only once did he look across the pine-covered ridge on his right, to the east, and wondered how long it would take a small group of men to march at night to Natzweiler.

It was late afternoon by the time he approached the hairpin bend on the road to Salm and the air was cooler in the shadows between the stream and the pine branches hanging over the track. He saw an old black Peugeot parked just off the road but no-one was around and he assumed it was the car Carole and Paul had come in. He opened the door of the Morgan, sat down and relaxed. He stretched his legs out to loosen them after his walk but he felt no pleasure in the day. Perhaps his father was clear of the charges but he had no proof and he was stung by the thought of Carole fussing over Paul up in the hills. He fished about in his pocket for the car key, reflecting on the sad uncertainty of an affair with a girl from a different background, one he did not understand. He looked forward to seeing Diana again.

He stuffed the key in the ignition and was about to turn it, when he caught sight of a movement out of the corner of his eye. Someone was walking briskly towards him from under the pine trees on the side of the road. He stared.

Axel Romm reached the car and said, 'They told me in Marmoutier that you were around. I guessed you'd be up here.' He was wearing a clean white shirt and had his hands deep in the pockets of a comfortable pair of trousers. His grey hair was ruffled and he looked almost friendly. However, a dark look in his eyes put Edward on his guard. He was not sure there was anything left to say to Romm. He kept his hand on the key in the ignition, ready to start the car and leave, and asked, 'Who told you?'

'The gendarmes, of course, and that woman up the road, at Salm. Who else?' Romm narrowed his eyes with the question.

Edward realised Romm had no idea that anyone else was around. Carole and Paul must have come separately though he wondered where they had left their car.

Romm jerked his head up the track to the high ground above them and said, 'I suppose you've seen the plane?'

Edward nodded. He said flatly, 'Everything's clear now. Your report blaming my father was a pack of lies.'

'I knew you'd come here eventually, after you stole things from my file,' said Romm. When Edward refused to be drawn, he added, 'And I particularly regret not being able to prove that you murdered Yaacov. You've obviously been taking lessons, young man.' Almost casually, Romm pulled his right hand from his pocket and Edward found himself staring at a large calibre short-barrelled revolver.

'What's the point of that?' he asked dully. Life was not fair. He felt drained after his fight with Paul and the walk downhill. The implication of this new threat, when he had thought everything was finished, was too much. He had tossed Paul's pistol away into the grass. So much for pacificism, he told himself. Why was everyone so obsessed with revenge?

'Take your choice,' Romm was saying. 'Yaacov or the fact that you've done nothing but poke your goddam nose in my affairs since we met, and now you know too much. You'll ruin me if you sound off about this and I'm not having that.' It would be too much like Denkmann winning twice over.

Romm's superior manner was intensely irritating and in spite of the revolver Edward looked up and snapped, 'How d'you explain the photograph of you and Carole's mother grinning at Ulric Denkmann, a Nazi and head of the SD?'

Romm's steady gaze faltered for a moment. Then he asked, 'Just what do you know about Operation Joshua?'

Edward watched the revolver and decided to tell Romm everything. At worst, it might give him time. Maybe he could distract Romm again, start the car and take off, maybe knock him over. He told Romm what he had learned from his father, from Paul Levi when he had been kidnapped, from Colonel Haike, from Fullerton who told him the purpose of the operation, and finally that he understood they had been forced to comply with the Germans to produce a radio game, culminating in a final fatal message which brought in the Hudson. While he spoke, he gradually slipped his hand up to the key in the ignition again. By the time he finished, his hand was firmly on the car key. He said, 'Denkmann laid out that ambush, didn't he?'

Romm nodded. Just as he thought, Edward knew too much. He rubbed a hand through his grey hair and regretted the whole affair, a faraway look in his grey eyes.

Edward moved his left foot towards the clutch and repeated, 'So, why were you so friendly with Denkmann?'

Romm took a deep breath. It did not matter any more what he said to Edward and he began to talk, wistfully

The Joshua Inheritance

at first. 'I met Carole's mother on leave after the fighting ended in the First War. She was very beautiful, exactly like Carole. But then you know that because you stole her photograph. We married and lived here, in Marmoutier, where we met Ulric Denkmann. He became a good friend. In those days, there was no Hitler and we were happy. Denkmann supported German claims on Alsace. He joined the Party and became a Nazi.' Romm's voice rang with bitterness. 'He had style, I admit, and was quickly promoted. I saw little of him but he arrested my wife in 1938. We were Jews, you see?' He shrugged. 'I tried to stay on as long as I could but I had to leave, for Carole's sake, and I took her back to America. That photograph you stole from my house was taken before the war, when we were friends.' Suddenly Romm slammed his bunched fist on the side of the car and shouted, 'I should never have been allowed on that goddamed operation. That bastard Fullerton knew it. He should never have let me join, but he let me persuade him because I was fluent and knew the area so well. Goddam it, if I'd been choosing men for the team myself, I'd have ruled me out at once. I was too involved. But you British love amateurs. Fullerton let me go even though he knew my wife was a prisoner here.'

'Any operator could have been caught by the Germans. Lots were,' said Edward as coolly as he could, unable to stop staring at the revolver as he inched his left hand towards the gear stick. Romm's face was suffused and he shouted, 'It wasn't my fault we were caught! It was your goddam father! He was so much the bloody British cavalry officer, so casual that he allowed the Germans to follow him back to our safe house. He had just recced this place, the landing strip,' Romm continued to shout, waving his left arm up the track, 'and they followed him back. Right when I was in the middle of sending a message. He was a bloody amateur. Typical goddam Limey.'

Edward shook his head. He was almost ready to start the car, but none of this was right. His father was cleared. Carole and he had been through it all. Besides, he recalled the lonely mountain route he had driven from Marmoutier to Salm and thought it would be almost impossible to follow anyone without being seen. He tightened his hand on the ignition key, and slipped his right foot on to the accelerator, saying, 'I think you were located by direction finders'.

'Nonsense!' Romm shouted, stepping back from the car. 'I was too good.' But he knew he had also been too old. That is what really hurt about the whole affair. He had taken immense care with his procedures to prove he was up to it but Denkmann had taken advantage of it. He yelled, 'Denkmann thought he knew it all, the bastard. He even buried the men he killed up there in the cemetery in Marmoutier, where Lisa and I had lived.' The sergeant in the gendarmerie had also told him Denkmann was dead, so now time was up for Edward, the only other person who knew the whole story. Abruptly he shouted, 'Get out of the car!'

Edward was completely ready for a racing start but he hesitated. What if the car stalled? The hesitation was enough. He was defeated. Romm was too far away for Edward to slam the door into him as he got out, too far to run at him when he did and not far enough away to start the engine and drive off without being shot. He had no chance. Slowly, his grip on the key and the gear stick relaxed and he climbed out. To his surprise, Romm gestured him a few paces away and took his place. A faint smile flicked over his thin face and he said, 'I shall shoot up my own car and drive off in this to say we were both attacked from the woods.'

The simplicity of the plan shook Edward. He stood in the middle of the layby with his arms hanging and waited for Romm to shoot him. An image slipped across his mind, of the SS waiting for their trucks in the same place, cheerful, like Romm, after their successful ambush, with the body bags lined up on the ground by the road.

Romm lifted the revolver to fire and reached forward to start the engine with his other hand. A blinding sheet of flame exploded in front of Edward's eyes, his senses were paralysed in the deafening blast and he felt himself lifted like chaff and hurled away on to his back on the road. Pieces of metal and glass showered down on him and all around like hail, and then there was silence.

He lay on his back with his eyes wide open staring at the blue sky and wisps of black smoke drifting away down the valley. The realisation slowly filtered through his shocked mind that he had not been shot but blown off his feet by a bomb. In his car. Paul Levi. It had to be. He raised his head to look round. The pines, the hills above them, the sound of the stream, everything was the same, except the Morgan. He struggled to his knees wincing at a stabbing pain in his back. The car looked as if a giant had stamped on it making it as open-topped as it could ever be, so that its sides were bent back over the four wheels which lay almost flat on the ground. Edward stood up and walked unsteadily towards the wreck. Inside, Axel Romm hung back over the driver's seat like a suit of clothes, his white shirt burned and ripped and his head grotesquely angled from his neck. Edward found he could not look at the lower half of his body. He felt sick. The sight was too much like the two soldiers in the convoy who had been mined in their truck. Briefly, it crossed his mind that those two soldiers had not deserved to die while perhaps Romm had. Anyway, the end-result was the same. Disgusted, he turned away, amazed at his own escape, trying to decide what to do.

On the slope by the Hudson Carole looked up when she heard the explosion. The sound was faint, blurred by the distance and the ridges between but quite distinctly a bomb blast. A feeling of utter horror seized her. She glanced at Paul who had quietened now his arm had stopped bleeding. She had tied a splint to it with strips of Edward's handkerchief and was about to make him start the painful walk back to their Citroën.

Paul stirred, watching her and she put her hand on his shoulder to stop him speaking. She listened intently, on one knee, staring in the direction of the valley, like a deer poised for flight and certain there is danger.

'Wasting your time,' said Paul hoarsely.

'What d'you mean?' she asked without taking her eyes off the pines on the ridge and wishing she knew what had happened.

'Serve him right. I told you we'd win in the end.'

Paul's words sank in slowly and she looked down at him. His face was grey with pain, his shirt and trousers filthy with dirt and blood but his eyes were alight with triumph.

Horrified, Carole whispered, 'You never went back for the camera. You went back to set that bomb, on his car!' There was no question in the words.

'I promised Matty Spurstein,' he said.

'Who?'

'The boy's mother.'

'You bastard!'

'Carole, you don't mean that,' Paul gasped, shifting to sit up.

'You stayed with me. Not him.'

Carole stood up and backed away from him. She had always known Paul was in the Irgun but until that day had assumed he was merely a spokesman visiting her father in Jerusalem. When she found out he had survived Operation Joshua, she wanted him to tell her how to find the Hudson and she felt sorry for him. He had suffered Orianenburg after the disaster and she felt responsible. Perhaps because of her father, perhaps because she had been involved in coding the messages that sent the team on its way to destruction. She felt sorry for his broken

The Joshua Inheritance

arm. She was nearly sick when Edward snapped it while they grappled on the ground. But Paul and she were far apart. She understood his commitment was honest, even admired it, admired the dangers he risked in his fight against a vast and powerful enemy, but she realised he liked explosives too much, even liked killing people, and he trod a path too remote for her to forgive. She shouted, 'I stayed to fix your goddam arm. That's all!' Frantically, she turned away hating herself for not going down with Edward, for leaving him the second time, and started to stride through the stiff long grass towards the pines at the end of the landing strip.

'Wait!' Paul shouted desperately. 'You can't leave me here. For God's sake!'

Carole never looked back. She was a nurse. She knew he might not feel like it, but he could walk. She quickened her pace, angry at the gentle tussocks which pulled at her feet, until by the time she reached the top of the track down, among the pines on the ridge, she was running.

Edward found Axel Romm's revolver as he shuffled across to the big black Peugeot parked on the side of the bend. The revolver was scratched but serviceable and he put it in his pocket. He supposed the police would come, probably the woman at Salm would fetch them, but he had no intention of waiting about for them. Not there. If they wanted him, they could find him and he would tell them all about Paul Levi. Meanwhile, one last thing remained to be done and then Operation Joshua was finished for good. Romm had reminded him of something that Carole had said, which Paul's sudden appearance had made him forget. He had to see where the other members of the team were buried, in Marmoutier cemetery.

Bruised and cut, he knelt down like an old man to inspect the underneath of the big Peugeot for explosive devices before he got in and started it. He laughed at himself, knowing it was ridiculous but feeling better for having done it. He climbed in and found the key in the ignition. Even after his inspection, he had to force himself to control a sickening feeling of apprehension and turn the key quickly. The engine purred.

The run through the Col du Donon back to Marmoutier was beautiful in the blue evening light. The air was clearer than it had been that morning and he could see for miles across the lush green valleys which opened out on either side. By the time the road dipped off the mountain ridge towards Marmoutier, the pines cast long shadows across the road and as the big car swung back and forth in wild hairpins he thought he heard another car way above, following him. He tried to imagine his father returning from his recce of the landing strip and wondered if Romm had been right. Maybe the Germans had followed him. And if they had, all Carole's theory about the radio game was wrong. Edward felt himself losing his concentration. He had been more shaken by the explosion than he first thought.

He slowed down, telling himself he would be a fool to drive off the edge of the narrow mountain road. He wound down the windows and rubbed his eyes to stay awake. He reached Marmoutier after seven as the sun dropped behind the pines on the hills around the town. The cemetery was easy to find, on the outside of the town as he drove in, surrounded by a high wall like so many in France. He pulled in to the side of the road in a cloud of dust and climbed out feeling awful. His bruises had stiffened terribly after an hour in the car. He glanced up at the elaborate wrought-iron cross standing on the wall, silhouetted black against the clear evening sky, pushed open the gate and walked inside.

To his surprise, the cemetery was well kept. Grass paths divided the marble tombs, monumental angels and statues which cast long shadows in the warm evening light. Edward moved slowly up the centre looking right and left for a group of graves together. He reached the back of the graveyard furthest from the road, uncertain which way to go, and chose to continue his search to the left. He found them at once, in the only corner of the cemetery empty of memorials. A few fresh mounds of earth, decorated with faded bunches of flowers and still lacking their headstones showed recent burials. Before that, among shiny new plaques, put up for local people who had died at the end of the war of natural causes, were fourteen clean white slabs of marble set up for the men of Operation Joshua.

Edward counted them in three rows. The Hudson's crew of four, including the gunner, in one row and the ten Commandos in two rows, perfectly spaced apart, each marble exactly the same distance from its neighbour as all the others. A final immaculate parade. The grass between the headstones was neatly clipped and in front of each, over the stomach of the dead man beneath, grew a small bush of evergreen rosemary. Unsure whether such perfection was irony on their last awful moments of life or a tribute to their death, Edward began to read the names carved on the stones.

He was so absorbed that he never heard Carole's car stop on the road nor her soft footfalls on the grass paths through the graveyard till she spoke behind him 'Edward?'

Perhaps because his back was uncomfortably stiff, he did not turn round. He said coldly, 'What're you doing here? Why aren't you with your patient?'

She said quietly, 'He'll live, but he was nothing more than a ticket to find the Hudson. When I heard the explosion, I ran down. I thought you were, I thought you might be . . .'

'Dead?' he finished harshly.

Yes. Like these, she thought, unable to answer. She was still not recovered from the shock of finding her father blown apart instead of Edward. She glanced past him at the graves, transfixed by the symmetry of the white headstones which seemed to catch the evening light.

Still refusing to look at her, he demanded, 'How did you get here? I saw no car on the road.'

'Paul hid our car behind the pines,' she replied. She had been so stupid not to have understood. They had both seen the Morgan but only Paul realised its significance and deliberately hid their car. 'He said it would be best to keep it out of sight to stop it being stolen.'

'And then he went back with some story of fetching the camera and fixed up the bomb?'

'I suppose so.'

The abject tone of her voice suddenly made him realise she had lost her father in the explosion. He stopped feeling sorry for himself and turned round. Her hair was loose, her face and neck were dirty with sweat from running down the track and streaked with the tears which had blinded her as she chased after Edward down the mountain to Marmoutier.

'I'm sorry,' said Edward gently. 'About your father, I mean.' He noticed she was not looking at him and repeated, 'I'm sorry.'

She focused on him again and shook her head. She said, 'There's nothing to be sorry about any more. He was responsible, for everything.'

Edward nodded, 'Yes, he told me. Denkmann arrested your mother. And he took you back to America. In 1938.'

Vehemently Carole said, 'No! She left him. She divorced him. As a little girl, I always suspected she hated him.' She pointed to a gravestone set away, beside the other local people who had died in Marmoutier these years ago in 1944. 'Now I know for certain.' The words carved on the simple stone were easy to read, '*Ulric Karl Denkmann, tué par la Resistance le 2 Dec 1944*' and underneath another line, '*et sa femme, Lisa Helène Denkmann. Tué le 2 Dec 1944.*'

The Joshua Inheritance

Dully Carole said, 'Those are my mother's names. She never had any intention of going back to him.'

Edward frowned and said dismissively, 'Denkmann was a Nazi. He wouldn't marry her, not if she was Jewish.'

To his surprise Carole laughed. 'She wasn't Jewish at all.' Her laughter was hollow and did not last. Quietly, she added, 'Maybe that's one of the reasons she left him, but I think really it's because she liked people with charisma and power. When they met, my father was a war hero and she fell for him. Later she realised he was an obsessive. They lived in the same house, he adoring her, she hating him for his meticulous insistance on detail. With the rise of the Nazis, she was fascinated by Denkmann's brutal prestige. My father, a Jew, could never accept it. Never. When we went to the States, he was determined to get back here. All the time he used the system, first in Washington, then in England, until he persuaded Fullerton to let him go on Joshua.'

Edward pulled the creased photograph of Romm, his wife and Denkmann out of his pocket. Now he could see Denkmann was in command, the cock on top of the heap, standing in his smart policeman's uniform with one leg raised on the steps of the police station and fully conscious that Lisa Romm had eyes for no-one else. Carole stepped over to look, brushing her hair from her face and bent close to Edward. 'I've never seen this before.'

'I thought you said you knew I'd stolen it?'

Carole shook her head adamantly. 'Of course I knew you'd taken my picture off the side-table, but my father just said some other pictures had been stolen, from his files. He never said what of. I've never seen this and I can see why he never wanted me to see it.' Her eyes filled with tears as the realisation hit home.

'Why? He said it was taken before the war, when you lived here.'

'Look at Denkmann's uniform,' she cried. 'His rank.

417

He's a SS Standartenführer. That's the rank he held at the time of Operation Joshua, when he was chief in Strasbourg. That picture was never taken before the war. It was taken in 1944.'

The implication was clear. Romm was quite obviously not a prisoner. He was willing, actively enjoying himself and smiling at some joke of Denkmann's perhaps. Edward asked quietly, 'It seems extraordinary that he could have collaborated? I'm sure they were caught, my father and yours, except your father never wanted to admit it. I can see why, but I can't believe he was willing, even then.'

'He wanted her back,' Carole whispered. 'He would have done anything to get her back.'

'Including agreeing to collaborate with a radio game?'

'Yes. While he meticulously sent back his security checks to say he was in trouble. To get us to stop listening to his messages, to cancel the mission.'

'And Colonel Haike never did.'

Carole nodded, hardly able to speak. Tears were streaming down her cheeks as she imagined the torture of her father's dilemma. She added. 'After they realised, Colonel Haike warned me never to tell anyone. He threatened me with all sorts of trouble.'

'Was that just before we met? In Whitehall on VE-Day?'

'Yes.' She looked up at Edward and he wiped her tears with his fingers.

She smiled. 'I agreed not to speak out, but I goddam intended to.'

Edward looked puzzled at her stained face gazing at him so intently.

Her voice was strong and determined. 'I copied all the signals he sent back. Every goddam slow and immaculate message. With the date, the serial and my comment that the bluff check and true check were omitted in each goddam case. I've got the whole record. We can show that he may have been playing the German game, but he was trying to tell us all the time. In his precise way.' A thought struck her. 'We even could have turned the radio game against the Germans if they'd believed him.'

'Wonderful!' Edward took her face in his hands and kissed her, elated at the thought of the reaction this would cause in London when he got back. Then he turned to the graves and said, 'These poor sods wouldn't have died if Haike and Fullerton had taken any notice of you, if the damned system had worked as it was designed to.'

Quietly he took her hand, bridging their bitter separation of more than a year, and they stood close together looking along the neat, clean rows of graves. They were both exhausted and filthy, Edward stiff with his bruises, but more relaxed than either could remember. Together they had solved the disgrace and suspicions which had hung over their fathers like a cloud since the war, and had found peace with each other.

Carole said suddenly, 'Have you noticed something about these men?' And when Edward shook his head, she pointed at the inscriptions, one after another, not at the names but at the emblem carved into the marble above their names. Each one was a Star of David. 'Not just Paul Levi,' she said, 'they were all Jews. Jews sent to free Jews.'

'No wonder my father went looking for them in camps like Belsen.'

'Those people in Belsen and the other camps, and these,' she gestured at the graves, 'are the real victims of the war. Not the survivors like you and me. We don't have the right to feel sorry for ourselves. Not ever.'

Without knowing why, he said, 'These are the old guard. We should salute them, for we shan't see men like them again.'

EPILOGUE

Edward spent the rest of his leave with Carole, in Switzerland, in a little wooden Gasthaus in a remote valley in the Bernese Oberland. During the warm sunny days, they went for long walks among the pines and meadows and forgot all thoughts of Joshua, Palestine, London and everything else which had conspired to separate them. In the evenings, invigorated with the fresh Alpine air and pleasantly exhausted, they sat down to enjoy good dinners of local meats and cheeses, looking out of the window at an incomparable view of green pastures, streams, rocks and snow-capped peaks. They drank rich fruity wine from the valley's vineyards and made love under clean white linen duvets. Edward had never felt more free and happy in his life and Carole nearly persuaded him not to go back to England, to the Army. He tried to persuade her to come with him, but she had things to clear up in Jerusalem, just as he needed to see his mother and also explain to Aubrey what had happened to his beloved Morgan. Their parting at Geneva airport was difficult, almost impossible, hardly sweetened by desperate promises that they would see each other again, soon, because neither could believe that a world still recovering from war, in which communications between England and Palestine were so slow, and which was threatened with new conflicts to which

Edward would inevitably be committed, could possibly allow them to re-create the simple happiness they had enjoyed in a sunny Swiss valley.

Paul Levi had not given up when Carole left him in the grass in the hills. He was made of tougher material. He remembered the place which they had chosen during the war as the emergency rendezvous, on the corner of a wood not far from the landing strip. He stood up, clutching his broken arm to his stomach, and forced himself to find it, thankful for the cool evening air as the sun went down. He found his memory was surprisingly good, maybe because he had spent hours learning the route before embarking in the Hudson two years before; and once he was on the move, he kept going and walked determinedly away in the opposite direction from the little village of Salm where later Sergeant Lescaut came with other police and found the remains of Axel Romm covered with late summer flies. By the time the police had trudged up to the Hudson, Paul was on a local train to Strasbourg and a day later he arrived at the clinic in Switzerland where they succeeded in fixing his arm.

By the time he returned to Haifa, Palestine had become Israel and was at war with the Arabs. Only a month after his fight with Edward, on 17 October, the British Colonial Secretary went to the United Nations and told the world that the British government would, 'not accept any settlement antagonistic to either the Jews or the Arabs or both which was likely to necessitate the use of force'. Britain was defeated. She gave up trying to find a solution between Arabs and Jews, relinquished the Mandate and washed her hands of the problem. By May 1948, when the last British soldiers left Palestine, over 10,000 people had died in the previous three months as Jew and Arab fought each other bitterly throughout the country.

On 14 May 1948, the Zionists declared the State of Israel in Tel Aviv and open warfare broke out at once. Paul Levi joined up and distinguished himself, recovering his

The Joshua Inheritance

self-esteem and afterwards securing a job for himself in the secret service of the new Israeli State. His work was endless. The Jews had won their first war with the Arabs, but the Arabs did not give up, nor did the killing stop.

Britain was humiliated in Palestine, but in 1948, though still exhausted by the Second World War and in desperate financial straits, there was no rest for her politicians or the Army. British eyes were quickly turned from the Middle East. In June, only a month after the Jews celebrated their new State, the Berlin Blockade and a twelve-year guerrilla war in Malaya began. Communism was the new enemy.

Back in England, Diana's distress at Edward's long absence was soon forgotten in her pleasure at seeing him home. She had genuinely missed him and he found her excellent company, more fun than he remembered before the war or even in Palestine. But he could not forget Carole. Worse, he heard no word from Carole and his telegrams to Jerusalem went unanswered. Even Angus Maclean could not help. He reported that the house in Hezron Street was closed and empty, nor could he glean any information from the US Consulate or from Carole's hospital.

In a fit of depression Edward volunteered for a posting to Intelligence. He reckoned he had something to offer. He had seen how the proper use of Intelligence had failed the British Army in Palestine, he had an aptitude for languages and he had taken part in the Special Squads, a new concept with potential, but ill-executed. The fight against the Jewish underground had been a bitter experience but he hoped the British Army had learned its lesson.

Later, Edward understood what he had meant by talking to Carole of the old guard. Trained British soldiers of the best kind lay in those neat rows of graves in Marmoutier cemetery. They died at the end of the war, among the last to die in the wartime British

Army, the old Imperial Army for which the new Israelis had sounded the death knell. Their type would never be seen again.

They had died fruitlessly, but committed to fight an evil everyone could understand. It did not matter that they were Jewish, for their deaths were not for political gain, not for the greed of empires or nation states, nor for the hypocrisy of competing religions. They had fought and died with hundreds of thousands of others of all nationalities and creeds: Jews, Catholics, Muslims, Buddhists; Australians, Americans, Canadians, Indians, Welsh, Scots, Irish and English; and many others. All of them had been on the same side, fighting oppression, together. They were the old guard. That was why he had saluted them.

And because times had changed in the short three years since they died, in the three years since Edward joined the Army. Palestine had seen to that.